TARGET OMEGA

TARGET OMEGA

A THRILLER

PETER

KIRSANOW

DUTTON

□

DUTTON
An imprint of Penguin Random House LLC
375 Hudson Street
New York, New York 10014

Ⓟ

LIBRARY OF CONGRESS CATALOGING-IN-PUBLICATION DATA
Names: Kirsanow, Peter N., author.
Title: Target Omega : a thriller / Peter Kirsanow.
Description: 1st ed. | New York : Dutton, 2016. | Description based on print version record and CIP data provided by publisher; resource not viewed.
Identifiers: LCCN 2016024490 (print) | LCCN 2016016031 (ebook) | ISBN 9781101985304 (eBook) | ISBN 9781101985298 (hc) | ISBN 9781101985311 (mass market)
Subjects: LCSH: Intelligence officers—United States—Fiction. | Terrorism—Prevention—Fiction. | United States. Central Intelligence Agency—Fiction. | GSAFD: Suspense fiction.
Classification: LCC PS3611.I769845 (print) | LCC PS3611.I769845 O44 2016 (ebook) | DDC 813/.6—dc23
LC record available at https://lccn.loc.gov/2016024490

Printed in the United States of America

1   3   5   7   9   10   8   6   4   2

Set in Warnock Pro
Designed by Alissa Rose Theodor

To Karola, Serge, and Solveig

Then out spake brave Horatius,

The captain of the gate:

"To every man upon this earth

Death cometh soon or late,

And how can a man die better

Than facing fearful odds,

For the ashes of his fathers

And the temples of his gods?"

—MACAULAY

CHAPTER ONE

THE WHITE HOUSE

JULY 17 • 2:18 P.M. EDT

M r. President, we should not commit to any irreversible course of action, not until we confirm the Russians' and Iranians' true intentions. And our missing operator is vital to such confirmation. We mustn't act before we locate him."

The president examined the faces of the core members of the National Security Council arrayed around the conference table in the Situation Room. Most registered anxiety, others disbelief, perhaps even fear.

Except for James Brandt. The national security advisor appeared calm, almost serene. But inside, he was rattled by the call he'd received only moments earlier.

"Elaborate, Jim."

"Are you familiar, sir, with the phenomenon surrounding the event known as Starfish Prime?"

"Yes, vaguely."

"The man I'm speaking of, the man we've assumed is on the run after committing numerous acts of unspeakable violence, possesses information that could thwart an event dwarfing Starfish Prime. We've got to find him, sir."

The president stared hard at Brandt. "What's the worst-case scenario if we didn't?"

Brandt appeared to stare right back at the commander in chief. "Not to overstate matters, sir, but the immediate end of the United States as currently constituted."

SIX DAYS EARLIER

There were thirty-five of them—twenty shooters and the rest labor—and they were within moments of acquiring a nuclear device.

Not just one nuke, but several. More than the West would ever, or could ever, expect. Enough to obliterate the entire population of their target and, if deployed shrewdly, to provide second-strike capability. Deterrence and insurance.

In less than two hundred feet they would enter the facility and would meet, at most, token resistance. There might be a brief firefight, but only for show, to fool the West.

They would load the devices on the flatcars they pushed before them. Then they would go to the extraction point, detonating explosives to cover their escape, making it look like the work of terrorists.

Less than two hundred more feet. Then victory and glory. They had trained for more than a year, rehearsed hundreds of times. They knew their assigned roles to the letter. They knew they would be celebrated. They knew they would be heroes.

What they did not know was that they would be martyrs, for less than a hundred feet behind them, death approached.

———

The tunnel ninety feet below the outskirts of Wah Cantonment was a serpentine affair, winding around hard rock formations for nearly eight hundred yards before coming to a stop beneath the nuclear weapons facility approximately two miles west of the Pakistan Ordnance Factories. From there, a laddered shaft led up to a concealed trapdoor in a seldom-used storage area in a remote part of the facility.

The tunnel wasn't what Mike Garin had imagined during the briefing on the flight from Ramstein Air Base in Germany. It was wide and tall and brightly lit, almost like a miniature metropolitan subway tunnel. The floor was smooth and level and the walls were carved into the earth at precise ninety-degree angles to the floor. It was built deep enough to minimize, if not completely evade, detection by the nuclear facility's vibration sensors or, for that matter, most any other monitoring device.

Not that such detection was likely. Nearly two hundred million US dollars had been paid to both corrupt officers and faithful confederates within and without the facility to ensure that no alarms would be triggered—or, if triggered, would not be reported.

Garin hated tunnels. Most operators did. Tunnels were telescoped kill boxes. No cover, no possibility of lateral movement. Therefore, no effective way to avoid incoming fire unless you were fortunate enough to be near one of the tunnel's twists and turns. Then you might be able to duck behind an earthen bend to avoid a direct frontal hit. But even then, you were just as likely to be struck by bullets ricocheting off the tunnel's walls.

Tunnels were death traps. No margin for error. Even tactical perfection provided little protection.

Nonetheless, Garin led his eight-member team swiftly and stealthily through the labyrinth, pausing before each turn to be sure no sentries were posted around the corner. Somewhere ahead, a force estimated to consist of at least two dozen highly trained, heavily armed men was using the tunnel to gain access to the facility.

If the intelligence reports were accurate, it was only about a hundred more yards before Garin and his team would reach the shaft leading up to the storage area. Accordingly, the odds of encountering the armed force grew with each step he and his men took. It was possible the force was already on its way back, having acquired the holy grail. If they had, and Garin's mission was unsuccessful, the world would soon be facing a crisis unlike almost anything previously witnessed.

Instinctively slowing the pace, Garin signaled his team to stop as they approached another bend angling toward the right. He flattened himself against the right side of the tunnel wall and slowly slid forward until he was able to peek quickly around the curve. Two sentries, standing shoulder to shoulder, alert, carrying KL-7.62s, and glancing expectantly down the tunnel in the direction of the facility.

Garin signaled his findings to the team, lowered his HK416, and after contemplating whether to leave it slung across his torso, lowered it gently to the ground. He withdrew his tactical knife with his right hand, braced for a beat, and then burst around the bend toward the sentry on the left. Garin jammed the knife deep into the right side of the man's neck, ripping its serrated blade across his throat and tearing through skin, muscle, cartilage, and veins as he severed the man's trachea.

The other sentry's brain hadn't yet begun processing the blur of carnage before Garin pivoted a full 180 degrees to his right and plunged the blade into the base of the second man's throat, just above his sternum. A jet of blood spurted from the cavity as Garin retracted the knife. Both sentries collapsed to the ground almost simultaneously, dead.

Elapsed time: a tick under two seconds. Speed, Garin maintained, kills.

He wiped his blade on the second sentry's trousers before sheathing his knife and shouldering his rifle again. He listened for any sounds of movement ahead, then motioned his team to advance.

Stepping lightly over the two corpses, the team moved cautiously and silently, the engagement with the sentries raising expectations of an imminent encounter with the larger force. As they rounded the bend, the tunnel straightened for a full thirty yards before disappearing around another right turn.

Garin sped up the pace. They were exposed while in the straightaway. Shooters shielded behind the bend ahead could cut them down with impunity. An underground slaughterhouse.

Within seconds they approached the break of the next turn. Garin signaled another halt and again went flush against the right wall, his team doing the same, single file, John Gates and Gene Tanski immediately behind him. Garin paused for a moment, alert for any sounds, any vibrations, any whisper of air that might betray human presence.

Nothing.

He darted his head around the corner to take a peek. Still nothing. Only the singular silence of a channel embedded within millions of tons of earth and rock.

Garin turned back slightly toward his team, pointed to himself, and nodded. Then he paused, braced, and spun swiftly around the corner.

Twenty-five feet in front of him stood a man brandishing a rifle who himself had just spun around a corner from the left.

The two men stood staring at each other, absolutely frozen, for two seconds that seemed like ten. Not a single breath, not so much as a blink or a twitch or a flinch between them. Squared off. High noon.

Then a second man began to emerge from the bend behind the point man. And a third.

Garin shot the point man with a three-round burst just above the bridge of his nose, the impact shearing off much of the top half of his head and the rifle's sharp report reverberating down the tunnel. The point man's body toppled backward to the ground.

There was utter silence for another full second, the surrounding earth having quickly absorbed the gunfire's echo. A moment later, John Gates appeared from behind Garin and shot the other two men with a level of precision even Garin could not have surpassed.

And then all hell broke loose.

CHAPTER TWO

CHALUS, IRAN

JULY 11 • 11:43 P.M. IRDT

He was drunk. Again.

To the casual observer, nothing about the Russian would seem amiss. His speech was slow but not slurred; the normally stern visage was more relaxed but still flinty. He was somewhat more talkative but not voluble.

But to a man like Hamid Mansur, who had spent more than three decades making a living—and staying alive—by reading people closely, it was apparent that his guest, reclining comfortably on a low white couch in Mansur's living room, was approaching the red zone of inebriation.

For Mansur's immediate purposes, this was a good thing. He had befriended the Russian scientist shortly after his arrival in Iran with the intent of gathering as much information as possible about what he was doing at the military installation within the mountains just south of Mansur's hometown of Chalus.

The Russian remained guarded even after consuming enough alcohol to fell a camel. But on each such occasion, he would reveal another small piece of the puzzle. It had taken the better part of a year, but Mansur had been able to collect enough disparate kernels of information from the Russian to conclude that the installation formed some part of Iran's nuclear weapons program, and the man sipping chilled vodka across from him was an integral part of that program.

Whatever was inside those mountains appeared to be nearing completion, and although important pieces of the puzzle were still missing, the latest piece filled Mansur with alarm and a compulsion to relay the information to a resourceful Israeli agent who would take appropriate action.

Among the residents of Chalus it was a poorly kept secret that shortly after Iran had begun negotiations with Western powers regarding the scope of its nuclear program, the facility located in the North Alborz Protected Area swarmed with Russians and North Koreans. With only one or two exceptions, the foreigners remained confined to the "research" facility. In truth, Mansur's guest, Dmitri Chernin, represented the sum total of the exceptions, a position accorded him due to his elevated status at the facility. A position, Mansur deduced, that was something akin to a project manager.

Yet even Chernin wasn't permitted to venture outside the heavily guarded gates of the installation without an escort, whose purported responsibility was to act as Chernin's driver, but whose real duty was to act as a minder, a spy, ensuring that the Russian made no unauthorized contacts with local residents or unknown individuals.

Mansur was not merely known to the Iranian regime, but occasionally proved himself quite useful. Now in his midsixties, he'd once been one of the more talented agents of the Sazeman-e Ettala'at va Amniyat-e Keshvar, or SAVAK, the ruthless Iranian intelligence agency under the shah. When the shah fell, Mansur was among the few former SAVAK agents not executed or purged, primarily because of his extensive and valuable network of contacts throughout the Middle East—particularly Israel—and he'd demonstrated a fidelity to each of Iran's supreme leaders since Khomeini. Vezaret-e Ettela'at va Amniyat-e Keshvar, or VEVAK, the *current* ruthless Iranian intelligence agency, used Mansur to gather intelligence from, and pass disinformation to, the regime's adversaries.

What the regime didn't know was that Mansur's professed allegiance was a charade—he'd detested most everything about the Iranian leadership since the revolution. So while feeding the regime inconsequential intel from the various intelligence services throughout the Middle East, he provided *useful* intel about the Iranian regime to those very same agencies. Mansur had even played a minor but indispensable role in one of the occasional setbacks that had beset the Iranian nuclear program over the years. And although it was a dangerous game, Mansur excelled at it, and it had provided him with a very comfortable lifestyle. One that, at least by Iranian standards, might even be considered luxurious.

Mansur was sufficiently concerned by what he'd heard from Chernin this evening that he planned to contact an Israeli named Ari Singer immediately upon Chernin's departure. But first, Mansur needed to draw as much information about the timeline from his guest as he could.

Assuming a pose of amiable indifference, letting Chernin believe he was controlling the conversation, Mansur asked, "So what will you do when it is finished?"

Chernin shrugged. "I am not sure it matters . . ." Chernin caught himself. "I am not sure, Hamid. I have been working, seemingly day and night, and I have not given it much thought. It will not be a matter of what I do, but of what I do not do."

"Retirement? Is that what you are insinuating? You are not that old, Dmitri."

"Every Russian is born sixty years old."

Mansur smiled. "You are fatigued, yes. I can see that for myself. Fatigue is not the same thing as age."

"It is worse." Chernin took another sip of vodka. "It steals one's optimism. Robs one of time. Makes one a coward."

Mansur sensed an opportunity. "How much more time, Dmitri? Years? Months?"

"Days."

And just like that, Mansur felt a stab of anxiety. Based on their conversations over the last few weeks, he knew Chernin's work was nearing completion, but he'd assumed at least a few more months remained. So had the analysts to whom Singer had conveyed Mansur's information. This development would dramatically alter timelines, if not strategies, in Tel Aviv. Mansur needed to bring the evening to a close so he could contact Singer. The elf needed to know this now.

Mansur made a show of examining his watch, appearing surprised. "It is nearly midnight. I have an appointment in Tehran in the morning," he lied.

The Russian waved him off and rose from the couch. It was his turn to lie. "I am about to leave, Hamid. Early start for me as well." He keyed his cell phone to alert his driver to pick him up. "Thank you, once again, for dinner. And the vodka. And the cigars." A playful pause. "Did I mention the vodka?"

"Thank you for the company, Dmitri. These days I have few occasions for interesting conversation."

Mansur guided Chernin down the narrow entryway to the door of the apartment, pleased that he was able to so easily manipulate Chernin into departing. Opening the door for the Russian, he clapped him on the shoulder and watched him go down the stairs with surprising alacrity and steadiness for someone who had consumed more than half a bottle of liquor.

What the wise old spy did not know—would not have believed—was that it was he who was being manipulated.

CHAPTER THREE

NORTH ATLANTIC

JULY 11 • 11:51 P.M. UTC

Barely ten hours ago, they had thwarted a catastrophe by a margin of mere minutes, but now, save for the taciturn man with the fierce eyes, they were at ease.

Five of the eight men reclining in the darkened cabin of the sleek Gulfstream G650ER cruising forty-two thousand feet above the black waters of the North Atlantic were in a deep sleep, aided by the white noise of the jet's twin Rolls-Royce engines. The two men seated in front, Cal Lowbridge and Manny Camacho, though awake, wore placid, almost trance-like, expressions. Only the man seated aft appeared alert and focused.

Camacho, the newest member of the team, nudged Lowbridge and nodded toward the taciturn man working on his laptop. "Check out the boss."

Lowbridge glanced back. "Vintage Mike Garin. Sleep's a nuisance."

"What's he up to?"

"Ask him."

"Tell you the truth, he scares me."

"Get used to it. It gets worse the longer you know him. I've known him for going on six years. Still gives me the yips."

Camacho nodded toward the man with a bulbous nose sprawled in the seat across from Garin. "Tanski, though, is dead to the world."

Lowbridge looked back again. "This plane goes down, grab that nose and use it as a flotation device." Lowbridge turned back to Camacho. "Go ahead. Find out what the boss is up to."

Camacho rose and walked tentatively to Garin's seat, crouching in the aisle next to him. Before Camacho could open his mouth, Garin, without looking up from the laptop, asked, "Finish your report yet?"

Flustered, Camacho stammered, "I was about—"

"We debrief as soon as we deplane. Leave absolutely nothing out." Garin looked up from the screen and locked a glacial gaze on Camacho. "Not one thing."

The conversation was over. Camacho rose awkwardly and returned to his seat as Lowbridge stifled a chuckle.

Gene Tanski, proud owner of a bulbous nose and other noteworthy anatomical features, stirred. The former Delta Force operator had known Garin longer than anyone else on the team.

"You enjoy doing that."

"Doing what?"

"Intimidating people."

Garin didn't respond.

"Why won't you tell the poor kid what you're doing?"

"He doesn't need to know."

Tanski leaned over to catch a glimpse of Garin's laptop screen. "Then tell me."

"Just trying to put down everything I can remember seeing on the bad guy's laptop before exfil."

"Mike, op's over. Mission accomplished. Job well done. Time to shut down the engines and catch some z's. We've been on fast-forward for the last forty-eight hours."

"We're missing something."

"We did exactly what they sent us to do. With flair, grace, and extreme prejudice."

"*They* didn't tell us the whole story, Gene."

"They never tell us the whole story. Ours is not to reason why . . ."

Garin shook his head slowly. "The thing is, I'm not sure just *who* it is who's telling us the story."

"You lost me, boss."

"Some of the bad guys in the tunnel were Ansar Corps."

"So?"

"Why is a file on Evan Dellinger on a laptop of an Iranian Ansar Corps colonel in an assault tunnel . . . underneath a Pakistani nuclear weapons facility?"

Tanski exhaled. "Still lost, boss. Who's Dellinger?"

"American physicist. Caltech, then Livermore, then MIT."

"Nuclear?"

"No. Quantum electrodynamics."

"Whoa. What the hell's that?" Tanski asked, and then quickly added, "No, forget it. Don't wanna know. I'm pretty sure my head will end up hurting more than it does now. I just wanna go home and grab a couple beers. Getting laid would be nice. But I'll settle for an Orioles game if they're in town." Tanski sank back into his seat. "What about you, Mike? We got some time coming to us, provided the bad guys cooperate. Any sex, drugs, or rock 'n' roll in your plans?"

"Going to Badwater."

Agitated, Tanski sat up again. "Are you freakin' kidding me? You're still on that? Be serious, hombre. You've never even run a marathon. And I know you haven't trained, at least not for that. Badass operator or not, can't be done. No way."

"Thanks for the encouragement."

"I'm being serious, Mike. That's what, five marathons nonstop? In the middle of the desert? That's absolutely, positively nuts. Suicidal, homicidal, fratricidal—all the freakin' cidals. Take my advice. Please. Don't do it."

"I'll think about it. Even so, I need to go out there to see Clint Laws."

"Ahhhh . . . the Professor of Death and Destruction. What for?"

"Not sure. He invited me out to the Ranch for a few days to kick back and tell lies. Said he wants to talk to me about Dan Dwyer and DGT."

Tanski shook his head. "Nobody kicks back at the Ranch. Telling lies, maybe. But no kicking back. Probably gonna make you an offer you can't refuse."

"I don't think so, Gene." Garin shifted in his seat so his face was flush with Tanski's. "You've been at this for a while, right?"

"Long enough. You know that. I've got at least five years on you, boss."

"Have you ever been sent on an operation where it seemed like the bad guys were expecting you?"

"All the time." Tanski examined Garin's face. "What are you getting at, Mike?"

"That tunnel was rigged. Why would they wire the tunnel if they were making a one-way trip to hit the nuke facility?"

"Are you saying they were tipped by someone on our side?" Tanski shook his head dismissively. "Nice cinematic flourish, Mike, but it doesn't compute. Look, with all due respect, you're overthinking this. They were probably going to collapse the tunnel onto any pursuers in case they had to make a fast retreat. Besides, outside of the president and Kessler, only a handful of people knew about the op."

Garin turned back in his seat. The plane dipped as it hit a pocket of turbulence. He closed the laptop and gazed out the window at the crescent moon.

"Right." He exhaled. "That's what worries me."

CHAPTER FOUR

The assassin was back in the United States.

The tall, lean figure with a patrician bearing, smoking a cigarette on the second-floor balcony of the large beach house overlooking the Atlantic, knew this because of the ringtone on his cell phone. The tone was reserved for one person alone.

Oddly, the patrician felt more at ease knowing the assassin was in the country. The man seemed to discharge assigned tasks with almost supernatural efficiency, and that gave the patrician a sense of comfort, security.

Despite the fact that the phone was encrypted and the house was clean, the patrician spoke sterilely.

"Yes."

"There was an issue."

"What kind of issue?"

"A matter of identification."

"Are you certain?"

"No. But there is, at the very least, a possibility."

"Then eliminate the possibility." The patrician paused. "*All* of the possibilities. Use our surrogates when feasible."

"That will be a challenge," the assassin replied. "The possibilities are . . . formidable."

"Quite right. But time is of the essence and all of the possibilities must be resolved quickly. That can only be done with a sufficient number of surrogates."

The connection was silent for a moment. The patrician understood that the assassin preferred to resolve the possibilities by himself; he wouldn't entrust it to surrogates, although he'd allow them to provide any necessary logistical support.

The assassin said, "It will be done," and severed the connection.

The patrician casually returned the phone to his pocket and flicked the cigarette butt onto the beach below. Calm for a man who had just unleashed hell.

CHAPTER FIVE

The assassin was pleased with the house he had chosen. A two-bedroom nondescript ranch, it sat at the terminus of a dead-end street, ensuring that there would be no passersby.

The house was separated from its only neighbor to the west by an eight-foot-high row of hedges and was set back sixty feet from the street. The yard on the east side of the house dropped into a thickly wooded ravine. There were no houses immediately across the street, only a wooded lot.

The assassin backed the black Ford Explorer into the driveway until the rear bumper was about four feet from the garage door. He exited the SUV, glanced casually about the perimeter of the yard, and proceeded to unlock the manual garage door, lifting it open in a single pull.

The assassin opened the hatch of the Explorer and examined the rolled-up carpet, most of which was encased in a yard-size black garbage bag. He pulled the carpet toward him and, once clear of the hatch, heaved it over his right shoulder. He carried the carpet into the garage, closing the door behind him.

The powerfully built killer gently laid the carpet on the concrete garage floor. Extracting a box cutter from his left rear pocket, he opened it and sliced the rope binding the carpet with a swift upward movement. Before standing, he pulled the weapon from the holster attached to his right calf and affixed a sound suppressor from his waistband.

The assassin stood over the carpet for a moment, his right hand holding the pistol loosely at his side. In the dim light he could detect a slow rhythmic expansion and contraction near the center of the roll. He placed the thick rubber heel of his boot at the crest of the roll and pushed hard, unrolling the carpet and exposing the man who had lain wrapped within.

The man remained motionless except for the steady rise and fall of his chest. Multiple strips of duct tape covered his mouth. Several more were wrapped around his ankles. His arms were bound at the sides of his torso.

The assassin stepped over the man toward a wooden workbench along the length of the west wall of the garage. The bench had a variety of tools, which he casually flung on the floor. He did the same to a row of shovels and rakes that were leaning neatly against the wall.

The clattering of the tools against concrete caused the man on the floor to stir. The assassin strolled over and looked into the man's face. His eyes registered a mix of fear and confusion. The killer understood. He had seen the look numerous times before. Each time, he had sincerely wished he would not have to see it again.

The assassin moved to the crown of the man's head. Bending down, he grasped the man's armpits and dragged him toward the east wall of the garage, where a six-foot pile of gray cinder blocks left over from the construction of a small backyard gazebo was stacked next to a push mower. The assassin noted that the man didn't even struggle against his restraints. That was unusual. The man was relatively young and strong, yet he put up less of a fight than many of the assassin's previous victims who had been older and smaller. Young Americans, he thought, were growing soft and weak. Lots of bluster and strutting, but fewer and fewer cowboys among them.

After positioning the man directly beneath the stack of cinder blocks, the assassin reached up and pulled one from the top. He lifted it over his head and prepared to drop it on the man's head. This elicited a more vigorous reaction from the target, who whipped his head back and forth as muffled noises came from the duct tape covering his mouth. The look in the man's eyes had evolved from fear to terror.

The assassin hesitated and then replaced the cinder block atop the stack. The man's agitation subsided a bit as the assassin assumed a relaxed stance, his head tilted slightly to his left as if regarding a puzzle. The two men looked at each other for a few seconds before the assassin drew the pistol from his waistband and shot the target an inch below the center of the forehead, the sound of the suppressed pop resonating in the garage resembling the abrupt release of a champagne cork.

The assassin inserted the weapon back into his waistband and picked up the shell casing from the garage floor as the doll-like eyes of the dead man held the assassin's gaze. They were all like that. First a pause, as if they would return to life again after recharging their batteries. Then oblivion.

The assassin looked about the tool-strewn floor once again. An artist practicing his craft. Satisfied, he retrieved the cinder block from the top of the stack and dropped it flush on the dead man's face, the corpse's head yielding with the soft crunching sound of compressed bone and cartilage. Then the assassin dropped another.

As a stream of blood pooled around the target's head, the assassin walked to the doorway leading from the garage to the kitchen of the house. Before entering, he pulled the box cutter from his pocket, extended his left arm, and with a slight wince made a longitudinal incision along the top of his forearm. He paused briefly. Then he walked into the kitchen, fixed himself a pot of black coffee, and leisurely sipped until the last drop of the brew was gone. It was the beginning of a very long night. And a new world order.

CHAPTER SIX

The raucous postrace atmosphere in the lounge of the Diamondback wasn't quite what the doctor would have ordered, but Garin hadn't felt better in weeks. Even though he hadn't been a formal entrant, he'd followed a caravan of vehicles from Mount Whitney Portal toward the watering holes about an hour's drive west.

He sat at the corner table on the raised level of the lounge, affording him an excellent view of the goings-on and a direct path to both the men's room and the exit. On the table in front of him was his fifth ice-cold beer of unknown provenance. They kept magically appearing in front of him and he dutifully consumed the contents.

After returning to the United States following the operation in Pakistan, Garin flew to the West Coast to participate in the Badwater Ultramarathon, unquestionably one of the most grueling physical challenges in the world. More than anything, however, Badwater was a test of will. To complete it, it helped to be one of the best-conditioned athletes in the world, yet ninety-nine percent of those individuals wouldn't even think of entering the race, let alone have the ability to finish it. It was 135 miles through one of the most unforgiving environments on the planet. Through the bowels of Death Valley and partway up Mount Whitney. Temperatures frequently soared to 120 degrees. The dry air sucked the moisture out of runners' lungs and muscles.

Garin hadn't trained for Badwater. At least, he hadn't altered his normal training routine. He planned to rely primarily on sheer willpower. To test himself. See how deep he could reach. How far his determination and discipline could take him.

Garin, however, had arrived too late to participate. Although disappointed, he acknowledged that Tanski was probably right. Relying on sheer willpower was lunacy. He'd probably have caused himself serious physical harm.

In the end, Badwater was still a *voluntary* test of physical and mental toughness. He wouldn't have been shot; he would've suffered no grievous wounds that nearly required amputation; no RPGs would've exploded about him. And he wouldn't have suffered the psychic trauma of having the contents of a teammate's skull splattered across his face—all of which he'd endured during the course of his career.

As Garin finished his beer, he sensed the presence of someone standing behind him. Perhaps it was a combination of the alcohol and self-confidence, but the usual alarms didn't sound and he made no effort to even turn around. In truth, his lack of urgency had more to do with simple calculation: There were only a handful of men in the world who had any hope of sneaking up on him undetected, and he was expecting one of them to join him at some point that night.

Luci Saldana was fascinated by the madman.

This was her third consecutive year acting as part of a support crew for Bob Janasek's attempt to finish Badwater. For the third consecutive year he'd failed, but this time he'd made it almost to the one-hundred-mile mark.

Luci and fellow support-crew member Vicki Starks made sure Janasek was properly hydrated, properly medicated, and resting comfortably in his hotel room before they proceeded to the Diamondback to party—for some, the primary attraction of Badwater.

And shortly thereafter the madman appeared.

What fascinated Luci most about the madman was that he had absolutely no business being here. He wasn't a distance runner. In fact, Luci doubted he had ever run even a half marathon, let alone an ultramarathon, and one in 110-degree heat no less. She knew this because Luci was a runner herself—mostly 10Ks and the occasional half marathon—and she was familiar with the distance runner's physique: muscular calves, lean but developed thighs, thin, almost emaciated torso and arms. The madman, however, was built more like an NFL running back or mixed martial arts competitor: six feet two inches, approximately 210 pounds, sprinter's legs, broad shoulders tapered to a narrow waist, and powerful arms—far too much muscle and upper-body weight to be carried over long distances.

The madman's name was Tom Lofton. He occasionally patronized the Dale City, Virginia, recreation center, where Luci worked the desk part-time while she was studying for her master's in physical therapy.

For the last year, Lofton had been coming in to work out once or twice a week. Unlike most of the other patrons, whose workout schedules rarely varied, Lofton never came in at the same time twice in a row. Sometimes he arrived at five A.M., other times at ten P.M., and a variety of times in between. Occasionally, he wouldn't show up for a week or two.

The rec center members who were distance runners would hit the treadmills for five- to seven-mile runs during the winter. In warmer months they would run several miles outside after some light weight training. Lofton's workouts couldn't be more different. Although they varied, each consisted of intense cross- or interval training. Numerous sprints up the steep hill behind the center followed by multiple sets of squats, dead lifts, power cleans, presses, and plyometrics, with virtually no rest in between.

Luci occasionally saw male rec center members, including some of the former Marines from Quantico who resided nearby, watch in fascination. Lofton's sessions were brutal, almost sadistic. But they weren't *distance* workouts. They were the workouts of someone for whom superb conditioning was more a matter of function than fitness.

The male members weren't the only ones to notice Lofton. Shortly after he began working out at the rec center, Luci noticed that the female members began paying more attention to their appearances. Day-Glo spandex shorts replaced drab sweatpants. Some sported new hairstyles and hints of makeup. They weren't daunted by Lofton's unpredictable schedule; they simply attended more often on the chance that he might be there.

The ladies were, however, frustrated by Lofton's apparent obliviousness to their presence. In the gym he was all focus and exertion.

Luci was one of the few people at the center to whom Lofton ever spoke, even if it was just a greeting. Luci found him courteous and respectful, not qualities she normally found among the good-looking guys she knew. And Lofton, thought Luci, was hot. Not in the soft, pretty-boy way some guys in school or the center looked; rather, he had an intense, serious appearance that suggested looks were not an acceptable substitute for accomplishment.

Despite what Luci believed to be the wrong training approach, it seemed Lofton had planned to make one of those accomplishments completing the Badwater course. Impossible. But those who knew him as Mike Garin wouldn't have bet against him. Not even his fellow operator Gene Tanski, whose long familiarity with him had produced something closer to reverence than proverbial contempt. They'd seen him go from challenge to challenge. Battle to battle. And prevail. Always. No matter the obstacle.

Luci was more than a bit disappointed when Lofton was unable to participate. On first seeing him at Badwater, she was hoping she would have a chance to get to know him after the race. In fact, had she known he was actually going to show up, she would've volunteered to put a support team together for him. The man had a story, and she was determined to find out what it was.

Vicki prodded her to make a move. Luci didn't need much encouragement. The interest was certainly there; it was more a matter of screwing up the nerve. Lofton wasn't the most approachable person. Not only did he have the demeanor of an executioner—albeit a handsome one—but when he spoke, his unnervingly deep voice tended to intimidate everyone within earshot.

Luci knew she was attractive enough. She was pretty and fit and, as the baby sister of four older brothers, was comfortable around men and knew how to make them comfortable around her. She had an infectious gregariousness that made everyone near her more talkative.

Luci had observed Lofton sitting alone in the corner of the lounge for the last hour. In that time she had fended off the good-natured advances of two members of other support crews, downed four beers, and toyed with three different opening lines to use on Lofton. She finally rose from her seat and told a giggling Vicki to wish her luck, when she noticed a tall, wiry man who looked as if he had just driven a herd of cattle to the rail yards approaching Lofton from behind. Luci took a few tentative steps forward before the trail boss took a seat opposite Lofton. He wore cowboy boots, jeans, and a black T-shirt that revealed Popeye forearms laced with a road map of veins and arteries. His hair and beard were the color of pewter and his deep-lined face was almost as taciturn as Lofton's. Whoever he was, he looked like a serious man who had seen and done serious things. Luci returned to her seat and ordered another beer.

The man who had sat across from Garin was Clint Laws, and although not truly a trail boss, he was, at least, a Texan.

The magic waitress placed beers in front of both men and nearly succeeded in escaping with Garin's empty when Clint placed his hand on her arm. "Darling, I truly appreciate the effort. I do. But is there any chance on your next trip back, those pretty little legs of yours might just bring me something a man all growed up might drink? I'm thinking Jackie, Johnnie, or maybe even Jimmy?"

The waitress gave Laws an easy smile and walked away more slowly than she had moved all night.

"Class. Real class," groaned Garin. "Your sorry butt's way too old for her, Clint."

"That's not what those hips say. And those hips don't lie."

Garin shook his head. Laws was not just a character but, quite literally, an original.

One of the first members of First Special Forces Operational Detachment-Delta, colloquially known as Delta Force, he had been among the pioneers to guide the continued evolution of modern asymmetric warfare.

The process of developing specialized unconventional combat units had begun as early as World War II and continued through the early sixties. By the time of US involvement in Vietnam, American special operations forces were well established.

But the need for a hyper-elite quick-reaction force tasked solely with neutralizing catastrophic threats to US security became critically apparent after January 17, 1966. On that date a US Air Force B-52 collided with a tanker during a midflight refueling over the Mediterranean. The B-52 disintegrated in midair and the four Mk-28 hydrogen bombs it was carrying fell to earth near the coastal town of Palomares, Spain.

Conventional explosive material inside two of the bombs detonated, scattering metallic debris below. The radioactive remains were almost immediately recovered and secured.

A third bomb was recovered wholly intact within hours of the incident.

The fourth bomb, however, couldn't be found.

Frantic, President Lyndon Baines Johnson ordered the deployment of scores of ships and planes, along with more than ten thousand troops, to search for the missing bomb. It took nearly three months before the fourth and final nuke was recovered in the Mediterranean at a depth of three thousand feet.

After an intense bout of awkward diplomacy with the Spanish government, the matter was quickly laid to rest.

Seemingly.

In fact, only *one* of the bombs reported destroyed by its conventional explosives had actually exploded. The other couldn't be found. Thousands of American troops and dozens of planes and naval vessels quietly continued searching for the missing bomb.

Obviously, recovering an American nuclear weapon intact would have been a huge intelligence coup for the Soviets, who had learned from an asset in the US State Department that one bomb was still unaccounted for. So they, too, dispatched troops to find the bomb. But in contrast to the massive US deployment, the Soviets sent only a fifteen-man squad of specially trained Spetsnaz GRU commandos, guided by a handful of KGB analysts.

Five months after the accident, the Spetsnaz squad located the missing bomb in the hills of a sparsely populated coastal area south of Carboneras, about twenty miles from Palomares. Within twenty minutes of the discovery, more than two thousand US Marines had the Spetsnaz team surrounded.

After an extraordinarily tense standoff lasting several hours, and a flurry of urgent calls between the White House and the Kremlin, disaster was averted when the Soviets surrendered the nuke.

The incident became the subject of numerous analyses by the CIA and DIA, both of which were astonished that a small team of Soviet special operators was more effective at finding and securing the bomb than a much larger American force, a force that also had the advantage of knowing the area and general conditions in which the bombs were lost.

Reports were written, recommendations made. But they were shelved for nearly two decades. Then, in October 1986, a missile tube on a Soviet Navaga-class nuclear submarine exploded in the Atlantic approximately four hundred miles east of Bermuda. Several US naval vessels were dispatched to the area, but before they could reach the sub, it sank eighteen thousand feet beneath the surface with an estimated thirty nuclear warheads.

Neither the sub nor its arsenal of warheads was ever recovered.

Thereafter, President Ronald Reagan tasked Vice President George H.W. Bush, a former director of the CIA, with forming a quick-reaction force modeled after the Spetsnaz squad and designed to interdict, recover, and/or destroy any loose or rogue weapons of mass destruction—regardless of the source. The vice president tapped a highly regarded special operator, Lieutenant Colonel Clinton Laws, to spearhead the development, recruitment, and training of the force and, ultimately, to command it. Laws handpicked a diverse team of some of the best tier-one special operators in the US military, putting them through an ungodly eighteen-month training program at a four-thousand-acre southern Nevada compound affectionately called the Ranch, a tongue-in-cheek takeoff on the CIA's own training facility in Camp Peary, Virginia, the Farm.

The process was arduous and consumed several years but took on greater urgency with the collapse of the Soviet Union and the nightmare possibility that nuclear weapons housed in former Soviet republics might be stolen by or sold to terrorists or state sponsors of terror.

Laws commanded the force for nearly a dozen years and upon his retirement continued to supervise training at the Ranch. The man he picked as his successor to head the team was killed under circumstances known only to the president and a few others. By then, Laws had already identified Mike Garin as the next leader of the team.

Laws ran both hands through his hair and sat back in his seat.

"Well, tell me about Pakistan, Chief."

Garin registered only mild surprise. "Who says I was in Pakistan?"

"*The Washington Post,* that's who." Laws pantomimed reading a newspaper. "Pakistani officials refused to comment on reports of an explosion and collapse of a tunnel at the nuclear facility in Wah Cantonment. The ISI, Pakistan's intelligence agency, assures that there was no breach of the compound. Reports continued to emerge of numerous bodies being pulled from the debris, reports strongly denied by Pakistani sources. . . ."

"When did you begin reading *The Washington Post*?" Garin asked.

"Opposition research, Chief."

"No, I mean when did you begin reading?"

"Ho, he's got jokes." Laws casually scanned the premises. "I'm guessing those weren't prairie dogs in that tunnel. So, should I assume you can neither confirm nor deny?"

"You know the protocols."

"I *wrote* the protocols. So, I say again, tell me about Pakistan."

"Check the after-action report. I'm sure Kessler would be happy to read you in."

Laws frowned. "That little Kraut's got no sense of gratitude. Every once in a while when he needs something, he'll feed me some useless intel and claim it's on an eyes-only basis. Usually nothing more important than directions to Burger King. But he acts like he just told me about the Manhattan Project. Other than that, the miniature little bastard treats me like a crazy uncle."

"Smart man."

"Not gonna throw me a bone, Chief? Something that'll make an old dried-up operator feel warm and fuzzy? Lord knows with your repulsive face repellin' the honeys, I'm not gettin' any tonight."

Garin smiled for the second time that night, a personal best. Laws was in some ways like an uncle, though far from crazy. He was something of a legend in the special ops community. Even though he'd been officially retired for more than a decade, the various US intelligence agencies still sought his advice and occasionally engaged more specialized services on a contract basis. He maintained an impressive network of contacts both overseas and domestic, well-placed individuals whom Laws had cultivated over several decades who would still return a favor thought long forgotten.

It wouldn't surprise Garin that Laws knew there had been some type of recent operation in Pakistan, although he wouldn't have gotten the information from Kessler. And he wouldn't have known the specific purpose of the operation or any of its details. Laws thrived on such information, but he knew there was almost no likelihood he'd get it from Garin. It was, after all, Laws who had scouted Garin more than a dozen years ago. Laws had plucked the former Ivy Leaguer from the midst of SEAL Qualification Training and set him on a path only a handful of men had ever followed. It was Laws who had harnessed the volatile mix of testosterone and adrenaline within Garin and tempered it with appropriate measures of training and discipline, forging an especially lethal instrument to be unleashed in the war on terror. The training had been more important than the discipline. Indeed, Laws had already heard from Dan Dwyer, an Annapolis football coach, about Garin's preternatural discipline. Many helped train Garin, but Laws was his mentor. And Garin was his prized pupil.

The magic waitress reappeared with a shot glass and a full bottle of Johnnie Walker Red. She placed the bottle and glass on the table, grinning at Laws all the while, causing Garin to marvel at the old man's way with women. As he watched her walk away, he conceded that there was, indeed, no deceit in those hips and recalled that Laws was celebrated among the special ops community for more reasons than one.

Laws poured himself two fingers and hoisted his glass to Garin. "Tell me something, Chief, and be honest. When did your sorry fieldcraft go *all* the way to hell?"

Before Laws could knock back the drink, Garin replied, "If you're referring to whether I noticed the guy sitting at the near end of the bar, blue trousers, gray blazer, white open-neck shirt, thick black hair combed back, copper complexion, two-day stubble, about thirty-five, five foot ten, maybe 185 pounds, who's been nursing a tonic water for the last hour and fifteen minutes and should have a sign taped to his forehead that says 'Which one of these objects doesn't belong?,' then I'd say it all went to hell the first day you took me to the Ranch."

Laws blinked once, put down the drink, and leaned forward, his forearms on the table. "I was referring, smart-ass, to that pretty little señorita with the long black hair and big brown eyes sitting at the other end of this dump, about twenty-seven, maybe five foot three, 105 pounds, yellow sundress, who looks to be charging hard through her fifth Bud and has been staring at you for the last fifteen minutes like she wants to have your babies."

For once, Garin thought, he had the old man. "You really didn't notice him, not until just now, did you?"

Laws threw back the scotch, grimaced, and exhaled forcefully. "Who? Mr. Obvious?"

Garin nodded, a self-satisfied expression forming on his face. The old master, starting to slip, had zeroed in on the lady and had completely missed the possible bad guy.

Laws slowly poured another drink and looked at Garin, a kid who thought he'd beaten his father at H-O-R-S-E for the first time. "You mean the Mr. Obvious whose black 2009 Ford Taurus rental car, Arizona tags RG53588, Nike gym bag in the backseat, is sitting in the parking lot?"

Garin's shoulders sagged visibly, his jaw taut in frustration. The old man had checked him once again, but he didn't dwell on being bested. He glanced at the man nursing the tonic water, then back at Laws. It had been drilled into Garin that if there is any question, there is no question; if a threat is possible, it is certain. The *possibility* of a sniper on the roof was the *certainty* of a sniper on the roof. To operate otherwise was to court disaster, if not death. His mentor caught Garin's hesitation and knew the conversation would turn more serious.

"Something I should know, Chief?"

"Just how big, exactly, was the Nike bag?"

Laws comprehended instinctively. "Big enough to carry say, a Dragunov, along with other assorted parting gifts."

Garin glanced over at Luci, who was gazing at him past the left shoulder of her third suitor of the night. "Clint, I'm going to ask you something. Now, just a hypothetical, understand?"

Laws, of course, understood perfectly.

"What would you do if you saw something on a milk run that you're not sure about? You *think* you saw something that's not supposed to be there, but you're just not sure?"

"Note it in the report, son. Let the analysts figure it out."

"But you're not sure what you saw."

"*What* you saw or *who* you saw?"

"Who. Well . . ." Garin paused. "I don't know if it's a who or a . . . Just something looked vaguely familiar. Like someone or something I should know. Just a possibility. That's all."

"You're a model of clarity there, Chief. If there's a possibility . . ."

"Yeah, yeah, I know, but really . . ."

"There are no—I repeat, I repeat, I repeat—no coincidences in this business, Chief."

Laws casually scanned the premises and then slid his chair closer to Garin. "That brings me to why I wanted to meet you here, Chief."

"I assumed it was for the simple pleasure of my company."

"I didn't want to talk by phone or anything else that could be monitored. And I didn't want to do this at the Ranch either."

"Something tells me you've had your own share of coincidences."

"Over the last three to four months, there's been an unusual number of operations gone bad. As a result, several warriors in the ground."

"Bad things happen all the time."

"Equipment failures, bad intel, weather, ordinary mistakes—sure. We expect those, plan for them. But being repeatedly outmaneuvered, as if the other side anticipated and planned for our moves, that doesn't happen by chance."

Garin didn't need to be sold. Just a short time ago he'd related similar suspicions to Tanski. "What kind of operators?"

"Tier-one."

"That would mean a JSOC-level problem. Maybe higher."

Laws nodded. "My guess is higher."

Garin raised his eyebrows. "Why's that?"

"Intuition. Experience. And certain commonalities."

"What commonalities?"

"Well, for instance, *cui bono*?"

"My guess is all of the failures benefit a certain bad actor," Garin said. "Let me guess: Iran, Russia, China, North Korea, or a major terrorist group?"

"Your guess is as good as mine."

"I seriously doubt that. But specifically, what commonalities?"

"The last three operations involved Crimea, Ukraine, and Syria."

"Geez, Clint. You didn't have to be that specific. Something tells me I'm not supposed to know that."

"You do now," Laws stated matter-of-factly. "What player benefits most from failed US ops in those locations?"

"President Yuri Vladimirovich Mikhailov."

"That's right, Chief. Probably a distant relative of yours. Lord knows he's ugly enough." Laws paused, then shook his head. "Then again, he's way too smart."

"So the Russians are running someone high enough in US military or intelligence to compromise code-worded direct actions. . . ."

"The Soviet Union collapsed. Russian ambitions never do."

Garin said nothing. He conceded Russian interest in Ukraine, Crimea, and Syria. But he couldn't fathom what interest they might have in thwarting his operation beneath a Pakistani nuclear weapons facility.

Laws studied Garin's face. "You're thinking how your little milk run in Pakistan plays into this. I haven't worked that out yet. Maybe it doesn't. But I figure if someone—whether Russian, Chinese, or Guatemalan—is compromising the highest levels of American intelligence and special ops, then they might be able to compromise Omega, too. And if you guys get compromised, well, we're screwed. The whole world's screwed."

"But to affect Omega, they'd have to compromise addresses far beyond MacDill or Bragg," Garin said, referring to the bases that housed US Special Operations Command and Joint Special Operations Command. "Those addresses are in Washington. There are one, two, three, tops. And they're very exclusive."

Laws nodded. "That's why I didn't even trust having this talk at the Ranch."

Garin drained the last of his beer. He nodded slowly to himself, then: "Looks like I've got work to do."

"You always do."

Garin looked at his watch. "My flight back to Reagan is at six A.M. Feel like giving me a lift to my hotel?"

"It's either me or Mr. Obvious."

Garin looked in the direction of the man in the gray blazer. The seat was empty.

CHAPTER SEVEN

A careful man is more likely to remain alive.

Cal Lowbridge was fastidious. He always carried a firearm, sometimes two, wherever he went. He carried his firearms hot but made sure to always safely lock away any weapons he wasn't using, magazine out, no round in the chamber.

Lowbridge was always checking his surroundings, his head seemingly on a perpetual swivel. Little escaped his attention. He rarely took the same route to a destination and constantly checked his rear- and side-view mirrors. Before parking his car, he circled the block at least once, sometimes doubling back twice to see if he was being followed. He never parked his car in the same spot and never near thick foliage. Both of his personal vehicles had remote keyless ignitions.

His apartment was protected by a cutting-edge security system installed by a civilian contractor who had once worked in the same capacity for the FBI. Best of all, he had Loki, his agile Doberman, who seemed to have bionic ears and treated nearly everyone but Lowbridge as a mortal threat.

Lowbridge was a celebrated insomniac. That in itself didn't present much of a problem, except that wherever he was detailed he was always being volunteered for first watch. Like most former SEALs, he had gone without sleep for at least forty-eight hours on multiple occasions. Unlike most former SEALs, he'd begun doing so long before he'd joined the teams and continued long after he'd left.

Lowbridge's baseline insomnia was compounded this particular night by his struggle to adjust to the time change from the preceding three days in Pakistan. Jerri, his long-suffering (as she continually reminded him) girlfriend, left the apartment at ten thirty P.M. to work the night shift as a charge nurse at Sentara Northern Virginia Medical Center. He watched a movie, read parts of two opaque novels, and cleaned Jerri's fish tank after she left. He was wide-awake at two thirty A.M. with no prospect of sleep on the horizon.

Fortunately, Loki seemed to share his master's affliction and was pleased to accompany him on a walk through the neighborhood. Lowbridge inserted a magazine into his Beretta 92S, chambered a round, and stuck the weapon in his pocket holster. Before leaving the apartment he checked the stove, turned off all but one light, set the security alarm, and locked the door. He climbed down a flight of stairs, paused at the doorway, and looked up and down the sidewalk. He noted the locations and makes of the vehicles parked at the curb and, verifying that there was no one silhouetted along the rooftops of adjacent apartment complexes, permitted Loki to precede him out of the building.

The night was warm, humid, and still. The only sound came from the faint buzzing of an overhead streetlamp. There were just two lights on in the windows of the rows of apartment buildings lining the entire block, no pedestrians on the sidewalks, and no motorists on the street. Perfect for walking an obedient yet aggressive dog.

Lowbridge walked slowly and with a slight limp, a consequence of an exceedingly tiny but painful piece of shrapnel in his thigh, acquired during the assignment in Pakistan. Calhoun, the corpsman, had removed the offending piece of metal, disinfected the wound, and given Lowbridge an antibiotic shortly after the team's extraction. He was given a clean bill of health upon arrival just outside Fort Belvoir for debrief and told to expect some stiffness and soreness for a while. Within a week or two he would be back to normal.

With no pedestrians, vehicles, or small animals to distract him, Loki was content to walk slowly at his master's side. Lowbridge paused at the end of the block and contemplated which direction to proceed. He decided to go right for no other reason than Loki had already begun moving in that direction. Loki's decision was based on his favorite oak, which he carefully inspected before marking his territory once again, part of an ongoing turf war with the seemingly incontinent black Lab that resided with his elderly owner in the duplex across the street.

Loki returned to Lowbridge's side and the pair made another right turn onto a largely unoccupied street where several houses had been left in midconstruction due to a persistent softness in the housing market. Jerri and Lowbridge had inspected one of the houses with an eye toward financing its completion and moving in. Cal estimated he had another year, at most, in Omega. He'd lost no more than half a step, but in his business that loss could be fatal. He'd had some feelers from security firms and private military contractors. Very good money. He'd long ago begun preparing for the transition, accumulating a decent savings. Leaving the team—the camaraderie, the sense of purpose—would be hard, but Jerri's biological clock (as she frequently reminded him) was ticking.

Loki nuzzled Lowbridge's hand in search of some treats. Cal dug into his left pocket for a biscuit, when Loki's ears perked and he began to emit a growl that immediately turned into a soft, plaintive yelp as a geyser of blood erupted from the top of his skull and he fell on his side.

Almost simultaneously, the hot sharpness of ballistic metal pierced the left side of Lowbridge's neck just below the jawbone. Astonished by the skill of his assassin, in the milliseconds before death the fastidious operator chastised himself for not thinking it peculiar that the neighborhood's nocturnal insects had remained still on this warm and humid night.

CHAPTER EIGHT

Clint Laws turned his big Suburban into the parking lot of Garin's hotel and stopped at the entrance.

"Where you headed from here?" Garin asked.

"A little R and R at Kings Canyon, then back to the Ranch."

"Any last words of wisdom?"

"Plenty, but your peanut brain couldn't remember them all."

"Then give me the condensed version."

"You should expect that they're coming after Omega, Chief."

"Who?"

"Don't know."

"Why Omega?"

"Looks like someone's compromising tier-one operations. If that's the case, Omega's the grand prize. So keep your eyes open. Take nothing for granted. Make sure your team's on alert, but don't communicate in any way that can be monitored or intercepted. I'll try to find out as much as I can when I get back to the Ranch. In the meantime, keep your eyes open."

"You said that already."

"Make sure you remember it."

Garin opened the car door. "Talk to you later."

As Garin entered the hotel, Laws drove out of the lot. Even if he had kept his own counsel, he would not have noticed the black 2009 Ford Taurus, Arizona tags RG53588, parked with its lights off in the darkened lot across the street.

CHAPTER NINE

For Miriam Camacho, life was good. In fact, she couldn't imagine it much better. Primarily because Manny was home. And Manny made everything, and everyone, better.

They'd been married for eight years, right out of high school in the Bronx, where they'd been high school sweethearts, a fact that had befuddled many of the other boys in school. Most of them thought Miriam was out of Manny's league. She was tall—nearly three inches taller than Manny—and gorgeous. Manny, on the other hand, was short and not much to look at. He had a big nose, huge ears, and riotously crooked teeth. But he had a big smile, a bigger heart, and an incessant, infectious laugh.

He was an indifferent student but he was a quick study and could do almost anything: install a transmission on a '68 Checker Marathon, dunk a basketball, repair an oil-fired furnace, do a backflip, fix a laptop, play the drums, bake a pie, pull a quarter from your ear.

But his primary talent was making people laugh, which, by the sounds wafting up the basement stairs, he was doing this very moment. It was the tinkling squeals of their little girls, Lillie, age five, and Ana, age three, plus the booming guffaws of Manny's giant teammate,

Eli Calhoun, age somewhere north of thirty. Equal opportunity laughter, spanning generations.

While Miriam prepared baked beans, potato salad, and corn in the kitchen, Manny grilled steaks on the patio outside the sliding glass doors of the basement rec room. It was a ritual begun shortly after his completion of BUD/S. Whenever he returned from a training exercise or an operation, he'd bring a different member of the team over for beer and steaks. That ritual, plus Manny's interminable pranking, made him the most popular member of the team.

He was on a new team now, a member for less than six months. Although Miriam didn't detect much difference from Manny's previous units, she sensed from his obvious pride that this team was unique. Upon learning of his qualification and selection, he'd acted as if he'd been named to a major league all-star team.

Eli was the second to last of Manny's teammates to partake in the ritual. Miriam liked him. A Texan, he was as big as Manny was small. Boulders for shoulders, tree trunks for legs. He had an open, guileless face and addressed Miriam as "ma'am." Judging by the sounds coming from the basement, he and Manny were getting along like long-separated brothers. Manny got along with all of his teammates that way.

Except for one. Manny's team leader, the star of the all-stars. He spooked everyone. Manny promised—no, warned—Miriam that he'd bring the man over after the next op. Miriam was curious to meet him. It was one of the few times Miriam had ever seen even a trace of apprehension in her husband's eyes.

Miriam heard a scramble of tiny feet coming up the stairs. As the basement door burst open, a peal of laughter emerged from the stairwell, followed by the beaming faces of Lillie and Ana, who breathlessly announced that Daddy and Uncle Eli needed more "brown juice" and pretzels. Fast. Right away. And while she was at it, they could probably use lots more of those chocolate cookies with sprinkles. For Daddy, of course. And Uncle Eli. He liked cookies. A lot.

Life was good. And joyous. And fun. And it was about to get even better. While Manny was away, her obstetrician had confirmed what Miriam suspected: She was pregnant again. About two and a half months along.

She hadn't told Manny yet. After a protracted debriefing, he'd come home late in the night and they'd celebrated his return in their usual way, falling hard asleep afterward. A few hours later she heard the girls' squeals upon discovering Daddy home and making breakfast in the kitchen. Pots and pans crashing, cups and dishes clattering, the smell of bacon and eggs swirling. Shortly thereafter Eli had arrived. Then more cooking and grilling and laughter.

She looked forward to telling Manny the news after Eli left. Manny wanted a boy this time, but either way he'd be ecstatic. Another crazy Camacho, all electricity and sparks and manic energy.

As Miriam busied herself getting more beer and snacks, the basement hysterics ebbed for a spell—Manny and Eli likely pausing to admire a three-run homer or an acrobatic double play on Manny's ridiculous seventy-two-inch screen. Or maybe Eli was quietly listening to the preamble of one of Manny's outrageous jokes. Regardless, soon there would be another eruption of laughter punctuated by hoots and howls and backslaps and foot stomps, the mere anticipation of which had Miriam giggling to herself.

She dispensed three cookies each to Lillie and Ana, tucked the six-pack under her left arm, grabbed the bag of pretzels with her right hand, and descended the stairs to the temporarily quiet basement. Upon reaching the fourth step from the bottom, the reason for the silence came into view. Light transmitted it instantly to her optic nerves, which relayed it to the deepest reaches of her brain, which refused to process it.

To her left, bright sunshine flooded through the sliding glass doors, a spiderweb of cracks radiating from two holes in the glass. To her right, Eli Calhoun lay faceup on the all-weather carpet Manny had put down just last month. Eli's eyes were open but there was nothing inside. On Eli's far side, sprawled across the tan leather lounge chair, was Manny, a single hole centered on the ridge between his eyebrows, just above the bridge of his nose. His eyes, too, were open. Behind him on the headrest was an explosion of hair, blood, bone fragments, and brain tissue.

A heartbeat later the cognitive regions of Miriam's brain finally permitted the signal from her optic nerves to be processed. A heartbeat after that, her legs went numb and she began to wobble.

Her obstetrician would later determine that Miriam's miscarriage was caused by the trauma of her falling down the remaining stairs to the basement floor. But Miriam would always believe it was due to the trauma of knowing that her life, a life that seemed to be reaching a crescendo, would never be good again.

CHAPTER TEN

DALE CITY, VIRGINIA

JULY 13 • 1:25 P.M. EDT

Garin had slept the entire four-and-a-half-hour flight back to Washington, D.C. So deep was his sleep that he was momentarily disoriented when awakened by the sound of the other passengers removing their carry-on bags from the overhead bins and exiting the aircraft. He looked around the plane and out the window, trying to get his bearings. Seeing the familiar outlines of Gate 10 of Reagan National, he rose carefully from his seat, surprised that he could move with relative ease. Maybe he was in even better shape than he thought. Or maybe it was the glutamine and turmeric he'd ingested before the flight. Not that he felt invigorated enough to tackle a fresh session of PT, but he didn't think he would need more than a day or two to recover.

Garin checked his watch as he moved through the terminal toward the parking facility. Just after one thirty P.M. Taking Laws's advice, he'd refrained from using any devices to contact the other members of Omega. Since they all lived within thirty miles of the District, his plan was to dump his gear at his apartment, then visit each personally. After they had been read on to the possibility that someone was compromising operations, they'd develop a course of action.

He bought a liter bottle of water at a kiosk, consumed its contents in a few seconds, and then bought another, placing it in the smaller of two gym bags for the drive home.

A blast of hot air met him as the sliding glass doors opened to the outside walkway. Locating his Jeep Wrangler Sahara on the first level of the garage, he stored his bags in the rear and retrieved the parking ticket partially wedged under the rubber floor mat. By habit, he examined the vehicle and scanned the entire garage before starting the engine. The place was full of vehicles but no other travelers. Saturday afternoon in July in the District. Hot, humid, and slow.

Before turning on the ignition, he hit a preset on his phone to check in with his support. Getting no answer, he drove out, heading toward I-95 South. He retrieved a La Gloria Cubana cigar from the glove box, lit it, and inserted a Jimi Hendrix CD. He fast-forwarded to "Voodoo Child" and turned the volume to its pulsating maximum, drawing the attention of the motorists he passed.

Michael Garin, clandestine warrior, hiding in plain sight.

To describe Garin's apartment as Spartan would be to assign an unwarranted level of luxury to it. The unit was located in one of a series of low-rise apartment buildings in a sprawling complex in Dale City, Virginia, approximately thirty minutes southwest of D.C. The complex catered to low-income families and had some of the lowest rental prices in the Washington metropolitan area. The majority of the complex's occupants were Latin American and the remainder equal percentages of whites and blacks. A fair number of the male residents were day laborers who congregated every morning at five at the 7-Eleven about two blocks south of the complex to be picked up by general contractors working throughout Prince William County.

Garin's apartment was a basement-level unit in Building C, directly accessible from the outside. It consisted of a living room that doubled as a bedroom, a small efficiency kitchen, a bathroom, and a five-by-five storage space. A single mattress lay on the floor next to a lamp and a neat stack of about a dozen history books. The only other furnishing was a metal folding chair that Garin would pull up to the kitchen counter to eat his meals. The refrigerator rarely contained more than milk and some fruits and vegetables, and most of the cabinets above the sink were bare, save for a few glasses and dishes. Above the refrigerator, however, sat an impressive array of nutritional supplements, energy drinks, and meal-replacement packs.

The entire living space was no more than four hundred square feet, a place to "flop" when Garin was in town, which was infrequently. The apartment made no statement about Garin other than his indifference to comfort and his affectless efficiency. It was only a fifteen-minute drive from Quantico to the west and Fort Belvoir to the east, and barely a quarter mile from the Dale City Rec Center on the other side of Minnieville Road.

The clusters of apartment buildings in the complex were separated by fairly large expanses of grass worn bare from the incessant soccer games played by his neighbors' kids. On Sundays the day laborers played on the largest such field, opposite Garin's apartment.

Since he was often away, Garin had few occasions to interact with the other residents of the complex, but he found them pleasant and likable when he did. He was an enigma to the adults and a subject of speculation for the kids. The young boys, some of whom tried to copy every nuance of his walk, were especially intrigued by him. Though they disagreed wildly about Garin's occupation, they were unanimous that whatever he did, it must certainly be something highly nefarious.

The leader of the twenty or so boys who lived in Garin's cluster was ten-year-old Emilio Val Buena, who lived with his mother and somewhat bookish older sister in the unit two floors above Garin's place. Emilio was smart and one of the better soccer players in the complex, but part of his elevated status was due to the fact that he was the only kid to have actually spoken to the mysterious Señor Lofton. In fact, it had been Emilio who had pried loose the name. From there, of course, it took very little for Emilio to embellish the routine salutations the two exchanged and report to his friends the details of Señor Lofton's many epic adventures. A trip to the gym became a rendezvous with a spy; a bruise on the arm signaled a battle with multiple assailants. Emilio could not know how closely he sometimes swerved toward the truth.

Emilio had taken an almost proprietary interest in Garin and jealously guarded his position as the complex's primary contact with the enigma. And like many kids, Emilio was an expert at surveillance, especially regarding goings-on in the complex. So it was Emilio who first spotted Garin's Jeep pulling into a parking space almost directly below the front window of the Val Buenas' apartment. Señor Lofton had been gone for nearly two weeks—enough time, clearly, to topple a small African nation or kidnap a crime boss's girlfriend. In fact, the two strangers Emilio had seen in the parking lot earlier that day were probably the crime boss's henchmen, coming to exact a terrible revenge on Señor Lofton.

Spotting Emilio in the window, Garin waved as he climbed out of the Jeep. The soccer fields were deserted due to the stifling midafternoon heat, the neighborhood kids having sought refuge in their air-conditioned apartments with video games for entertainment.

Garin pulled his bags from the back of the Jeep and glanced back up to Emilio before proceeding down the concrete steps on the west side of the building that led to his apartment. Emilio stood before the window with a look of concentration, or perhaps one of anticipation, on his face. Interesting. Random bits of information floated through the part of Garin's brain devoted to self-preservation. An odd club patron, a Nike bag in the back of a rental car. If there is any question . . .

Garin slowed his pace, taking note of his surroundings again before wedging the smaller of his two bags into his armpit so that he could remove his Oakleys and insert the key into the door. Garin shut his eyes for a moment to acclimate them to the dark apartment and then opened the door.

Light from the blazing sun spilled in a rhomboid pattern across the carpeted floor and reflected dimly off the suppressed Makarov PMM held in the outstretched hands of a figure obscured by shadow. Garin sprang forward furiously, knocking the intruder backward as a round tore into the gym bag under Garin's right arm. As the two crashed to the floor, Garin seized the weapon with both hands and ripped it from the intruder's grasp as the man's head bounced off the floor. Rolling swiftly to his left off of the momentarily dazed assailant, Garin landed on his back facing the open door. Standing there, as Garin intuited, was the assailant's partner, his figure outlined in the doorway against the streaming sunlight. Garin squeezed the trigger four times, striking the second man twice in the head and twice in the upper torso. The figure dropped limply to his knees and fell forward onto his face. Garin immediately shifted his aim to his left, where the first assailant was struggling to sit up. Garin fired two shots into the man's chest. Then, springing to his feet, Garin stood over the man's motionless body and fired a round into the bridge of his nose.

Garin crouched slightly with the weapon grasped in both hands before him, tracking across the room from left to right. He then strode quickly toward the second assailant, the Makarov trained on his body, and kicked the man's weapon clear. Garin reached down with his left hand and pulled the body clear of the doorframe. After turning on the adjacent light switch, he shut the door and looked about the tiny apartment, the scent of cheap aftershave filling his nostrils. He paused to gather himself and moved quickly to check the bathroom and closet.

Satisfied that the apartment was clear, Garin looked at his watch: 2:45. He estimated that he had no more than fifteen minutes before the team backing up the pair lying dead on the floor would arrive to see why they hadn't checked in. They clearly weren't amateurs, a matter made plain by the fact that, despite his suspicions, he had failed to detect the second assailant. Although he hadn't seen any signs of another crew in the vicinity when he drove up, he had to assume that another team was watching the apartment.

Garin again hit the call key for support on his phone and waited. Nothing. He quickly disconnected and repeated the action. Same result. Garin didn't have time to dwell on his inability to contact his team's support. Instead, he methodically searched the bodies for any identification. Nothing. No licenses, no credit cards. Not even a cell phone. Even their faces yielded little: perhaps Mediterranean, but beyond that, no specificity. He went to the window next to the doorway and peered through a slight part in the drawn curtains for any evidence of surveillance. Again, nothing.

Garin began to feel a dull pain in his ribs that had been shielded by the gym bag when the first assailant had discharged his weapon. He was fortunate that the bullet hadn't even pierced the bag, having been slowed by the presence of several hardcover books, a water bottle, running shoes, and assorted gear packed tightly inside. It was unlikely that the ribs were broken, but the ache was sure to remind him of the encounter for a few days.

He went into the closet, where a black gym bag nearly identical to the one that had just saved him was stored on a shelf above the clothes rack. Garin placed the bag on the kitchen counter and, facing the door, unzipped the side compartment. The next person to come through that door uninvited would be met by the unfriendly contours of the SIG Sauer P226 that Garin pulled out. Opening the bag's end compartment, he found a suppressor and two extra magazines and stuffed them into his pockets. He pulled back the slide to check the chamber and placed the pistol on the counter.

The bag was a survival kit, a fail-safe of sorts. It contained items essential for Garin's short-term existence in case he was cut off and on his own. He had used it—or more accurately, taken it with him—once before, for an assignment that required a lightning insertion into an Eastern European city without any preparation or staging whatsoever. As it turned out, he'd left the bag aboard the transport plane since he'd been able to make arrangements with local contacts for supplies.

The bag contained approximately fifty thousand dollars in cash—ten thousand of which was in dinars and euros—multiple IDs, credit cards in various names, a US passport for Thomas Lofton as well as a French passport for Andre Duvalier, a Glock 17 and several magazines, a tactical knife, a toiletry kit, QuikClot, a secure cell phone, and a couple of changes of underwear, socks, shirts, and pants.

Garin tried calling support once more. Nothing except a hum. Anxiety gradually began to replace frustration as he decided that the circumstances dictated he abandon Laws's advice and try to contact his team immediately by phone. He hit the first of several preset numbers stored on a coded contact list. Rod Mears. Another hum. He looked at his phone as if he expected it to provide a written explanation for his lack of success and then hit the next number, Joe Calabrese. A hum. Eli Calhoun—hum. Cal Lowbridge—hum.

The muscles in Garin's jaw tensed with each unsuccessful attempt to reach the members of his team and he began pacing the length of the counter as he dialed. Manny Camacho—hum. Gene Tanski . . . Garin stopped pacing. The phone was ringing. A sense of hopeful relief crept over him, only to be replaced by growing urgency as it continued to ring without answer. Garin disconnected and went to the last preset: John Gates—hum.

Garin's mind rifled through the plausible reasons for his inability to contact anyone from Omega. None was pleasant. He quickly cycled through the calls once again, this time leaving Tanski for last, and once again, only Tanski's number rang and rang.

Garin examined his watch: 2:53. He considered his situation. An attempt had been made on his life by two men of indeterminate nationality. They were professionals. He was unable to reach either his support or any of the men he'd last seen only a few days ago when they had returned after a successful, highly sensitive DA in Pakistan. His working assumption, at least for purposes of self-preservation, was that the rest of his team was dead and someone wanted him dead also. He hadn't the slightest idea who that someone might be. If he tried to contact anyone outside of Omega for help, he might reveal his whereabouts to the very person behind today's events.

It was time to move. There was at least one open door left: Gene Tanski's phone was still ringing and he lived less than thirty minutes away. If Garin couldn't reach him by phone, he would have to reach him in person.

Garin took the SIG and gym bag off the counter and stepped over the bodies of the two dead men as he went to the door. The matter of disposing of the corpses would have to be addressed later. He peeked out the window again before slowly opening the door, pistol held at eye level. He examined the entire area outside the apartment for several seconds before putting the weapon into the pocket holster on his right and covering it with his shirt. In similar circumstances he sometimes had a gnawing sensation that he was about to be struck by a sniper's bullet, the only solace being that he would be dead before he even heard the shot. He knew the feeling wouldn't go away until he was no longer in open space.

Turning left, he walked briskly up the concrete steps to the parking lot, this time stopping to check the undercarriage of the Jeep before jumping in and turning the ignition. When he pulled back from the curb, Garin saw Emilio appear at the window above. As he shifted into drive, Garin gave a casual wave, prompting Emilio to return the gesture enthusiastically, a broad grin covering his face.

As the brake lights of Garin's Jeep disappeared around the corner, Emilio stood vigil by the window, putting the finishing touches on the latest Señor Lofton yarn.

CHAPTER ELEVEN

Olivia Perry wasn't surprised by the news she'd just received, but that did nothing to diminish her bitterness. There was simply no defensible reason for what was going to occur at Turtle Bay, yet few were even aware and fewer still seemed to care.

Olivia had been excited when she'd accepted the offer to be an aide to National Security Advisor James Brandt, her former advisor at Stanford. Moving to D.C. and being at the fulcrum of important global developments promised to be exhilarating. Although the move was a significant advancement in her career, her first few months on the job proved to be largely an exercise in mind-numbing tedium.

Her primary charge had been to monitor and analyze Russian commercial transactions and overall economic development for any hints of their strategic ambitions. Old-fashioned Kremlinology had been resurrected due to President Mikhailov's increasing bellicosity and adventurism.

But she found nothing scintillating there. It appeared that in some respects the Russians were reverting to the disastrous practices of a command economy. Over the last couple of years they'd produced massive quantities of run-of-the-mill electrical equipment, only to have it all sit idly in row upon row of enormous warehouses scattered throughout the vast country. They'd manufactured enough generators to power a medium-size European country, but there was no corresponding market. Two decades after the collapse of the Soviet Union, Russia, it seemed, still hadn't mastered the vagaries of supply and demand.

Moreover, the spike in US natural gas production due to new drilling techniques was depressing Russian economic growth. Hydrocarbons, after all, had been responsible for nearly forty percent of Russian GDP growth over the last decade. But the US natural gas boom was lowering world gas prices and undercutting Russian gas exports to Europe. Gazprom, the mammoth Russian gas company—indeed, the largest in the world—had suspended liquefied natural gas production at the Shtokman field in the Arctic because of plummeting prices. They were now forced to look to burgeoning Asian markets for salvation.

There was something about the Russian economy that bothered Olivia. Something annoying, like the irritating whine of a mosquito flitting about her ear, looking for a place to alight. It kept buzzing whenever she was concentrating on another task. Buzzing to remind her to pay attention. To take a closer look.

Olivia stared gloomily out the window of the Peet's Coffee near the Old Executive Office Building, where she'd spent most of the day gathering information and preparing analyses for Brandt regarding the positions of various nations on the escalating tensions between Israel and its Middle Eastern neighbors. Earlier in the week, the IDF had conducted strikes on a number of Hezbollah strongholds in southern Lebanon in retaliation for a blizzard of rocket attacks on the Golan Heights over the preceding four days. Although a dozen Israeli civilians had died, the international media became aroused only when one of the IDF's strikes had resulted in the inadvertent deaths of approximately eight Palestinian civilians whom Hezbollah rocketeers were using as human shields. The familiar pattern of outrage and denunciations

followed, beginning, of course, in Tehran and Damascus and concluding in Moscow, Brussels, and Paris.

The buzzing in Olivia's ear persisted.

The United States was one of the few nations that stood by Israel's
use of force. President Marshall issued a statement of unequivocal
support for Israel's right to defend itself and caused a minor tempest
when he demanded the UN investigate possible Hezbollah culpability
for the deaths of the civilians.

Of course, the president's demand went nowhere. In contrast, the
draft resolution condemning Israel for the strikes and demanding no
further incursions by the IDF into southern Lebanon rapidly picked
up support.

Carole Tunney, the US ambassador to the UN, had spent the last
two days trying to prevent the resolution from being brought up for a
vote of the General Assembly. For a while it appeared the resolution
might be tabled, but by midafternoon on Friday, momentum began to
shift in favor of the draft.

Olivia was monitoring developments for Brandt from Washington.
At approximately one thirty in the afternoon Tunney's assistant informed Olivia that the UN would indeed vote to condemn Israel. Far
worse, the resolution was expected to call for Israel to pull back all
forces to its 1967 borders, to be enforced by threat of economic sanctions.

Olivia was disgusted. This was not simply a diplomatic insult to
the United States. It had the potential to be a national security debacle
for Israel. Requiring Israel to pull back to its 1967 borders would give
Israel's enemies command of the Golan Heights, exposing much of
Israel's population to rocket attacks. Olivia thought it highly unlikely
that Israel would comply with the resolution and that an economic
boycott would strengthen the hands of Hezbollah, Syria, and Iran, en-
couraging them to become even more aggressive and increasing the

possibility that Turkey and even Egypt might join the fray. Israel could find itself in the ultimate dilemma: either face possible annihilation or unleash its nukes.

And the buzzing became louder.

Olivia had called Brandt to relay the developments at the UN. Brandt, who was with the president when Olivia called, received the news with his typical reserve. He agreed that the proposed resolution was breathtakingly irresponsible but was fairly confident the United States and Britain would prevail upon Egypt to stand down.

Olivia ordered an iced coffee and pondered what Brandt would recommend to the president if the resolution passed in the next seventy-two hours. She probably knew how his mind worked better than anyone, but despite his orderly and precise thought process, he was sometimes unpredictable—which was when he often came up with his best ideas.

Taking a long sip of coffee, Olivia finally yielded to the buzzing. Despite the urgency of the Middle East crisis, her mind kept returning to the puzzle of the Russian economy. In the midst of an economic downturn, they kept producing commodities no one wanted. It was as if the laws of supply and demand had been suspended. It made no sense, especially with the decline of their energy sector.

The buzzing came to a crescendo and abruptly stopped. The energy sector.

While world energy markets were struggling and energy prices were volatile, something peculiar was going on with Russian energy production. Olivia had first noticed it when scanning some unremarkable satellite surveillance photos of industrial sites. Nothing exotic in the photos, just fuel storage depots, tanker trucks, and pumps. But there were multitudes of them. And that was a problem. An as yet undefinable problem.

Olivia had no idea how big that problem was about to become.

CHAPTER TWELVE

DUMFRIES, VIRGINIA

JULY 13 • 3:35 P.M. EDT

Garin drove his Jeep onto a gravel access road about a quarter mile east of Jefferson Davis Highway. A shallow, heavily wooded ravine separated the access road and the backyards of the houses in Gene Tanski's development.

Garin parked in the tall, reedy grass on the side of the access road so that the Jeep wouldn't be readily visible to passersby, although it appeared the road was rarely used. He headed cautiously down the side of the ravine and through the woods toward Tanski's backyard; in brown cargo pants and a tan T-shirt, he could've blended better into his surroundings, but at least he didn't stick out.

He held the SIG at his right side. Crossing a small creek at the bottom, Garin ascended the opposite side of the ravine and could hear the sound of a lawn mower somewhere over the crest. It was unclear whether the sound was coming from Tanski's yard or that of one of his neighbors, but as Garin climbed closer to the top of the hill he allowed himself to hope that Tanski was still alive. He'd known Tanski longer than any of the other members of the team. They had been on numerous deployments together in some of the most hostile territories imaginable. A former Delta staff sergeant, Tanski was one of the toughest and most resourceful operators in the nation's covert arsenal.

Once, on a mission in Yemen a little more than two years earlier, Garin had been momentarily stunned by an RPG that had exploded only a few feet away from his position. He was conscious, barely so, but immobile. The concussion from the same explosion had knocked Tanski off his feet and blown his M4 from his grasp. Tanski and Garin's defensive position just inside a vacant storefront was charged by four screaming combatants who believed one or both of the pair to be either dead or disabled. As the combatants stood over Tanski and Garin, ready to administer a coup de grâce, Tanski pulled his combat knife from his boot and in one motion sliced the femoral artery of the assailant closest to him, and as the man fell in agony, Tanski pulled him on top of his body, using him as a human shield. He then took the man's AK-47 and, with smooth precision, shot the remaining combatants dead before they had even processed what was happening. Garin had passed out shortly thereafter. When he regained consciousness moments later, the combatant with the severed thigh was also dead. Garin never asked Tanski whether the cause of death was bleeding or something else. There was little need.

Unsure of the exact boundaries of Tanski's property, Garin headed in the direction the lawn mower sound was coming from. When he got within twenty feet of the top of the hill he knelt down and crawled slowly until he was only a foot or two from the crest. There, he paused and then looked behind him and to each side for signs of any other human presence. He was alone.

The noise from the mower was fading gradually as Garin, flat on his stomach, looked over the top of the hill. The property was about two hundred feet wide and bordered on either side by rows of towering pines.

Garin could see the back of a man on a riding mower heading

toward the rear of the house about seventy yards away. The red cap he was wearing was pulled down low over his head, making it difficult for Garin to tell whether it was Tanski or someone else, but as the tractor began to turn around on the return pass, the man's profile, dominated by a bulbous nose broken in countless bar fights, left no doubt it was the former Delta operator.

Garin rose from his stomach and got to his feet, relieved to see his friend unharmed.

Seeing Garin, a puzzled look came over Tanski's face. What the hell was his boss doing coming up from the ravine with a weapon at his side, looking as if he had been doing some weekend recce? Hadn't he just gotten enough of that crap in Pakistan? As it would for any operator with Tanski's experience, the unexpected fired his synapses, prompting his eyes to dart about the vicinity.

Garin returned the SIG to his pocket holster and raised his hand to wave when he saw a strong gust of wind blow Tanski's cap off his head. Tanski began to wobble drunkenly in his seat and then collapsed off the tractor, the pressure sensors in the seat automatically shutting the machine off and bringing it to a halt. Tanski's cap lay several feet from his body. There was, however, not even the slightest breath of wind.

Garin dove to the ground, pulled out his pistol, and crawled quickly backward into the tree line at the top of the ravine. He should've been able to hear a rifle shot over the drone of the tractor and concluded that the sniper must have used a suppressor. Blood was now covering Tanski's entire face and it was clear that the top of his head had been torn off. Garin scanned the surrounding area and listened for movement. By the direction in which Tanski's cap was blown off, Garin estimated that the sniper was positioned somewhere to Garin's left, the vector suggesting no more than eighty to one hundred yards away.

Garin resisted the temptation to run toward Tanski's body. There was nothing he could do for him, and the sniper would be able to cut him down easily in the open field. Instead, he continued to listen for sounds of the assassin making his retreat—branches snapping, the crunch of leaves underfoot. He heard and saw no signs whatsoever of the gunman. Had the sniper seen Garin stand up a split second before shooting Tanski? Garin thought it unlikely. The sniper had probably had Tanski in his scope for several seconds before taking the shot and with his concentration on his target wouldn't have seen Garin. Garin wondered, however, whether the sniper had noticed the confused expression on Tanski's face just a moment before the shot. He should have, and if he was good, he wouldn't dismiss it. If he was good, he would wait a moment. He would try to determine if Tanski had spotted something—a person, an animal—or if his target had just remembered a forgotten errand. He would wait until he was reasonably certain there was no one else in the vicinity before making his exit.

The sniper would be the first to move. He had no evidence that anyone was around, and he held the weapon that killed Tanski. When someone came looking for Tanski, they would come looking for him, too. So Garin kept his head down and waited for a moment. And listened.

It took less time than Garin expected. Within a few minutes his trained ear heard the barely perceptible sound of fabric against underbrush. He looked in the direction of the noise and saw movement approximately one hundred yards down the ravine. The sniper *was* good—he had moved an appreciable distance through dense woods making nary a sound. Garin crawled back behind the tree line and rose to his feet. He couldn't get a clear visual on the sniper but detected a slight movement of branches and leaves. He momentarily raised his weapon in the direction of the movement but considered the noise the discharge would make reverberating through the ravine and stopped. Given the distance, and with all the trees and brush in the way, the odds of hitting the sniper with a pistol were poor. If he was going to alarm the neighbors and alert law enforcement with gunfire, he'd better make it worthwhile. He decided to pursue the sniper and see if he could get a clear shot.

Garin scrambled down the ravine toward the creek as fast as he could while making as little noise as possible. At the same time he kept his eyes trained in the direction where he'd seen movement and prepared to hit the ground if he saw a raised rifle or heard a shot.

A minute later Garin crossed the creek and paused to listen for movement. He saw and heard nothing. He climbed the other side of the ravine rapidly, once again feeling the sensation of being in a sniper's sights. If the sniper had gotten near the crest, he might easily be able to pick Garin off.

He emerged from the ravine about sixty yards north of where he'd hidden the Jeep. As he turned toward the vehicle, he heard tires spinning on the gravel access road, as if someone was trying to leave in a hurry. Sprinting through the tall grass, he could see a cloud of dust billowing upward approximately one hundred yards south of the Jeep. Upon clearing the grass, he leveled his weapon at the receding car, the rear of which was completely concealed by a curtain of the chalky dust kicked up from the gravel.

Garin held his fire. He couldn't shoot what he couldn't see. For the moment, Tanski's assassination would go unavenged.

And Garin's predicament had worsened.

CHAPTER THIRTEEN

NORTHERN VIRGINIA

JULY 13 • 5:42 P.M. EDT

Tanski's assassination confirmed Garin's initial suspicion that someone had taken out his entire team, but part of him insisted on remaining in denial. After all, how could seven of the most skilled operators in
the world, plus, apparently, their support, be eliminated so effectively?
Who had that kind of capability? What was the motive?

So after leaving Tanski's he drove quickly to the residences of each
and every member of Omega and its support team to confirm whether
they were dead or alive. First, Cal Lowbridge's, where an inconsolable
Jerri gave Garin the news. Then to Manny Camacho's, where an am-
bulance crew was in the process of taking his wife, Miriam, to the
hospital and a neighbor hovering nearby explained that the cops had
found the bodies of Manny and someone named Calhoun. Garin
made an anonymous call to the Prince William County Sheriff's Office after finding Rod Mears lying on his side on his kitchen floor, the
back of his head blown away.

And on it went—Joe Calabrese, the members of the support team—
yet after each confirmation, Garin held out hope that someone had
escaped the slaughter.

But any remaining doubt evaporated when he drove to John Gates's house in Dumfries, to check the last member of Omega. Garin stopped a block from his destination. The place now consisted only of a brick fireplace and damaged chimney surrounded by smoldering embers that had once been Gates's home. Much of the yard was surrounded by yellow police tape. Two yellow fire department SUVs were all that remained of the crew that had extinguished the blaze several hours earlier. Several arson investigators and technicians were picking through the rubble. Garin knew, if they hadn't already done so, they would soon find the remnants of Gates's body. And he knew that he was now the only surviving member of Omega.

Garin turned the Jeep around and headed back to his apartment in Dale City. He needed to tend to the grim matter of body disposal. He considered dispensing with the chore—in the big picture, neatly getting rid of the corpses of two killers didn't exactly qualify as a high-priority item. On the other hand, in the summer heat the bodies would begin decomposing and the stench would lead to their quick discovery and yet another problem Garin didn't need.

The Saturday evening traffic on I-95 North was moving slowly. Garin, normally impatient, barely noticed, consumed by the events of the day. As he drove, it occurred to Garin that perhaps the only person he could trust now was Clinton Laws. The old soldier's counsel and assistance might be essential to staying alive. So while the traffic inched along, he punched Laws's number and waited. The phone rang but there was no answer, unusual for Laws. He disconnected and hit redial. Again no answer.

Garin took the Dale City exit and proceeded west on Dale Boulevard toward Minnieville. It didn't take long for him to determine that body disposal wasn't going to be on tonight's agenda. Well before pulling into the apartment complex off Minnieville, he could see a number of official-looking vehicles surrounding his building. When he drew closer he could see more than a dozen individuals in distinctive blue FBI jackets standing on the grass immediately outside the open door of his apartment. Several floodlights shone on the entrance. Milling about just beyond the circle of FBI agents were dozens of apartment residents. Several Dale City police officers were standing next to cruisers occupying the parking spaces where Garin's Jeep had been just a few hours earlier.

Flitting about the perimeter of the crowd was Emilio, searching for gaps in the ranks of the curious for a view into the apartment. Unsurprisingly, it took the hyper-vigilant Emilio only a few seconds to notice Garin's Jeep seventy yards away in the drive off Minnieville. Garin put a finger to his lips, and Emilio, barely able to contain himself, gave a slow conspiratorial nod in response. That act alone would assume mythic proportions in the next Señor Lofton tale Emilio would tell his friends.

Garin carefully examined the scene for anything amiss, anything that might provide insight into who was behind the attack on his team. No one seemed out of place. Everyone appeared to be either law enforcement or residents of the complex. But one thing seemed obvious: Whoever had directed the attempt on his life, having failed, was now setting him up to take the fall. No one had seen him kill his two assailants. No one had cause to call the police, let alone the FBI. And no one had cause to enter his apartment. Yet the place was overrun with law enforcement. Someone wanted the authorities to know he had killed the two men whose bodies were now being carted out of the unit.

Fortunately, a search of his apartment would yield nothing related to Michael Garin. The apartment was leased to Thomas Lofton, and any identifying information found inside—credit cards, bills, passport, were in that name. All of his neighbors knew him as Lofton, and any check on the description of his Jeep or its license number would return Lofton as the owner.

In hindsight, Garin knew it had been a mistake to leave the Makarov in the apartment while he checked on Tanski, but even so, any fingerprints the FBI lifted off the weapon, or anything else in his apartment, would belong to Thomas Lofton. That would be fine if the matter were confined only to the local police and the FBI. But when his prints were checked against the BCI database, alarms would be triggered in certain quarters. There was a select group of individuals who would immediately know that the FBI's suspect was Michael Garin, and it was unclear how those individuals would react; they were, after all, the only ones who knew the identities of the Omega team and where they could be found. As Clint Laws would say, there were no coincidences in this business.

The thought of Laws prompted Garin to punch the old man's number into his cell phone again. Still no answer. Laws not answering once was happenstance. Failing to answer twice was unusual. Three times signaled an emergency. Garin's mind reflected back to a man in gray slacks and a blue blazer nursing a tonic water in the lounge of the Diamondback.

At the moment it appeared everyone who had a close association or recent contact with Garin was now dead or unreachable. Which made Garin's stomach plummet when he realized he hadn't thought to call his sister, Katrina.

Garin knew he should go dark. Whoever was methodically finding and executing some of the finest operators in the world had impressive capabilities. Garin's phone was supposedly secure, but he had to assume that whoever was responsible for today's carnage had the ability to intercept and track his communications. US intelligence agencies could easily do so, and it was certainly possible that someone within the community was involved. Regardless, he had to take the risk of contacting his sister. Then he would make sure to disappear.

Keeping an eye on the scene outside his apartment, Garin punched Katy's number on his cell and waited. After four rings it went to voice mail. He disconnected and redialed. Same thing. And just like that, his anxiety spiked. He had to go to Ohio to check on Katy and her family. He couldn't fly; security cameras and credit cards would reveal his whereabouts, so that left driving.

Garin put the Jeep in gear and, as Emilio watched, put a finger to his lips again in reminder. Coconspirators executing a classified mission. Emilio kept his hands at his sides and gave a slight, surreptitious nod of acknowledgment.

Garin turned the Jeep around. There was little doubt that whoever had tried to kill him this afternoon would try again. But he was going to make sure his sister and her family were safe. And then he was going to kill every single person responsible for today's slaughter.

CHAPTER FOURTEEN

WASHINGTON, D.C.

JULY 13 • 6:00 P.M. EDT

The Red Top cab dropped Olivia in front of Brandt's modest yet stately redbrick colonial near the Columbia Country Club in Chevy Chase, Maryland. Many high-level political appointees, upon first arriving in the capital, take months to find a suitable residence in the D.C. area, some remaining in hotels or sharing apartments with friends until they do. Not James Brandt. With his typical Teutonic efficiency, he had located this gem in less than a week after his appointment as NSA.

Olivia proceeded up the winding walkway, lined with a rainbow of tulips, to the front door. A small security camera connected to a facial recognition system locked on her as she pressed the intercom button on the right side of the doorframe.

After a few moments the door buzzed open and Olivia stepped inside. She was greeted affably by Arlo, Brandt's mammoth black-and-tan German shepherd. The dog raised his muzzle to be petted by Olivia. The two were fast friends, having spent long hours together while Olivia worked on her dissertation with Brandt back at Stanford.

Brandt's voice floated from somewhere down the hall, informing her that he was in the library. Arlo led Olivia down the Persian rug–covered passageway past a sunroom and into a large study lined from floor to ceiling with hundreds of books, a few of which had been authored by Brandt. He was seated next to a small fireplace in a plush, high-backed leather chair in a pensive pose well familiar to Olivia. His brow was furrowed and his chin tilted slightly upward, resembling an artist's rendering of an ancient philosopher contemplating a profound dilemma.

The Oracle. The title was first applied to Brandt when he was a young White House aide more than two decades earlier, shortly after he had written a white paper predicting the fall of the Berlin Wall and the collapse of the Soviet Union. This, at a time when the State Department, CIA analysts, and prominent political science professors were all claiming both that the Soviet economy was strong and that the Kremlin's hold over the Eastern Bloc was unbreakable. Not much later, the whiz kid wrote a widely derided op-ed for *The Wall Street Journal* warning that militant, radical Islam had supplanted communism as the greatest threat to the West. In particular, he noted the destabilizing influence in the Middle East of a little-known despot by the name of Saddam Hussein, and his probable interest in Kuwaiti as well as Saudi oil fields. At the time, Hussein, regarded as a potential if distasteful ally, was at war with Iran. A short time later, Iraq invaded Kuwait.

And on it went. Brandt's prescience drew the envy of rivals and the admiration of nearly everyone else. It was believed that he was first given the title of Oracle not by an admirer but derisively by a jealous colleague in Brandt's own department at Stanford. Now in his midfifties, Brandt radiated confidence. Some of that had to do with his appearance: Tall, with an aristocratic face, thick eyebrows, and a rather large head topped by perfectly trimmed white hair, he had deep-set arctic-blue eyes that conveyed the unflappable bearing of someone who's used to almost always being the smartest person in the room.

"Olivia, it is my fervent hope that I've angered some young man by summoning you here on a weekend." Brandt held his pose, a look of mischief passing across his face. Olivia smiled, an act that had an electric effect on nearly every man she encountered. She sat opposite Brandt in an identical chair. An antique coffee table separated the two.

"You're the only man in my life, Professor."

"And that, darling Olivia, is precisely what I'm afraid of. I may take up more of your time than I should, but that's no excuse. You really need to get out. Have fun, and I don't mean writing an analysis of the Chinese navy's blue-water fleet or some such thing. There are a lot of fine men here in Washington, smart, successful. You can't just focus on work as if you're back at school. You need to live your life."

Brandt's tone was playful, but there was an element of fatherly admonition to it. Olivia's own father had died when she was seven. He had been one of the first black players to integrate Bear Bryant's football team at the University of Alabama. He had met Olivia's mother, a native of New Delhi, while on a church mission in India. They returned to the United States and, after attaining their respective degrees, got married and taught high school mathematics in Chicago. When Olivia, their only child, was born, they moved to Minneapolis, where Olivia grew up—raised by her mother in a sheltered environment after her father died in a car accident.

A math prodigy, Olivia attended Stanford and had been a physics major until taking an elective course in international strategy taught by Brandt. Brandt instantly recognized her intelligence and plucked her from the physics department, setting her on the path of geopolitics. Blind from birth, he had remained unaware of her stunning looks for years, until the accumulated weight of appreciative remarks by envious colleagues made it plain that his assistant's brains were rivaled by her beauty.

"I *am* living my life. This is precisely the life I choose to live," Olivia replied. "Besides, it's not as if I don't see *any* men."

"Olivia, seeing them as they pass you getting off the Metro doesn't count. I mean going out to dinner, maybe a Nats game." Brandt turned a palm up, a gesture that prompted Arlo to rest his head on his master's knee and nuzzle his leg.

"Professor, look, I've been here for less than two months. Give it some time."

"Whatever came of that introduction Carole Tunney made to that TV anchor, the one that makes every story sound like the first moon landing?"

"They're all like that."

"Well?"

"Not to put too fine a point on it, but he's an idiot."

Brandt decided to drop the subject. Forming relationships had never been easy for Olivia. Some men were too intimidated by Olivia's looks to even talk to her. That, combined with Olivia's painful shyness, resulted in a social life that consisted primarily of the receptions following speaking engagements at colleges and think tanks. "Anyway, thanks for dropping by on short notice. I just want to go over a couple of things that I need addressed rather quickly." Brandt placed a slippered foot on Arlo's back and slid it back and forth.

"How's the president doing?" Olivia inquired.

"Checked into Walter Reed after I met with him. No jokes, please. He's a bit fatigued, as you might imagine."

Olivia was new to Washington, but she wasn't naïve. The president of the United States didn't just check into Walter Reed on a Saturday afternoon because he was a little tired. He must be suffering, at bare minimum, from fairly pronounced exhaustion. She did not, however, press Brandt for details, but rather moved on to the draft UN resolution.

"Where do you want to begin with the resolution?"

"Let's put that aside for a moment," Brandt said. "It's going to pass, not as a formal resolution that we could veto but probably as something else, and there's nothing we can do about it. His strategic options are limited. None of them painless."

"It might still be helpful if I give you my observations on the players behind the draft resolution."

Brandt nodded. If his protégé thought something worth mentioning, it usually was. "Go ahead, Liv."

"Well, the usual factions developed; France made a show of being reasonable and unbiased before throwing Israel overboard; Muslim nations were intransigent; African nations moved as a bloc. But in the last few days a pattern began to develop. Any tweaks to the condemnation language were the joint work of Russia and Iran. Not Iran and Syria, or Saudi Arabia and Egypt, but Russia and Iran."

Brandt shrugged. "We've seen that on some other matters."

"True, but not to this degree. The Iranians haven't made a move all week without the Russians. Their envoys were joined at the hip the last two days."

Brandt tilted his head slightly. "So what do you make of it?"

"Perhaps nothing. But I get the strong sense that the Russians have dual objectives here."

"You've worked with me long enough to know I suspect the Russians *always* have dual objectives, if not triple or quadruple objectives. The trick is figuring out the one that's most important to them. Any theories?"

Olivia shook her head. "Inchoate. I was hoping you might have some."

Brandt took his foot off Arlo's head and thought for several seconds. "Right now all I've got is gut instinct and bits of seemingly unrelated information. They may, in fact, remain unrelated. But there's one piece that seems odd. It may be wholly unconnected to anything going on in the Middle East or UN. In fact, it probably is. But the timing's curious."

Olivia wasn't used to Brandt being so opaque. "Timing of what?"

"Late this afternoon, just before you called me at the White House, we—the president and I—were informed that at least seven American special operators have been assassinated in the last twenty-four hours, all in the D.C. metro area. That in itself is, to put it mildly, alarming. Apparently, these men were extremely good at what they do. Getting to one or two of them would be difficult. Killing seven in one day would be nearly impossible."

"What is it exactly, that they do?"

"That's part of what I asked you here for. I wasn't even aware of this team prior to today. Apparently, the information about the team and its mission is 'compartmentalized,' and I wasn't in the compartment, at least not yet." Brandt tilted his head as if contemplating an absurdity. "I suppose it's partially a function of my being on the job for only seven weeks."

"You don't know anything about the team's purpose?"

"Nothing beyond what the president told me this afternoon after he got the news from DCI Scanlon. From what I understand, this is a select unit charged with preventing the proliferation of WMD."

"I take it they don't do it by means of diplomacy," Olivia said.

Brandt placed a foot atop Arlo's head again. "Correct. They do it by direct action."

"Isn't there some overlap? DEVGRU is trained to deal with loose nukes. Delta also has a WMD disposal element."

Arlo groaned contentedly as Brandt rubbed the dog's head. "Not really. Any overlap is strictly around the edges. This team's sole mission is to act as a counter-WMD task force. A strike force. Some of them *were* SEALs or Delta. Possibly SAD. They were handpicked to serve in the unit because they had unique capabilities and, to be trite, they were identified as the best of the best."

"Then who could've possibly taken them out?"

"Indeed. Even the KGB in its heyday probably couldn't have pulled this off, at least not without significant logistical support that would be very difficult to conceal. And the KGB scrupulously avoided killing Americans on American soil. Even the vaunted Mossad couldn't kill all of the perpetrators of the Munich Olympics massacre in a single day."

"Who had operational authority over the team?"

"I can't be sure. They were formed as a unit under the Joint Special Operations Command and, I think, occasionally detailed to the CIA. But I bet you won't find them in the CIA's budget, or the DIA's, or anywhere else for that matter. I'm not even sure the team has—had—a name."

Olivia was mystified as to what, if anything, this had to do with the draft resolution. The assassination of an elite team of special operators—no matter how astonishing—had no bearing on what would happen in New York at the beginning of the week.

"I assume you'll tell me in your own time how the UN resolution and the assassinations are related." It was a declaration, not a question. "In the meantime, what do you need me to do?"

For his part, Brandt sometimes understood Olivia better than she understood herself. He suspected that without being fully conscious of it yet, she already was beginning to sense the direction in which he was going, and might even get there before him.

"The leader of the team hasn't been accounted for. Everyone else is dead. Naturally, he's now the prime suspect," Brandt said.

"One man killed all seven? Just a moment ago you said that even the KGB and Mossad would've had a hard time duplicating what happened. I'm sorry, Professor, that doesn't make any sense," Olivia said, shaking her head.

"Under most circumstances, I'd agree. But I'm told this man is something of a remarkable fellow."

Olivia cocked her head, dubious. "He would have to be more than remarkable to pull off an operation like that. Who told you?"

"Who told me he's remarkable?"

"Yes."

"The president."

"The president? No disrespect, Professor, but I find it difficult to believe the president of the United States is even remotely aware of the identity of a lone member of the vast special operations intelligence community, no matter how remarkable. What did he tell you about this man?"

"Just that he's talented and his name is Michael Garin," Brandt replied. "Oh yes. And that Scanlon says there's some evidence of Garin's culpability. It appears two bodies were found shot dead in an apartment in Dale City, leased to a Thomas Lofton." Brandt raised his hand to fend off the obvious question. "Lofton is a pseudonym Garin sometimes uses. The FBI says the placement of the shots indicates the shooter was likely a pro."

"So I take it the bodies belonged to two members of the WMD team," Olivia said flatly.

"Actually, no. As yet, they're unidentified. And Garin is nowhere to be found."

"I can see why his disappearance doesn't look good." Olivia's eyes narrowed. "But did anyone consider that the two bodies are those of the assassins? I mean, isn't it more likely that Garin killed two unknown attackers in self-defense, as opposed to seven elite operators? What would be his motive for killing his teammates?"

"Liv, that's precisely what I want you to find out."

"You've lost me," Olivia said, a distinct note of exasperation in her voice. She was used to Brandt making seemingly unrealistic demands, but detective work wasn't part of her portfolio.

"I'd like you to gather as much information about Garin and his team as you can. Someone had a reason for killing that WMD team. The more we know about Garin, the more likely we'll discover the reason. And that reason might have some bearing on the crisis in the Middle East."

Brandt, four moves ahead again.

"The FBI's main objective is to find and apprehend Thomas Lofton," Brandt continued. "They don't yet know Lofton is Garin. That's a call for Scanlon to make."

Olivia studied the designs on the rug under her feet as she pondered

Brandt's statement. "Care to give me a hint of what you think I might find?"

"I'm not sure even I know, because right now, all I have is suspicious timing."

"What's so suspicious about the timing? The Middle East is *always* in crisis. Using that logic, any event that occurs at any time would be suspicious because it would always coincide with a Middle East crisis."

"Liv." Brandt smiled. "Don't be coy. I learned about the assassinations of the WMD team a few hours ago. You learned about them five minutes ago. But if I know you—and you know I do—you're already starting to draw some of the same conclusions I have."

Olivia had to admit to herself that as Brandt and she spoke, the chessboard was becoming clearer: tensions in the Middle East that could erupt into a major conflict, the threat of the use of WMD always hanging in the air. And now a WMD task force virtually wiped out. Brandt was right. Getting as much information about the last surviving member of that force might yield some clues.

Olivia nodded. "I'll do my best. Any recommendations on where I should start?"

Brandt shook his head. "You always know what to do. I'll leave it to you."

Olivia, sensing from experience that the meeting was at a close, rose to leave. Arlo got up to escort her out.

"And, Liv?"

"Yes?"

"Try to get as much information as quickly as you can. Garin doesn't sound like the kind of man who leaves any loose ends. I have a feeling that a lot more bodies are going to start dropping soon. And a lot of information will drop with them."

CHAPTER FIFTEEN

G arin drove to the rear of the U-Store-It facility off of Dale Boulevard and parked the Jeep out of sight of both street traffic and
the security camera hanging under the western eave of the building.
He picked up a discarded newspaper and approached the camera per-
pendicularly so he could remain out of its range.

Garin had to ditch the Jeep. It was registered to Thomas Lofton, and
the police and FBI, if they weren't already searching for the vehicle,
would be doing so shortly. He walked to the storage bay he rented—
unit 53—at the northeast edge of the facility and lifted the overhead
door, revealing a navy-blue 2006 Crown Victoria. The registration form
in the glove compartment stated that it belonged to Mark Webster.

Garin opened the trunk and lifted the carpeted bottom that covered the well housing the spare tire. Inside were a variety of supplies
and an arsenal of weapons and ammunition sufficient to wage a small
but respectable war, including an MP5 submachine gun, a Taurus 608,
a Glock 17, a couple of tactical knives, several flash bangs, and even a
vanity Desert Eagle. He retrieved several nutritional bars and a bottle
of water and closed the trunk.

Garin opened the passenger-side door and pulled a soft leather case from the glove compartment. Inside he found a current driver's license for Mark Webster along with several major credit cards in Webster's name. He would use the credit cards only in an emergency—relying on cash instead. Removing the Lofton license and credit cards from his pocket, he threw them onto the floor of the Jeep and doused the vehicle with a five-gallon container of gasoline. When he was done, he threw the container onto the floor of the Jeep, too, before lighting a match.

As Garin pulled out of the empty lot in the Crown Victoria, he glanced once in his rearview mirror, seeing nothing but an eruption of orange-yellow flames consuming the vehicle.

Good-bye, Señor Lofton.

CHAPTER SIXTEEN

Dmitri Chernin sat glumly at the black metal desk in his office, a large glass of Smirnoff and a fully loaded Tokarev before him. Although it was only nine A.M., he was on his second glass of vodka. The Tokarev, which had formerly belonged to his father, was prominently displayed to deter anyone who might express disapproval of the alcohol.

Chernin sometimes imagined himself a beleaguered character in a Chekhov play. It seemed his life consisted only of work, responsibility, discomfort, and disappointment. Any moments of joy were confined to childhood memories and, even then, were fleeting. And there was little prospect of joy in his present station in life.

Chernin's office was a small box with a linoleum floor and concrete walls painted a ghastly shade of green. Beneath an overhead fluorescent light, two metal cabinets stood in the corner near his desk, which faced the door leading to a catwalk above the floor of the main facility forty feet below. The floor-to-ceiling window adjacent to the door permitted him to see much of the enormous work space.

In addition to the vodka and gun, a secure phone and computer sat on the desk. The computer screen displayed data indecipherable to almost anyone but Chernin and told him that the work taking place outside his office was slightly ahead of schedule, an impressive achievement given the numerous setbacks the project had endured. Chernin was effectively in charge of the facility. Although he had no formal title, all operational authority ultimately rested with him.

Chernin, however, took no satisfaction in the project, in part due to his boss, Aleksandr Stetchkin, head of the Twelfth Chief Directorate of the Ministry of Defense and second only to President Mikhailov as the most feared man in all of Russia.

Stetchkin was perpetually displeased with anything and everything related to the project. When work was temporarily halted because the centrifuge operations at Natanz had been sabotaged with faulty parts, Stetchkin accused Chernin of indolence. After Chernin patiently explained that nothing could proceed without the enriched uranium, he was charged by Stetchkin with insubordination and docked a month's pay. When a minor earthquake again required a cessation in operations until the structural integrity of the supply tunnels could be verified, Stetchkin blamed Chernin for lack of foresight. Chernin declined to ask how he was supposed to forecast earthquakes.

By any other measure, Chernin had performed brilliantly. But Stetchkin was a man for whom no performance was adequate until the objective was successfully met.

Chernin wondered what his boss would do to him if he knew how he really felt about the project. Chernin saw no benefit to Russia in helping the Iranians. On the contrary, he saw only problems down the road. The mullahs' wrath was directed at Israel and the West today, but Chernin believed it was only a matter of time before they trained their sights on Russia, too. After all, it wasn't as if Iranians and Chechens had no common purpose. These fanatics believed they were destined to dominate the world. The project was a major step toward fulfilling that destiny, and the mullahs maintained that they were divinely inspired to build it. Indeed, they took enormous pride in its construction.

Except, the Iranians didn't build it. The critical parts came from Germany, Belgium, and France. The technicians came from North Korea. And the design, management, and even some of the uranium came from Russia.

Moreover, Chernin had nothing against the Israelis. The tiny state never threatened to annihilate anyone. They weren't out to take over the world. When he looked into the eyes of an Israeli, he didn't see the seething hatred he often saw in the eyes of the lunatics here.

Not that Chernin disliked the Iranian people generally. He found most of them to be little different from people everywhere—friendly, industrious, and concerned about their families. He had made several friends here, including one of his closest—Mansur, with whom he shared a fondness for premium cigars, Smirnoff, and Iranian caviar.

The mullahs and their followers were another matter. They didn't even attempt to hide their contempt when he interacted with them. His presence was tolerated only because they needed him; without him they couldn't achieve their goal. Once it was achieved, he would be seen as just another infidel, with little to distinguish him from the apes and pigs that inhabited Israel and the other countries in the West.

Chernin had abandoned most pretenses by now. At first, he hid his drinking, in large part because Stetchkin had forbade it as offensive to the Iranians. But as his antipathy toward the hard-liners grew, Chernin made a show of drinking openly, daring anyone to say anything to him. The Tokarev was an additional touch, an affect in which he secretly found great humor.

Soon the project would be completed. Most of the essential work was already done. He estimated that they were only days away from being fully functional. Then he would go home, stroll down Nevsky Prospekt, and look at women who weren't covered from head to toe in burlap bags.

The phone buzzed. Chernin picked up the receiver with his right hand, took a swallow of vodka from the glass in his left, and prepared to listen to an inventory of his infirmities. To his surprise the call was brief and Stetchkin was not unpleasant, probably because the project was under budget and all but complete. Stetchkin even encouraged him to take the day off, one of only a handful over the last year. Chernin was going to do just that. He grabbed the Smirnoff and headed over to Mansur's for an afternoon of palatable food, strong tobacco, and mild inebriation.

CHAPTER SEVENTEEN

BRECKSVILLE, OHIO

JULY 14 • 1:11 A.M. EDT

Few who knew Michael Garin could imagine him as a vulnerable young boy, but from infancy through adolescence, he had been undersize and frail, a favorite target of the larger boys, and even some of the older girls, in school.

Garin had been born nearly three months premature with respiratory problems requiring him to remain in the hospital's intensive care unit for several weeks. Even after he was discharged, his parents rushed him to the emergency room for any number of ailments, and for the first nine months of his life he seemed perpetually attached to IVs and breathing tubes.

His parents rarely permitted him to venture outdoors. When, by age four, his illnesses became less frequent, Garin begged his parents to let him go outside to play with the other children in the neighborhood. The spindly boy was eager to make friends, and he did so fairly easily. Unfortunately, he attracted antagonists as well. His quick wit allowed him to parry taunts from bullies, his responses often making them look foolish.

The physical abuse, however, was something he couldn't handle alone. So, after his third or fourth bloody nose, it was up to Katy—

recognized as the most fearsome kid, male or female, in the neighbor-hood—to protect him. No one challenged Katy Garin, and anyone who hurt her little brother in any way suffered swift and painful retri-bution.

Mikey, of course, was properly mortified to be under the protec-tion of his older sibling, a girl, no less. He gradually withdrew to the confines of his room rather than face the looks of derision from his peers. There, he spent his days reading everything from his parents' outdated *Collier's Encyclopedia* set to the old Great Books series his mother had won in an academic competition as a teen.

Garin had an affinity for history, but his real aptitude was in sci-ence and math. He spent hours gazing through a microscope Katy bought him for his ninth birthday and rigging crude chemistry ex-periments, usually in attempts to create small explosions.

He was, undeniably, a geek. When the boys in his sixth-grade class began playing organized football, Mikey, too small to join, spent his time preparing exhibits for the middle school science fair. When the others attended dances in the school gym, Mikey busied himself with algebra problems.

By the time he reached high school, a growth spurt negated any further need for Katy's protection. Indeed, by tenth grade he was al-ready a second-team all-conference running back and far and away the fastest, strongest, and most respected athlete in his school. As Katy put it, from geek to freak in just over two years.

But it was at this very point when Garin would need Katy most. She'd come home from college to attend a postseason awards banquet with Garin and their parents. Returning home from the event, their car was struck head-on by a driver under the influence. Garin's par-ents were killed instantly. Garin suffered a concussion, several broken ribs, and numerous cuts and contusions. Katy walked away from the collision practically unscathed.

By chance—with an assist from advances in technology—the

emergency room visit revealed something the countless NICU exams hadn't: Garin had a congenital heart defect. It was likely he'd never see his fortieth birthday, maybe not even his thirty-fifth. Katy was with him when he got the news. It was the first and last time he'd ever seen her cry.

But just for a minute. Then she gathered herself, asked the cardiologist where she could find the chapel, and followed him out of the examination room. After he deposited Garin's chart at the unattended nurse's station, she deftly retrieved the exam results from the file, stuffed them in her purse, and checked the desktop computer, verifying that the results hadn't yet been entered into the system. Thanks to Katy, they never would.

Katy dropped out of college to look after Mikey until their grandfather arrived from Europe nearly a year later. By then, Garin was an all-state running back and excelled at most everything he tried. Katy had drilled into him that he needed to treat the heart anomaly as an opportunity, a blessing. Everyone else, she insisted, was so occupied with evading death, prolonging life, that they missed living. They put things off, didn't take risks, thinking they'd always have another chance, a better opportunity down the road.

Mikey, on the other hand, could concentrate purely on living every second as if it were his last. Taking risks he otherwise wouldn't. Keeping absolutely nothing in reserve. He couldn't afford to procrastinate, to say "maybe later" or "someday." Everything took on greater urgency. People, places, and events became more vivid, more intense, more consequential. He needed to pack all of his life into half the time he'd thought he had.

Katy was right. As the grief of their parents' death gradually receded with time, Garin had found the knowledge of his limited life span . . . liberating. He could take the brakes off. After all, he had almost literally nothing to lose. He was never irresponsible, but he had an indomitable quality bordering on recklessness. He had far fewer guardrails than his peers. Ironically, it made him feel almost inde-structible, invincible.

After their paternal grandfather—Pop—arrived, Katy had planned on reenrolling in college, but their parents' death benefits were meager, so she helped Pop get settled, took an administrative job at a local hospital, advanced quickly, and never looked back. She and Pop were the only ones who knew of Garin's condition, Katy's theft having apparently erased any record of it. Katy, protecting Mikey's interests well into adulthood. Now, on a hot July night two decades later, it was Garin's turn to play protector.

It took Garin nearly six hours to drive from Dale City to the Cleveland suburb where Katy lived. As he approached the intersection of her street, he could see that it had taken someone less time than that to station surveillance outside her home. Two Ford Tauruses were parked on opposite ends of Katy's block, the light from the streetlamps outlining the heads and shoulders of two men sitting in each.

Garin drove past Katy's street to the block behind her backyard, about fifty yards from the house itself. He turned left and parked across from the tall wooden fence that stretched across the end line of her property.

Garin sat in the car for a moment, surveying the surroundings. There were no other vehicles on the street.

The two cars on Katy's street couldn't be FBI. At this point, the bureau likely was still looking for Tom Lofton of Dale City, Virginia, who had absolutely no connection to Katy Burns of Brecksville, Ohio.

Garin had no idea who the sentinels out front were. He thought it unlikely they were somehow connected to his two assailants from yesterday afternoon. No one could coordinate and move that fast. Whoever they were, if any harm had come to Katy and her family, Garin would know whom to kill first.

Garin switched off the dome light. He got out of the car, closed the door gently, and scaled the back fence. Dropping to the other side, he quietly made his way past the swimming pool toward the sliding screen door at the rear of the house. A low, soft light was on in the living room. As Garin neared the screen door he could hear the sound of a television. He pulled his SIG from his pocket holster and paused at the door, listening for signs of any intruders inside the house. From where he stood he could see down the hallway leading to the front door, next to which was the security alarm panel. The light was green, signaling that the system wasn't armed.

He expected the sliding screen door to be locked and was concerned when it slid open. He crept slowly into the sunroom and then into the kitchen. The living room was to the immediate left. His brother-in-law was seated on the couch facing the TV, his back to Garin. Joe was watching an old black-and-white movie and didn't appear to be under duress. Garin felt a mild sense of relief, though he had already surmised that his sister's family was safe, at least for the moment. Unless they were spectacularly incompetent, the sentinels wouldn't have parked out front if they had caused harm inside. And if they had any involvement in the elimination of Garin's team, they clearly weren't unskilled.

But neither were they perfect. Maybe they had only a limited number of men, but their failure to cover the street behind Katy's house might allow Garin to get Katy's family to safety. First, however, he had to approach Joe without causing cardiac arrest. Katy and the kids were probably asleep upstairs. Garin decided to turn on the kitchen faucet, leading Joe to think someone had come downstairs for a drink of water.

Hearing the sound of running water, Joe asked, "Katy?" Getting no reply, he turned around and saw Garin standing next to the sink. Joe's reaction was ideal: He was dumbstruck.

Garin raised his hand to signify that Joe should remain silent. "Joe," Garin said quietly, "sorry to startle you. Take a second to reorient yourself and I'll explain."

Joe looked as if he was trying to blink away the confusion. He stood as Garin came into the living room. "Mike, what's going on? You scared the hell out of me." Joe looked at the pistol Garin held at his side and with greater urgency asked, "What the hell is going on?"

Garin got right to it. "Joe, I know this is going to sound bizarre, but I want you, Katy, and the kids to be prepared to leave the house in five minutes. Here's the situation: Less than twelve hours ago, two men tried to kill me and I'm certain whoever sent them intends to finish the job. Several people close to me have also been killed in the last day. Right now, there are at least four men parked in the street outside your house who I suspect are shooters." He paused for a moment to allow Joe to process what he had just said. "I don't think they're after you or your family. They're hoping to get me. But I can't take any chances, so I need to get you out of here."

As a former command sergeant major who had served three tours in Iraq, Joe knew that at some point Garin had had some type of involvement with special operations. His wife's brother would frequently disappear for varying periods of time and upon his return respond evasively to any questions about his trip. Joe had long since stopped asking questions and had told the kids Uncle Mike was some kind of big-game or treasure hunter. For her part, Katy had no illusions about what her brother did. She knew him better than anyone in the world and she was sure that in one way or another he was going after some very bad men.

Joe began to move to the staircase down the hall to get his family. As he did so, he turned partially toward Garin. "Mike, why not just call the cops?"

"Can't do it, Joe. I wish I could tell you more, but I can't. I know it's tough, but please trust my judgment on this."

"Can't you at least tell me where we're going?" Joe asked.

"To a safe place not far from here."

As Joe went up the stairs he bent down and, peering between the rail posts, nodded at Garin's weapon. "Mike." Garin understood and put the SIG in his pocket.

"Don't turn on any lights," Garin cautioned. "And bring your sleeping bags and some extra clothes."

Garin moved to the side of the front door and kept an eye on the sentinels. Within seconds after Joe had disappeared up the stairs, Garin heard the squeak of a box-spring mattress and muffled voices. The only word he could distinguish was "When?" uttered by Katy. She sounded more curious than alarmed. A few seconds later, he heard several feet padding about and the faint rustle of clothing.

As Garin peeked out the window he saw the passenger-side door of the vehicle to the right of the house open. The dome light didn't come on. Garin's hand gripped the pistol in his pocket as he watched a man in a dark polo shirt and trousers walk across the street to a head-high row of hedges, probably to relieve himself. He appeared about five foot ten and 175 pounds. As the man disappeared between two hedges, Garin looked for any activity from the other sentinels. A few moments later, the man reemerged, his face turned toward the house. There wasn't enough light to identify any features other than two large jug ears.

Seconds after the man got back into the car, Garin heard the muffled pounding of several feet coming down carpeted stairs. The three kids, each clutching a sleeping bag, descended. Four-year-old Kimmy came down first, followed by Nicholas, six, and Alex, eight. It was clear that they were excited to see their uncle Mike and believed they were embarking on some grand adventure. Despite having been awakened only minutes earlier, each was alert and grinning like it was Christmas morning. They gathered around Garin at the foot of the stairs. Smiling, he knelt and gave them each a hug.

Katy followed a few steps behind, carrying a large duffel bag. Her expression was one of concern, but she smiled fleetingly as Garin rose to give her a hug. Behind her, Joe was carrying a matching duffel bag.

"Guys," Garin said to the kids, "go wait in the living room for a second." They shuffled off obediently.

Garin turned to Katy and Joe standing in the hallway. "Katy, I'm sorry," Garin said. She frowned as if offended that Garin thought it necessary to apologize. The tall brunette was smart, mentally tough, and utterly devoted to her little brother. Garin liked to tease her that she was at least partially responsible for making him the son of a bitch he was. "Joe fill you in?" Garin asked her.

Katy nodded.

"We need to move quickly. I'm pretty sure they're only after me, but for all I know, those guys outside are just waiting for backup before they move in. My car's on Elmwood, behind the house. I'll lead us out the back, take up a position next to the pool, and provide cover until you and the kids get to the back fence. Wait for me there. Don't go over the fence until I catch up and make sure it's clear."

"Do you need me to cover too?" Joe asked.

"What are we talking?"

"Shotgun. I've got a Benelli Nova Pump in the basement."

"We'll scare the kids if we come out heavy."

"No, they'll love that," Katy countered. "We'll say we're hunting for bears or something." *Katy Burns,* thought Garin, *suburban mother of three and part-time commando.*

"All right," Garin said. "I'll still lead us out, but instead, Joe, you cover the rear. Car's a Crown Vic. It'll be tight, but it should fit all six of us. We go in thirty seconds."

Katy went into the living room to tell the kids they were going camping and to keep an eye out for bears and coyotes. Joe retrieved the Benelli from the basement. Garin checked on the sentinels one last time. They appeared to be in their cars.

Garin looked back down the hall toward the sliding screen door, where Katy's family was gathered, and felt nervous. Once they went out that door, they would be exposed. If the sentinels spotted them, their assignment could turn from surveillance to execution. Garin regularly placed the lives of highly trained warriors in danger, but placing the lives of family members in jeopardy was far more difficult.

Garin stepped out the sliding screen door and scanned the perimeter of the yard before waving Katy and the kids forward. Joe came out last, duffel bag strapped over his left shoulder, shotgun cradled across his chest and right arm, and closed the door behind him.

Garin heard a soft thump that came from somewhere up front, possibly the closing of a car door. He held his arm up, motioning for everyone to stop, the kids hoping that some mythical creature might be nearby. Looking at Joe, Garin jerked his head to the left, indicating that Joe should look around the side of the house to see what was going on out front.

Joe glanced quickly to the front yard. Seeing no change there, he turned around, shook his head, and motioned for Garin to proceed.

Once everyone was over the fence, they crossed the street to the Crown Victoria. Garin popped the trunk and they placed the bags inside. Then they piled into the car, Joe literally riding shotgun, with Katy and the kids in the back.

"When I say 'go,' everyone close your doors, *gently*, at the same time," Garin instructed. "Go." The doors closed in unison, one soft *thump*.

"Everyone in back put your heads down so the bears don't know how many of us are in the car," Garin directed. It didn't make sense, but neither did hunting for bears in the middle of the night in suburban Cleveland.

Garin started the car, drove to the next intersection, and turned right—away from where the sentinels were parked. After driving for a minute, checking the rearview mirror for any signs of a tail, he gave everyone permission to sit up, which the kids also took as permission to speak. A fusillade of questions was fired, most of which dealt with why Uncle Mike was taking them bear hunting in the middle of the night. Since Katy had proposed the story, Garin decided to let her handle the questions. As she did, he turned to Joe and said, "I'll tell you as much as I can when we're outside the kids' earshot."

"Mike, where are we going?"

"A place no one else in the world knows about," Garin replied. "If they're capable of finding us there, we never had a chance to begin with."

CHAPTER EIGHTEEN

NORTHEAST OHIO

JULY 14 • 2:05 A.M. EDT

They had been driving for several minutes on an isolated two-lane road in the Cuyahoga Valley National Park approximately thirty miles south of Cleveland when Garin turned left onto a dirt path barely wide enough for the Crown Victoria to pass. As he drove along the rough ground, brush and tree branches scraped along the sides of the car. The middle of the path was overgrown with tall weeds and was crisscrossed with low-hanging vines from adjacent trees.

After they'd driven for nearly half a mile, the path ended. They drove up a slight grade for another two hundred yards until the density of the trees prevented them from proceeding farther. About seventy-five feet ahead, barely visible through the foliage, was a small cabin in a miserable state of disrepair. The steps leading to the porch were rotting away, the porch railing was askew, and the two front windows were broken. Nailed to a tree twenty-five feet from the front door was a superfluous NO TRESPASSING sign that Joe surmised had been posted sometime during the Hoover administration. Next to the tree was something that at one time may or may not have been a well.

Joe turned to Garin with a look that said, "You're kidding me."

Kimmy asked the obvious question. "Mommy, why are we stopping *here*?"

"I'm not sure but I'm hoping Uncle Mike is about to tell us there's a Holiday Inn behind this house."

Garin turned off the lights and engine. They were instantly enveloped in total blackness.

"It's not as bad as it seems," Garin declared as he opened the car door. "Follow me. Be careful, and watch your step. There's a lot of exposed roots."

The other doors opened and the Burns family emerged from the vehicle with trepidation. The kids' expectation of an exciting Uncle Mike adventure had been replaced by doubts about his sanity.

Garin produced a flashlight from the trunk and led Katy's family to the cabin's front door. Katy couldn't imagine any reason why the door would be locked and, indeed, her brother simply pushed it open and entered, floorboards sinking beneath his feet.

The family gathered inside the entrance as Garin swept the flashlight around the room as if to assure them that there were no skeletons strewn about the floor. The space in which they stood was about twenty feet by twenty feet and dominated by a large wooden table in the center. A few chairs were scattered about and there was a freestanding metal washtub against the wall to the right. An old-fashioned woodstove stood against the wall to the left. The short hallway on the opposite side of the room led to two smaller rooms, one of which appeared to have been a bathroom at one time.

"Mike," Joe said, "I didn't see any utility lines connecting to the house."

"Right. No electricity. No telephone. No gas or water lines." Garin gave Katy the flashlight and said to Joe, "Give me a hand."

He walked over to the table and placed both hands under one end. Joe did the same at the other end. Garin tilted his head to the left and the two men moved the table several feet in that direction. Garin then returned to where the table had been, bent down, and pried loose a handle that was flush with the floorboards. He pulled, and a three-by-five section of the floor rose, secured at one end by well-oiled hinges. Garin laid the section on the floor and extended his hand toward Katy for the flashlight. "Follow me. Be careful going down the stairs."

The family descended a dozen stairs as Garin turned on a switch on the nearest wall. The low, somewhat comforting humming sound of an unseen generator was followed by the flickering of bright fluorescent lights on the ceiling. When finally steady, the lights revealed a room nearly twice as large as the one above. The walls were plastered and painted off-white, the same color as the thick, all-weather carpet covering the floor. The place was furnished with two leather couches and a polished wood table surrounded by four comfortable-looking chairs. A large flat-screen television hung on the opposite wall. A few feet to the right of the television was a hallway that led to a bathroom, bedroom, and pantry.

Kimmy, Nicholas, and Alex began running around the room as if they had discovered an underground amusement park. Joe and Katy slowly moved about, examining the amenities.

"I'll get your stuff," Garin announced, and disappeared up the stairs. By the time he returned, Joe and Katy had determined that the place was the size of a small one-level home and surprisingly comfortable. Dropping their bags on one of the couches, Garin cataloged the bomb shelter's features.

"As you've probably guessed, the electricity is provided by a couple of generators, with enough fuel for a couple of weeks of normal use. The TV is only for DVDs and games, stored in the cabinet underneath. The pantry has a microwave and enough canned foods and other non-perishables for a couple of months. There's also a mini-fridge back there if you want to store leftovers, but it will take a while to get cold after you turn it on.

"Water comes from a well, and the switch for the pump is next to the sink in the pantry. Unfortunately, the water for the bathroom sink and shower is cold, but in the summer it's not too bad. There are also about a hundred gallons of bottled water back there if you don't like the taste of well water."

"Geez, Mike," Joe said. "This is survivalist heaven. What the heck is this place for?"

"A friend of mine who doesn't believe in coincidences once told me that in my line of work it's a good thing to be able to completely disappear, go to a place where absolutely no one can find you, not even those you think are your friends. Unfortunately, now that you know about this place, I guess I'll have to get another one."

Joe whistled. "Mikey, I'm not going to ask what line of work requires you to have a place like this. I have a general idea, but I suspect you're way off the radar screen."

The kids were already playing video games and Katy had wandered off toward the pantry.

"Joe," Garin said, walking over to a metal locker behind one of the couches, "come here. I want to show you something."

Garin spun a combination lock on the locker. "Three–thirty-two–seventeen. Got it?"

Joe nodded. Garin opened the locker, revealing an M4 rifle, a Beretta M9, and dozens of magazines of ammunition.

"You can store the Benelli in here so the kids can't get to it. Besides, you won't need to use any weapons unless you've done something exceptionally stupid. No one knows about this place except me. I bought the cabin above us from an estate, using a cutout. My name's not on the deed, and the previous owners have been dead since the Great Flood. You're in the middle of a national park and not even park rangers come up here. It's not on any utility grid and it's built so it doesn't give off any noticeable heat signatures. Just don't go outside or use your cell and no one could possibly find you."

"How long are we staying here?" Joe asked.

"*You're* staying here a few days. I'll be leaving in a few hours, once you're settled in."

Katy returned from the pantry. "Leaving for where?"

"I haven't worked that out yet. I need a secure location I can operate from, somewhere no one will know to look for me while I figure out what's going on and take care of the problem. I can't do it from here without compromising your safety."

"Mike," Joe said, "I have a job. I can't just disappear. I've got to let them know something."

"I'll call your job for you first thing tomorrow and tell them a relative died and you're taking funeral leave to attend services in Texas. Maybe take a couple extra vacation days." Garin smiled. "Hell, Sergeant Major, they're scared to death of you. They won't ask any questions."

"Michael," Katy said firmly, "after all this, we deserve to know. Just what *is* this problem you need to take care of?"

Garin paused to gather his thoughts. He was determined to tell Katy and Joe everything he could without compromising their safety or violating his oath. Through no fault of their own, their lives had been endangered. Ironically, even if he were inclined to disclose classified information, the truth was, he knew very little about what was going on.

"I'm afraid there isn't much more beyond what I've already told you. But I'll try to give it some context. I work with a group of individuals who are very careful and very skillful. In fact, you won't find a more capable group in the world. These are not ordinary men. Yet it looks like every single one of them has been killed in the last day. One of them, a longtime friend, was assassinated right in front of me.

"Not only that, but it looks like others close to me have been killed, including someone who used to be my boss. I saw him just last night, so I assume I must be the common denominator. My best guess is that they're killing everyone to whom they think I disclosed something they want kept secret."

Katy and Joe were listening intently, their expressions growing increasingly anxious.

"For what it's worth, I don't think that includes you. They know I wouldn't disclose classified material to you. But I can't be absolutely certain of that. That's one of the reasons we can't call the cops or FBI. Whoever is behind this has tremendous resources. If we went to the authorities, there's a fair probability that the bad guys would find out and then be able to locate you. They could then use you—possibly even kill you—to get to me."

"And the other reason?" Katy asked.

"The FBI is looking for me already. Two men tried to kill me in my apartment this afternoon. They failed; I didn't. The FBI found the bodies. *Someone* told the FBI to look there. Obviously, that someone had sent the attackers in the first place. Therefore, that someone wants me dead and wants the FBI to think I'm somehow involved in the deaths of my friends."

"Is there someone other than the FBI you can go to?" Katy asked. "Whoever it is you work for, couldn't you just go to them and give them the facts?"

"Problem. The individuals who provide us direction and logistics are all dead. So, at this point, I have to assume everyone's a possible bad guy until proven otherwise."

"Are you saying the government could be involved?" Katy asked.

"No, that's not what I'm saying. Contrary to popular belief, the government does not have a general policy of assassinating its citizens on American soil. But there may be someone in the government who's working with, or for, the bad guys. In fact, it's a near certainty. That's the only way they could've pulled off what they did. So, before I contact anyone for help, I have to be sure—at least as sure as I can be, given the circumstances—that the person's clean."

The look on Joe's face was that of an unsentimental realist. It was clear that he was skeptical the matter would be resolved favorably.

"But, Michael. Why?" Katy asked. "Do you have any idea *why* this is happening?"

Garin's mind flashed to an image he thought he'd seen in a tunnel in Pakistan a few days ago. More accurately, it was a series of images he'd definitely seen but had difficulty placing or comprehending. He believed, however, that he knew someone who could help him get some answers.

"I don't know. There are three possible reasons why we were targeted: to retaliate for something we did; to prevent us from doing something in the future; or to erase something we know. Maybe it's a combination of the three. My hunch is that someone is trying to erase something we know. That's why they also targeted my old boss. They think I might have told him something."

"Mike, this doesn't sound like you can get the answers by yourself. And definitely not in a few days," Joe said.

Garin lowered his head slightly, conceding the point. Then he looked at his sister. "Sorry, Katy. You didn't ask for this. You shouldn't be burdened with this. It's not your fight."

Katy glanced at her husband and then took a step closer to Garin, an intense look on her face. She spoke in a quiet, controlled voice, but her tone was insistent. "I don't want to hear that sorry crap, Michael. We're hiding in a damn bunker. In the United States of America. My kids' lives are in danger." She pointed her right index finger at his chest, jabbing for punctuation. "You go on offense *right now.* Find out who these bastards are and take it to them. No excuses. That's what Pop would do. That's what Pop would expect you to do. He would expect you to make things right. And it seems to me that means making absolutely sure that the people responsible for all of this can *never* do it again."

CHAPTER NINETEEN

CRYSTAL CITY, VIRGINIA

JULY 14 • 10:15 A.M. EDT

The morning haze didn't burn off until well past nine. The forecast promised temperatures in the mid- to upper nineties, with oppressive humidity. The sidewalks were nearly empty and the traffic sparse. It was a slow, lazy Sunday morning in July in Washington, D.C.

Olivia Perry was scouring the classified briefing materials from the National Counterproliferation Center regarding US WMD protocols. Before leaving Brandt the previous evening, she had asked him to call the Office of the Director of National Intelligence and request any information he could provide on US efforts to contain the spread of weapons of mass destruction and any information available on an individual by the name of Michael Garin.

Olivia's only concession to its being a Sunday morning was her casual attire and her decision to work from home. She wore a pair of white cotton running shorts and a tank top and sat on a cushioned deck chair on the small balcony of her apartment overlooking the Pentagon. A cup of espresso sat on a circular coffee table next to her laptop and a manila file folder.

The requested information had arrived by courier at Olivia's apartment in Crystal City shortly after eight A.M. It consisted of a CD and a thin manila folder. The CD contained the material on WMDs. The folder contained information about Michael Garin.

Olivia hadn't expected that the information the DNI sent over would be anything more than generic, open-source information. She wasn't disappointed. Most, if not all, of the data could've been obtained through a diligent Internet search.

Still, the material saved Olivia a considerable amount of research time, and given Brandt's desire to get as much information as quickly as possible, it was a useful starting point.

Olivia began by reviewing the WMD data on the CD. She was already familiar with much of it. SEAL Team Six—DEVGRU—based in Dam Neck, Virginia, was trained in WMD. As was Delta Force. No mention was made of any WMD task force assigned to destroy or otherwise compromise the WMD programs of rogue nations and terrorists. No mention was made of anyone named Michael Garin or Thomas Lofton. Olivia would have thought it a spectacular breach of security if there had been.

The only references to the destruction of WMD programs was a file on the CD that consisted of publicly known or suspected WMD programs that had been delayed or destroyed by deception or force. The majority of these, unsurprisingly, related to actions taken by Israel against some of its neighbors. A nation faced with existential threats didn't have the luxury of engaging in detached deliberation about the pros and cons of destroying a murderous dictator's nuclear weapons program. Among the actions were the bombing of Iraq's Osirak nuclear reactor in 1982, the bombing of Syria's al-Kibar nuclear reactor in 2006, and several acts of sabotage against Iranian nuclear facilities in the last several years. It was widely rumored that the attacks on the Syrian and Iranian programs had been accomplished with American assistance, but there was no evidence confirming such rumors.

After Olivia completed a review of the data on the CD, she opened the file on Garin. The contents were so sparse as to be mildly amusing.

Had Olivia not been informed by the president's national security advisor that Garin led an elite team of operators tasked with destroying renegade WMD programs, the file would've caused her to think Garin was nothing more than an honorably discharged veteran with six years of service in the US Navy. In fact, it appeared from the file that Garin's last military or government service ended nearly ten years ago.

According to his file, Garin had enlisted in the Navy at age twenty. He had been stationed at several bases, including Coronado, California, where he had gone through BUD/S and SEAL Qualification Training as a member of Class 226. He didn't become a SEAL, having failed to complete the course. He was discharged sometime thereafter. That, and a three-by-five black-and-white file photo, constituted the complete official record of Michael A. Garin's service to his country.

The file was practically useless. Sitting back in her chair, Olivia gazed at the Air Force Memorial in the distance and plotted her next move. She wasn't a private investigator and Brandt hadn't charged her with acting as one. She had suggested to Brandt that he simply requisition Garin's entire file, but he dismissed the idea as unproductive. Even if he knew what agency Garin worked for, without presidential clearance all he was likely to get back would be a heavily redacted, compartmentalized file. And Brandt wasn't inclined to go to the president's bedside at Walter Reed and pester him for the file of some GS-14 who might be able to shed some light on the not-unexpected cooperation between Russia and Iran on a resolution condemning Israel. Afterward, Brandt, sensing that Olivia felt chastened by her naïveté, apologized and reassured her that he, too, was struggling with the ways of Washington bureaucracy.

Olivia decided to follow up on Garin's tenure in BUD/S and SQT. Since that was the beginning of his special operations training, and since he evidently was still in some form of special operations, she thought it could be fruitful to explore any connections between Garin's SEAL training and his current occupation. She planned to start with finding out who the instructors for Class 226 had been. Maybe one or more of them still had a relationship with Garin.

But first, Olivia decided to try something easy. She Googled him. It took her ten minutes of scrolling through hundreds of dead ends before she linked to a fifteen-year-old article in *The Cornell Daily Sun*. It was a sports-section report on the Cornell football team's 21–17 victory over Yale. A free safety by the name of Mike Garin had returned two interceptions for touchdowns, including the game winner. She scrolled to the bottom of the piece, where there were a series of game-related photos including one of a Cornell player standing next to a stocky, tough-looking man who appeared to be in his mid- to late sixties. The caption read "Big Red Star Congratulated by Biggest Fan."

Because the player in the photo was wearing a helmet, Olivia couldn't be sure if Mike Garin, Cornell football player, was Mike Garin, special operator. She hit the link under the player's name and a few seconds later a page of statistics and honors appeared. This Garin was six foot two inches, 210 pounds, and had been honorable-mention all-American, as well as all-Ivy. Olivia knew enough about football to recognize that it was uncommon for an Ivy Leaguer to be named an all-American—even an honorable mention. She thought it even more uncommon, however, for an Ivy Leaguer to be a lethal commando.

At the bottom of the page it showed that Cornell's Garin was from Cleveland, Ohio.

She hit the link under Cleveland and more honors appeared—this time from high school. By his senior year, Garin had been a second-team high school all-American in football and small school division state four-hundred-meter champion in track.

Her father having played at Alabama, Olivia knew full well that high school all-Americans generally got scholarship offers from major powers such as Alabama, Ohio State, and USC. It was unusual for someone like that to end up at an Ivy League school with its rigorous academic requirements and lack of athletic scholarships. This Garin, whether or not he'd gone on to become the special operator Garin, was a peculiar specimen.

Olivia went to the bottom of the page, where there was a grainy photo of a taciturn high school football player standing beneath goalposts on a football field. Olivia took out the photo from Garin's file and placed it next to the photo on the computer screen. Both subjects had black hair, although the adult Garin's was short and the high schooler's was long and curly. Both had angular features and pugilistic jaws. But it was the intense, purposeful look in their eyes that convinced Olivia that the two Garins were almost certainly the same. It was a look uncommon for the Ivy League elite. It was, thought Olivia, the rather chilling look of a man capable of taking another man's life.

Olivia spent another half an hour looking for more information on Garin before returning to the *Cornell Daily Sun* article. She reread the article carefully for anything she might have missed. She then went to the link for Garin's college stats and to his high school stats. Olivia noticed that she had missed the link underscoring the term "all-American."

She clicked on the link and was directed to an article from *The Plain Dealer* describing the recruitment of area high school stars by various college programs. She read the paragraph that mentioned Garin:

> *After receiving offers from a number of programs, including Ohio State University, Michigan, and Notre Dame, the Blue Devils' Mike Garin narrowed his choice to the Naval Academy and Cornell, before ultimately choosing the latter. "We were really disappointed," said the Academy's Dan Dwyer, who had recruited Garin heavily, "but we wish Mike the best of luck. He's going to be a fine college player."*

There was nothing more about Garin in the story. Olivia got out of the chair and stretched. Standing with her hands on her hips, she looked down at the computer screen and contemplated taking a short break before running down the instructors for Garin's BUD/S and SEAL Qualification Training classes. That would take a lot of time, she thought, and even then she might not get anything more useful than what she had just learned on the Internet.

She decided that she should call Brandt and give him a heads-up that progress on the assignment was slow and she was skeptical of finding any substantive information on Garin. The *Cornell Daily Sun* article was fifteen years old, the *Plain Dealer* article even older. And any information gleaned from Garin's BUD/S instructors would probably be more than a decade old. Olivia opened the sliding glass door and stepped from the sweltering July heat into the air-conditioned kitchen. She poured herself another cup of espresso and searched for her cell phone, which, miraculously, was in the first place she looked. She punched the speed dial for Brandt. It rang twice before she abruptly disconnected and placed the phone down on the kitchen counter next to a stack of the last week's editions of *The Washington Post*.

Olivia stared at the newspaper as if trying to remember where she had put her keys. A few moments later she walked back onto the balcony and looked at the laptop screen, which still displayed the *Plain Dealer* article. "'We were really disappointed,' said the Academy's Dan Dwyer . . ."

Olivia hurried back inside and rifled through the stack of newspapers until she came to Thursday's edition. She opened the first section and leafed through the pages before stopping at page five. There, at the top of the page, was a story titled "President of DGT to testify Monday before the Senate Select Committee on Intelligence." Olivia traced her index finger down the column until it rested on the phrase "DGT president Dan Dwyer, a former Navy SEAL, maintains that the company's contracts with the Defense Department—" Olivia's cell phone interrupted. The caller identification indicated it was Brandt.

"Olivia, I understand that you called."

"Professor, let me call you back in an hour. I've got to talk to a man about a SEAL."

CHAPTER TWENTY

Garin stood in the pantry of the bunker, sipping his second cup of strong black coffee and waiting for the caffeine to work its magic. He'd spent much of the night thinking about what was happening and who was behind it. When he had finally crawled into his sleeping bag, he had planned on taking a brief nap before heading to upstate New York in the morning, but the effects of the Pakistan op and the previous day's events conspired to keep him asleep past noon, and when he rose, he was much stiffer than he'd been the day before.

The rest, however, was beneficial. His energy level was good and his mind clear. Joe had recommended that Garin use the old Burns family farm in Spencer, New York, as his base of operations. Joe had grown up there, but after his parents died, he and his four siblings, who had dispersed across the country, used it only occasionally as a family vacation home. Because the property had been held in trust under the name Craigy-Creek Farms for nearly two decades after probate of their parents' estate, there was no paper trail connecting the place to the Burnses. They allowed a local farmer, an old family friend, to grow corn on a portion of the land in return for performing the odd maintenance job. Since Garin had no connection to the place, no one, including the FBI, would ever think to look for him there. Garin decided it was perfect.

Katy came into the pantry and gave him a bear hug. She seemed in good spirits given the circumstances.

"Michael, you gotta tell me, how in the world did you build this place? I mean, setting aside the whole idea that anyone would ever *need* something like this, it's amazing you did it by yourself."

"I didn't."

Katy looked slightly puzzled. "But I thought you told Joe that no one knows about it."

"No one does."

"Okay, wise guy, stop it."

"Pop helped me. More accurately, I helped Pop. He worked on it almost nonstop for nearly two years. I helped him when I could between deployments. The cabin above already had a cellar. We made it a little larger and Pop did most of the rest. He finished it less than a year before he died."

Katy had a faint smile of wonderment on her face. "I saw him every day. I would go over to the house to fix sandwiches, his favorite soups, do laundry. I had no idea. He never said a thing."

"I guess when you go through the kinds of things he went through, you know how to keep things to yourself. In many respects, this place was his idea. My old boss used to say guys like us needed to be able to disappear at a moment's notice. But he was talking about holing up in some fleabag motel in Tangier or Bangkok. Pop said if people can see you—even people who don't know you—your enemies can and will find you."

Katy shook her head, still trying to comprehend how her grandfather could have kept a project like this secret from her. "That tough old SOB. So when he died, no one else besides you knew the place existed."

"To tell you the truth, I'm not sure I ever expected to use it. It was more a security blanket than anything else. I'd come up here every once in a while—usually when I was in town to visit you—and do a little upkeep. But it was mainly out of respect for all the work Pop put into it, not because I actually thought I had to keep it ready for action."

Garin led Katy back into the main room, where Joe and the kids were wrestling on the floor. Upon seeing Uncle Mike, the kids ran over and performed their ritual of hugging his legs.

"Before I go, just a few things you should know. The temperature stays pretty constant, but if you need to run some fresh air through, just turn on the air for a few minutes, preferably at night. The exhaust is under the porch so no one should see it, but don't take any chances."

Joe held up his hands. "Mike, not going outside is going to be tough, especially for the kids."

"I know, but people do it all the time—subs, air raid shelters. That doesn't make it any easier, but you'll adjust. Now, if you feel you absolutely must get out or you'll kill each other, do it at dusk. The park closes at nine P.M. Heck, I've never seen anyone anywhere near this place, but to be safe, we have to presume someone is looking for us in the park and that they're using all of the resources at their disposal. Thermal, drones, nightscopes, the works."

"Thermal? Drones? Are you serious?" Joe sounded incredulous.

Garin chose his words carefully in front of the kids. "Taking out my team was the work of extremely serious, sophisticated people who are involved in something extremely big. They will spare no resource."

For the first time since last night, both Katy and Joe had worried looks on their faces, as the gravity of the situation continued to sink in. Garin tried to reassure them.

"Look, I'm not without resources either, and they're very good. When I get to Spencer, I'll begin putting them in motion. I know you don't think it can be done in a few days, but believe me, it can.

"Joe, in the locker I showed you last night there's a bunch of cell phones with prepaid minutes. Don't use them unless you've been discovered. Don't even turn them on. They're programmed to call only one number. That number will bounce the call all over before relaying it to me. Wherever I am in the world, you'll be able to reach me."

"But what if you need to reach us?" Joe asked.

Garin thought for a moment. "Turn on the phone for five minutes at six A.M. every day. If I need to reach you, I'll call then. You know what, I'll call then anyway just to check in. Otherwise keep the phone off unless you *must* call me."

"What if you don't call at six?"

Garin remained silent. Joe understood.

Garin bent down to hug the kids good-bye and then gave Katy a kiss. He shook Joe's hand and, before climbing up the stairs, whispered, "I know you'll take care of my sister and the kids, Sergeant Major. Just try not to scare the living hell out of the bad guys."

CHAPTER TWENTY-ONE

CRYSTAL CITY, VIRGINIA

JULY 14 • 3:34 P.M. EDT

Olivia was encouraged by the progress she was making. A contact at the Pentagon had provided her with Dan Dwyer's unlisted phone number as well as a cell number.

Dwyer was the president and cofounder of DGT, a closely held, sprawling security services firm. Though slightly less than a decade old, it was one of the premier private military contractors in the country. It drew many of its field personnel from special forces and clandestine units—American as well as foreign—and it regularly discharged highly sensitive duties for both public and private sector clients.

Despite the firm's propensity for secrecy, Olivia was able to glean useful kernels of information from a two-year-old *Wall Street Journal* profile on Dwyer. The salient points in the article were that he had been a BUD/S instructor at Coronado at the same time Garin was there and that it was unclear to which SEAL team he had been attached. That left open the possibility that Dwyer had been a member of SEAL Team Six and involved in WMD disposal.

Olivia called Dwyer's home number. There was no answer and the call didn't go to voice mail or an answering machine. She then dialed his cell and he answered instantly.

"Dwyer."

Olivia, somewhat surprised to have reached him, decided to be direct. "Hello, Mr. Dwyer, my name is Olivia Perry. I'm an aide to National Security Advisor James Brandt."

Dwyer was equally direct. "Hello, Ms. Perry. I know exactly who you are. I read at least one essay coauthored by you and Professor Brandt in *Foreign Affairs,* the one on cyberwarfare strategies."

Olivia was caught slightly off guard. For some reason she had expected Dwyer to be reticent, if not outright hostile. "Mr. Dwyer, I'll get right to the point, and admittedly, it may sound somewhat peculiar. In the next day or two we expect the United Nations to vote on a Russian-Iranian resolution condemning Israel's actions in the latest Middle East crisis. Without going into detail, we have some concerns about what the Russians and Iranians are up to and we think that a friend of yours could help us address those concerns."

"What friend?" Dwyer's tone was still friendly, but there was now a hint of guardedness to it.

"I can't go into it over this call. To be honest, I'm not even certain he is a friend of yours, but I have reason to think you know him."

"Why not just call this person directly?"

"We can't locate him."

There was a pause before Dwyer asked, "Is this urgent? I'm sorry, that's obviously a very silly question. The Office of the National Security Advisor doesn't call on a Sunday afternoon unless it's pretty important. What can I do for you?"

"I'd like to ask you some questions about your friend—acquaintance— in person. I know this is short notice, but I see you live near Mount Vernon. That's not that far from me. I could be at your house in forty-five minutes. It shouldn't take much of your time. Jim Brandt would be very grateful."

"Unfortunately, Ms. Perry . . ."

"Call me Olivia."

"Deal. You can call me Dan. Unfortunately, I'm spending the rest of the day with my attorneys, who happen to be seated across from me right now. They're very well dressed, very well groomed, and very well paid. I have no doubt I'm being billed as we speak. I'm appearing before the Senate Select Committee on Intelligence tomorrow morning and my lawyers and I need to go over my testimony so I don't use an inordinate number of expletives or accidentally perjure myself. By the way, when did the Senate start holding hearings on Mondays? I have no doubt the only reason they're doing it is to screw with my weekend."

Olivia couldn't help being amused. Dan Dwyer sounded like a character. "Is there another time you would be able to meet?"

"How much time do you need again?"

"Whatever you can give me."

There was a moment of silence, and then Dwyer said, "My testimony is at ten A.M. Why don't you join me here for breakfast tomorrow at, say, seven thirty A.M.?"

"Excellent. Thank you very much. I'll see you then."

"Remember to bring your appetite."

CHAPTER TWENTY-TWO

The scenic drive south along the western shore of Cayuga Lake reminded Garin of his college days, when he would travel from Cleveland to Cornell at the beginning of each semester. On his left, boat and fishing docks appeared sporadically, extending into the smooth waters long rumored to harbor a Loch Ness–like creature. Rising to his immediate right were miles of low hills covered with the vineyards of Finger Lakes wine country.

The sun had just dipped below those hills as he approached Spencer from the north. The eastern sky was already midnight blue and the few passing motorists had turned on their headlights.

According to Joe's directions, the Burns farm was another four to five miles south down Route 96 and then another half mile east along a narrow undedicated lane named Turnberry Road. The farmhouse was on the right and was the sole residence on Turnberry.

Garin would employ the same maneuver he'd used at Katy's house and continue south past Turnberry to the next road, approaching the Burns farm from the rear. As he got closer to Turnberry, the road dipped downhill into a shallow valley darkened by the surrounding hills, which absorbed the last remnants of twilight. He slowed as he passed Turnberry but saw nothing. The road disappeared into blackness less than one hundred yards from the intersection.

It was nearly another mile before Garin reached an undedicated gravel road that branched to the left. Turning onto the road, he drove another half mile, searching for an opening in the woods that lined both sides. He found a gap between two large oaks on the left and drove between them and over bumpy ground until coming to rest fifty feet from the road. Garin turned off the lights and ignition, got out, and satisfied himself that the car was invisible from the road. He opened the trunk and took out his M4 rifle, flashlight, and a gym bag containing clothes, toiletries, and nutritional bars.

As he walked north toward the rear of the Burns farm, he contemplated using the flashlight, but his eyes quickly grew accustomed to the darkness, allowing him to navigate safely through the woods, provided he moved slowly.

He walked for approximately a quarter mile before coming to a clearing. Standing at the edge of the tree line, he could see the rear of the Burns farmhouse another quarter mile or so beyond a grassy field that looked like it might have sustained livestock at one time. On the left, or west, side of the house was a fairly sizable barn. On the east side was a large field of corn that ran north from the tree line toward Turnberry half a mile away.

The farmhouse was completely dark. Garin saw no vehicles or any signs of human activity. He put the gym bag and flashlight down, raised the M4, and scanned the surroundings through its scope. The place was vacant.

As he continued to peer through the scope, Garin's ears picked up a familiar rhythmic sound over the horizon. He trained the scope above the farmhouse's roof and quickly identified the source of the sound. Sweeping swiftly toward the farm from the north were four aircraft, the configuration of which Garin immediately recognized as that of an MH-6 Little Bird helicopter.

Garin retreated into the woods and sank to the ground as the Little Birds skimmed the tops of the trees north of the house and banked over the cornfield before descending to within a few feet of the grassy field. Each of the four helos carried four passengers—two riding pods on each side—besides the pilot. The four carried rifles with collapsible stocks. They were outfitted in all-black tactical gear, Nomex balaclavas covering their faces and night-vision goggles over their eyes.

The figures leapt to the ground almost in unison. Six fanned out with impressive precision and rushed the farmhouse, weapons raised. The remaining ten formed a perimeter approximately fifty feet from the house and barn and then fell to the ground, weapons trained on the building. The overall scene, even to an experienced operator like Garin, was nothing short of mesmerizing.

Garin watched with a mixture of fascination and foreboding as the raiders methodically checked the buildings. From a distance, their highly coordinated movements appeared choreographed, almost balletic. There was no hesitation, no wasted effort. Garin knew he wasn't watching a local SWAT team, not even a crack one. Before him, he saw the uncompromising proficiency of a world-class special operations unit.

This was both a bewildering and an ominous development. There were only five in the world who knew Garin was here, and those five people were in an undetectable bunker that only he knew about. How did the team presently going through the Burns farmhouse know to look here?

A faint feeling of dread came over Garin as he analyzed the possibilities. The most straightforward answer to his question was that the team got the information from Joe or Katy, but Garin thought the odds of anyone having located the bunker in the seven hours since he'd left it were practically zero. Even less when combined with the odds of prying loose the information from the sergeant major, or the even lower odds of extracting it from Katy. But that, of course, was before the kids were factored in. Using them as leverage increased the likelihood of disclosure to a near certainty. But again, only if the bunker had been detected. The problem was that Garin wouldn't be able to reach Joe for another eight hours—possibly the longest eight hours of Garin's life.

The other option was nearly as remote. To be plausible, it required his pursuer to have not just vast resources, but exceptional luck. Of the millions of possible locations for Garin to go to, someone had to conclude that Garin would choose an all but abandoned central New York farmhouse belonging to the family of his sister's husband.

Either way, Garin thought, he was facing a formidable adversary.

The team searched the premises for twenty minutes before boarding the Little Birds and departing in the direction from which they'd come. Garin remained prone and checked his watch. A little more than seven hours before he could contact Joe. Until then, there was nothing he could do. He wasn't going into the house; he couldn't take the risk. He laid his rifle at his side and continued to watch the area. Twenty minutes later he drifted off to sleep.

CHAPTER TWENTY-THREE

NORTHERN IRAN

JULY 15 • 7:12 A.M. IRDT

Chernin scanned a series of reports prepared by the various task managers on the project as he ran an electric razor over the stubble on his chin. He paused to sip some coffee from a large mug and rub the sleep from his eyes. He had slept barely three hours.

Chernin felt no ill effects from the previous evening's cigars and vodka. In fact, despite having consumed nearly twice as much vodka as Mansur, Chernin was still going strong, hinting at the importance of his work without revealing any details, when the latter had begun drifting off to sleep.

Chernin had spent most of the morning reviewing weekly reports. He took satisfaction in the knowledge that this could very well be the last series of weekly performance reports he would need to review. The time was approaching for him to go home. After a series of tests, the project would be certified at the local level. The Iranians were so anxious to get under way that they would likely certify anything, but Chernin's superiors in Moscow would make the final assessment and their standards were far more exacting.

Chernin's standards were just as high and he was confident that all systems would pass inspection. Then, if all was in order, the project would be prepared for execution in a little more than three days. It would be, as the Americans liked to say, a game changer.

CHAPTER TWENTY-FOUR

Garin scratched himself awake sometime after five A.M. He was covered with fewer insect bites than he had expected, but the one on the back of his neck itched worse than any he had gotten during a miserable month he'd once spent in the Colombian jungle.

The eastern sky was a light yellow and the house and barn were readily visible. They appeared freshly painted and well maintained. A rear door was open—having been kicked in during last night's raid. It was the lone sign of what had occurred hours before.

Clearly, Garin needed to find somewhere else from which to operate. He had plenty of cash and at least one false ID that no one in the government knew about, so theoretically, he could rent a hotel room and work from there.

But the events of the last forty-eight hours, especially those of last night, had spooked him. It seemed wherever he went, with the exception of the bunker, his adversaries followed. Or, as in the case of both his apartment and his sister's house, they *preceded* him. They seemed to be everywhere. Pop was right: If someone can see you, your enemies can, and will, find you.

Garin decided it was best to return to the Washington, D.C., area. After all, he had gone to Ohio only to secure his sister's family, and he had come here only to operate freely, with minimal chance of detection. He would find out in a few minutes whether he had accomplished the first goal. Last night proved that he wouldn't accomplish the second. At least in Washington, he had a potential resource that might produce some answers. So far, he had none.

Garin grabbed his rifle and was about to get up when, on the grassy field approximately one hundred yards in front of him, the ground began to move. He remained still as the ground took the shape of a man slightly taller than Garin, with a stocky, muscular build, holding an M110 sniper rifle. The sniper wore a ghillie suit that had allowed him to blend in with the foliage. Had the sniper not moved first, Garin would have never detected his presence. Had Garin moved first, he would most certainly be dead right now. The raiders had left the sniper behind as a fail-safe. Garin had missed him completely last night, and that made the sniper very good.

The sniper was facing north, his back to Garin. It appeared as if he was speaking into a communication device. After placing the device in an unseen pocket, he stretched, arched his back, and removed his balaclava. He appeared to be adjusting something on his rifle. Garin, a paranoid about scope glare, flipped the antireflective cover on the scope of his rifle to prevent any reflected light from giving away his position. Only a few moments later, he could hear the distinctive sound of an approaching Little Bird over the horizon. The craft appeared, hugging the treetops of the woods north of the farmhouse. Garin calculated it must have been stationed only a few miles away. It banked east and then swept over the cornfield before coming to rest midway between Garin and the sniper.

As the sniper turned to board the craft, Garin's stomach tightened. Although he was nearly the length of a football field away, Garin was fairly certain that he was looking at the face of one of the deadliest snipers in the world.

His name was Congo Knox. He was unforgiving. And he was Delta Force.

CHAPTER TWENTY-FIVE

NORTHEAST OHIO

JULY 15 • 5:59 A.M. EDT

Joe Burns sat at the table next to the stairs leading from the bunker to the cabin, the Benelli Nova Pump next to him. He had turned on the cell phone a few minutes early in anticipation of Garin's call. Joe wanted to be sure not to miss it.

Katy and the kids were asleep in the bedroom, Nicholas in a sleeping bag on the floor and the rest sprawled in various directions across the mattress. Joe had gotten little sleep during the night. His family had already gone to bed when he thought he heard muted noises coming from aboveground. He had remained absolutely still for a long period of time, hoping to be able to discern the source of the sound, but was unable to do so. There seemed to be a couple of faint thumps and a barely noticeable vibration. He had heard no voices, but the noise definitely didn't originate from anywhere within the bunker. He had been sitting next to the stairs ever since.

The cell began to vibrate. He picked it up immediately and simply said, "Mike."

"Sergeant Major, you have no idea how good it is to hear your voice." The evident relief in Garin's voice telegraphed that something had happened.

"Mike, what's the problem? You sound on edge. Not like you."

"A little matter like having the entire law enforcement apparatus of the United States gunning for you can have that effect." Garin caught himself. "Joe, sorry, I don't mean to be sarcastic. I was worried someone might've found you."

The reception in the bunker was poor, but Garin had Joe's complete attention. "What happened?"

"I won't go into details. We have to keep the call short. But I have reason to think the military may be somehow involved in looking for me."

"They can't, Mike," Joe said unequivocally. "*Posse comitatus.*"

"I know. But some people arrived at the farm last night and they sure didn't look or move like local law enforcement." Garin paused. "No matter. I'll handle it. I was just concerned that they found me by getting to you."

A pause. "I heard noises coming from outside last night."

The edge returned to Garin's voice. "What time, where did it come from, and what did it sound like?"

"Around midnight from somewhere outside. I can't be certain where. I don't think it was from inside the cabin. It's hard to describe the sound—not voices. Barely audible."

"Did you go outside at any time last night?"

"Yeah, but we followed your instructions and waited until dusk. We were only out for ten or fifteen minutes and stayed within one hundred feet of the cabin."

"Don't go outside again. I seriously doubt anyone was looking for you," Garin said unconvincingly. "But let's not risk it. You're safe in the bunker. It's made out of steel and concrete. Nobody can get in. Remember to keep the hatch locked. If you hear voices or noises again, close the air vent until it goes away."

Joe understood without the need for elaboration. Gas. "Will do," Joe said.

"I'm getting off now. I'll call you again tomorrow. On second thought,

I'm not going to call you anymore. No sense giving them a signal. You call me if there's an emergency. Now, turn off the phone and take out the battery."

"Hey, Mike?"

"Yes."

"Remember to call my job."

CHAPTER TWENTY-SIX

The cab dropped Olivia before a massive black wrought iron gate. On either side of the gate were eight-foot-high redbrick walls that appeared to run the entire length of the street. Somewhere beyond the tall barrier sat Dan Dwyer's house. The only things visible from where Olivia stood were a long, winding driveway lined with neatly trimmed hedges and at least a dozen varieties of spectacularly colored flowers.

Olivia was a few minutes early for the meeting. She searched the gate in vain for a camera, buzzer, or intercom. As she reached into her purse for her cell, a golf cart driven by a serious-looking man in his early thirties came down the driveway. A sidearm was visible in a holster on his right hip. The gate automatically opened inward as he neared.

"Good morning, Ms. Perry. My name is Matt. Mr. Dwyer is on the east patio. If you'll join me, I'll take you there."

Olivia climbed in and Matt drove up the driveway, passing a series of fountains, miniature waterfalls, and ponds along the way. After riding for nearly a quarter mile, they rounded a perfect circle of hedges and came to a large manicured lawn punctuated by geometrically shaped plots of brilliant flowers. Sitting one hundred yards beyond the expanse of emerald grass was a series of wide-terraced, marbled steps—similar in appearance to those in front of the Capitol Building—that led to Dwyer's four-story home.

Matt turned the cart to the right and proceeded up an asphalt ramp to the east patio, where Dwyer was seated in a cushioned redwood chair, looking at his smartphone. He wore a blue suit, white shirt, and bright yellow tie. Standing ten feet behind him in front of the French doors leading to the house was Matt's clone, also wearing a firearm on his hip. On the table in front of Dwyer were several carafes of coffee, pitchers of various juices, a plate of Canadian bacon, sausage, and scrambled eggs, baskets of rye and wheat toast, bowls of nearly every fruit imaginable, and several platters of assorted pastries.

Dwyer looked up when the cart approached and rose to his feet, a broad grin on his face. He appeared to be in his midforties, easily six feet five inches tall, and had the build of a recently retired NFL offensive lineman. He still looked fairly fit but could stand to lose a few pounds. He had a large head and short, thick hair so blond it appeared nearly white.

"Hello, Olivia," Dwyer said enthusiastically as she got out of the cart. Holding up his phone, he said, "I've been reading more of your work: Russia's effort to reconstitute the Soviet Empire by extorting the former republics, one by one, with natural resources. Interesting stuff. You're a regular Junior Oracle."

Olivia smiled and extended her hand. She was inclined to like Dwyer. There seemed to be little, if any, artifice about him. "Thank you again for meeting me," Olivia said. "Especially since you're testifying this morning."

"I'm happy to do it. I'm an admirer of your boss. He's not the standard-issue cloistered academic who thinks everything wrong with the world is America's fault. A serious man and a rigorous thinker. Understands that there are some real bad guys out there, and we can't pretend they don't exist.

"Besides," Dwyer added, pointing at Olivia's driver, "when Matt over there heard me mention your name on the phone yesterday, he practically begged me to invite you over. He's made a major pest of himself. Embarrassing, really. He's seen your picture in the *Post* and insists you're a goddess not of this realm."

Both Matt and his clone were smiling unabashedly. As was Olivia. Dwyer's affable nature made it hard to be offended by him.

Dwyer waved his hand theatrically across the table. "What would you like?"

"Just some coffee, thank you. Black."

Dwyer appeared crestfallen. "You didn't bring your appetite. And we went to all this trouble."

Dwyer poured her coffee and gestured for Olivia to sit in the chair next to him. "So you have a problem with the Russians and Iranians. Don't we all. Decent caviar, though. Caspian. Unfortunately, probably seventy percent petroleum. What can I do to help?"

Olivia hesitated, glancing at Matt and his clone.

"Guys," Dwyer said, tilting his head to the door. The two vanished inside the house.

"See those things over there that look like bug zappers?" Dwyer asked, pointing to two oblong metal objects flanking the patio. "They prevent long-distance electronic eavesdropping. Beyond state-of-the-art. A generation ahead of anything the NSA pukes have even thought about. So feel free to speak as openly as you'd like."

Olivia got right to it. "The Russians and Iranians have been working closely together during this latest crisis in the Middle East." Olivia paused. "I know, no surprise there. But Professor Brandt thinks that something out of the ordinary may be brewing and that Michael Garin might be able to shed some light on the situation. No one can find him, so we're attempting to get as much information about him as we can to see whether that may provide some answers."

Dwyer steepled his fingers under his chin. "Why can't anyone find him?"

"We understand Mr. Garin leads, or led, a military or paramilitary unit of some kind. I don't know the name of it or even to what branch or agency it's attached—"

"Olivia," Dwyer interrupted, "no need to talk code. As you might expect, I've signed a Classified Information Nondisclosure Agreement. I may be privy to more classified information than you."

Olivia nodded. "It's a counter-WMD strike force. And every member of the force—seven in all—except Garin, has been found assassinated in the last forty-eight hours. He's the chief suspect and the subject of a massive FBI manhunt—although I don't think the FBI knows it just yet."

"I don't follow."

"As of yesterday, the FBI was still looking for someone named Tom Lofton, an alias Garin used. Maybe they've connected Lofton to Garin by now, I don't know. But I don't think they know about the weapons of mass destruction angle."

"What does any of this have to do with the Russians, Iranians, and the Middle East crisis?"

Olivia looked slightly embarrassed. "I'm not quite sure. Professor Brandt has a theory, but he tends to keep such theories close to the vest until he has more information."

"The Oracle," Dwyer declared dramatically. "Sees patterns where others see puzzles. What's *your* theory?"

"I'm still working on it. But I think that Israel could get hit by something bigger than anyone expected."

"I don't know what I can tell you about Mike Garin that will be of any use," Dwyer said, shrugging.

"It could be something that seems irrelevant to you, but it might be a thread that leads to answers. For example, do you know where he's traveled recently? Has he been to the Middle East? Has he said anything about the situation in the Middle East? What has his training been focused on?"

"I haven't seen Mike in some time, Olivia. I wouldn't have any idea."

Olivia tried a Hail Mary. "You were DEVGRU, right? Black Squadron? Weren't you involved in recovery of nuclear material?"

Dwyer remained silent, putting his hands in his lap.

"Do you know anything about what Garin was up to in the last few months?" Olivia asked.

"I recruited Mike to come to the Naval Academy to play football. A few years later, I was one of his instructors when he was in BUD/S. I've had a couple of beers with him in the years since. I don't know anything about what Mike's been doing the last few months. I can tell you one thing, though, Olivia. Mike Garin did not kill those men. You tell that to Jim Brandt. You tell that to the FBI."

The sudden intense look on Dwyer's face projected a mixture of loyalty and protectiveness. Because there was so little artifice to Dwyer, Olivia thought she detected that he was being less than candid about his relationship with Garin. Not deceitful exactly, but also not completely forthcoming.

"Mr. Dwyer . . ."

"Dan," Dwyer reminded her.

"We're not out to get Michael Garin. In fact, I don't know him, but I'd tend to agree that he had nothing to do with the assassination of his team. I'm told Garin is very talented, but for one man to assassinate seven . . . It doesn't seem feasible.

"It really comes down to this: The Middle East is currently on a trip wire; it's no mystery that the Iranians would like to wipe Israel off the face of the earth; to do so requires deliverable WMD. Garin is the sole surviving member of a highly specialized counter-WMD team. It's quite possible the rest of the team was killed by someone trying to prevent information from getting out. So Michael Garin, consciously or not, may have knowledge that someone desperately wants covered up. Information that may concern WMD that could be used against Israel. I don't need to tell you the implications of such use."

"No, you don't. I've been warning Senate Intelligence about those implications for some time. Everyone acts like if they ignore the problem, it'll go away. It won't and it's not. It's at our doorstep. Right now."

Matt appeared at Dwyer's elbow. "Sir, Jack Elliott's here."

"That's my lawyer, Olivia," Dwyer explained as he rose to his feet. "I'm going to a barbecue in the Hart Senate Office Building, and I'm the main course. Matt will be happy to see you out. I'm afraid I haven't been much help to you. I don't know what to say." Dwyer shrugged apologetically.

Olivia stood and shook Dwyer's hand. "Thank you for your time, Dan, and good luck with Senate Intelligence. Let me know if something occurs to you. And if it does, let me know fast. Given how quickly things are developing in the Middle East, I don't think we have very much time."

CHAPTER TWENTY-SEVEN

CENTRAL NEW YORK STATE

JULY 15 • 8:40 A.M. EDT

A sign over the convenience store promised sixteen ounces of the best coffee in Broome County for only $1.19. Judging by the number of cars parked along the store's front curb, the claim appeared highly exaggerated.

Garin had subsisted on protein bars and water for the last twenty-four hours. He would've preferred a breakfast of eggs, home fries, toast, and coffee while comfortably seated at a table in the roadside pancake house he had passed thirty minutes ago, but having spent the night sleeping in the woods, he thought he would spare the other patrons the dubious pleasure of his company.

Garin parked as far from the other vehicles as possible and reached under his seat for his pistol. He shoved it into the waistband holster at the small of his back and covered it with his shirt.

The gym bag in the passenger seat contained nearly fifty thousand dollars in cash. He unzipped it and pulled out two hundred dollars, a baseball cap, and sunglasses. He put on the cap and glasses and popped the trunk. No need to give a curious thief any ideas; before entering the store he put the bag in the trunk and locked the vehicle.

The interior of the store was a frigid contrast to the rising heat and humidity of the morning. Garin first searched for any security cameras inside. He spotted cameras on each end of the back wall, one near the entrance to the restroom and another over the cash register. The cashier, a plump woman in her early twenties, pointed helpfully to the back, where pots of coffee were lined up under several coffee machines.

Before heading for the coffee, Garin grabbed one of the small baskets near the door and proceeded down the first aisle, filling it with an assortment of powdered doughnuts, candy bars, and other junk food. He was usually scrupulous about his diet, but he believed that it was a good idea to defer on occasion to the body's natural cravings for unadulterated junk.

Garin faced the store's floor-to-ceiling exterior window while shopping for chocolate bars, giving him a clear view of the parking lot, where a man with jug ears was getting out of the passenger side of a Ford Taurus. He appeared Middle Eastern, as did the driver.

As the man walked toward the entrance, Garin noticed the second Ford Taurus in the back of the store's parking lot, about fifty feet directly behind the Crown Vic. Two men were seated in the car watching the storefront.

The sentinels.

They wouldn't try to kill him here. They would wait until he drove to a more secluded area somewhere down the road. Right now, they were simply keeping tabs on him. Jughead would browse around the store until Garin left. Then one of the cars would leave ahead of Garin, in the direction that he had been driving before he'd stopped at the store. A second car would follow behind Garin. They would stay far enough from Garin's car not to raise his suspicions, but close enough to strike at an opportune moment. Garin would not give them that opportunity.

Jughead moved casually about the store, feigning interest in an item and then moving on. He was weaving up and down the narrow aisles, gradually making his way toward the rear of the store, where Garin was pouring himself a large coffee.

As Garin busied himself with finding a lid and cup sleeve, he examined the periphery to locate the only other customer. He was looking at the newspapers at the front of the store, his back to Garin. The cashier's attention seemed to be absorbed in some paperwork.

The sentinel strolled down the aisle next to where Garin was putting the finishing touches on his coffee. Garin placed both the coffee and his basket of junk food on the counter and, with a look that conveyed that he'd just remembered something else he needed, walked to the aisle where Jughead was inspecting packages of AAA batteries.

Garin made a show of searching the shelves as he approached the sentinel, who looked up and politely smiled as Garin drew near. Garin returned the smile with a nod and a violent thrust of the three middle fingers of his left hand into the sentinel's throat, crushing his windpipe. In a smooth motion, Garin caught the sentinel around the waist before he collapsed, and lowered him gently to the floor. The man emitted strained wheezing sounds, choking futilely for air as Garin wrapped his right arm around the man's head and his left around his neck. With a brutal twist he snapped the sentinel's neck, killing him instantly.

Garin rose to check the premises. The other two occupants were oblivious to what had just occurred. There was no doubt, however, that a review of the security recording would reveal a muscular man in a cap and dark glasses assaulting a somewhat smaller Middle Eastern man.

He grabbed the sentinel by the back of his collar and dragged him silently across the floor, around the corner at the end of the aisle, and into the employees' restroom, where he deposited him on the floor of the stall. Garin checked for a pulse in the sentinel's neck and, satisfied that he was dead, rummaged through the dead man's clothes for any identification. Finding a wallet in the sentinel's right rear pocket, Garin stuffed it into his front pocket, though he would be surprised if it contained any useful information. He took his SIG from the small of his back and inserted it into his waistband in front, making sure it was covered with his shirt before emerging from the restroom.

The other patron had left while Garin was stashing the body. Garin casually collected his basket and coffee and went to the checkout register, where the cashier rang up the sale and placed everything but the coffee in a paper shopping bag.

Garin knew his next move would be more difficult. It had to be executed before the remaining sentinels began wondering about the whereabouts of their cohort. It also depended on the angle of the rear- and side-view mirrors of the jug-eared sentinel's driver.

Garin exited the store, turned left, and walked unhurriedly to his car, pretending not to look at either of the two Tauruses. Cradling the shopping bag and coffee in his left arm, he dug into his pocket for the car keys and pressed the button to open the trunk. He put the coffee on the roof of the car, then placed the bag in the trunk, where he quickly unzipped his gym bag and removed a suppressor. With his back to the vehicle containing the two sentinels and angling slightly away from the vehicle to his left, he swiftly affixed the suppressor to the SIG. As usual, a round was already chambered.

Garin closed the trunk. Holding the weapon against his right leg, he turned and began walking briskly toward the sentinels in the vehicle directly behind him. Through the front windshield Garin could see a momentary look of puzzlement cross their faces, changing into wide-eyed expressions of terror as they spotted the SIG in Garin's hand and realized what was about to happen.

Garin raised the SIG in one fluid motion and quickly fired three shots at each man. He immediately pivoted to his right and sprinted toward the other Taurus, his eyes fixed on its rear- and side-view mirrors for any indication that the remaining sentinel had seen what had happened. If he had, he reacted too slowly. Garin put three more shots through the rear window of the vehicle, striking the driver twice in the head and once at the base of the neck. Through the shattered window Garin saw the man pitch forward against the steering wheel, a curtain of blood and brain tissue splattered across the front windshield.

Garin returned the pistol to his side as he walked back to his car and scanned the area. There was no sign that anyone had witnessed the events of the last ten seconds. Although there were no security cameras on the exterior of the store, Garin was under no illusion that the police, and later the FBI, wouldn't instantly conclude that the muscular man in a ball cap and sunglasses who had crushed the trachea of the jug-eared shopper was the same one who had assassinated the three men in the parking lot. Just like that. Four corpses in Broome County.

Garin retrieved his coffee from the roof of his car, got in, and placed the weapon under his seat. Looking in the rearview mirror, he could see the splintered windshield of the Taurus, the two dead men reclining against their respective headrests. They appeared strangely at peace.

He took a sip of impressively awful coffee before driving out of the parking lot, casting a quick glance through the store window, where the cashier remained engrossed in her paperwork. Garin would've preferred to have spared one of the sentinels for interrogation but couldn't risk having another patron drive into the parking lot and report the gruesome sight of three dead men slumped in their cars. It would take only a few minutes for the local cops or sheriff to arrive and put out an alert for a man matching his description. He estimated that he had twenty minutes to get rid of the car, ball cap, and glasses, alter his appearance, and secure another means of transportation.

As he drove, Garin realized that he was becoming accustomed to being in a sustained state of bewilderment. It seemed no matter where he went, someone was able to track him and employ various hunters. The sentinels had already been in place outside of Katy's house when he arrived, even though the FBI had no idea they were looking for a Michael Garin. The only person besides himself who had known about the bunker was dead, yet it seemed someone may have been snooping around the cabin shortly after he left. Then an elite assault team conveyed by military helicopters showed up at the Burns farm, defying odds that would dwarf winning a multistate lottery. And finally, the sentinels from Katy's house had tracked him to a convenience store in central New York.

Garin could only assume the sentinels followed him to the store using some form of tracking device. But since there was nothing in his bags, the device would have to be inside or attached to the car. How someone had managed to place a device in or on a vehicle that had been locked in storage for more than a year was a puzzle he would have to ponder later. Right now, Garin needed to get rid of the vehicle so it wouldn't be an easy target for either the authorities or the sentinels' associates.

And he had to do it quickly. He had the uneasy sense that a clock was ticking, although toward what he had no idea.

CHAPTER TWENTY-EIGHT

WASHINGTON, D.C.

JULY 15 • 9:30 A.M. EDT

Dan Dwyer arrived thirty minutes before the hearing was scheduled to begin. He sat on a leather couch in Room 211 of the Hart
Senate Office Building, waiting to be summoned through the imposing vault-like double doors of the Sensitive Compartmented Information Facility of Hearing Room SH-219, the space wherein the most
consequential secrets of the world were discussed. A young man sat at
a desk opposite him, typing earnestly on a keyboard.

With Dwyer was his attorney, Jack Elliott, instantly recognizable
to cable news junkies as the man invariably seated next to whoever
was testifying that particular day before an investigative body of the
federal government on a matter of national interest. Elliott's expensive
but rumpled suits, unruly white hair, and exploding waistline camou-
flaged a quick and precise mind that regularly outmaneuvered the
congressmen before whom his clients appeared.

And Dwyer regularly appeared before congressmen. As DGT had
grown exponentially over the last eight years, so had the interest of
some congressmen in nearly every aspect of his business. A few of
them had serious questions about the enterprise and the extent to
which it was replicating, if not usurping, the role of the military in

fighting the war on terror. But the majority of politicians simply saw DGT as a useful foil, a shady, rapacious outfit that not only soaked up large amounts of federal revenue but soiled America's reputation overseas. For the latter cohort, DGT was the Great White Whale. Whoever harpooned it would be a hero to the country's antiwar movement and could use it as a springboard to higher office.

If DGT was the Great White Whale, then the man who had just walked into the room was Captain Ahab. Julian Day was counsel to Senator Harlan McCoy, chairman of the Senate Select Committee on Intelligence. Princeton undergrad. Yale Law. Smart and tenacious, he had been responsible for unearthing evidence leading to the conviction and imprisonment of nearly a dozen military contractors for matters ranging from massive overbilling to the killing of civilians in war zones. During his nearly two decades on the committee, he had accumulated a wealth of institutional knowledge and innumerable contacts, allowing him to establish something of a fiefdom in Intelligence. As a result, a mere call or e-mail from Day's office often generated substantial bouts of anxiety and paranoia in contractors, other staffers, and even some congressmen.

Day was determined to uncover evidence of scandal and misconduct by DGT and had spent the last several years demanding that DGT produce nearly every imaginable document related to its business for inspection and nearly every one of its executives for testimony. So far, all he had been able to discover was that DGT was an efficient, well-run organization that fulfilled all of its contractual responsibilities to the government.

Day was a short, thin man in his early forties with small, clever eyes behind stylish glasses. His appearance was the opposite of Elliott's in almost every respect. He wore expensive, closely tailored suits that never seemed to wrinkle and always sported a precisely knotted tie. His thinning light brown hair was perfect, not a strand out of place. He had a permanent sneer on his face and he did nothing to mask his contempt for Dwyer.

Entering the room behind Day was another committee counsel, Elizabeth Riley, a tall, attractive redhead who once had a crush on one of Dwyer's key executives, a fact that infuriated Day and, as a result, delighted Dwyer.

Day didn't look at Dwyer as he spoke to Elliott. "Jack, there have been some developments over the weekend that require today's hearing be postponed. Senator McCoy asked me to convey his apologies for the short notice and inconvenience, but we wonder if you'd be kind enough to spend a few moments with Elizabeth and me to answer some questions informally?"

"Hello, Julian," Dwyer said cheerfully. Day ignored him.

"Julian, we will do whatever we can to accommodate the interests of the committee." Elliott glanced at the young man behind the desk. "We came here today to testify about the matters set forth in your letter to Mr. Dwyer last Thursday. We sent a large number of documents to the committee in advance of Mr. Dwyer's testimony. We spent a considerable amount of time preparing for the hearing, time that took Mr. Dwyer away from the business of running his company. Would you care to tell us why the hearing's postponed and what kind of questions you'd like Mr. Dwyer to answer?"

Day pointed to the door leading to an adjacent room. "Why don't we step in here?"

The four filed through the door to an unused hearing room. Riley closed the door behind them. Day and Riley sat on one side of a rectangular, dark-wood witness table. Dwyer and Elliott sat on the other.

"Okay, Julian, what's going on?" Elliot asked.

"The short, unclassified version is this: The hearings have been postponed because there's been a significant complication to our counter-WMD capability." Day turned his attention to Dwyer. "Your old friend Michael Garin appears to be in the middle of it."

Dwyer concentrated on Day but remained silent. Only a handful of people associated with the committee were familiar with Garin. Some of them viewed him with at least as much hostility as they viewed DGT.

"Why did that require postponement of the hearing, and what's Garin's involvement in all of this?" Elliott asked.

"Jack, you know I can't get into all that. Suffice it to say the committee is dealing with the potential ramifications of the 'complication.' It's a matter of some urgency. As for Garin, the FBI has just determined that he was connected to the shootings of two men in Dale City. It's believed Garin may be the reason for the complication."

"Hell, Julian, why don't you just send us a note about what's going on in Sanskrit? You want our cooperation and that's the best explanation you can give us?"

Dwyer put his hand on Elliott's shoulder and looked at Day and Riley. "What do you want to know?"

"Have you had any contact with Garin recently?"

"Julian," Elliott interjected, "do you think we're completely daft? That I just passed the bar last week? You just told us Michael Garin's the reason for a complication to national security. I assume that means he's a person of extreme interest to the FBI and the Department of Justice. And you expect me to allow my client to testify about whether he's had contact with the man?"

"He's not testifying, Jack. This is informal."

"That doesn't mean a damn thing," Elliott said dismissively. "Clearly, the FBI is looking for him and I have no doubt he's considered a fugitive."

"Hold it, Jack," Dwyer said, raising his hand. Dwyer gazed at Day. "I haven't seen or heard from Mike Garin in months. I have no idea where he is. He has no relationship whatsoever to DGT. But get one thing very straight, Julian. Mike Garin is not a 'complication.'"

"Perhaps you're too blinkered to see what he and others like him have done to America's image abroad," Day retorted. "They hate our imperial exploitation of their resources, our reckless destruction of their lives and property. Our imposition of our values on their societies. Putting them in the Guantanamo gulag. Mike Garin and those like him destroy their way of life and in the process do incalculable damage to the nation's reputation. To them, he's death personified. They hate America because of him and his ilk and yet they're vilified for simply wanting to stop him."

"Simply stop him? Those weren't temporary restraining orders that flew into the World Trade Center and Pentagon, Julian. And in case you missed it, that was *before* Mike Garin ever even *thought* about a career in raping and pillaging."

"Dan," Elliott said, trying to restrain his client. The big man waved him off.

"Mike Garin is one of the reasons you can sit up here and act like you're the last defender of democracy on earth. Flatter yourself all you want. But don't make the mistake of thinking Mike Garin is a complication to anything or anyone except our enemies."

"Michael Garin," Day retorted, disdain punctuating each syllable, "the very *idea* of Michael Garin, is a disgrace to international law and the constitution."

As if a light switch had been thrown, Dwyer's neck and face instantly turned crimson. "You have no idea what he's done for this country, the Constitution and, oh yes, your precious international law."

"Please enlighten me."

"Read his file," Dwyer shot back. "But I guess you already have. That's probably why you can't stand him. Makes you feel kind of puny, doesn't he? Kind of reminds you of the shower room after gym class."

Elliott closed his eyes. "Dan . . . ," he said quietly.

"Oh, I was just getting started, Jack. I was going to ask our fearless Julian how many terrorists he's killed, captured, or defeated today with those lethal subpoenas of his. But I'll let little Julian and his friends talk the issue to death. It's what they're good at. It's all they're effin' good at."

Riley spoke for the first time as Day sat rigidly, his face flushed.

"Senator McCoy was hoping that you might have talked to Mr. Garin recently. He knows the two of you go back several years. If there's anyone Mr. Garin would talk to, it's likely to be you." Her voice was conciliatory. "Would you please let us know if he attempts to contact you?"

Elliott said, "Elizabeth, we'll certainly take the request under advisement. We want to be of assistance. As I said, we'll do whatever we can, consistent with the law and my client's interests, to accommodate the committee."

"Elizabeth," Dwyer added, "if Mike Garin contacts me, I'll make sure to let him know how highly Julian speaks of him." Dwyer, grinning menacingly, turned to Day. "Don't wet your pants, Julian. If Mike Garin comes after you, it'll be painless. It'll happen so fast you won't feel a thing. Not one thing."

"Please let us know if you hear from him," Riley repeated evenly.

"Are we finished here?" Elliott asked, eager to get his client out of the room.

"Yes," Riley said. "We'll e-mail you when the hearings have been rescheduled."

"Thank you, Elizabeth." Elliott turned to Day. "But this time with a little more notice? My client has a fairly substantial business to run." Dwyer and Elliott rose to leave.

"Dwyer," Day said, "this is a very serious matter. Tell Garin to make arrangements to present himself to the FBI. Otherwise something bad will happen."

Dwyer paused in the doorway and turned toward Day. "To you or to the FBI?"

CHAPTER TWENTY-NINE

A ri Singer had spent more than thirty years in intelligence, primarily in the field. During that time he had never been shot, never been stabbed, suffered no broken bones. He had never had so much as a scuffle. This was remarkable for someone who worked for an intelligence service whose operations exposed its people to a high degree of risk more frequently than any other service in the world. It was even more remarkable for someone who had operated in Beirut for much of the eighties, Iraq in the nineties, and both Syria and Iran in the last decade.

Over the course of his career, Singer had seen the nature of intelligence gathering evolve, in large part due to advances in technology. Although he was privy to only a portion of Mossad's impressive technological resources, he knew that the kind of capabilities presently available would've been considered science fiction when he first began his career. Nonetheless, Singer believed technology could never be a substitute for face-to-face human contact. The look in the informant's eyes sometimes provided more information than a month's worth of calls intercepted by satellites and decrypted by computers.

Singer believed there was one tool more valuable to a spy than any other. Most of the vital information he'd collected over the years came from its frequent use. When used correctly, it seldom failed, and it wasn't as risky as blackmail, as hazardous as undercover work, or as unpleasant as coercive interrogation.

Singer believed that the most valuable intelligence he had acquired in his career was the result of the judicious payment of money. Information was a commodity like any other. It had a market value like any other. The trick was in being able to accurately appraise both the commodity and the person who possessed it. Come in too low and a higher bidder might snatch it from you. Come in too high and you might scare off the potential seller by causing him to think the commodity was more valuable than his life. Singer's ability to appraise both the information and the seller was uncanny.

Singer had accurately taken stock of Mansur shortly after the Iranian Revolution. Both Singer and Mansur were young intelligence agents then. Mansur was a reasonable man with a new family. Singer was an accommodating man with a lot of money. Even better, a lot of American dollars. The two did business regularly. Mansur supplied useful, if not earth-shattering, information about the political strength of the Iranian regime, its alliances with foreign powers, its support of Hamas and Hezbollah, and the state of its weapons programs. The latter had been the focus of Singer's concern the last five years.

One of their more recent collaborations had resulted in the identification of the chief of cyberwarfare for the Islamic Revolutionary Guard Corps. IRGC's cyberwarfare division was believed to be responsible for the Shamoon virus that had damaged hundreds of Aramco's computers. They had also hacked the systems of several US banks as well as a highly classified system of the US Navy. Shortly after Mansur had conveyed the chief's identity to Singer, the cyberspy had been assassinated by a motorcyclist who had attached a magnetic bomb to the chief's limousine while in transit.

Mansur might not have grown rich from the arrangement, but he had become very comfortable. And Singer, despite resembling a story-book elf, had become regarded as one of Mossad's most effective agents.

Mansur's participation in the arrangement was no longer fueled primarily by money. His wife had passed away after a brief illness a decade ago; his two sons were now physicians in London. He had few expenses and had amassed a sizable savings. Financial concerns had now been eclipsed by patriotic ones. So, for the last six months, Mansur had been supplying Singer with information concerning a joint project involving the Iranian military and the Russians. The information was nebulous at first, but judging from the description of the project's location and the level of security surrounding it, both Singer and Mansur knew that it was a matter of extreme importance to the Iranian regime.

The project was being constructed under a small mountain in the North Alborz wilderness area. That fact alone suggested that it might be related to Iran's nuclear program. It was well known that the Iranians had spread their program throughout numerous fortified underground facilities to shield it from preemptive strikes from the United States and Israel. There was an Iranian uranium enrichment plant at Natanz, another at Fordow, a conversion facility near Isfahan, and two nuclear plants at Bushehr that were supplied by the conversion facility at Ardakan and centrifuges at Tehran's Sharif University.

Hamid Mansur was unable to confirm that the project was related to the nuclear program, but he reported that several vertical shafts—which he presumed were large freight elevators leading to the underground facility—had been constructed near the base of the mountain. Also, a railroad tunnel moved massive pieces of cargo into the mountain.

The vertical shafts were of particular concern. Singer could see no good reason the Iranians would need both a railroad tunnel and freight elevators to supply the facility. Satellite images revealed little, but Singer always believed it was best to assume the worst. And to him, the worst case was that the "vertical shafts" Mansur talked about were not freight elevators, but missile silos.

Singer had arrived in the early evening at the spot Mansur and he had agreed on during their last meeting. It was as Mansur had described: a copse of trees exactly five and a half miles east of the bus depot in Chalus, off the Tehran-Shomal Freeway. It stood at the edge of flat farmland along a seldom-used rural road. There were no dwellings within several miles. If anyone approached, they would be seen long before their arrival.

Singer had arrived on a Vespa motor scooter that he had rented in Chalus. In the distance, he could see another scooter approaching. It would take at least a few minutes to arrive. Singer passed the time leaning against one of the trees, smoking a Marquise.

Mansur stepped off of the scooter just as Singer stamped out the embers of his cigarette. The two shook hands and, speaking in English, got right to business.

"Chernin says the project is ahead of schedule," Mansur said.

"When will it be ready?"

"He was not specific. But very soon. Days. A few weeks at the most. My friend, it appears you may be correct. A missile is involved, perhaps more than one. I do not know for sure. When Chernin drinks too much, he is sometimes difficult to understand."

"Did he indicate what kind of missile?"

"No. Perhaps he did and I did not understand him. He said that the solid-fuel rocket caused fewer problems than what the North Koreans had been working with."

"Liquid propellant, I presume?"

"He did not say."

"What else?" Singer asked.

"He is looking forward to going home. He has no quarrel with the Israelis."

"Did he say what he means by that?"

"No. Chernin never elaborates. And when he is asked a question about something he just said—if he's asked for more information—he immediately stops talking and changes the subject, as if he realizes he has said too much. But the project clearly troubles him."

"Did his driver wait for him this time?"

"No. Not for the last two times."

Singer tapped another Marquise out of the pack and offered it to Mansur, who declined with a shake of his head. Singer lit it and inhaled deeply.

"What do you think?" Singer exhaled skyward.

"I believe, my friend, that the people who run my country are about to do something very stupid. I believe the Russians are stupid to help. Their stupidity, however, is exceeded by that of the West."

"Hamid, for God's sake, stop talking in Persian parables. Are you saying that the missile's payload is nuclear?"

"Clearly, that is the objective. But I do not think that they are there yet," Mansur answered.

"Why, then, does Chernin say the project is ahead of schedule? What does he mean?"

"I may be mistaken, of course, but I think he was referring to the missile, not the payload."

"Hamid, you see, that's where I think you're wrong. I believe the objective is to have a functional, deliverable nuclear device. And once they have that, they intend to obliterate Israel."

"You are such a pessimist. Always such a pessimist."

"It's better to be a pessimist. That way, I'm rarely disappointed. Chernin wouldn't be talking about returning home unless both the missile and the warhead were nearly ready to go."

"Everything I hear says they are not yet capable of producing a deliverable nuclear device. The faulty centrifuges, the random accidents, set the program back even further than the IAEA estimates," Mansur said.

Singer picked a bit of tobacco from his tongue. "Those 'estimates' were sheer guesswork. They haven't the slightest idea where Iran's program stands. Neither does the CIA. For three years they were saying

Iran had discontinued its nuclear program. Then, suddenly, nuclear sites are popping up all over the country. The IAEA and UN have consistently underestimated Iran's nuclear progress, and forgive me for suspecting that their underestimation was intentional. If they say your country is one year from having deliverable nuclear capability, I'd bet it's actually one month.

"Considering what you've told me, I'd say Iran will be a nuclear power within days or weeks, if it is not already. And by nuclear power, understand something, Hamid: I mean being able to deliver and detonate a functional nuclear payload. We estimate they already have a nuclear device, probably more than one. We believe they can already *detonate* such a weapon—however crude—but we need to be absolutely certain it's functional and deliverable before appropriate action can be taken. There can be no mistake."

Both men stood silently. The sky was darkening and night quickly approached. Singer gazed pensively at the large orange half-moon cresting over the horizon.

"When can you see Chernin again?"

"I must be careful, Ari. I cannot overplay my hand. You know how these things are. His driver is security. Chernin calls me every few days. He hates the food in the compound, so he comes to my place to drink my vodka, fill his stomach, and smoke my cigars. I cannot push."

Singer dropped the half-smoked cigarette to the ground and put it out with his foot. The look on his face was uncompromising. "Hamid, I have to ask you to do whatever you can to get him to come over to your place and give you more information, any information that would provide greater certainty as to what we're dealing with, so appropriate action can be taken. We can't afford to make mistakes—either of action or inaction."

"You understand that this will be risky," Mansur said. "If I ask too many questions, if I appear too interested, he will stop talking. Worse, for me, my inquisitiveness might come to the attention of VEVAK."

"Hamid, I understand fully what I'm asking. I wouldn't ask if I thought we had more time or another way. But if we don't confirm what we're dealing with, the consequences could be catastrophic. After the failure to find large weapons of mass destruction dumps in Iraq, no Western nation will move on Iran without verification of the project's status. This restraint would allow Iran to complete the nuclear missile and strike Israel. Think about that. Do you think Israel, though devastated, wouldn't launch everything it had at its enemies? Your country would cease to exist. Period. And who knows what other actions would be triggered? Once nukes start flying, there's no way to predict where, or if, it will stop. It's a risk you must take. And, although I don't think it needs to be said, you will be compensated in proportion to the risk."

Hamid smiled sardonically. "Dead men have little use for money." He quickly added, "Make no mistake, I will gladly accept your generosity. But I recognize what must be done, regardless of the fee. It is just that I am not eager to die while so young and handsome."

"Hamid, dear man, we're no longer young. And you were never handsome."

Singer reached into his pocket, produced an envelope, and handed it to Mansur.

"Thank you," Mansur said without examining the contents. "I will meet you here in two days, but one hour earlier. If I am not here, it is because I am dead, or will be soon." Both men knew the last comment was superfluous.

Singer shook Mansur's hand. It was not the handshake of a concluded business transaction. The two men stood for a moment and regarded each other before Hamid climbed onto his motor scooter and drove into the twilight.

CHAPTER THIRTY

After the meeting with Day and Riley, Dwyer decided to go home. He had cleared his calendar for the day, anticipating that the hearing would take several hours. When he arrived, he went straight to his library, sat in his recliner, and wondered how Washington had come to be dominated by the Julian Days of the world.

Dwyer was mildly surprised when the phone on the credenza next to him rang, for it rarely did so. Nearly everyone called his cell. He picked up the receiver and listened as a series of digits were recited before the line went dead.

Dwyer rose to his feet and walked quickly out of the library, down the hall, and down two flights of stairs to the subbasement. At the bottom of the stairs was a long, wide hallway with a series of doors on both sides and one at the end. Dwyer walked to the end of the hallway, where he punched a four-digit code on the touch screen next to a thick metal door. There was an electronic chirp and then a heavy click as the door unlocked.

As Dwyer entered, lights came on automatically and the door swung shut behind him. The room was the size of a large conference room. Arrayed along the walls was millions of dollars' worth of some of the most advanced communications technology in existence. Dwyer had the ability to establish secure links with individuals anywhere in the world. A large video screen on the wall opposite the door provided videoconferencing capabilities. The walls of reinforced steel were thickly padded and acoustically designed to absorb any sounds emanating from the room. An electromagnetic curtain surrounding the room precluded any form of electronic eavesdropping.

Dwyer settled into a deep-cushioned captain's chair in the center of the room and waited impatiently. Nearly five minutes passed before a light flashed on the phone embedded in the right armrest of the chair. Dwyer picked up the phone and said, "I assume I don't have to tell you that you are, once again, in an impressively deep pile of excrement."

"It's good to talk to you, too," Garin said.

"Is there anyone in America who *isn't* looking for you?" Dwyer asked.

"I doubt it. But what do you hear?"

"This morning I got a visit from an aide to James Brandt. Yes, *that* James Brandt. National Security Advisor James Brandt. She—the aide, world-class babe, by the way—tells me Brandt wants to know everything there is to know about one Michael Garin. They think you're somehow connected to the crisis in the Middle East and something the Russians and Iranians might be cooking up. They know I recruited you to Annapolis. And they know I was one of your instructors at BUD/S."

"What did you tell her?"

"That I haven't talked to you in months. Afterward, I sauntered over to make a special guest appearance at Senate Intelligence. But it's canceled because an urgent complication has come up regarding our country's counter-WMD capability. Instead of the privilege of testifying, I get to spend quality time with the lovely and talented Julian Day, who informs me that, in fact, *you* are the complication. Apparently, you've captured the attention of the entire intelligence establishment, and most anyone who matters in law enforcement."

"Tell me about it," Garin said.

"Oh, I'll do just that. For what it's worth, I'm told the FBI has figured out that you're somehow involved in a matter of two corpses in the otherwise tranquil and bucolic suburb of Dale City," Dwyer said. His tone went from jocular to serious. "This is as bad as it gets, Mikey. What can you tell me?"

"That it's even worse than you think. It's not just law enforcement that's after me. I have reason to believe Delta Force is involved, too."

"As bad as things are, Mike, I think you have a seriously inflated view of your importance. Delta can't do domestic operations. You know that."

"I also know that someone has the capability to take out seven members of my team and make it look like I did it. They also seem to have the ability to track me anywhere I go. And they've sent two separate teams to kill me."

Dwyer focused on the last item. "So I suppose sometime soon someone's going to tell me about a second set of corpses." It was not a question.

"Probably," Garin replied. "I'm going to give you a description and you tell me your reaction: sniper, African American, dark complexion, about six feet four and 220 pounds. Shaved head. Goatee with kind of a pointed tip—"

"Congo Knox," Dwyer said before Garin could finish.

"And now, genius, just who is he with?" Garin asked.

"Delta."

"He was gunning for me this morning."

"If Congo Knox were gunning for you, I wouldn't be talking to you right now. You'd be in a rubber bag."

"He didn't see me," Garin explained. There was silence on the other end. Garin knew Dwyer was considering the import of what he had just heard.

Dwyer exhaled slowly. "Okay. What do you need?" A note of fatalism had crept into his voice.

"First, for you to stay alive. Nearly everyone I've been in contact with the last forty-eight hours is dead. They—whoever 'they' are—are going to come after you. In fact, you were probably at the top of their kill list because of our history. But your palace guard has probably made things a little more difficult for them. Regardless, get even more security."

"Matt and Carl can handle anything that comes up," Dwyer assured him.

"No, they can't. I remember Matt and Carl. Let's see, Matt's former Australian SAS. Carl's former Recon Marine, right? Sharp, tough. But these guys who were after me, whoever they are, took out Gene Tanski right in front of my eyes. They got Camacho, Gates . . . everybody. Don't take any chances. Double up. Don't go anywhere without a detail."

"Are you saying Congo Knox will be after me, too?" There was a hint of concern in Dwyer's voice.

"I don't think so. My guess is that whoever targets you will be Middle Eastern. Now that you've told me that the national security advisor is suspicious of the Russians and Iranians, I would guess they're likely Iranian."

"Okay, I'll increase security."

"Second, I need a place to stay in the metro area."

"You're staying here? Not smart," Dwyer said.

"I'm not staying there. That is, I'm not there now. But I'm coming back. Look, they've found me wherever I go. It doesn't matter where I am. Somehow they show up. So I may as well be where I can fight back."

Dwyer thought for a second and using the code for a DGT safe house said, "Alexandria Four. Do you need me or someone else to meet you there?"

"No. Do I need a key or does it have electronic access?"

"Key."

"Leave the key taped to the lid of one of the garbage cans in back. How's the place stocked?"

"The place is Metz on the Potomac. You could hold off the Third Army for weeks," Dwyer replied. "Mike. Listen—"

Garin cut him off. "Dan, I know exactly what I'm asking. I'm asking you to jump into the impressive pile of excrement with me. You're aiding and abetting someone the FBI is looking for. Day and the rest of those sanctimonious clowns have already painted a target on your back. Putting you in this position isn't something I'd do by choice." Garin exhaled. "But it looks like I've really hit the trifecta here. I've got the FBI, foreign-looking bad guys, and Delta after me. At minimum. That means someone's up to something very big and very bad."

"But that's not what I'm concerned about," Dwyer stressed. "Well, okay, it's *one* of the things, but it's not what I was about to get into. I was going to ask, is there anyone in a position of authority you can trust? Someone up the food chain who can help?"

"No. I'm a grunt. I don't have friends in high places. You know that. And even if I did, I don't know who may be involved. But that brings me to my third point. What do you think of Brandt's aide—what was her name?"

"Olivia Perry."

"What do you think she really wanted from you?"

"Just what she said. I think she's sincere. She and Brandt believe the Russians and Iranians are up to something. More specifically, they think Iran may be poised to use weapons of mass destruction—probably a nuke against Israel. Since you're the counter-WMD guy and your entire team was assassinated—well, I guess they think it's all related. For what it's worth, she thinks you had nothing to do with your team getting wiped out."

"What do you think she would do if you told her that you've been in touch with me?" Garin asked.

"You mean, do I think she would go to the FBI?"

"Yes."

"I only met her for a brief time this morning. But if I had to guess, I'd say she's indifferent about going to the FBI. She wouldn't do it if she thought it would compromise her ability to get a handle on what the Russians and Iranians are doing," Dwyer said. "Want my advice? Let me talk to her. You need all the help you can get, and even then it may not be enough. You need an ally who's more plugged in than a broken-down former SEAL."

Garin thought precisely the same thing. There was, of course, significant risk to engaging anyone in a position of authority. But even if she did go to the FBI, she wouldn't be able to tell them where he was, only that he'd been in contact with Dwyer.

"I'm inclined to agree," Garin said. "Not that I'm eager to get you in trouble, Dan, but having Brandt in my corner would be very helpful."

"The question is, do you have anything that could be useful to Brandt?"

"I might," Garin said. "But let's not give them everything at once. Let's proceed cautiously and see how they react."

"What do you want me to do?"

"Call her back. She wants to know about me? Tell her what you know."

"What should I say is the reason for my getting back in touch?"

"That I called you. Hell, be up front. I told you to contact her, but I need help, and in return, I'm willing to provide as much information as I can."

"I'll call right away. Anything else?"

"No. Thanks. Anyway, I've got to get off. Too much time."

"This call is secure," Dwyer said with a bit of indignation. He had spent a considerable sum ensuring that his calls couldn't be monitored.

"No such thing. I'll be in touch. One last thing. It looks like my former mentor is dead," Garin said softly, referring to Clinton Laws. "Make an anonymous call to the National Park Service or the police department closest to Kings Canyon. Tell them to look for a body along a road."

CHAPTER THIRTY-ONE

MOUNT VERNON, VIRGINIA

JULY 15 • 3:55 P.M. EDT

Brandt had been right, as usual.

After leaving the morning meeting with Dwyer, Olivia had stopped briefly at her apartment before going to Brandt's office in the White House. She had informed Brandt that Dwyer had provided little useful information, but it seemed as if he might be holding back. Brandt predicted that Dwyer would be in touch again soon with more information. The first meeting had merely served as an opportunity for Dwyer to assess Olivia. Sure enough, a few hours later Dwyer called Olivia for another meeting.

Matt and his clone, whose name, Olivia learned, was Carl, arrived shortly after three just outside of the Old Executive Office Building to pick up Olivia in a Lincoln Town Car. Olivia didn't know it but the vehicle was heavily armored, with bulletproof windows. Olivia sat in the rear. Matt and Carl, sporting light-colored summer-weight clothing and wide grins, sat in front. Their regular duties weren't nearly as enjoyable as escorting someone like Olivia Perry.

When they arrived, Dwyer was in the library, talking on his cell. He motioned for Olivia to take a seat and pointed to refreshments on the coffee table. Matt and Carl left, but a short, wiry man with a Glock at the small of his back stood in a hallway immediately outside the library. On the patio beyond the French doors directly behind Dwyer, Olivia could see another man. He was wearing a white T-shirt, beige cargo pants, and sunglasses. An exotic-looking rifle of some sort was slung across his chest.

Olivia sat in a chair and looked at the photographs perched along several shelves of the bookcase closest to her. Some of the photos were of the Navy football team. A few more were of Dwyer and several other men in fatigues, standing on a beach. The largest was of Dwyer in a hospital bed, smiling and giving a thumbs-up signal despite the fact that he was covered with discolored bandages and looked as if he'd been caught in a hay baler.

Olivia looked back at Dwyer, the tone of his voice indicating that the call was coming to an end. Dwyer disconnected, walked over with a slight limp, and sat across from Olivia. "Thanks for coming over again. Too hot to sit on the patio this afternoon."

"What about the guard outside?" Olivia motioned toward the window.

"He's used to hot weather." Dwyer grinned. "Believe me."

"I notice that you seem to have more security this afternoon than you did this morning. I hope you haven't concluded that I'm some kind of threat."

Dwyer kept grinning. "Well, you certainly present a distinct hazard to Matt and Carl. Actually, I put on more security at the insistence of Mike Garin." Dwyer examined Olivia's face for reaction. If she was surprised, she didn't show it.

"When did he do that?" Olivia asked casually.

"You seem to have expected that he'd call."

"We thought he might," Olivia said. "Michael Garin's facing daunting odds. He needs help. There was a fair probability that he'd reach out to you because you're his friend, and you have substantial resources."

"But what made you think that I'd contact you again?" Dwyer asked.

"A hunch. Despite your not inconsiderable resources, Garin was likely to figure that being on good terms with James Brandt might be very helpful also. Garin would try to barter what he knows for whatever goodwill Mr. Brandt can provide. It was logical that he would call you and you, in turn, would call us," Olivia explained.

Dwyer stared at Olivia. The Oracle's apprentice was one quick study.

"But Mike was concerned you would go to the FBI if he asked me to contact you."

"Certainly, that was one of the things he had to consider," Olivia agreed. "But after he weighed the probabilities, he'd conclude that we're less interested in the FBI than we are about Russian-Iranian WMD. And to be safe, Garin wouldn't play his entire hand at once. He'd tell us just enough to keep us occupied and interested. This way we wouldn't go to the FBI, even if we were so inclined, until we got all the info he could provide." Olivia sat back and crossed her legs. "So, what can you tell me?"

Dwyer smiled and began to wonder if his calls were, in fact, secure. Garin, Brandt, and Perry seemed to be reading from the same script. "What do you want to know?"

"Well, as they say, we don't know what we don't know. So why don't you start from the beginning? Mr. Brandt believes that sometimes seemingly irrelevant pieces of information can be useful. There may be things about Garin that neither he nor you think are pertinent, but might provide clues to what's going on in the Middle East."

Dwyer reached toward the table in front of him and poured a glass of iced tea. Long Island vintage. He offered it to Olivia, who shook her head. He took a sip before proceeding.

"Olivia, the first thing you have to understand is that I'm not a Mike Garin encyclopedia. Despite the fact that I'm a friend—I'd like to think a pretty good friend—there are big gaps in my knowledge about him."

"Understood," Olivia said. "We don't expect you to know everything, of course. Just tell me what you do know. You recruited Garin to the Naval Academy, correct?"

"That's right. Mike was a hell of a football player and a good all-around athlete. He could've gone anywhere, but he was cursed with a serious, almost debilitating affliction."

"What was that?"

"Brains. In addition to the big football schools, Mike was being recruited by Annapolis, West Point, and the Ivies because of his grades and board scores. He chose Cornell, and as you probably know, he did pretty well there academically and athletically."

"But he left after less than three years."

"Not quite. He didn't just leave. He got his degree. But he wanted to go into the service."

"Did you have anything to do with that?"

"No. He did it on his own. Believed he had a duty. It may not be fashionable, but he really believes in 'duty, honor, country.' The next time I saw him was at Coronado. He was a member of a BUD/S class and I was an instructor. Do you know anything about BUD/S?"

"Sure, I've seen the movies, the TV shows. They're everywhere. Cottage industry. I understand it's some of the toughest military training on earth."

"No, ma'am," Dwyer corrected, "it's *the* toughest training. The media really don't capture how tough. Yeah, you may get some pushback from some of the other elite units around the world—SAS, Sayeret Matkal, Spetsnaz, GSG-9—but don't listen to them. The dropout rate in BUD/S and SEAL Qualification Training is extremely high. The thing is, there's really no way of telling who's going to make it and who's not when a new class first arrives. Some of the toughest, meanest, fittest SOBs drop out before Hell Week, and some guys with the faces of angels go all the way through. What you have to understand about success in the teams is that it's a function of mental toughness. Show me a SEAL squad and I'll show you eight men who have never quit, and will never quit, anything in their lives."

"Where does Garin fit, SOB or angel?"

"Both. Mike's one of the mentally and physically toughest men I've ever met. But he's somewhat of a warrior-poet paradox. He's a Grade A predator and yet he's pure Boy Scout. Goes to Mass, prays the Rosary, rarely curses. But he can drink you under the table without so much as pausing to breathe, then rip out your liver to replace the one he just ruined. A *ruthless* Boy Scout, but a Boy Scout nonetheless. One of his mottos is Patton's line, 'Better to fight for something than live for nothing.' I mean, the guy's got *mottos*, for cripe's sake," Dwyer said, grinning. "He knows when to pivot, when to stand down. He's very savvy, and he understands gray areas. That said, he really belongs in the twelfth century. Age of chivalry. Where everything's black and white."

"How can the Big Bad Wolf also be a Boy Scout? Especially after all he's done?"

Dwyer brightened theatrically. "Thanks so much for letting me play amateur psychologist. It's my true calling."

"Seriously."

Dwyer shrugged. "The Big Bad Wolf wasn't always big and bad?" Dwyer offered. "When I recruited him for Annapolis, I was a grad assistant on the Navy football team, something to keep me occupied while I was recuperating from two broken legs."

"How . . ."

"Don't ask. Training accident." Dwyer made air quotes with his fingers.

Olivia blinked acquiescence.

"When you recruit players, you're actually recruiting the whole family—Mom, Dad, siblings, girlfriends—to encourage them to get the recruit to sign with you."

Olivia nodded. "My father played for Bear Bryant."

"No kidding? Really? Then you know how it goes. I got to know his sister, Katy, pretty well. Major babe, though she's probably even tougher than Mikey. Over beers she tells me Mikey was a runt as a kid. Their mom had serious complications when pregnant with him and his twin. Doctors recommended she abort. Mikey was born almost three months premature. His twin died in utero. Mikey spent a long time in the NICU before coming home. Grew up undersize for most of his childhood, chronically ill. He wasn't a Big Bad Wolf back then. He was prey, not predator."

"That wouldn't necessarily turn him into a Boy Scout. Some people might be resentful or vengeful once they got strong and healthy."

"Look," Dwyer said. "That's about the limit of my psychoanalytic abilities. All I know is Mike is *not* someone you want as an enemy. You definitely want him on your side."

"But he never became a SEAL. If he's so smart and tough, why did he drop out?"

"He didn't. Not technically, at least. Mike was going through all the evolutions during BUD/S and coming out at, or near, the top in all of them. He was definitely a candidate for honor man of the class. Push-ups, pull-ups, running. Didn't matter how much or how many. He just kept plugging. Never lagged. And he seemed oblivious to the cold— getting wet and sandy all the time. Everybody else is frozen, teeth chattering. Guys were dropping out like flies. But there he was, with that determined look in his eyes. I'll tell you, it can be unsettling. We sometimes get star athletes that come through. Many of them, most of them, can't hack it. Not only could Mike hack it; he *thrived.* No, he didn't DOR. He went to SEAL Qualification Training. But then he just disappeared."

"DOR?"

"Drop on Request. Anyone dropping out just places their helmet on the grinder—an asphalt area—and rings a bell. No questions asked. Mike didn't do that. He didn't ring the bell. Like I said, he was in SQT and then he was just gone." Dwyer shook his head as if still trying to sort out what happened. "Mike's disappearance stunned the rest of the class and the instructors. Naturally, there was some talk—not much; we don't dwell on those things. But people were trying to figure out what happened. We asked around a little. No one knew anything.

There was some speculation that he got sheep-dipped, but that was about it."

Dwyer noticed Olivia's eyebrows knit in confusion. "Sorry. Sheep-dipped. Some thought he might've been snagged by the OGA—the CIA—and trained at the Farm, Camp Peary," he explained.

"He wasn't?"

"Hell, I still don't know."

"When was the next time you heard from him?"

"The next time I heard *about* him was more than a year later. Rumors of Garin sightings. One night, back when I was with Task Force 121 looking for Saddam Hussein, some guys came back to Baghdad Airport buzzing about how they got ambushed, but some guy with an M4 shows up out of nowhere and takes out eight of the enemy. When the smoke clears, he's gone. But one of the guys who knew Mike from BUD/S claims it was him."

"Was it?"

"Who knows? I asked Mike about it once and he just got quiet like he always does."

"Like you did when I asked you about DEVGRU this morning."

Dwyer pursed his lips. "Anyway, over the next year and a half, I heard the occasional Garin story. Someone saw him in the Ma'laab District in Ramadi. Then all the way over in Kandahar. And the stories." Dwyer rolled his eyes. "The stories got more and more ridiculous."

"What do you mean?"

"I mean, they sounded like he was Batman or something: Garin wipes out ten al-Qaeda fighters with a dull can opener; Garin leaps tall buildings in a single bound. Unbelievable stuff."

"You're confusing superheroes," Olivia needled. Dwyer could see that Olivia was becoming absorbed in the story despite its marginal relevance to Iranians and Russians. "Was it really Garin?"

"Again, don't know. Sounded over-the-top. But operators aren't generally given to hyperbole."

"Do you know what Garin was supposedly doing in those areas, presuming it was him?"

"He never told me. But clearly, he was killing bad guys."

"Do you believe the stories?"

"I believe one of them, that's for sure."

"Why's that?"

"Because I was there."

CHAPTER THIRTY-TWO

NORTHEASTERN AFGHANISTAN

AUGUST 28, 2004 • 1:12 P.M. AFT

The crevasse ran deep and long, high in the Hindu Kush. A short distance ahead, no more than a two-hour walk, was the mountain that intel had identified as the safe haven for Taliban fighters who had been harassing allied troops for the last three weeks, often with devastating effect.

Lieutenant Dan Dwyer led his team cautiously through the narrow passage, alert for any signs of the enemy's presence. This was their territory and they knew how to remain hidden in the rocky crags and nooks until it was often too late for allied patrols to react.

The crevasse was perfectly constructed for ambush, with only one avenue of retreat. To the team's left was a steep four-hundred-foot slope, behind which the midday sun was already beginning to disappear, casting hideous shadows throughout the canyon floor. On the right was an imposing wall of rock that rose more than three hundred feet at a sheer ninety-degree angle. Between the steep wall and the more gradual slope, the floor of the crevasse was no more than forty feet wide, with massive boulders throughout.

Every single member of the team preferred not to be walking this path, but there were no practical alternatives. Most of the terrain surrounding the safe haven was impassable and the only other plausible path was controlled by the Taliban.

Dwyer and his men—Chief Petty Officer Terry Cipriano, Petty Officer Ron "Cochise" Coleman, and Petty Officer Bob McKnight—had been in the mountains for three days and had yet to encounter any of the fighters they were looking for. Consequently, with each passing minute their tension grew. Each wanted to get out of the crevasse as quickly as possible, shake the sensations of claustrophobia and being watched, and have room to maneuver. They felt straitjacketed in this place.

As they approached a cluster of boulders, Dwyer heard Coleman whisper behind him.

"Boss. Ten o'clock high."

All four slowed and looked midway up the slope to their left, squinting as the blinding sunlight framed the crest.

"Don't see anything," Dwyer said quietly.

"Me neither," McKnight concurred.

Coleman stared at a spot on the slope. "Seeing ghosts, I guess," he said, shaking his head. "Light gets funny up here."

"You just keep right on looking for ghosts, Cochise," Dwyer said, turning back to Coleman. "This place—"

Before Dwyer finished the sentence a 7.62×39mm round tore through Coleman's throat, nearly severing his head from his neck. Almost simultaneously, McKnight took a round in his left shoulder, and Dwyer's left thigh was also struck. Ground sausage.

The three SEALs dove behind the cluster of boulders a fraction of a second after Coleman's body collapsed to the ground. A storm of gunfire chased them, slamming against the boulders for several seconds before halting abruptly.

Cipriano peeked quickly around one of the boulders to scan the slope and then looked back to a grimacing Dwyer. "Looks like the last scene from *Butch and Sundance* out there. I'd estimate forty-five to fifty. That I can see."

"Shame. Gonna be a shitload of graves for them to dig." Dwyer nodded at McKnight, who was inspecting his wounded shoulder. "How you doing, Bobby?"

"Pissed."

"We've got a couple of seconds before they start coming down that slope," Dwyer said. "Terry, take care of Bobby's shoulder."

Instead, Cipriano sprinted out to Coleman's body and began dragging it behind the boulders. Dwyer cursed as he watched from behind the boulder and saw Cipriano get hit in his left hip, a spray of blood and bone marrow temporarily blinding the team leader.

"What the hell," Dwyer said. "You don't believe in waiting for cover?"

"Just assumed you knew I'd go, boss."

"You okay?"

Cipriano's eyes were bloodshot with pain. "Never better."

"Okay. Then patch us up, quick as you can. Bobby, get on the radio. We need evac right now. Otherwise, there's going to be a whole mess of dead Taliban up here."

Dwyer took another peek up the slope. The enemy was using rocks and shrubs for cover. He detected no movement. He knew that would change quickly.

"Radio won't work, boss," McKnight informed. "Canyon walls. We need to get out of here."

Dwyer knew the team wasn't getting out of there anytime soon. They were going to be pinned behind the cluster of boulders, backs literally to the wall, unless they could thin out the opposing force substantially.

"All right," Dwyer said, "they know if they come directly down the slope at us, we'll pick them off from behind these rocks. So any second now, they're going to start fanning out to try to flank us. We can't let that happen. You see them move laterally, you take them out. Got it?"

Cipriano and McKnight nodded.

"Maintain fire discipline," Dwyer continued. "No matter how hot it gets. Make each shot count—"

Dwyer was cut off by the thunderous noise of gunfire from dozens of AK-47s reverberating off the canyon walls. Shards of rock torn from the boulders screamed past them like swarms of jagged dragonflies.

Dwyer spun to his left and fired single shots at two Taliban trying to flank the team's left, felling both. Cipriano and McKnight, manning the right flank, each fired bursts at enemy moving to the right. Two more fell.

Even though the enemy's ranks had been reduced, their fire increased. The SEALs had to pivot from behind the rocks, acquire their targets, fire, and return to cover within seconds. All in the face of withering, incessant fire.

Yet they were doing so with lethal accuracy. The Taliban were determined to outflank them, but every attempt was thwarted.

Even so, the enemy was inching closer down the slope. If they couldn't outflank Dwyer's team, they would eventually charge them en masse. And Dwyer knew that the enemy's sheer numbers would overwhelm three shooters, no matter how accurate they were.

But the three warriors kept fighting, steadily and methodically acquiring targets and taking them out.

The fight had raged for nearly two hours when the rate of fire *increased,* as if they'd just landed at Omaha Beach. Dwyer was braced against the rock wall, slamming a new magazine into his weapon, as McKnight edged out to see what was going on.

"I got good news and bad news, boss," McKnight said.

"Give it to me."

"The good news is, cavalry's here. Bad news is, it's theirs. Maybe another fifteen to twenty."

A bullet ricocheted off the back wall and passed through Cipriano's left shoulder, leaving a shallow wound. He emitted an angry growl and kept firing. At the same time, two Taliban, firing furiously, charged across the floor of the crevasse. Dwyer spun from behind the rocks and cut them down with two torso shots each, but not before catching some shrapnel in the meat of his left biceps. He dropped his M4 momentarily but willed himself to raise it and fire several more rounds to keep the Taliban at bay.

Four more men charged, screaming loud enough to be heard over the cacophony. Cipriano fired a fusillade, killing them all, and retreated behind the boulders.

Cipriano caught Dwyer's eye and nodded toward McKnight. Though upright, he was leaning hard against the boulders and appeared dazed, on the cusp of losing consciousness. He was soaked in blood. He'd been hit several times during the course of the fight but was determined to keep going.

Dwyer and Cipriano glanced at each other. The math wasn't hard. They didn't have comms. No one knew their position. They'd spent most of their ammunition, and the Taliban seemed willing to sacrifice as many bodies as necessary to get the job done. It was just a matter of time. But they would never quit fighting.

Dwyer winked at Cipriano and moved over to McKnight, patting him on the shoulder.

"Take a blow for a minute, Bobby. We got this."

He lowered McKnight to a sitting position on the ground and propped him up against the wall.

McKnight stared straight ahead. "Just for a minute, boss. Then I'm back in the fight."

Dwyer stood and prepared to reengage when Cipriano, providing cover, looked back to him with a puzzled expression.

"Hear that?"

Dwyer did. Interspersed among the cracking sounds of the AK-47s were several single shots from a different weapon, followed by wails of agony.

Dwyer and Cipriano darted their heads around opposite sides of the boulders and saw several Taliban falling. The two SEALs turned back toward each other with quizzical expressions. Then more single shots, more cries of pain, accompanied by frantic shouting.

Again, the two glanced around the boulders. Dwyer couldn't see where the fire was coming from—the glare from the sun's corona sinking behind the slope obscured the view. And once more, the two turned to each other.

"What the hell?"

"They're dropping like flies, boss," Cipriano declared with a hint of a smile. "Gotta be a whole squad of our guys up there. Maybe more. And not missing. Not missing at all."

"Maybe Delta. Or Six." Dwyer looked at McKnight. "Hear that, Bobby? Hear that? Hang in there, buddy."

McKnight smiled and nodded painfully.

Cipriano whooped and spun around the boulder, firing. Dwyer did the same. The Taliban had broken cover trying to evade the shots coming from the top of the slope, and were now sandwiched by Dwyer and Cipriano below.

Dwyer and Cipriano were jacked. The momentum had shifted dramatically. Fire discipline was out the window. They were pumping rounds at the enemy with glorious abandon.

And then they saw him.

Cipriano noticed him first. At the very top of the ridge, silhouetted against the sunlight. Not a squad. Not even a team. Just one man, on one knee, in a firing position. Exposed, yet obscured by the blinding sunlight. Calmly taking out one, two, three—six, seven, eight Taliban in a matter of seconds, then pausing to slap in a fresh magazine, seemingly indifferent to return fire, and then taking out more.

Cipriano pivoted to Dwyer. The two blinked at each other with expressions of disbelief. Cipriano began laughing almost maniacally, then turned, gave another triumphant yell, and resumed firing.

The attention of the Taliban now was focused almost exclusively on the threat from the top of the slope. Dwyer watched as the man rose, his figure framed but still obscured by sun glare, and began slowly descending toward the Taliban, firing as he went. Confident, as if he believed himself indestructible. Under any other circumstances, Dwyer would have considered the move inexplicably reckless, almost suicidal. But Dwyer conceded that to the Taliban, who were being slaughtered apace, it probably looked ominous. Dozens of them lay strewn across the slope.

The figure continued down the slope, picking off the enemy with deadly efficiency. Merciless. *Whoever this guy is,* Dwyer thought, *he's badass, stone-cold.*

The remaining Taliban, now numbering no more than eight or nine, took off at a full sprint to Dwyer's right down the crevasse, firing everything they had while making their escape. Dwyer and Cipriano fired after them. A couple more went down.

Less than a minute later, the echoes faded; the crevasse was silent. The Taliban were gone and the spectral figure continued his descent, stopping to check the Taliban lying on the ground with his HK416, making sure they were dead. He looked to Dwyer like a farmer checking to see if his tomatoes were ripe.

As the figure approached, Dwyer and Cipriano moved tentatively toward him from their position behind the boulders. When they were about twenty paces apart, Dwyer came to a dead stop.

"I don't effin' believe this."

"What?" Cipriano asked.

"Mike effin' Garin."

Cipriano was incredulous. "You know this guy?"

"Mike?" Dwyer called. "Mike Garin?"

The man's face, shrouded by long curly hair and a thick black beard, was deeply tanned and weather-beaten. But there it was—the unmistakable intensity in his eyes. Garin acknowledged Dwyer with an almost imperceptible nod as he scanned their wounds.

Dwyer rushed forward and gave him a bear hug, then turned to Cipriano and in a voice that sounded like he was announcing the winner of the Ms. America Pageant said, "Mike effin' Garin!"

In a quiet voice, Garin responded, "Let's get you squared away and out of here."

CHAPTER THIRTY-THREE

Olivia realized she was leaning forward in her chair while listening to Dwyer, her forearms resting on her knees. She straightened self-consciously. "He must've been more than a little surprised to see his former BUD/S instructor and football recruiter. What else did he say?"

"Nothing. All business. He looked at our wounds and knew we needed evac, pronto. But we needed to get out of the canyon to higher elevation so our comms could work. He didn't have any. He's up there by himself in some of the most hostile territory in the world and the son of a bitch doesn't even have a radio. Says it got hit by fire a while back. Anyway, he puts Ron's body over his shoulder and we start climbing the slope.

"Now, it's about four hundred feet—steep—to the top, and we're already at altitude. Thin air. But he's carrying Ron, plus gear, and not even breathing hard. The only thing he didn't do was hum 'The Battle Hymn of the Republic.'"

Olivia laughed, which prompted Dwyer to laugh in turn. The reason for Dwyer's protective behavior toward Garin earlier in the day was becoming clear. The former BUD/S instructor didn't merely respect his former pupil; he seemed almost in awe of him.

"It took us a while to get to the top. We were in pretty bad shape. But we get there and I radio in and a little while later, in comes a Chinook. We get loaded up and ready to go and Mike just walks away. The rest of us are yelling at him, asking him what the hell he's doing, and he just says, 'Gotta go.' I tell him to at least take some comms and toss a radio to him. He just nods and takes off. Said maybe sixteen words the whole time. Everybody in that bird just looked at each other."

Olivia glanced at the photograph of Dwyer in a hospital bed.

"Yeah, that's me at Bagram right after all of this," Dwyer acknowledged.

"Did he ever tell you what he was doing up there?"

"No. Playing avenging angel, I guess."

"Michael the Archangel."

"Mike never talks about any of those stories. But I suspect he was hunting high-value targets." Dwyer put down his glass of Long Island iced tea. "Well, I'm sure you thought that story was totally useless."

"Well, it doesn't tell me anything about Garin's connection to the Iranian/Russian matter, but it did give me insight into the man. He's certainly not your standard-issue cog in the country's war machinery, is he?"

"I tried recruiting Mike again a year later, this time successfully," Dwyer said. "I left the teams shortly after my recovery at Bagram. My leg was messed up pretty bad and I couldn't hack it anymore. So, while recuperating, I got the idea to form DGT and convinced Mike to be one of my partners."

"Garin helped found DGT?" Olivia asked. "I remember reading in the materials that he went to work for a military contractor. I didn't know it was DGT."

"Yep. Like I said, the man's got more than a few working brain cells. I guess he got tired of sightseeing in the Hindu Kush. My original idea was to provide logistical support for diplomatic missions. I saw that fighting a couple of wars had stretched the military's capacity pretty thin. So we went to the Department of Defense, and then State, and someone decided to give us a try." Dwyer shrugged his shoulders.

"A small contract at first that kept Mike, Ken Thompson—our other partner—and me busy for only about sixty days, providing an escort detail for some State Department people who were helping the Iraqi parliament get on its feet. Then, just as that contract was about to expire, we got another one to do the same thing for the USAID folks in Kabul.

"We were limping along for another month until Mike got the idea to go big. He somehow secured us a line of credit and bid on a big DOD contract to provide security for civilians in several locations throughout the world. We won and were off to the races. Then he got us to start diversifying—providing materiel, personnel, making ourselves indispensable to the global war on terror. We grew fast. It didn't take long for Thompson to cash out. He's sunning himself on a tropical island somewhere. Not long after, Mike left too, but not before making a pretty decent bundle of cash."

"Why did he leave?"

"His grandfather had just died," replied Dwyer. "Mike revered him. Said he was twice the man Mike was."

"I thought operators don't generally engage in hyperbole," Olivia said.

"Yeah. I had to think about that one for a while too. But around the time of his grandfather's death, the country was going through another period of self-flagellation. A large part of the media and political class claimed that the US was the locus of evil in the world, that we'd brought all the bad stuff, all the terrorism, on ourselves by being so imperialistic, chauvinistic, and racist. Blame America First."

"I saw it among some of my colleagues. Individuals who didn't realize how good they had it and, more importantly, why it was they had it so good. Disparaging the things that gave them their security, their privileged status, their very ability to criticize," Olivia said.

Olivia smiled upon seeing Dwyer's surprised reaction. It was rare to encounter a civilian with a cold-eyed understanding of the real world.

"I think Mike felt bound to defend the country he and his grandfather loved. As I said, he's a Boy Scout. He wanted to be in the fight. He wasn't content with supporting it. The things the talking heads were saying about America were what his grandfather had actually experienced in the Soviet Union."

"Wait," Olivia interjected, letting it sink in. "His grandfather was a Soviet émigré?"

"Right. As I understand it, he was an officer in the Red Army, fighting in Germany during World War II. When the war ended, the political officers adjudged him to be anticommunist, or at least an insufficiently zealous communist, and he was arrested, destined for death or a labor camp. Somehow, he escaped and made his way to the American sector in Germany. A few years later, he came to America."

"Garin's family is from Russia," Olivia said as if pondering an unfinished puzzle.

"Mike still has some distant relatives there," Dwyer said, hoping to add a piece.

"Go on."

"Mike thought it was his obligation to both his grandfather and his country to serve the latter as best he could," Dwyer said.

"So he became part of the counter-WMD strike force."

"It was pretty clear diplomacy wasn't containing the spread of WMD," Dwyer said. "A.Q. Khan was selling nuclear know-how to anyone with enough cash; the North Koreans were doing the same. Chechens were trying to get their hands on uranium. Every thug between Syria and Burma had nuclear designs."

"And the UN does nothing but pass toothless resolutions," Olivia added. "The IAEA is at best worthless and at worst enabling. There's no meaningful penalty for violating nonproliferation treaties."

"The administration—the one preceding Clarke's, that is—understood that negotiations to prevent the development of WMD have only been used by rogue regimes to play for time until they acquired WMD capability," Dwyer said. "The administration also knew that even if tough sanctions were imposed, they would find a way to circumvent them. So direct covert action was needed."

"And the strike force was created," Olivia finished. "But why not simply use Delta or SEAL Team Six to do the job? They're already trained in nuke detection, recovery, and disposal."

Dwyer said, "The strike force isn't designed for detection and recovery. Its sole task is to seek and destroy."

"Does it have a name?

"I don't know. I can tell you that I've heard the name Omega once or twice. I'm not sure if that's the unit's official designation or if it's what the unit members called themselves."

"Omega," Olivia repeated. "Makes a perverted kind of sense. The last resort before oblivion."

Before Dwyer could respond, the piercing sound of a commercial-grade security alarm startled Olivia. A gun materialized in Dwyer's hand and the compact bodyguard appeared at his side in an instant, weapon drawn. The guard outside had his rifle up at the ready.

Dwyer seized her elbow and pulled her roughly in the direction of the hallway.

"Come with me," Dwyer commanded. "*Now.*"

CHAPTER THIRTY-FOUR

Garin parked the Crown Victoria at the edge of a crowded shopping center lot in Binghamton, New York, and surveyed the parking area across from a convenience store that sold lottery tickets—a liquor store next door—and waited, counting on the beneficence of human nature. It would take a while, but inevitably someone in a hurry would park outside one of the two stores to get a ticket, a few sundries, or maybe some spirits—leaving their car unlocked and relieving Garin of the problem of breaking into a vehicle in broad daylight.

Sure enough, within mere minutes a stout, lumpy man in his forties, wearing shorts, flip-flops, and a stained white T-shirt, struggled laboriously from a Volkswagen Jetta that was much too small for him and that he parked in the fire lane in front of the liquor store. A bonus: The man was gracious enough to leave the car running. Just a quick pop into the store for a pint of Jim Beam, maybe a pack of Marlboros from the convenience store, and then back home to finish the tile grout in the bathroom. No worries.

Garin, carrying his gym and rifle bags, was already halfway between the Crown Vic and the Jetta by the time Lumpy had disappeared into the liquor store, its windows placarded with ads obscuring the view from the inside. Garin casually scanned the lot before sliding smoothly into the driver's seat and driving out of the lot. He was already on the access ramp to Interstate 81 southbound by the time Lumpy emerged from the liquor store and stared blankly at the space where he'd left the vehicle, as if it would magically reappear if he just concentrated hard enough.

Garin drove the Jetta south on Interstate 81 until he spotted an Avis location on the outskirts of Scranton, Pennsylvania. He put the keys and, like a good Boy Scout, five hundred dollars in cash in the glove compartment of Lumpy's car before locking it and leaving it in front of the Avis building.

Garin rented a blue Ford Fusion, driving within five miles of the posted speed limits to Washington, D.C., stopping only once to change clothes in the restroom of the gas station a few blocks from the Avis.

The traffic into Washington was fairly light until he reached the madness of the Beltway. He arrived at the safe house in the evening. The house was a small, slate-gray, two-story town house wedged between two others that were nearly identical. He circled the block once looking for anything out of the ordinary before parking along the street a little less than a block away.

Garin collected his bag from the trunk and proceeded up the narrow walkway along the side of the house to the rear. A row of three dark green plastic trash cans stood next to the back door. Garin found the house keys taped to the lid of the middle can and let himself in the back door. Recalling the security code from his days at DGT, he punched it into the touch pad inside the door and found himself in a small kitchen. Curious, he opened the door to the refrigerator and found it stocked with plenty of meats, fish, fruits, vegetables, and sports drinks.

Garin dropped his bag on the floor and performed a methodical sweep of both floors of the premises. A short hallway with a half bath to the right led from the kitchen to a living room at the front of the house. A large rectangular mirror hung over a small fireplace to the right. A narrow wooden staircase led to the second floor, where there were two bedrooms at opposite ends of the hallway. A laptop sat on the desk in the smaller bedroom. There was a modest full bath between the two bedrooms.

Garin returned to the kitchen, where he found the basement door next to the stove. He flipped the switch on the wall and went down eight steps to a small, unremarkable cellar with a concrete floor, a washer-dryer combination at the far end, and a freezer along the right wall. Garin opened the freezer. Dwyer was right; the house was well stocked.

Garin went back upstairs and spent the next hour preparing a dinner of spaghetti, Italian sausage, and tomato sauce with a small mixed-greens salad. While waiting for the water to boil, he took his bag up to the master bedroom and unpacked. He placed his shaving kit in the bathroom and laid out its contents on the counter next to the sink before returning downstairs to finish cooking.

It was his first meal in three days that didn't consist of protein bars or junk food. Garin devoured two large plates of spaghetti and sausage and washed it down with more than a quart of Gatorade.

After a long, hot shower, he emerged feeling fatigued but much better. He looked forward to finally getting a good six hours' sleep in a comfortable bed, but first he inspected the items from his shaving kit that he had placed on the sink counter. The contents consisted of a nose-bridge mold, a lens case carrying blue contacts, and a molded lower lip. A pair of black-framed glasses would complete his disguise.

Garin's somewhat inchoate plan involved altering his appearance. Despite having done so on several occasions, he wasn't particularly creative or elaborate. Garin understood that subtle changes to one's face would throw all but the most perceptive observers. More important, given the ubiquity of security cameras in the District, altering his facial symmetry would stymie facial recognition programs.

Garin walked into the small bedroom, turned on the laptop, and logged in using an old passcode from his time with DGT. He called up a map of the District with the locations of all the hotels. After study-ing the map for a few seconds, he magnified the area around Four-teenth and K, using the cursor to slowly move the map from east to west, then north to south. He then switched the application to a satel-lite view of the same area, gradually zooming in on the Hamilton Crowne Plaza on the northeast corner of the intersection. He exam-ined the building from the top and front for several moments before shifting to the National Labor Relations Board building next door to the left, circling its perimeter using Street View.

He then went to the NLRB website and viewed the members' office numbers on the eleventh floor. Satisfied, Garin shut down the laptop, walked to the next bedroom, and after placing the SIG under the frame, lay down to rest.

Tomorrow he was going on offense.

CHAPTER THIRTY-FIVE

Several hours later, Olivia was still on edge.

When the security alarm had sounded, Dwyer and one of his bodyguards, whose name, Olivia learned, was Ray, had hustled her into a small vault-like room in the subbasement of Dwyer's house. The room was equipped with multiple surveillance monitors that permitted them to view every corner of the estate. Olivia watched as approximately a dozen armed men supported by two canine teams covered every inch of the grounds. They found nothing.

A large alarm monitor next to the surveillance cameras displayed a facsimile of the grounds divided into twenty sectors. Sector 17, the easternmost portion of the property near the street, was lit red, indicating a breach in the area. Olivia could see the dogs become agitated as they searched the grounds; they had picked up the scent of someone who didn't belong. Whoever it was, however, was long gone.

Dwyer manipulated a mouse on the console in front of the surveillance monitors and a digital recording of Sector 17 began to play back, beginning ten seconds before the alarm had gone off. When the replay reached the time of the alarm, Dwyer enhanced and froze the image. At the top left corner of the screen, the head of a man was visible above the stone wall that surrounded the estate. The right side of the man's face was obscured partially by a tall hedge near the wall.

Dwyer magnified the image of the intruder as far as he could without losing resolution. He was olive-skinned and appeared to be in his early to midthirties. No distinguishing features were readily apparent.

Dwyer played the recording in real time. The intruder remained visible for approximately two seconds. Olivia thought he looked composed, despite the shrieking of the security alarm.

"See that?" Ray said in a clinical voice as he pointed to the intruder's image. "He's not startled by the alarm. It doesn't look like he was trying to get in. And he doesn't seem to be in any hurry to take off. He knew exactly what he was doing."

"A probe," Dwyer said.

Ray nodded in agreement. "He wasn't testing the security system. He knows we've got security and that it's good. He was testing our response."

"Gauging manpower and response time. Looking for weaknesses and opportunities," Dwyer said. "We've probably been under surveillance for a while. They won't try anything here. He'll go back and tell his friends it's a no-go."

"If they're going to make a move, it'll be elsewhere," Ray agreed.

"But haven't they blown it?" Olivia asked. "Haven't they lost the element of surprise?"

Dwyer shook his head. Olivia's question was logical and Dwyer avoided any hint of patronizing her. "If they're any good, they know not to underestimate their opponent. They'll operate from the premise that we've already been alerted to the possibility of an attack. So for them to be successful, it's much less about surprise now than it is finding the right spot and the right time. They probably took photos of all of our men."

Dwyer recalled the intruder's image on the monitor and froze it. He turned to Ray. "What do you think?"

"Could be," Ray said.

"Could be what?" Olivia asked.

"It's not the best image," Dwyer said, "but our friend here could be Iranian. Admittedly, he could be two dozen other nationalities, but we can probably rule out ethnic Norwegian."

"Do you think they know I'm here?" Olivia asked.

"They know you're here but they probably don't know who you are," Dwyer replied. "Whoever's watching this place is likely rank and file and doesn't know you're an aide to James Brandt. If they did, they might've decided that attacking was superfluous."

"Why?"

"Mike says someone's killing just about anyone he's talked to over the last few days. The logical inference is that someone thinks Mike has information they don't want disclosed to higher-ups in our government. You, Olivia Perry, are definitely a higher-up. So, if they know you're Olivia Perry, aide to the national security advisor, from their perspective the cat must already be out of the bag. There would no longer be a reason to come after us. The issue's moot."

"Not really," Olivia argued. "It doesn't necessarily follow that just because Garin told you, and you told me, that the higher-ups *believe* Garin. After all, Garin's wanted by the FBI for killing two men in Dale City."

"He's probably going to kill more before we figure this all out," Dwyer added, judging this wasn't the time to tell Olivia that Garin had already dispatched several more Iranians.

"What?"

"Mike thinks he's being tailed by more Iranians, so he might have to act," Dwyer said, easing slowly toward the truth.

"When were you planning on telling me this?"

"I was getting to it before we were interrupted by our friend there," Dwyer said, pointing to the surveillance monitor.

"Is this how Garin typically solves problems? By killing people?" Olivia's exasperation increased as she spoke.

Dwyer paused as if seriously considering the question. "Pretty much," he said, and shrugged.

"Dan," Olivia admonished, "this isn't funny. Your friend can't go roaming the countryside killing people. That's not a prescription for enhancing his credibility. Where are those brains of his you keep talking about? He's in very deep—"

"Excrement," Dwyer finished. "Yeah, I told him the same thing this afternoon. He's a big boy. He knows exactly how this would look. Mike would kill them only if they were about to kill him. His brains aren't very much use if he's dead."

Olivia softened a bit. "But he's—"

"No buts, Olivia," Dwyer interrupted. "Mike is our best bet at determining exactly what's going on with the Iranians and Russians. And clearly, based on the events of the past few days, something serious is going on. Understand one thing, though." Dwyer leaned forward in his chair and pointed a finger at Olivia. "Mike is going to kill more people before this is over. If he doesn't, he's dead. So be prepared."

There was a buzz. A security monitor showed Matt and Carl standing outside the door to the vault. Dwyer pressed a button and the door opened.

"We've combed the grounds and the perimeter's secure," Matt said. "We've also alerted the police. They'll do a standard drive-by. Would you like us to escort Ms. Perry home?"

"Ms. Perry will be joining us for dinner and will remain here tonight," Dwyer said. Dwyer turned to Olivia. "I hope you don't mind. I'm not that fond of the idea of you being in your apartment tonight. Unless you can wrangle an invitation to spend the night at the White House, this is the most secure residence you'll find in the Washington metro area."

"I guess this is where I'm supposed to politely decline and say I don't need the protection, but after everything that's happened, I'd be foolish not to accept the offer. The only problem is, I don't have any toiletries or change of clothes. Something tells me, though, that's not going to be an issue?"

"No. We should have everything you'll need, and if we don't, I think you can probably convince Matt to make a run to the closest store," Dwyer assured her. He gestured ceremoniously toward Carl. "This gentleman makes the best gumbo outside Louisiana, and it tastes just as good in the kitchen as it does in the formal dining room. So if you don't mind, why don't you join us there in about an hour?"

"Sounds good," Olivia said, looking forward to the chance to gather more information about Garin's adventures in Iran. "Can you show me to my room?"

"Matt will be happy to. Since Carl will be doing the cooking, Ray will go along to keep an eye on Matt." All four of the former special operators were grinning like schoolboys. Olivia smiled too.

"Oh," Dwyer said as an afterthought. "And watch out for Max."

"Who's Max?"

CHAPTER THIRTY-SIX

The best palliative, Chernin found, was to keep repeating to himself the phrase "Just a few days more." He repeated it both in his mind and out loud. He repeated it when one of the Iranians would give him a hateful look for drinking vodka. He repeated it when the North Korean technicians asked the same infernal question for the hundredth time. He repeated it most often when his boss, Stetchkin, called.

There remained little substantive work for him to do. He had come in under budget and ahead of schedule. For that, Stetchkin had rewarded him with a series of threats and rebukes, reciting all of Chernin's deficiencies. But Stetchkin had also made good on the bonuses, deposited timely in Chernin's account and in the correct amounts. And a premium, of all things, was added to the last bonus.

The bonuses and premium would permit Chernin a comfortable retirement. He would be able to fulfill his plan to buy a small place in the warmest village he could find on the Black Sea. He would read, boat, and make leisurely excursions to scenic destinations throughout southern Europe. He would, in short, stop living like a character from a Chekhov play.

The anticipation of these pursuits should have lifted the spirits of a man in Chernin's position. Instead, he became more depressed as his time on the project drew to a close.

Chernin was a pragmatist, a realist. And a pessimist. He lacked a capacity for self-delusion. As such, he understood clearly that the cause of his depression was the project's imminent success. He had presided over an enterprise that would result in the deaths of hundreds of thousands, perhaps millions, of innocents. The fact that he was being generously rewarded for his brilliant management of the project depressed him further still. The project was an abomination. Profiting from it was evil.

During the early stages of the endeavor, its potential consequences were too remote in time to give Chernin much pause. Then, as work proceeded, the scale of the damage the project would cause continued to make the effects too enormous to grasp.

But now the project was complete. And although Chernin had no capacity for self-delusion, he had a healthy capacity for avoidance. He tried to ignore the purposes of what he'd been working on for the last three years. But he could avoid them no longer.

Chernin wasn't a man given to frequent introspection. He rarely gave much thought to whether he was a good man, a bad man, or something in between. He was more concerned with survival than self-evaluation.

Lately, however, he'd asked himself what kind of man gives his best efforts to an endeavor that would cause horrific suffering. For a while he had compared himself to those who had worked on the Manhattan Project. Those scientists had created a terrible instrument that had extinguished tens of thousands of lives indiscriminately and instantly.

But his inability to engage in self-delusion ensured that the comparison was short-lived. Those men had created a terrible weapon for the purpose of bringing a war to an end, to ultimately save the estimated millions of lives that would have perished with an invasion of the Japanese mainland. Chernin's work had no such noble purpose, regardless of the deranged rationalizations of the mullahs in Tehran or the sterile explanations of the schemers in the Kremlin.

At another point, he thought a better comparison might be to the crew of the *Enola Gay*. After all, like them, he was simply carrying out the orders of his superiors with no real knowledge of the ramifications of such orders. But again, the crew members of the *Enola Gay* were on a mission to end a war, not start one. Chernin quickly resigned himself to the fact that the most apt comparison was to the engineers of the Final Solution, those efficient ciphers who asserted at Nuremberg that they were merely following orders. And that really depressed him.

He resorted to vodka more frequently. It helped temporarily, but afterward he would often be even more despondent. At such times he would occasionally stroll along the catwalks outside his office, silently cursing the circumstances that had placed him here with these insufferable wretches.

In the last few months he had found a rather unlikely companion with whom to commiserate. Although Chernin had mentioned a few irrelevancies about the project to Mansur, it was the North Korean technician, Dong Sung Park, in whom he most frequently confided.

Most of the North Koreans were a source of aggravation for Chernin. They seemed perpetually intent on demonstrating their competence in missile technology. They weren't shy about giving unsolicited advice and recommending changes in protocols. Even by Russian standards, they were abrupt and undiplomatic.

Park was different. He was quiet and unassuming. Despite the fact that he was in his early thirties and had no apparent connection to the leaders of the North Korean regime, he was the head of his nation's missile contingent, supervising men much older and with more seniority. In the rigid North Korean hierarchy, that fact alone spoke volumes.

What set Park apart from the rest of the North Koreans, however, was his attitude toward the project. Like Chernin, Park had serious misgivings about the endeavor, its purpose, and the involvement of the Iranians. Because Park was painfully cautious, even for someone who had spent his entire life under a mercurial totalitarian regime, it took several months of daily interaction with the man for Chernin to begin to recognize that Park might not necessarily agree with the party line.

In the last few months, Park had begun opening up to Chernin and the two had come to place a good deal of trust in each other. Each loved his respective country, if not his leaders, deeply. Each had an immediate superior who was a vainglorious tyrant. Each despaired that the project was a monument to miscalculation at best and to lunacy at worst.

Other than Mansur, Park was the only person in Iran whose company Chernin didn't merely tolerate, but actually enjoyed. Although Park had a reserved demeanor, Chernin found that his coworker could become quite animated when talking about matters other than missiles. Chernin learned that Park was an avid boxing fan who seemed to know more about Joe Louis, Muhammad Ali, and Manny Pacquiao than most biographers. He was also, of all things, an amateur poet, albeit a rather horrid one. And he was something of a vodka snob, claiming, impossibly, that soju was superior to anything Russian.

Once, over a presumably inferior bottle of Smirnoff, Chernin asked Park about his family. It was the first time Chernin had ever seen Park's expression anything other than placid. Even though they were alone and, Chernin believed, outside the range of any monitoring devices, Park lowered his voice to a whisper. Chernin realized the whisper wasn't to avoid being overheard, but rather to suppress rage. The members of Park's immediate family—his mother, father, and two older sisters—were all dead. Park declined to talk about their deaths other than to say that it had something to do with their having provoked the displeasure of the North Korean regime, an offense that didn't actually require an overt act. Park had lived with a cousin since the age of fourteen.

Chernin had heard Park's story many times before in Russia. It preceded the knock on the door. The arbitrary arrests of loved ones. Disappearances without explanation. Angry recriminations. Then resignation, powerlessness.

Like Chernin, Park had no interest in annihilating Israel or anyone else. He took great pride in his work and understood that his life depended, literally, on the successful completion of that work. But Park had gone through some of the same historical comparisons as Chernin and concluded that he, too, bore uncomfortable similarities to the efficient ciphers at Nuremberg.

Chernin was sitting at his empty desk in his drab office, comforting himself with the thought that he would be in Iran only a few more days, when Park entered. His face, for only the second time that Chernin had known him, expressed agitation.

"Good morning, Dmitri," Park said in unaccented English.

"Good morning, Park. You look displeased. What troubles you?"

Park sat in a metal chair on the opposite side of the desk and scooted closer. He asked in a low voice, "Your friends are not satisfied with my work?"

Park was referring to the two dour Russian engineers and a guidance expert who had arrived unannounced overnight and had begun inspecting the missiles and tracking systems without asking Chernin's permission. Furious, Chernin confronted them but backed off upon being told that Stetchkin had sent them to make a final inspection, and if Chernin had any questions, he should direct them to the tyrant.

"They're here only to give us the final seal of approval. It has nothing to do with the quality of your work," Chernin said.

"I am not so sure. They will not permit me to follow them or watch what they are doing. They are very secretive. I do not like it."

"You worry excessively. They will send a good report back to Moscow and Pyongyang. You have done a splendid job. We have all done a splendid job. You'll go home and be justly rewarded."

Park sat silently for several seconds studying the ugly green walls. He looked up and said, "Then, if I may be presumptuous, let us mark the occasion with two of your cigars."

Chernin didn't need to be prodded. He opened the upper left-hand drawer of his desk, pulled out a metal carrying case, and opened it, revealing an array of cigars. He held up two. "Macanudos," Chernin announced.

Park nodded his approval. The pair left Chernin's office and turned right, walking along the catwalk suspended more than forty feet above the workplace floor. The giant facility was eerily quiet, save for the sound of a couple of Towmotors and a distant hissing noise. There were only a few technicians in the facility—mostly North Koreans with a smattering of Russians—compared to the hundreds that had populated the facility during the height of operations.

Chernin and Park walked approximately a hundred feet to a freight elevator that ascended two hundred feet to a pillbox-like structure that sat on the southern slope of the mountain housing the project. They held their proximity badges up to a sensor near the sliding metal exit. The doors opened and the pair walked outside into a parking lot and past several more guards, two of whom were sitting in a jeep to the right of the doors. The guards acknowledged Chernin with a curt nod.

Chernin handed Park one of the Macanudos as the men strolled toward the fence-enclosed perimeter of the parking lot, a good fifty yards from the guards' position. Chernin removed a cigar clipper and lighter from his pocket, snipped the ends of both cigars, and lit Park's before lighting his own.

Park faced away from the surveillance cameras located at regular intervals atop the fence and looked at the brown mountains in the distance.

"Dmitri, I'm not going home," Park said bluntly.

Chernin wasn't surprised. He had sensed in the cavern that a troubled Park wanted to talk and that the cigars were a mere pretext. "What are you going to do?"

Park answered the question with a question. "You do not want to go home either, do you?"

"I want to go home very much. Truthfully, I cannot wait to leave this place," Chernin said.

"You cannot wait to leave this place," Park agreed. "And neither can I. But you do not want to go home."

Chernin didn't respond. He puffed slowly on his cigar and waited for Park to continue.

"You are not a crazy man. You are a smart man," Park said.

"The two qualities are not mutually exclusive."

"You can see what is about to happen here," Park continued. "What is happening is sheer idiocy. It is incomprehensible. Our governments are vastly underestimating the consequences of this action. They think there will be retaliation only against Iran. They are tragically mistaken."

"Our governments have not mistaken the lack of resolve in the West, however," Chernin noted. "America and Europe are dissolute. Weak. Yes, they may not confine their retaliation to Iran, but only Iran will be struck militarily."

Park nodded. "That may be so. But many will die here and in Israel. The world economy will be in shambles, in chaos. Our countries will not be insulated from the effects."

"My bosses believe that after the dust has settled, we will be positioned to pick up the pieces and to profit. We have resources—oil, gas, minerals—that the West must have. They must deal with us," Chernin said.

"The only reason anyone must deal with my country is to buy stability. We produce nothing. We cannot even feed ourselves. The only thing of consequence that we have is our military—our nuclear capability."

"That is a very big reason."

"But the people will remain destitute, probably more so when our role in the project is revealed, as it eventually will be." Park shook his head. "There is nothing for me to return to except misery. I will *not* go back."

"What do you plan to do? Your security people are everywhere. You cannot just refuse to go back. And even if you could, where would you go?"

"Anywhere but North Korea. Perhaps I will eventually find my way to the South. But first, I must get out of here."

"You cannot get out of Iran without considerable assistance. Who do you know who can help you?"

"*You* can help me, Dmitri."

Chernin appeared incredulous. "Me? What can I do? My security people watch me as closely as yours watch you. Besides, I have no means to get out of this country."

"But your friend Mansur," Park said. "He is a man of some means. As you describe him, he is a resourceful fellow. He might be able to get us out of here and to a safe place."

"Us? Whatever gives you the idea I am going with you? My country has compensated me very well. I plan to have a very comfortable retirement and forget all of this—as you put it—idiocy."

"I will not be able to forgive my role in this matter," Park said. "It is an impossibility. I will have partial responsibility for one of the great atrocities in history. And you will as well, Dmitri. There's nothing we can do about that now. The project is complete. The Iranians will get their wish; they will destroy Israel. It is not my wish. I have no animosity toward the Jews." He gave Chernin a sidelong glance. "And neither do you."

Park's intensity was somewhat surprising to Chernin. "And what will you do when you escape North Korea? Spend the rest of your life in a monastery atoning for your sins?" the Russian asked derisively.

"Nothing we do for the rest of our lives can atone for this, Dmitri. You know that. You know that very well. We will live with what we have done. That is our punishment. Our lives will be hell. But we need not live in hell."

"Spoken with all of the flourish of bad poetry."

"You fool no one with that cynical façade, Dmitri. Especially me. If I can get out of here, I will go to Central or South America. Maybe, after a time, to South Korea. I will disappear. I will, as you say, atone—as much as anyone can atone for something like this."

The two men stood silently for several moments smoking their cigars and gazing at the barren landscape beyond the security fence. Chernin was momentarily tempted by the thought of disappearing somewhere in South America. He could buy a villa on the ocean, read, and sail. He would drink vodka, eat well, maybe find a woman. Above all, it would be warm; *he* would be warm. And then, one day, a soulless young assassin from Moscow, or perhaps Saint Petersburg, would put a bullet in the back of his skull while he was sitting in a local cantina. The North Koreans might not find Park. But the Russians would surely find Chernin. It's what they did. It's what they'd always done.

He turned to Park, a note of fatalism in his voice. "I will contact Mansur. If he is available, we will meet with him at his home this evening. You can discuss your plans with him. But you must be careful. There are eyes and ears everywhere."

"Thank you. But what about you, Dmitri? What will you do?"

"You are a young man. You have most of your life still ahead and reason to seek something better. I, on the other hand, have lived most of my allotted time already. I have little to look forward to other than a measure of personal comfort and safety." Chernin dropped his cigar, barely smoked, to the ground. "So, I will live on the Black Sea and, like a good Russian, contemplate all of my regrets," he said matter-of-factly. "And then, after considering each one in turn, I will die."

CHAPTER THIRTY-SEVEN

Garin parked his car in the underground garage beneath the National Labor Relations Board building, on Fourteenth and L. Before getting out of the vehicle he put on a ball cap and replaced his sunglasses with black-framed spectacles. He'd already donned the contacts and nose and lip molds. Garin emerged from the parking garage carrying a shoe box–size, gift-wrapped package. He turned left onto L, made another left onto Fourteenth Street, passed the NLRB entrance, and went into the Hamilton Crowne Plaza, where he checked in. Having done that, he returned to the National Labor Relations Board building, where he presented himself to the Homeland Security guards at the security desk in the atrium.

"I'm here to see Member Halliday," Garin announced.

A female guard pushed a pen across the desk and pointed to the registry. "Sign here. ID, please."

Garin handed the Virginia license bearing the name Mark Webster to the woman, who placed it in a small metal box. "You can pick this up when you return," she said.

Garin signed the registry while a male guard picked up the phone, pressed four keys, waited a few seconds, and said, "Mr. Webster to see

Member Halliday." The guard listened for a few seconds and then looked at Garin. "What's the purpose of your visit?"

"I'm here to deliver a gift from an old friend of Mr. Halliday. Looks like it's supposed to be a surprise."

The guard repeated the information to the person on the other end of the line and then nodded. "His assistant will be down momentarily," the guard informed Garin.

A few minutes later the elevator doors at the far end of the atrium opened and a stern-looking blond woman in her fifties walked briskly toward the desk. "You have something for Member Halliday?"

Garin held up the package. "The sender says I'm supposed to deliver it personally. I was told it's some type of surprise or gag gift from a college friend of his by the name of McLain. He insists that I bring it to Member Halliday and then call Mr. McLain to confirm delivery." Garin waved a piece of scrap paper with the fictional telephone number of the fictional sender.

"Member Halliday isn't in right now," the woman said, a fact of which Garin was already aware, having called each of the board members' offices just a short time ago. "I can make sure he receives the package."

Garin affected the pose of a diligent deliveryman. "Ma'am, Mr. McLain insists I deliver it and then call him, you know? He gave me a pretty good tip to make sure. Look, you can walk me up to his office so I can put it on his desk. Then I can call McLain and tell him 'mission accomplished.' Okay?"

Halliday's assistant tilted her head to one side and shrugged. "Sure. Follow me."

"Sir, step over here, please." The male guard held up a metal-detector wand and motioned for Garin to step forward. Garin complied, raising his arms perpendicular to his sides as the guard waved the wand over Garin, the gym bag, and the gift box. The guard then opened the gym bag and gave the contents a cursory inspection before motioning for Garin to proceed.

Garin followed the assistant to the bank of elevators, where she pressed the button for the top floor, which housed the suites of the five members of the NLRB. She guided him to Member Halliday's suite to the far right of the elevator bank. They entered the wood-paneled reception area and walked into Halliday's expansive office with a view of Thomas Circle. Garin placed the gift box on the desk, then pulled out his cell phone, dialed a number, and said, "Mr. McLain, this is Mark from SpeedEx delivery. Just want to confirm that the package has been delivered to Mr. Halliday as you instructed."

Garin disconnected and turned to the assistant. "Ma'am, thanks so much. I'll get out of your way now. I can find my way back downstairs." The assistant smiled and returned to her desk in the reception area. Garin walked out of the suite, the door closing automatically behind him. The eleventh floor was quiet. No one was in the hallways as Garin strode to the door next to the elevator bank. He glanced around briefly before opening the door and ascending the stairwell one flight to the rooftop of the building.

Garin took off the black-framed spectacles and put on his sunglasses as he emerged into the bright sunshine. The rooftop was flat, enclosed by a chest-high brick wall. He walked to the southern side of the building and stooped under the metal overhang of an air-conditioning unit. He leaned forward against the brick wall and looked across the alleyway that separated the NLRB building from the Hamilton Crowne Plaza.

The sidewalk in front of the hotel had the usual level of pedestrian traffic for late morning. There was no unusual activity on either Fourteenth or K Streets, or Franklin Square on the opposite side of the hotel. Garin estimated it would be no more than another five minutes before that changed.

He used the time to remove the contacts and facial molds and put on a dark blue cap and shirt retrieved from the gym bag. To anyone viewing him from a distance, he would resemble a member of a SWAT team.

Garin then scanned the surrounding buildings for the location most favorable for a sniper covering the exits to the hotel, quickly concluding that the two best spots were the PNC Bank across from Franklin Square and the roof of the Tower Building on the northwest corner of Fourteenth and K. He would keep an eye on those locations.

The first sign of activity occurred a few minutes later. *That didn't take long,* thought Garin. Several dark-colored vans appeared along both Fourteenth and K Streets. Two parked across the street from the hotel entrance along the northwest curb of K Street. Another parked along the southwest side of the hotel. The last one that Garin could see parked directly below him in the alley separating the NLRB building and the hotel.

Almost simultaneously, more than a dozen DC police cruisers formed a perimeter extending approximately two blocks from the hotel. Garin presumed there was also a van behind the hotel, although he couldn't see it from his location.

The vans remained parked for a couple of minutes without anyone getting out of them. Then a nondescript dark-colored sedan pulled up behind the van parked in front of the hotel. Two men in business suits who looked to Garin as if they had just auditioned for Hollywood roles as FBI agents got out and entered the hotel. Contemporaneously, six FBI agents in SWAT gear and armed with what appeared to be MP5s followed the suits into the hotel. They would conduct the search for Garin.

The SWAT teams from the other vans Garin could see fanned out along the sidewalk to surround the hotel at equidistant intervals. D.C. police appeared and placed roadblocks at the intersections of Fourteenth and K, and Fourteenth and L, to direct traffic to two detours at Fourteenth and I and Thomas Circle. Alarmed pedestrians didn't have to be told to get out of the way as they scrambled as far as they could from the FBI perimeter.

Garin now heard the sound of a helicopter approaching from the west. He was fairly confident the air-conditioner overhang would shield him from the view of the helicopter's occupants but retreated slightly from the wall so that no portion of his body protruded from the shelter.

This is quite a production, thought Garin. The numbers of SWAT personnel seemed to grow even larger over the next thirty seconds. Another dark sedan was waved through the roadblock at Fourteenth and K and came to a halt in the middle of the street in front of the hotel. The passenger door opened and a figure familiar to Garin got out. He wore a dark business suit and an air of authority. His name was Jack Sakai, the head of the FBI's Hostage Rescue Team. Garin had met him several years ago during joint training exercises at Quantico. The heavy hitters were coming out to get Garin.

The Hollywood Suits emerged from the hotel and met Sakai on the sidewalk, where they engaged in an animated discussion. As they did so, Garin checked the surrounding buildings again, leaving for last the two sniper-friendly spots he had previously identified.

Atop the Tower Building across the street a curious maintenance man watched the proceedings below. In a tenth-floor window of the adjacent office building an office worker in a white shirt and red tie did the same. Garin slowly panned to the sniper-friendly locations. He saw nothing at the first but noticed a barely perceptible anomaly at the second. On the roof of the PNC Bank building, there was what appeared to be a slight discoloration in the otherwise dark gray metal façade of a window washer's carriage. Only a skilled observer in a position precisely level with the PNC rooftop would've had just the right angle and cast of light to spot the discoloration.

While keeping his binoculars trained on the anomaly, Garin adjusted the focus carefully. He then closed his eyes for several seconds to dilate his pupils. When he peered through the binoculars again he thought he could make out something that might be a man. On the other hand, it could very well be an odd-shaped blotch of faded paint on the carriage. A Rorschach test. For anyone else, it was faded paint. For Garin, it held the potential for death.

Garin ignored the activity in the street below and remained focused on the Rorschach test. He didn't move. He didn't blink. He concentrated on slowing his breathing, so that his gaze remained steady. He stared at the single spot for several minutes, willing some form of movement. Nothing.

Garin remained patient. His attention stayed fixed on the Rorschach despite an urge to wipe away an annoying bead of perspiration that perched on his right eyelid. He ignored the helo circling overhead. He disciplined himself to avoid looking down at the FBI teams on the street below. And he waited. Yet the Rorschach remained unchanged.

A moment before Garin was about to end his surveillance, a thread of sunlight reflecting off the windshield of the circling helicopter splayed for a millisecond across the carriage. In that millisecond, Garin caught the unmistakable face of one of the most lethal men in the country's arsenal of covert operators. Approximately thirty hours ago, Garin thought he'd seen that face in a field in upstate New York. Now, seeing it a second time left absolutely no doubt in Garin's mind as to whom it belonged. Congo Knox, Delta sniper.

Sergeant Knox's exploits and capabilities were legendary. He could hit the proverbial eye of a mosquito in a hurricane at a thousand yards and disappear while standing at attention at midfield during the Super Bowl. He had more than eighty confirmed kills and an even larger number of probables. His longest recorded kill was nineteen hundred yards, using a fifty-caliber McMillan TAC-50. A man with such skill probably considered it an insult to be assigned such an easy target. Whoever had sent him believed there could be absolutely no margin for error.

Knox's face and form disappeared with the flash of light caused by the helicopter. Garin scanned the area immediately surrounding the carriage and saw nothing. As he had in upstate New York, Knox was probably working without a spotter.

Knox, Garin reasoned, was positioned in the hide atop the PNC Bank to take out Garin once the FBI had him in custody or, perhaps, when Garin attempted to escape from the hotel. Either way, it was clear that Knox and the FBI weren't working in tandem. The FBI wanted Garin alive. Someone else wanted him dead. *That* someone was giving Knox orders.

Garin looked back down at the entrance to the hotel. Sakai and the Hollywood Suits were still talking. The helicopter continued to circle overhead, and at the roadblock at Fourteenth and I a few blocks away, a television news sound truck appeared seconds later. The Hollywood Suits reentered the hotel as Sakai remained standing on the sidewalk, looking like a man waiting impatiently for a delayed train.

Garin resumed scanning the surroundings, hoping that he would find some clue as to why a large contingent of an elite FBI division as well as a Delta Force sniper were pursuing him. Crowds of pedestrians, emboldened by the lack of anything dangerous occurring in the last ten minutes, were beginning to form behind the roadblocks at Fourteenth and I and Fourteenth and Thomas Circle.

Methodically scanning the crowd, Garin noticed something odd about a solitary figure standing at the far right of the barricade at Fourteenth and I. The man stood with his hands thrust into his pockets, looking intently at the entrance to the hotel. His demeanor was different from that of the other spectators. His face was serious. He wasn't there for entertainment or out of curiosity. He looked like a man performing a job.

The man's physical appearance also caught Garin's attention. He appeared very fit under a white polo shirt and tan trousers and had a bearing Garin recognized. The man was either former or current military. Elite military.

Garin examined the man's face closely. Something about his face seemed artificial, yet somewhat familiar. He wore an Orioles cap and sunglasses and had an unfashionable blond mustache.

It was the mustache. It didn't fit the face. It was as fake as the facial molds Garin had worn moments earlier. Someone didn't wear a fake mustache, especially one as unflattering as that, unless his aim was the same as Garin's had been—to avoid facial recognition. Whoever the man was, the capture or killing of Michael Garin was certainly drawing an interesting crowd.

Renewed activity at the hotel entrance caught Garin's attention. The Hollywood Suits had reappeared and were in heated conversation with Sakai. The trio's hand gestures and overall body language conveyed exasperation. Garin surmised that the Hollywood Suits were telling Sakai that the search of the hotel had thus far revealed no signs of a dangerous rogue operator wanted for multiple murders in Virginia and New York.

Garin returned his attention to the figure at the Fourteenth and I barricade. The man also appeared intrigued by the exchange between Sakai and the Hollywood Suits, so much so that he removed his sunglasses for a better look.

The man had wolf's eyes. Predatory. The feeling of bewilderment Garin had felt the last few days returned even more forcefully.

The man Garin was looking at was dead. At least he was supposed to be. Burned to ashes. He was John Gates, Omega operator. His corpse had been exhumed from the smoldering remains of his house in Dumfries. Garin had seen the destruction himself. He had learned all of his teammates, including Gates, were dead. Yet Gates was now standing in half-assed disguise behind a police barricade waiting for Garin to be apprehended by the FBI.

Garin shook his head. He had staged the Crowne Plaza check-in for the specific purpose of flushing out who was after him, but he hadn't expected to be more perplexed after the maneuver than before.

Garin knew why the FBI was after him, and through Olivia Perry, by way of Dan Dwyer, he might be able to obtain information on the FBI's activities. He might even have a contact point in Sakai, who appeared to be running the show. As for Congo Knox, Garin couldn't very well walk up and ask him why Delta was trying to kill a US citizen in apparent violation of the law. But Garin might get some information, if not an explanation, from Perry and Dwyer.

Gates, however, was another matter entirely. His return from the dead raised even more questions than the appearance of Congo Knox. Why was Gates reported dead? What purpose did it serve? How did he know Garin had checked into the Crowne Plaza?

It was the last question that troubled Garin most. Someone within the law enforcement or intelligence community had to have informed Gates that a man using Garin's credit card had checked into the hotel, and that information had to have been conveyed instantaneously. Someone within those communities was helping Gates maintain the fiction that he was dead.

Garin could think of no innocent reason for doing so.

There was nothing else to gain from staying on the roof of the NLRB building. But he wouldn't be able to leave until the FBI's search was completed and the roadblocks were removed from the surrounding streets. That might take another twenty or thirty minutes, possibly more. He might as well put the time to productive use. Garin took out his cell phone, punched in a number, and recited a series of digits.

CHAPTER THIRTY-EIGHT

For Dwyer, the last forty-eight hours had been largely consumed by all things Garin.

The call from his former partner came seconds after Dwyer had settled into his chair in the subbasement communications room. Dwyer pressed a button on the armrest to connect.

"Where are you?" Dwyer asked Garin.

"In town. Watching the FBI search for someone in the Crowne Plaza. Up on the rooftop a short distance away is a jolly old soul. Not Saint Nick, but a scary elf from Delta. Pretty sure he's not there to deliver presents," Garin replied.

"My, but you're a popular fellow."

"More popular than you know. Even the dead are coming out to see me today."

"Anyone I know?"

"About two blocks down around Fourteenth and I is a man who's a ringer for my old Georgian team member," Garin said, referring to Gates, a native of Augusta.

"Impossible. The Georgian is confirmed dead. They dragged him out of the ashes of his house after it burned to the ground."

"What do you mean *confirmed* dead?"

"I mean he's not breathing. Horizontal. Cold to the touch. They pulled his body—what was left of it—from his house. And there wasn't much left of the house, either."

"How do they know it was the Georgian?"

"You think someone snuck into his house while he was away, set it on fire, and then decided to take a nap in his garage?"

Garin became slightly annoyed. "C'mon, buddy, you know what I mean and I don't have much time. Forensics. DNA. Did they confirm it was Gates?"

"DNA sampling confirms significant traces of his blood in the garage."

"What did the body look like?"

"Like it had been through a fire. Very little, if any, flesh remained. An accelerant had been used. Extreme heat. Primarily skeletal remains."

"Did they check dental records?" Garin asked.

"They couldn't. Apparently, he was shot once in the forehead right at the bridge of the nose. He fell next to a stack of cinder blocks. One or two fell flush on his face, pulverizing much of his skull, including his teeth. No way to do a meaningful comparison. Besides, after they checked the blood sample, they probably figured there was no need."

"Very convenient," Garin scoffed. "Crushed skull, burned corpse, blood helpfully spilled for forensics examiners. Whoever that poor guy was, he wasn't the Georgian. He was planted there to make everyone believe he was the Georgian."

"Well, you just might be right," Dwyer agreed, nodding slowly as he thought about it. "Everyone thinks you snuffed your whole team. Who else had the knowledge and skill to pull that off? Who else could've gotten so close to a group of elite operators? And, just to be sure, they—whoever's trying to pin this all on you—even shot the fake Georgian right at the bridge of the nose. Your signature. The question is, why?"

"And who? But look, I can't discuss that now. I've got to get out of here and somehow find the Georgian. He should be able to provide some answers."

"Before you go, two things," Dwyer said quickly. "I got a call late last night. Your hunch was right. They found the Professor of Death and Destruction by the side of the road in Kings Canyon. He'd been shot twice and thrown—or fell—down a hill off Generals Highway. Somehow the tough SOB crawled up that hill and lay at the side of the road, where some hikers found him."

Garin winced. "How is he?"

"Not good, buddy. He was out there for more than three days. He lost a lot of blood. Exposure, dehydration. One of my West Coast guys is at the hospital right now. He can't get any information from the medical people, but the cops have told him what they know."

Garin's jaw tightened. He respected Laws more than any living being in the world. From feared instructor to close friend, Laws had taught Garin more than anyone, except Pop. The two mentors were alike in many ways. Outwardly mean, physically tough old bastards with impossible standards who unapologetically expected you to meet those standards. Men who had a clear, unsentimental understanding of the world and those who populated it. Laws, Garin knew, had been targeted because of their close association, the possibility that vital information had been shared.

"Keep me updated, buddy," Garin said quietly.

"Just so you know, my guy says the Professor has got tubes going in and out of every orifice in his body, and he's mostly unconscious. The cops say during moments of lucidity he tries to talk."

"Tell your guy to find out what he's saying. Whatever he says, let me know. Don't discount anything."

"All he's said so far, strangely enough, is that he's bored. Either he's not all there or the wicked Laws humor can overcome even the most life-threatening wounds."

"That's *not* what he's saying," Garin countered. "I guarantee it. He's trying to tell them something useful. Tell your man that the Professor has very important information. Hell, ask our newfound friends in high places to send one of their specialists over there to find out what he's saying. Damn it, the man's not delusional or being funny. This isn't the first time he's been near death. He's a pro. He's trying to convey information—probably about who did this to him."

"Will do. That brings me to the second point. I had a very long talk with our 'friend.' I think she's someone who's actually on your side. Given the crap you're in and that you're generally a pain in the ass, I'd say that's a pretty big deal."

Garin thought for a moment. "What about her boss?"

"Well, obviously, I can't be certain. But he's the one who sent her over here in the first place. And if she has any influence, I think he'll be sympathetic. Do you want me to put him in touch with you?"

"No. But you can tell her I'm in D.C., and you can tell her everything I've told you." Garin paused. "And tell her I need their help *now*. If they can't call off the FBI, at least tell them to call off a certain sniper. He's military, and that's illegal. They should have some pull with that."

Garin hesitated before adding, "And ask them to at least tell the FBI my version of what's going on."

"And if the FBI asks where they got information about a wanted fugitive?"

"I wouldn't worry about that. Our friends are smart. They can just say they've heard from sources. Nothing wrong with that. It's not like they're aiding and abetting."

Dwyer wasn't wholly convinced but saw little harm in making the request. "Okay. Anything else I can do?"

"You've done plenty. But don't get any ideas that I owe you or anything like that." Garin disconnected.

Dwyer immediately hit another button and placed a call to Olivia Perry.

CHAPTER THIRTY-NINE

A rlo guided James Brandt through the halls of the White House, Secret Service agents parting to permit them to pass.

Brandt had just come from a short briefing for Vice President David Wilson, who was stepping in for the president while the latter was convalescing in Walter Reed. Wilson had quizzed Brandt on his take on the imminent UN resolution sponsored by the Russians and Iranians but seemed only mildly interested in what Brandt had to say. It was almost as if Wilson was just going through the motions, which past occupants of the office have, in colorful fashion, described as the primary function of the position.

Olivia Perry was waiting in Brandt's office when he arrived. "Good morning, Olivia. Your meeting with Mr. Dwyer was productive?"

After patting Arlo on the head and taking a seat in one of two chairs in front of Brandt's desk, Olivia wasted no time with pleasantries. "Michael Garin is being set up by the Iranians to take the fall for the assassination of his team. The most rational motivation for the Iranians to do so is to facilitate their intended use of WMD against Israel."

Olivia's lack of equivocation drew a loud chuckle from Brandt.

"Whoa, whoa, slow down there. No other possibilities, Olivia? None at all?"

"There are always possibilities. But my conclusion is the most logical probability," Olivia asserted.

Brandt chuckled again as he scratched Arlo behind the ears. His aide had rarely suffered from self-doubt or second-guessing when it came to her work, the product of usually being right. "Tell me how you came to that conclusion."

Olivia related her conversation with Dwyer in exacting detail: Garin's peculiar disappearance from BUD/S and SQT; the Garin apparitions in various operational theaters; his Russian heritage; the Omega team; his probable operations in Iran; the Iranian assassins; and the possible involvement of Delta Force. Olivia became most animated while describing the rescue of Dwyer's SEAL team in Kunar Province.

The national security advisor listened intently, his sightless blue eyes directed toward Olivia's face. Arlo lay on the floor throughout, making groaning noises, as if bored.

When Olivia was finished, Brandt sat pensively for several seconds, mental wheels in motion. When he spoke, it was in a sedate, almost grave tone.

"Well, I've learned one very important thing beyond all doubt."

"What's that, Professor?"

"That Ms. Olivia Perry—the woman who, despite her intimidating intellect and looks, was by far the shyest woman on campus—has a crush on the rough-and-tough Mr. Michael Garin, gentleman, scholar, and American action hero." Brandt paused dramatically. "Finally."

Brandt burst into laughter, causing Arlo to sit up alertly and place a paw on his master's lap. Although he couldn't see it, Brandt correctly sensed Olivia's discomfort, causing him to laugh harder and, in turn, Arlo to bark excitedly. Brandt's secretary appeared at the door to investigate the commotion. A flustered Olivia waved her away.

"I'm sorry," Brandt said as he gasped for air. "It's just that your tone was so *earnest.* I don't believe I've ever heard you so impassioned, Ms. Perry."

"I'm simply reporting what I believe to be the relevant facts." The indignation in Olivia's voice was unmistakable.

"All right, okay," Brandt said, catching his breath. "Just having a little fun at my protégé's expense. In truth, what you've told me may be useful."

Olivia watched as Brandt's demeanor quickly became more serious. She'd seen the transformation many times before. Brandt, having processed disparate bits of data, was about to make an analytical leap, arriving at a destination others would find only in hindsight.

"I gather you don't think my conclusions are sound."

"No, no," Brandt assured her. "They are. I think that Mr. Garin is being set up by the Iranians to cover, or distract from, their intended use of WMD. Also, I do think that we may be looking at an attempt to obliterate Israel during the conflict. I doubt, however, that the Iranians have the assets or capability to pull off the elimination of Garin's entire unit on American soil. Too sophisticated. The Russians might be a different story. Given their cooperation with the Iranians on the UN resolution, we have to assume the Russians are, indeed, involved. But to what end? What do they hope to gain from the Iranians' strike against Israel? What's their next move? And how do we stop it?"

"In the long term, perhaps very long term, Russia would benefit from chaos in the Middle East. Oil and gas prices rise, benefiting the Russian treasury and consolidating its power over not just the former Soviet republics, but Eastern Europe and anyone else dependent on Russia for energy," Olivia said. As soon as she did, she noticed the buzzing was back. *Warehouses, fuel depots, oil tankers.*

"That's correct," Brandt said as if he were responding to a student in class. Olivia sensed that Brandt's mind was on something more. Two chess moves ahead.

"Professor, we need to talk to Garin."

"Obviously, yes. The president needs to be advised on the next move once the UN resolution passes. And it most certainly will. We're making critical policy in a dangerous informational vacuum. The secretary of state says one thing, Defense tells him another. And I prefer that his options aren't reduced to only military ones. But for that we need information. Something we can confront the Russians with and deter them. Mr. Garin may be able to supply that intel, whether he knows it or not. I'm afraid, however, that things are moving rather quickly, Olivia. So please impress upon Mr. Dwyer the urgency of our request. We don't have much time. The Congress and leadership are saying ten things at once. We must give the president clear, concrete counsel. We have little, if any, room for error."

In her mind, Olivia kept turning over images of Soviet-era industrial equipment sitting unused in various locations throughout Russia. Unused and, by all indications, not even being moved to market. At a time when the Russian economy needed a large infusion of revenue.

This, Olivia thought, was economic idiocy reminiscent of the old five-year plans. Worse, given today's just-in-time market dynamics.

Olivia rose from behind the desk in her tiny office in the Old Executive Office Building and went for a contemplative stroll, the staccato click of her heels echoing through the long corridors of the massive edifice. She worked out problems better while walking.

Russian president Mikhailov and the oligarchs were getting quite good at capitalism—especially the more rapacious strain. They were too shrewd to devote precious resources and industrial capacity during an economic downturn to producing commodities no one bought. Olivia shared her boss's suspicion of all things Kremlin. When in doubt, presume they're up to no good.

She stopped in midstride. She should've been working on matters related to the UN resolution, but it struck her that the idle Russian equipment might have some indefinable bearing on what was going on in the Middle East. And in order to make that determination, she needed more information. She knew just where to get it.

Olivia returned to her office and called her friend Laura Casini, a former Stanford classmate, now an analyst at the National Geospatial-Intelligence Agency. Laura picked up on the first ring.

"Casini."

"Need another favor, Laura."

"I am *not* double-dating with you again just so you'll have another first-date buffer."

Olivia laughed. "C'mon, you had fun and you know it. Did what's-his-name call you back?"

"I'm pretty sure mastering the complexities of telephone technology presents an insuperable challenge to what's-his-name."

"Laura, you and I both know you're way past the point where brains are a prerequisite. Just about any testosterone-based life-form should do."

"You should talk. The only time you ever see men without their pants on is at the gym. And I bet your legs have better muscle tone than theirs. Anyway, what do you need?" Casini asked.

"Satellite images for the last six months of the industrial sectors of Murmansk, Vladivostok, Arkhangelsk, and the Volga from the Caspian to thirty miles upriver, to start."

"To start? That's an indigestible amount of data, Olivia. Not to mention a very big ask."

"I wouldn't ask if it wasn't a matter of national security."

"Yeah, well, you need a new line. You've only been in office a few months and it's already old."

"Can you send it to me at OEOB?"

"Nope. You're going to have to come here. Besides, if you want the kind of resolution needed to make sense of the images, you really need our equipment."

"I'm e-mailing the coordinates as we speak. I don't need all six months. Just pull, say, January 14, April 14, and July 14."

"Okay," Casini replied.

"When can I see them?"

"When can you get here?"

"I'll be there within the hour."

O livia stood behind Laura Casini as she typed on a keyboard. A grainy image of what appeared to be some kind of industrial plant situated on a riverbank materialized on the seventy-two-inch monitor before them.

"I have no idea what that's supposed to be," Olivia said.

"Neither do I," Casini agreed. "But watch this."

Casini played with several more keys and manipulated the mouse, and the screen projected a vivid image of an industrial park on the northeast outskirts of Murmansk, Russia.

"Holy cow," Olivia said.

"Only nerdy Midwestern girls say 'holy cow,'" Casini said as she resumed typing.

"Guilty."

"If you think that's impressive, watch this."

Casini moved the mouse and clicked an icon in the upper left quadrant of the screen. The resolution became even clearer, as if Olivia were standing on the roof of one of the warehouses in the photo. She could see the watermarks on the tar paper covering the roof of the warehouses to the left and the blades of the exhaust fans on the roof of the factory to the right. But Casini wasn't finished.

"You didn't hear it from me, but these images are courtesy of the next-generation KeyHole spy satellites that the administration says we never built. The KH-13. As you can see, unparalleled resolution. Now watch this."

Casini clicked another icon, magnifying the shot so that Olivia could see startlingly clear images of the cigarette butts strewn about the warehouse roof.

"New magnification software," Casini informed her, smiling. "Radical stuff."

"What do you make of those?" Olivia asked, pointing to rows of objects in the yard next to the warehouse.

"Standby or backup generators. Commercial grade. Three-phase, probably thirty kilowatts."

"I count rows of ten by twenty on the ground pallets and an equal number on the flatbed truck pallets. Four hundred generators. Is this the January 14 shot?"

"It is," Casini replied.

"Go to April 14, please, Laura."

Another photo of the warehouse appeared.

"Okay. There are a lot more flatbeds than before and . . ." Olivia paused to count. "Rows of twenty by twenty. I'd say there are twice as many generators than in January. Can we go forward to a couple days ago?"

A few seconds later, an image showed rows of generators filling the entire yard, with a caravan of flatbeds streaming down the adjacent road.

"Looks like production—and shipment—has increased dramatically over the last six months," Olivia said. "Now, can you show me the industrial sector of Vladivostok, same time progression?"

Seconds later, the screen displayed a view of a mammoth industrial park. Casini dialed down to a series of structures flanking a rail yard, then applied the magnification software.

"Heavy electrical cable. Spools and spools of it," Olivia whispered to herself as she inspected the image. "Go to April, then July."

Casini did so. There was more cable in April than in January, and still more in July, Towmotors loading them onto a nearby freight train.

"Now Arkhangelsk, please."

Seconds later, a January shot of an industrial area located near the port city appeared. Casini scanned for data points similar to the images of Murmansk and Vladivostok and then magnified and sharpened the resolution.

"Don't know what that is, but it looks like some kind of electrical equipment," Olivia said. "April, please."

April appeared on the screen. "More of whatever it is," she said. "July, please."

July came on the screen. "Tons of it, now on forklifts being loaded onto trucks."

"Have any idea what this means?" Casini asked.

Olivia shook her head. The buzzing was getting louder. "Not yet," she replied, only half-truthfully. "But it can't be good."

CHAPTER FORTY

Rapidly moving lead-gray clouds hung low to the west as Garin navigated around Dupont Circle, careful to remain several cars behind a white Chevy Blazer proceeding north on Connecticut.

By the time the FBI had abandoned its search of the Crowne Plaza, the man resembling Gates had disappeared from his post behind the Fourteenth Street barricades. Fortunately, Garin had spotted Gates getting into the passenger side of a white Chevy Blazer parked along the curb on Fourteenth Street. The barricades had impeded traffic for several blocks around the hotel, allowing Garin to retrieve his own car and keep the white Blazer in his sights as it drove north onto Connecticut.

Despite being only a few car lengths behind the Blazer, Garin was unable to tell how many occupants were inside because of the SUV's darkened windows.

Just as the traffic began to disperse along the spokes of Dupont Circle, the winds picked up and the clouds exploded, releasing waves of hard-driving rain. Though the traffic had lightened considerably, it slowed once again as the rain reduced visibility to barely two dozen feet. Garin could just make out the outlines of the Blazer as he leaned over the steering wheel and peered through the windshield.

The traffic continued to disperse as drivers sought refuge in side streets and parking lots adjacent to Connecticut. Within five minutes Garin found himself directly behind the SUV. He quickly resigned himself to the fact that there was nothing he could do but continue to tail the vehicle or lose it. He hoped that the heavy curtains of rain would provide cover, but Garin's hopes evaporated seconds later as the Blazer's rear tires spun wildly and it began to fishtail as its driver floored the accelerator. It shot forward and separated from Garin's car, disappearing into the rainstorm. Garin also sped up, and within a few seconds he reacquired his target, now slightly more than a block ahead of him.

The two vehicles raced along the nearly deserted street at speeds approaching seventy miles per hour. Garin realized he had no plan. He'd hoped to at least follow the Blazer undetected until it reached its destination and then improvise, depending on the circumstances. If he could apprehend Gates, he'd try to do so. If not, he'd observe and acquire whatever intelligence he could.

Now, however, he was in a damn high-speed car chase. The element of surprise was gone. He wasn't going to be able to gather intel without the subject's knowledge, and the number of potential outcomes had just multiplied.

Ahead, the Blazer swerved to the left around a slower vehicle. Garin did the same, holding his breath as he felt his car hydroplane momentarily until he eased off the accelerator and regained traction. No sooner had he done so than he saw the Blazer jolt upward as it ran over a large tree branch deposited in the street by powerful gusts of wind. Garin instantly recognized that his vehicle lacked the clearance to duplicate the Blazer's action. Instead, he drove around the branch, struggling to maintain control as his left rear tire caromed against the curb on the lane divider. He slowed and swung back onto the northbound lane, losing visual contact with the Blazer in the process.

Again, Garin accelerated, the muscles in his upper body taut from almost losing control of the vehicle. A few seconds later, he could make out the rear of the Blazer as it approached Chevy Chase Circle. He was gaining on the vehicle when it swerved around another slower vehicle, Garin pursuing closely behind. As the two vehicles swung around the circle back into the northbound lane of Connecticut, the Blazer's taillights flashed. Garin stomped his brake pedal to avoid rear-ending the SUV, causing the back of his car to spin to the left until it was nearly perpendicular to the curb. Garin turned into the skid, righted the vehicle, and avoided slamming into a westbound taxi, horn blaring, as it crossed the intersection.

The chase was barely three minutes old, but the tension of the near collisions made it seem far longer. Garin guessed that the Blazer's occupants were heading for I-495, but he had no idea what their plan was from there.

Garin caught a break less than a quarter mile later when the Blazer swerved to avoid a Volvo that had come to a complete stop in the northbound lane, its driver deciding it was safer to flash the emergency lights and wait out the storm than to navigate blindly down the narrow street. The Blazer skated across the center line, then across the southbound lane, and catapulted over the curb onto a grassy expanse between two light-colored brick houses. Garin braked as he watched the SUV pitch to its left and tip onto its driver's side as it landed in the vacant lot, its wheels still spinning furiously.

Garin came to a stop on Connecticut, approximately fifty yards beyond where the Blazer had come to rest. A few seconds later, the passenger-side door opened upward, and one of the occupants struggled to climb out. Garin could barely see through sheets of rain as he sprang from the car and was met by a volley of gunshots that were wildly off target.

The Volvo, a block back, did a U-turn and sped off.

Garin scrambled to the passenger side of the car and knelt next to the right front wheel well. Peering over the hood, he saw one of the Blazer's occupants jump to the ground as a second occupant climbed out of the same passenger-side door. Garin drew his SIG from his waistband and cursed as he realized his extra magazines were in the gym bag in the trunk. With visibility severely reduced in the blinding rainstorm, he'd have to make his shots count.

The din from the rain, wind, and thunder nearly drowned out the next round of gunshots coming from the direction of the SUV. The shots came nowhere near Garin, who saw the figures of two men, neither resembling Gates, in front of the SUV, pistols aimed in his direction. Garin fired two rounds in return, designed merely to pin them down and prevent them from making a run for it. To Garin's surprise, one of the men collapsed to the ground, a round having struck him in the right kneecap. Even under the best of conditions, Garin couldn't have replicated that shot.

Both men returned fire, this time several rounds striking the Fusion. Garin waited a beat before popping just above the hood of his vehicle and squeezing off two more rounds, at least one of which appeared to strike the wounded man in the chest, dropping him face-first into the wet ground. The other man took cover behind the Blazer, firing a shot in the Fusion's direction as he moved.

Garin had two concerns. The first was making sure the man behind the Blazer didn't escape. Garin couldn't see him and was afraid that he might use the Blazer to conceal a retreat into the wooded area directly behind him.

The second concern was the police. Although the violent storm had obscured the car chase and gunfight, at some point cops were going to show up. Perhaps in a matter of minutes. The driver of the Volvo was probably calling 911 at that very moment. One way or another, Garin had to bring this to a conclusion fast. That was unlikely to happen as long as he remained behind the Fusion and the other man had the protection of the Blazer.

Garin decided to force the issue by moving forward and drawing fire. Two large oaks on the other side of the street would provide sufficient cover if he could just get to one of them. The first oak was on the tree lawn immediately adjacent to the street. The second was about ten yards beyond the first, in the direction of the Blazer.

After looking to see if there were any cars approaching, Garin checked the Blazer and sprinted across Connecticut to the first oak twenty yards away. As he reached the tree lawn, jets of dirt spit from the ground, three bullets slamming into the earth a few feet in front of him. He safely reached the tree without returning fire.

The upended vehicle was another thirty yards in front of him. The man behind the vehicle was undisciplined with his fire. Garin didn't know how many rounds the man had expended but thought he might have only a few shots left. If he could be forced to empty his magazine, Garin might be able to get to him before he had time to insert another.

Garin fired another round at the SUV and, just as he'd hoped, the man behind it fired back, twice striking the tree behind which Garin hid. Garin then ran to the next tree but was disappointed when he drew no fire. In the driving rain Garin couldn't determine the make of the man's weapon, but it was clearly a nine-millimeter semiautomatic. Depending on the type, the number of rounds could vary and he might still have cartridges left. If Garin guessed wrong, he'd be dead.

With each passing moment, Garin's options were dwindling. Even if his adversary had spent his magazine, he could seat a second one in the next couple of heartbeats. And if Garin didn't move now, the Chevy Chase police might arrive, dumbfounded to find the most wanted man in America engaged in a gun battle in one of the wealthiest communities in the country near an upended SUV—next to which, of all things, lay an inert Iranian.

Garin charged for the Blazer, firing two shots as he closed the twenty yards between the tree and the target. As he rounded the front of the vehicle, he dove to the ground and rolled to his right, the SIG gripped firmly in both hands and extended in front of him ready to fire. But there was no one to shoot.

Garin leapt to his feet and swiftly checked all sides of the Blazer. The man was gone. As Garin had feared, he had escaped into the wooded area.

The man couldn't have gotten far in the seconds since his last shots, but Garin didn't have time to track him down. Instead, he turned his attention to the vehicle. He looked through the windshield, but it didn't appear that there were any occupants left within. To be sure, he climbed up to the passenger-side door and carefully peered inside. Empty. He opened the glove box for any identifying documents. It, too, was empty.

Garin hopped down and stuck his weapon into his waistband. The rain was beginning to lighten up. He was soaked and covered in mud. From where he stood, he could even see several bullet indentations in the side of the Fusion, which the friendly Avis rental agent would likely find somewhat unacceptable. Garin stooped and turned the dead man onto his back. He didn't recognize the face but thought it looked vaguely Middle Eastern. Rifling through the man's pockets, Garin feared he'd have no more information than when he'd begun the chase. But as he pulled a piece of paper from the man's left front pocket, Garin thought, *Perhaps not.*

CHAPTER FORTY-ONE

Mansur didn't look anything like Park had imagined. The Iranian was shorter and heavier than expected, his face softer and more open. He looked less like a former member of a ruthless intelligence service and more like a successful hotelier, or a restaurateur nearing retirement.

Mansur's apartment was modest but nicely appointed and well kept. It was the apartment, thought Park, of someone well-to-do who didn't care to advertise his wealth.

Chernin and Park each sat on comfortable leather chairs in front of a simple but elegant mahogany coffee table. Before Park was a cup of tea. Before Chernin was a glass of Smirnoff, a baked orange peel resting at the bottom.

Mansur sat opposite them on a low, plush couch that was startlingly white. He sipped from a bottle of water between puffs on a Cohiba. To Park, the cherubic Mansur appeared the picture of contentment.

When Chernin had called earlier in the day, he had casually informed Mansur that he was bringing Park along. Although there had been no discussion about the purpose of the visit, the astute Mansur surmised that he would likely hear some type of business proposition that evening. Three intelligent men who had lived their lives under three of the most repressive regimes in the world didn't gather to engage in idle conversation. A favor would be asked; a price would be discussed. If there was agreement, a plan would be formulated.

Yet to this point—twenty minutes into the evening—the conversation had, in fact, been idle. The comparative climates of Russia, Korea, and Iran; their respective cuisines; the World Cup. Park corrected Mansur on the number of rounds it took Ali to dispatch Jerry Quarry in Atlanta. Mansur, believing he knew more about Ali than the champ himself, was surprised but delighted.

Mansur was in no hurry. He understood that the rhythm of the conversation would soon turn to the true purpose of the pair's visit. It was best to let the discussion flow until the visitors felt comfortable. They would broach the subject when ready.

For his part, Park had been ready from the moment he'd entered Mansur's apartment. He had no use for small talk and preferred to get right to the point. But he deferred to Chernin. This was his friend and he knew the optimal time to make the request. And the time came soon enough.

"Hamid," Chernin said in an offhand tone, tilting his head toward Park. "My friend here believes you may be of assistance to him. I've told him you are a very resourceful fellow who can make certain arrangements if the consideration is right." Chernin arched his brow. "Is this a good time to talk about such arrangements?"

Mansur understood the question perfectly. He went to great pains to ensure that his apartment was secure. He swept it regularly himself using his own equipment and countermeasures generously financed by Mossad. With the flick of a switch his windows would vibrate to frustrate laser mics. Even so, when discussing business in his home he was careful to use vague terms.

"This is a good time to talk. It is always a good time to talk carefully," Mansur replied.

Both Park and Chernin understood. One of the few advantages to living in societies where paranoia was a virtue.

"We have been working in your country for some time but have not had much opportunity to see the sights or appreciate the culture," Chernin continued innocuously as Mansur rose and flipped what looked like a light switch next to the sliding glass doors leading to the outdoor balcony. "Can you suggest some places for us to visit before we return home?"

"Certainly, Dmitri," Mansur replied as he pulled a straight-backed chair to within inches of Chernin and Park before speaking softly. "What do you need?"

Park looked at Chernin, who nodded. "In the next few days my business here will be concluded," Park said, matching Mansur's hushed tone. "I need someone who can arrange travel out of Iran, preferably to somewhere in Central America. But at bare minimum, out of Iran. If necessary, I can make my own way to my ultimate destination."

"That can be arranged."

Park was a bit taken aback. This was going faster than he'd expected. He had anticipated a litany of reasons why his request would be impossible to fulfill, a recitation of the dangers, a recommendation that he abandon the idea. He didn't know what to say next. Chernin intervened.

"We can be ready to leave in forty-eight hours. Our work is done. We're simply filling out forms and smoking cigars. We're scheduled to return home in days. As you know, we have the ability to leave the compound for brief periods but we are under constant surveillance. The man who brought us here this evening—the driver—is attached to Iranian Quds Force. It will be difficult, but we can evade him. Sometimes the driver is Russian SVR. That will make it harder, but I still believe it can be done. I have been coming here for several months now, sometimes twice a week. To them it's inconsequential, boring. This has caused them to become lax," Chernin said.

Mansur nodded as if thinking. He was, but about how to steer the conversation toward the project. It was evident that the window for obtaining any more information was closing. He could no longer afford subtlety.

"As I said, Dmitri, this can be done. But I will be frank. I am less concerned about the difficulty of getting you out of Iran and to your destination than I am about the consequences of my actions—to me, that is."

Park, having expected from the outset to engage in customary Persian haggling over price, believed this was Mansur's opening gambit. "I am prepared to pay a very generous amount and bonus for your help, Mr. Mansur. That should not be an issue, I assure you. I will pay one hundred thousand American dollars plus costs. Half up front, half upon my arrival in Costa Rica or wherever my destination may be."

Chernin glanced at Park, an eyebrow raised.

Mansur smiled. "I am not talking about price, Mr. Park, although I welcome your offer. I am talking about my life. Literally, I am afraid."

Park looked mildly confused. "You have done such things before, have you not?"

"Yes, yes," Mansur said, waving a shroud of smoke from his face. "There is always a risk when dealing in contraband—human or otherwise—and especially in countries such as ours. The risks may vary, but they are risks nonetheless. This, however, is different." Mansur looked at Chernin. "Dmitri, I have enjoyed our time together. I do not have many occasions these days to socialize with individuals who are, shall we say, 'worldly.' What little I have learned from our conversations leads me to think you gentlemen are involved in a matter very important and extremely dangerous. That means my involvement with you would be extremely dangerous. Before I agree to help you, I must know precisely how dangerous. And whether I must then make my own arrangements."

Chernin and Park stared at each other for several seconds. Mansur knew that each was contemplating what, if anything, to reveal about their work. For Park, any personal constraints on full disclosure should've disintegrated once he'd made the decision to defect. He no longer had anything to lose. The only reason to maintain any level of secrecy was the effect disclosure might have on Chernin, who would return to Russia. Mansur resisted the urge to tell both men that Park's defection actually gave Chernin the perfect cover. If their secret somehow got exposed, everyone—the Russians, North Koreans, Iranians—would think it was Park, the defector, who had talked.

Chernin was thinking exactly the same thing. The Russian knew that Mansur would be killed, undoubtedly after a long and brutal torture, if the Iranian regime discovered that he had any involvement in Park's defection. Mansur deserved to embark on this endeavor with his eyes open. He needed to know precisely what risks the endeavor entailed. But Chernin, product of the Soviet Union, needed assurances of his own.

Chernin said in a slow, deliberate cadence, "Let us, as you said, be frank. I understand your need to assess how much risk you are assuming by helping us. And you are correct; we are involved in a matter of extreme importance to our respective countries and, accordingly, a matter very dangerous." Chernin leaned forward, his eyes narrowed. "I will tell you what I believe you need to know. But first, let me be very clear about something. Yes, we have talked about some interesting things. I have told you . . . well, not much, but more than a little of what we are doing up in the mountains. But I'm not as stupid as I may appear." The tone of the scientist's voice became oddly chilling.

Mansur began to protest, but Chernin calmly raised his hand to silence him. Park shifted uncomfortably in his seat before Chernin resumed speaking. "I have never suffered under the illusion that what I've told you stayed in this apartment. After all, you're former SAVAK." Chernin paused and glanced about the room. "You live very well, despite not having any visible source of income. It is, therefore, probable that you have sold some of what I've told you to an interested party or parties—possibly American, but more likely Mossad."

Mansur had a pained look on his face. "Dmitri . . ."

Chernin held up his hand again. "No need for explanations or apologies," Chernin said dismissively. "I truly hope you did not think that what I told you was the result of a tongue made loose by vodka. I am not some undisciplined fool. What I told you was intended for not just your ears."

Expressions of surprise covered the faces of Mansur and Park. Park because he couldn't imagine the stoic Russian would say anything whatsoever about the project to Mansur, and Mansur because he had not for a moment considered that Chernin's revelations about the project were intentional.

Chernin drew even closer to Mansur. "What we're doing, my young friend and I—the missiles—is an abomination. Perhaps I did not know that at the beginning; my superiors never revealed the purpose of the project." Chernin shrugged, his lips drawn into a scowl. "What can I say? We are Russian. Everything is a secret. *This* is a *very big* secret. And the more I have learned, the worse it is."

Mansur smiled in admiration. This had never happened to the old spy. He had been played by his clever friend, someone with no intelligence experience whatsoever. Over the course of their time together, Mansur believed it was he who had been manipulating the Russian.

"It is only in the last few weeks that the essential purpose of our work has become manifest," Chernin continued. "Yet from fairly early on, it has been my aim to alert the West that something troubling was coming. And I found a reliable conduit in you, did I not?"

Mansur dropped all pretense. He was dealing with a man who was far more sophisticated than Mansur had imagined. "You have, Dmitri. I never put you in any danger. I never revealed the name of my contact. Nor did I provide any identifying information that could be traced to you."

Chernin casually sipped his vodka, staring at Mansur. He understood the last statement was untrue. That was the nature of such things.

"Mossad?"

Mansur didn't respond.

"Hamid, you must never reveal your source. Of course, I do not need to tell you this. It is your expertise, your life's work. I simply say it for emphasis. If you were to ever reveal my name, the source of information could then be tracked back to you."

Chernin knew he now had an unshakable ally.

Mansur gave two quick nods. "Yes. Your life and mine, I'm afraid, are dependent on one another."

"Correct. As obvious as that is, it is important, I think, for us to acknowledge it. If either of our governments learns that what I am about to tell you has been transmitted to the West, what remains of our lives will be worse than hell."

"If it is that bad, then I suspect I'll have to make arrangements to leave the country myself," Mansur said.

"You'll need to leave the country not only for helping my friend," Chernin said, "but because it will be an extremely dangerous place in which to live."

Park's eyes flitted from Chernin to Mansur as they spoke. "So you will help?" he asked.

"The Iranian regime is insane," Mansur replied to Park. "And I suspect the consequences of their insanity are about to be visited upon my country in a catastrophic way. I would do what I can to make achievement of their goals more difficult. So, of course I will help you. But first you will help me by supplying the details of the project in the mountains. I will then immediately make arrangements for your departure." Mansur looked back to Chernin. "Dmitri, if you're not also leaving, what will you do?"

Chernin did not reply immediately but took another sip of vodka. "I have received a good deal of compensation for my work on the project and I plan, quite unoriginally, to use it to retire to a dacha on the Black Sea. I will be safe—in fact, more than safe. I will be celebrated as a national hero."

Mansur reached forward and clasped Chernin's hand. "Should you change your mind, I can arrange passage for you also."

Chernin smiled. "Always looking for a fee, Hamid."

"No fee, Dmitri," Mansur said earnestly. He looked to Park. "And now that we have come to the subject of price, Mr. Park, no fee for you, either. Use the money to disappear so that you'll never be found."

"Thank you," Park said, "but I could not—"

"No need to thank me. Thank the Israelis. I will make your arrangements before you leave tonight. They do not know it yet, but they will be paying your fee, and quite a fee it will be."

CHAPTER FORTY-TWO

EASTERN SHORE, MARYLAND

JULY 16 • 3:30 P.M. EDT

Julie Webber had worked as a rental agent for Terrapin Estates for four years. During that time she'd seen scores of people in colorful outfits, many covered with sand or mud. The rental units, after all, catered primarily to anglers and crabbers who spent the week or weekend trying their luck on Maryland's Eastern Shore.

The man standing before her was soaking wet and his pants and shoes were caked with mud. Julie barely registered his disheveled appearance, however, because he had the body of a gladiator. Most Terrapin Estates patrons were balding, middle-aged men with paunches who couldn't have spiked her interest had she spent the last decade in solitary confinement. So she patiently accommodated the man's inquiries despite the fact that company policy forbade giving out customer information.

"Sir," Julie said sweetly as she viewed the desktop computer screen, "we don't show any rentals to Bobby Martin. Could he be under another name?"

Garin made a show of looking puzzled. He'd come to Terrapin to track down the people who had been trying to kill him the last few days. The piece of paper he'd retrieved from the dead Iranian in Chevy

Chase was a paper napkin bearing the local address of a Phillips Crab and Lobster House about a quarter mile down the road from the Terrapin Estates rental office. A friendly Phillips waitress hadn't remembered anyone fitting the dead Iranian's description, but she helpfully pointed out that a number of her customers were renters from Terrapin. Garin traveled over to the rental office and made up Bobby Martin and a story about joining Bobby and his fraternity brothers for a few days of drinking and fishing.

"Maybe the rental's under the name of one of my other buddies," Garin said. "Do you remember a party of five or six guys checking in?"

"I don't. But they could've checked in late afternoon after I'm off. Any party larger than five would probably be in either the Anne Arundel or the Severn. Those are our biggest units—four bedrooms and a rollout in the living room. They can comfortably sleep eight."

"Could you check to see if anyone's checked into either of those cabins?" Garin asked. "The guys probably arrived a few days go. I was supposed to join them earlier but couldn't get away from my job until now. And unfortunately for me, they've probably drunk up all the beer already."

Julie moved the mouse and clicked the icon on the screen for Severn. "This might be them. Yep. Eight guys. Checked in to Severn a few days ago. Rental's under the name Joe Jones."

No points for originality, Garin thought.

"It looks like maybe some more of your friends checked into the Anne Arundel, too," Julie continued as she manipulated the mouse. "Seven other guys checked in at the same time as the Severn boys. But they checked out on Saturday. Is a Jim Smith one of your fraternity brothers?"

"Yes," Garin lied. "I didn't think he was coming down." Joe Jones and Jim Smith. The Iranians hadn't wasted any effort on cover names, but they had sent an army to kill Garin and the rest of his team. Garin guessed that the seven who had checked out of the Anne Arundel on

Saturday consisted, in part, of the four-man team Garin had killed in Broome County, New York.

"Is there anything else I can do for you, Mr. . . . ?"

"Webster. No. You've been a great help. Do you mind if I go over to the Severn and check on my friends?"

"Will you be staying?" Julie asked hopefully. "The rental fee for an additional person is only eighty-five dollars per day."

Garin pulled out his wallet and handed Julie ten twenties. "That should cover two nights. Do you mind if I fill out the rental agreement and get the receipt later?"

"No need to fill out a separate agreement. The one signed by Mr. Jones will suffice. I'll just put an endorsement on it noting the new number of guests," Julie said as she pulled out a drawer in a beige filing cabinet behind her. "But you'll need your own key."

Garin smiled as he took the key from Julie. A bit of charm to soften the mendacity. He hoped he wouldn't cause any problems for her by damaging any of her nice cabins. "Maybe I'll see you again in the next couple of days."

Julie intended to make sure of it. "Do you need help getting to the Severn?"

"If you just point me in the right direction, I'm sure I can find my way."

"Turn right as you go out the door. Go an eighth of a mile down the access road until it dead-ends. Then a left down the hill toward the bay. It's right on the water. Parking in the rear."

"Thanks," Garin said as he walked toward the door of the rental office.

"Julie."

Garin turned. "Pardon?"

"The name's Julie. Shorter than writing 'the hot blonde from Terrapin with the great ass' in your diary."

Garin smiled and walked out the front door.

The approach to the cabin would be problematic. Garin didn't know how many Iranians were in the cabin, or their security arrangements. Some of them could be on sentry duty or patrolling the surrounding woods. Although the cabins had a fair amount of distance between them, other residents nearby would easily be able to hear any gunfire coming from the Severn. And given the clothing he was wearing, Garin couldn't easily conceal a weapon with a suppressor attached.

Terrapin Estates was hilly and densely wooded. Most of the cabins ringed the bay, with approximately a hundred yards between them. A dirt path sloped from the access road to the Severn, a distance of approximately two hundred yards. Approaching the cabin on the dirt path would be suicide. Instead, Garin threaded his way carefully through the trees and brush leading to the rear of the cabin. When he was within thirty yards of the building, he lay on a soft mat of pine needles and surveyed the surroundings.

The cabin was a relatively modern two-story wooden structure. A wide porch wrapped around the exterior and a large deck spanned the width of the second floor. A simple wooden door flanked by two large windows covered most of the building's rear, allowing a view of the upper portion of the first floor and through the windows to the blue-green waters of the bay.

For several minutes Garin saw no movement within the cabin or in the area immediately adjacent to it. Then a bearded man dressed in black cargo pants and a light gray T-shirt appeared in the center of what appeared to be the kitchen. He was powerfully built. Garin put his height and weight at approximately six feet four inches and 250 pounds. He looked as if he was placing a kettle on the stove.

A few moments later the bearded bull disappeared in the direction from which he came, only to be replaced by a smaller, athletically built man dressed in garb similar to the bull's. The smaller man helped himself to the kettle's contents and disappeared in the same direction as the bull. Neither man appeared to be armed.

Garin remained prone for several minutes before advancing slowly toward the cabin, pistol drawn, using the trees and brush for cover. He was able to see enough of the interior to determine that there probably were no more than two or three men inside the cabin. He wanted at least one of them alive.

Garin proceeded to within a few feet of the back door. He could see the head of the smaller man, who was seated on a couch in a living room to the right. As Garin was beginning to calculate the time it would take him to enter the cabin and disable the Iranian, he felt a powerful blow from behind and found himself airborne, the SIG jarred from his grasp. He crashed onto the porch with the bull landing on top of him, momentarily stunned.

Garin had only a second to register his amazement that the big man had gotten the drop on him before powerful blows began raining down with relentless speed. Then he felt the sharp cold point of a knife pressing against the side of his neck, just under his left ear, as he lay prone.

"Up on knees. Slow. Hands behind head."

The bull spoke passable English. Garin complied. In a matter of seconds the Iranian would discover his good fortune upon realizing the man kneeling before him was the lone surviving member of Omega. He wouldn't hesitate to jam the knife into Garin's neck and slash the jugular and trachea. Watch the slow, gurgling death. Mission accomplished.

There are six points on the human body that, if struck by a blow from an average-size man, will render one incapacitated. Garin knew every single one. But for a man the size of the bull, the best bets were the eyes, throat, and testicles. Given his position, the latter target was Garin's only option.

In a rapid, fluid motion, Garin twisted his head to his right, away from the knife, spun on his knees, and sent a vicious uppercut to the bull's groin. Although he was doubled over, the knife remained in the stunned Iranian's grip. Before he could regain his senses, Garin, now standing, slammed a right hook into the man's temple that caved in the occipital bone of the left eye. That blow was followed by a left up-percut that pulverized the man's jaw and drove several bits of teeth into his throat.

Although the Iranian still remained upright, the motor functions on the left side of his body were effectively gone. His eyes were glazed, the look of a man nearly out on his feet. Now it was Garin who sought to bring the encounter to a swift and merciless end. Grabbing the back of the Iranian's skull with both hands, Garin pulled the man's head violently downward at the same time he thrust his right knee upward into the man's face. The impact whipped the bull's head backward, his body suspended momentarily in a half-upright position before crash-ing face-first onto the porch.

Garin dropped to one knee and turned the bull on his side. The big man's eyes were wide, searching. In a low voice Garin said, "You're strong. But not strong enough. Your mistake was standing too close. Playing executioner. Like back home. And hesitating. Even a second. Speed kills." Garin drew a bit closer and whispered, "You would've died anyway. But you would've had a few more seconds. Should've stuck with killing civilians."

To be sure the man would pose no further problem, Garin stepped on the back of the man's neck, grabbed his forehead with both hands, and wrenched his head backward, snapping the neck at the base of the skull—an inelegant but effective move Garin had learned years ago from Clint Laws.

The light went out in the bull's eyes. Garin wondered which of his teammates this particular Iranian had killed, but the thought was quickly interrupted by the sound of cracking branches. He looked up and saw the athletically built Iranian running north through the woods, parallel to the shore. Garin cast about for the SIG, but failing to immediately locate the gun, he decided he had scant choice but to ignore another bit of Laws's training and give chase to the Iranian without first securing his weapon.

The smaller Iranian had nearly a seventy-yard head start. Garin figured the man was unarmed and alone; otherwise, there would be little reason for him to flee. He bounded through the woods at a full sprint, hurdling fallen trees and dodging standing ones without breaking stride.

But Garin swiftly gained ground. The former track athlete was much faster than the Iranian, and he was closing the gap despite the lingering effects of Pakistan and the damage done during his hand-to-hand combat with the bull just moments ago.

Garin fixed his eyes on the Iranian's legs. The strides were shortening, almost imperceptibly, but shortening nonetheless, the lactic acid building in his quads. Soon the air would sear his lungs. He was beginning to run out of steam; Garin was not. The pair had covered about a quarter mile. They passed behind several other cabins, the gap between the two narrowing to only thirty yards. The Iranian began glancing over his shoulder, a telltale sign that he was nearing exhaustion. He would begin slowing more rapidly now. Running at a full clip for more than a quarter mile was the province of only highly trained athletes. It was Garin's territory. He'd have the Iranian and his secrets in the next three hundred yards, if not sooner.

Garin's legs churned harder, gliding over a large fallen tree and jumping across a small creek. He was close enough now that he could see the strain and growing apprehension on the Iranian's face, now colored deep red, pools of purple on his cheeks. Garin could hear his desperate gasps for breath. Shallow. Fast and irregular. He was through.

The dense canopy of leaves began to disperse and the somber twilight of the woods began to brighten. As he reached the crest of the hill, Garin heard a sustained hiss. Speed on wet asphalt.

The two men hurtled down the other side of the hill, Garin now within a few arms' lengths of the Iranian. Suddenly the brush dispersed, revealing a two-lane highway. The startled Iranian's momentum drove him directly into the path of an eighteen-wheel flatbed moving at sixty miles per hour.

As Garin dropped to a baseball slide to stop his forward motion, he could hear the impact of the truck's grille against the Iranian's body. Garin skidded to a stop on the shoulder of the highway, barely a foot from the right lane. Car horns blared. Tires shrieked as the flatbed braked to a halt.

Garin lay on the shoulder for several moments, his breathing hard—a result of both physical exertion and adrenaline from narrowly averting his own collision with oncoming traffic. He was amazed the crash and sudden stop by the flatbed hadn't resulted in a pileup.

The Iranian's body had been catapulted into the median more than 100 feet away and the truck had come to rest approximately 250 feet down the highway. A growing number of cars were now stopped behind the truck. Garin picked himself up and began jogging toward the Iranian's body.

The driver jumped out of the cab to inspect the carnage. Dozens of other drivers were emerging from their vehicles as well.

When Garin reached the body, the driver was standing over him, badly shaken; his jaw was slack and perspiration was streaming down his face. Several motorists were standing about, seemingly reluctant to approach any closer than thirty feet from the body, the carnage acting as a repellant.

Their reluctance was understandable. But for the clothing, the Iranian's corpse bore no resemblance to anything human. The impact with the flatbed had pulverized his skeleton; blood and internal organs were strewn over the pavement from point of impact to where the body lay.

A few of the motorists had their cell phones out, calling to report the accident. Garin made sure that no one was photographing the scene before he approached the Iranian's remains. Not surprisingly, no one wished to capture the hideous sight for posterity.

The police would be arriving within minutes and the gathering crowd would no doubt identify Garin as somehow being involved in the incident. Not needing to add the Maryland State Police to the list of law enforcement searching for him, he moved quickly. Kneeling next to the body, Garin was able to identify what appeared to be trouser pockets amid the mass of blood, bone, fabric, and tissue.

More than two dozen onlookers stared in astonishment at the apparent callousness of the disheveled, dangerous-looking stranger who rifled through the dead man's pockets, crossed the highway, and walked briskly into the woods. Garin was heading back to the Severn. He needed to retrieve his SIG and quickly inspect the premises. He'd killed several Iranians over the last two days, yet he was no closer to determining why they had wiped out his entire team. Nor why he was targeted for assassination by Delta Force. If the answers didn't come soon, any remaining luck he had was certain to evaporate.

CHAPTER FORTY-THREE

WASHINGTON, D.C.

JULY 16 • 5:15 P.M. EDT

The Edgar in the Mayflower Hotel was one of the better places to people watch in Washington, D.C., although that wasn't the principal reason Dan Dwyer frequently had dinner there.

It wasn't uncommon to see a senator or cabinet official strolling through the promenade that led from the reception area to the ballrooms past the restaurant. Talking heads from the various news shows and eggheads from the numerous think tanks were also habitués of the bar.

What drew Dwyer to the Mayflower, however, was the likelihood of encountering at least one stunningly attractive woman there, languidly sipping Chambertin Grand Cru while waiting for one of the rich and powerful to ask if he could join her. Dwyer took mischievous delight in the fact that he, the youngest of a struggling Wisconsin dairy farmer's four sons, was now among the richest and most powerful.

Dwyer held no illusions about the reason for his current appeal to women. He had boyish good looks for a middle-aged man, yet even fifteen years ago, when he was forty pounds lighter and his face reflected the intensity of an active SEAL, Dwyer's luck with women came nowhere near that of most of his warrior brethren. Women tended to view Dwyer more like a funny, protective big brother than a smooth lothario. But now that his photograph had accompanied more than a few newspaper and magazine articles speculating his wealth to be in the hundreds of millions, women ranging from Hollywood starlets to horse-country socialites suddenly realized that he was intellectually stimulating and physically irresistible.

The woman for whom Dwyer was waiting this evening rivaled even the most beautiful of the starlets and socialites who fawned over him, but she seemed immune to Dwyer's newfound allure. With Olivia, he was, once again, the funny, protective big brother. In turn, Dwyer viewed her almost like the brainy yet vulnerable little sister he never had, though he readily conceded that no one in his family looked remotely as good.

Dwyer was deciding whether she needed to be protected from the lethal good looks and altar-boy charm of a certain special operator. It was becoming apparent to Dwyer that Olivia's interest in Mike Garin went beyond the professional. Kid sisters should not, Dwyer believed, consort with stone killers, no matter how smart and courteous they might be.

And there she was, standing at the hostess station at the entrance to the restaurant. She wore a simple, sleeveless blue-black dress that matched the color of the lustrous hair that fell in abundant cascades to the small of her back. Nearly every pair of male eyes in the room fastened on her face. For a moment, Dwyer reconsidered. Maybe it was Mike Garin who needed protection.

As the hostess escorted Olivia to Dwyer's table, his cell phone vibrated. He threw an apologetic wink at the hostess and answered the call in violation of the restaurant's prohibition against cell phone use. He was happily indulged by a waitstaff accustomed to Mr. Dwyer's ridiculously generous tips.

Dwyer listened intently, rising absently as Olivia came to the table. He disconnected as they both sat down. "Haven't seen you in ages," Dwyer said with his standard mischievous grin.

"It's still not funny, Dan. I thought that some sort of wild animal had gotten loose in your house." Olivia was referring to Max, Dwyer's geriatric, overweight, and excessively friendly Newfoundland, which had the run of Dwyer's residence. The previous night, Dwyer, Matt, and Carl had rushed upstairs upon hearing Olivia's shrieks to discover their guest—looking magnificent in a white cotton nightshirt that fell barely to midthigh—attempting to barricade herself in the bathroom against Max's overly enthusiastic greeting. Prying the enraptured Matt and Carl from the scene proved nearly as difficult as removing Max.

"That was one of my guys in California," Dwyer said, patting the breast pocket in which he had just stowed his cell phone. "Thanks to the help of a sheriff's deputy who was a former swim buddy in the teams, he was able to spend several hours in the hospital room of Clint Laws, Garin's old boss. Laws was shot and in pretty bad shape. He was in and out, mumbling things no one could understand. Garin was right, though; that tough old bird wasn't talking about how bored he was."

"You've lost me. What do you mean?"

"Laws had been shot and left for dead at the bottom of a ravine near Generals Highway in Kings Canyon. Wounds in the head and chest. Professional," Dwyer said, shaking his head in disgust.

"Anyway, the old man refuses to die," Dwyer continued. "Crawls up the ravine to the side of the road, where a couple of hikers find him. They call 911 and Laws is life flighted to Community Regional Medical Center in Fresno. When they get him there, he's barely conscious, on the verge of death. Everyone thinks he's babbling incoherently about how bored he is. Delusional." Dwyer looked up and waved off the waiter, who had appeared at Olivia's elbow, before continuing.

"Except for Mikey. He insists Laws is trying to tell us something. Turns out he was, but I'm not sure what."

"Exactly what did your man tell you?" Olivia asked.

"Earlier this afternoon, he calls to say Laws described the men who hit him. Two Middle Eastern–looking dudes. Called one Mr. Obvious or something. Then the nurses come in and chase my guy off, but he gets the sheriff's deputy to intercede and goes back in. Laws was unconscious for a long while, but a few minutes ago he told my guy that he overheard the two guys who shot him talking while they were standing over him, thinking he was dead. They were talking about reporting in to someone named Taras Bor."

"Taras Bor doesn't sound like a Middle Eastern name," Olivia said. "More like Russian or Ukrainian. Given the circumstances, though, my guess is Russian. It looks like the UN isn't the only place where Russians and Iranians are working together."

"I don't know why, but something tells me I should know that name," Dwyer said pensively. "I'll run it through our databases to see if we get any hits. It would probably be a good idea for you to do the same. See if you can get CIA, NSA, and everyone else to run the name. He may be the one who orchestrated the assassination of the Omega team."

"The Russians working with the Iranians on the UN censure resolution is one thing. There are certain advantages to Russia in an unstable Middle East. But assassinating America's counter-WMD strike force—if that's in fact what they did—is another order of magnitude," Olivia said.

Dwyer summoned the waiter, who was waiting patiently out of earshot. "Olivia, why don't you have some dinner? You can't solve the Middle East crisis and usher in a golden age of world peace on an empty stomach."

Olivia ordered the free-range chicken breast. Dwyer ordered a glass of ginger ale.

"You're not eating?" Olivia asked.

"As you've probably noted, I can stand to miss a meal or two."

Once the waiter left with their order, Olivia asked, "Have you heard anything more from Michael Garin?"

"As a matter of fact, I have. He's in the District."

"When did you talk to him?"

"Late morning, which means he's been running around unsupervised for the last five or six hours. And that means there's a pretty good chance he's engaged in some mayhem."

"That raid on the Crowne Plaza had something to do with him, didn't it? On the news they said that traffic was backed up for hours as a result."

"That was him." Dwyer nodded. He looked down as if pondering a dilemma. "Look, I told you earlier that Mike might have to kill more men before this is over. You should know that he's eliminated at least half a dozen Iranians in the last two days. Maybe more by now."

"*What?*" Olivia's outburst drew the attention of surrounding diners. She immediately lowered her voice. "Six Iranians now? What could he possibly be thinking?"

Dwyer wasn't especially surprised by Olivia's reaction. The last she'd heard, Garin had shot two men in Dale City. She was smart enough to conclude that Garin had done so in self-defense. But the body count was adding up. It was difficult for a civilian to absorb.

"Olivia, I told you, this is what Mike does—"

Olivia cut him off. "You mean start mini-wars on American soil? Reenact the Saint Valentine's Day Massacre?" Although her voice was hushed, her tone was one of exasperation. She'd invested valuable time with this band of former special operators. They had impressed her as responsible and civilized. Now it appeared that Garin was nothing more than a rampaging thug shooting up the countryside. Relying on such a man was imprudent, to say the least.

"Before you get all righteously indignant," Dwyer said firmly, "you just might want to consider the circumstances. Mike's entire team has been wiped out. His mentor was shot and left for dead. Multiple teams of Iranian assassins have been hunting him for the last several days."

Dwyer's voice became sharper and more strident with each word. He liked and respected Olivia. She seemed to have an admiration for the military sometimes lacking among many of the people who traveled in her circles. But even someone as grounded as Olivia often had difficulty appreciating the terms under which men like Garin operated.

"Not only that, but his own government is trying to kill him," Dwyer continued, noticing Olivia's eyebrows arch upon hearing the statement. "That's right. And I'm not talking about the cops or the FBI. Someone's decided that Mike is sufficiently dangerous that he needs to be taken out—no Miranda rights, no trial, no judge, no jury—just killed immediately, no questions asked. Like some rabid animal that needs to be put down. So you might want to consider forgiving him for acting in self-defense when teams of assassins come gunning for him."

Olivia's demeanor quickly changed from prosecutorial to contrite. "Look, Dan, you guys get enough crap without having to hear it from someone like me. I get it. I do. I just reacted to hearing the number—six men killed." Olivia paused and shook her head. "But I'm having a hard time believing that the United States government is trying to kill Michael Garin. What makes you say that? What evidence do you have?"

"Mike told me that two nights ago in upstate New York, more than a dozen men, armed to the gills, came looking for him. They came on military helos. Not only were they armed to the teeth, they moved like military. Mike was able to identify one of them. He's a Delta Force sniper."

"Delta Force?" Olivia said incredulously. "Dan, seriously, no one in government could give that order. Not even the president."

"Well, someone gave it. Mike saw the sniper again this morning. He was outside the Crowne Plaza during the FBI raid, poised to hit Mike if he made an appearance."

Olivia sank into the back of her chair as she processed what she'd just heard. The waiter returned with their drinks and a basket of bread. Olivia waited until he left before speaking.

"I have to say I don't think this is something I'm at all equipped to handle. I'm an aide to the national security advisor. I can talk to you about the implications of the START II Treaty on missile defense or what side the US should take in the Kashmir dispute. But this"—Olivia shrugged, palms upturned—"this is spook stuff, serious spook stuff. What am I supposed to make of this?"

"Help Mike, Olivia."

"Help him how? What can I possibly do?"

"You work for a man who has the president's ear. You don't have to interfere with the FBI investigation. Just tell them the truth. Tell them Mike was set up in Dale City, that it was self-defense. And that you have credible evidence that Delta Force has targeted him."

"Do I? Do I have credible evidence? Listen to what you're saying. I'm supposed to go to the FBI and say, 'Hey, guys, that Michael Garin you're looking for was set up by an Iranian hit squad, the same squad that wiped out the US counter-WMD strike force. They're still trying to kill him, as is Delta Force, by the way. So cut him some slack, okay?' Is that what you expect me to say?"

"It's precisely because you're an aide to Brandt that they'll take it seriously. They need to start looking for the real bad guys."

"What do I say when they ask me where I got the information?"

"That you got it from one of the Pentagon's biggest contractors; a guy who's got multiple clearances; a guy who's been vetted a thousand times by the FBI, DOD, and a half dozen committees of Congress. And who's witty, charming, and exceedingly handsome."

"They'll ask me for a name, Dan. If I don't cooperate, they'll hit me with obstruction."

"Tell them it's Dan Dwyer. Hell, tell them Mike's been calling me on a regular basis. I've got nothing to hide."

"They'll want to know where Mike is. Do you know where to find him?"

Dwyer hesitated. "I know where he was last night, but he's probably not there anymore."

"You provided him with a place to stay, didn't you?" An adult remonstrating a child.

"He's probably not there anymore," Dwyer repeated.

Olivia sighed. Arguing with Dwyer was futile. The type of man who became a Navy SEAL was the type who would die before quitting almost anything, even an argument. But beyond that, he was right. The FBI needed to know the facts. Whatever the Russians and Iranians were up to, it had to be bad.

"Even if they go for it, they'll want Garin to turn himself in," Olivia said.

"Fat chance."

"They'll tap your phones, monitor your e-mail," Olivia said, a final parry before yielding.

"Let them try. My systems will have them so screwed up they'll end up listening to the French prime minister placing an order for truffles with his mistress's chocolatier."

"Okay," she relented. "I'll give it a shot. I'll talk to the FBI about the Iranian operators, about Michael being set up. I need to clear it with Jim, but I think he'll be okay with it. But the issue of Delta is another matter entirely. I don't even know where to begin there—they'll seriously doubt my credibility, if not my sanity. No one, I mean no one, can give an order to American military to kill Michael Garin on American soil, except in the most extraordinary of circumstances. And even if someone had, no one will ever admit to it. It could only have come from the highest levels. We're playing with fire here, Dan. Four alarm."

The waiter returned with Olivia's entrée. Again, Olivia and Dwyer paused until the waiter departed before resuming the conversation.

"I understand about Delta," Dwyer said. "Start with James Brandt. Tell him about Delta first. See what he thinks. Let's see if the Oracle has a solution. But make it fast. Mike's out there by himself. I'm not so worried about the Iranians, but Delta is a concern even for Mike Garin."

"Now, in return for doing this, I want to talk to Michael directly," Olivia insisted.

"I don't think Mike will object. In fact, I think he'll be happy to do so. Next time he calls . . ." Dwyer paused as he watched the hostess lead Julian Day and another man to a table at the other end of the restaurant. Day sat with his back toward Dwyer, while his dinner companion sat facing him. While Day's appearance was reptilian, the other man's was amphibian. His short, squat frame, bald pate, and bulging eyes made him resemble a bloated frog.

Dwyer had seen the man before but couldn't place him. "Excuse me a moment, Olivia." Dwyer pulled out his cell phone and aimed the camera at the frog.

The Mayflower was a good place to people watch. And surreptitiously take pictures of them.

CHAPTER FORTY-FOUR

Garin ascended the stairs to the master bedroom of the house that Dwyer contended he wasn't in. In his right hand was a flash drive he had retrieved from the pocket of the athletic Iranian as he lay on the highway on the Eastern Shore.

Garin had conducted a quick sweep of the Severn after leaving the scene of the accident. He had retrieved his SIG but had found nothing else of note. In fact, it appeared to Garin that the Iranians had concluded their stay. The refrigerator contained just two bottles of water and a plastic container with the remains of some kind of meat. The closets were empty. He found no weapons of any kind. The keys to a Ford Explorer parked outside the cabin were on the kitchen counter.

After checking the Iranians' SUV for any obvious booby traps and surveillance, he wiped down the Fusion and left it at Terrapin Estates in favor of the Explorer. Since he couldn't be certain the Explorer didn't have any hidden tracking devices, he parked the vehicle several blocks from the safe house and would abandon the vehicle as soon as he could secure another one.

The flash drive might yield a wealth of information about what the Iranians were up to or it might reveal nothing. Garin was skeptical that it would be of much use. Over the last few days, questions seemed to multiply in inverse proportion to answers. All he knew was that for some reason, someone wanted Garin and his team dead, and that someone had somehow motivated actors as disparate as the FBI and Iranian operators to get the job done.

Garin settled into a cushioned swivel chair before the laptop in the master bedroom. He paused before inserting the flash drive into the portal and examined the innocuous-looking device. Not long ago he had assisted a team that had used such a device to set back the Iranian nuclear program by at least two years. The device had contained a worm that had wreaked havoc on the computers controlling, among other things, the centrifuges that had processed uranium.

The Iranians hadn't been careful. Garin would be. He thought about what he'd seen in Pakistan. He'd survived scores of operations by being prepared. Caution dictated that he take an additional step before examining the contents of the flash drive. He picked up a secure cell phone and called Dan Dwyer.

CHAPTER FORTY-FIVE

The blood on his face was noticeably warm, a thought Chernin found somewhat odd given the circumstances. He also thought it strange that his heart rate was stable and his mind was calm and focused. Although this wasn't the first time he'd killed someone, it was the first since the Afghan war almost three decades ago, and then his target had been hundreds of feet away, not seated next to him in a cramped Subaru.

After leaving Mansur's apartment, Park and Chernin had returned to their waiting automobile. Chernin knew immediately that something was amiss when he saw that the Quds Force driver wasn't alone. Seated next to him was a stocky, bearded man Chernin didn't recognize but who had the familiar sneering look of another secret police thug. The man must have entered the vehicle while Park and Chernin had been in Mansur's apartment.

Chernin's suspicions had increased when Park approached the vehicle without so much as a hitch in his stride or a glance at Chernin. The presence of a second man in the vehicle hadn't seemed to faze the hypercautious North Korean in the least.

No Russian, however, would take the unexpected appearance of the second man as anything other than a bad sign. Over the last century untold thousands of disappearances had been preceded by something seemingly innocuous but slightly out of the ordinary: the sudden appearance of an old friend; the Lada idling across the street. Some Russians made preparations for the fateful day; others thought preparation a wasted effort. The result, after all, was almost always the same.

Nonetheless, Chernin believed in preparation, however futile. And he wasn't in Russia. In the two dozen or so steps from the entrance to Mansur's apartment building to the waiting vehicle, Chernin had resolved to act without hesitation upon the slightest confirmation of his suspicions. Any window of opportunity, if there was one at all, would close in an instant. He wouldn't have the luxury of deliberation.

All doubt that something was amiss was erased when he and Park had climbed into the backseat of the car. Before he had even closed the door, Park had begun speaking.

"He told Mansur everything about . . ."

Whatever else Park was going to say was cut off by a bullet to his temple from Chernin's Tokarev. It was followed by two bullets to the back of the driver's head and two more to the face of the second Quds Force thug, who had turned toward the backseat when Chernin began firing.

The three men now slumped in various poses, their blood spattered across the interior of the Subaru. Chernin, unsure of the source of the blood trickling down his left cheek, absently wiped it with his free hand as he scanned the three bodies for signs of life. Seeing none, he replaced the Tokarev in his waistband and covered it with his shirt.

Although no lights had come on in any of the low-rise apartment buildings lining the street, Chernin was certain that the blasts from his pistol had awakened many, if not most, of the residents. Some were probably peering through the blinds while standing in their dark apartments to avoid detection. Mansur must have heard the shots too.

Chernin needed to move quickly, before the authorities arrived. He performed a cursory check of the corpses' pockets and he ripped open Park's shirt to see if he was wearing a recorder or transmitter. He wore neither. A quick glance in the glove box and under the seats revealed nothing.

Chernin gave momentary consideration to moving the car but concluded doing so would accomplish nothing. The bloody vehicle would be found soon enough. The police would be the first to arrive, perhaps within minutes. VEVAK wouldn't be far behind. Clearly, security at the project, whether Iranian or Russian, had concerns about Chernin's friendship with Mansur. To test Chernin, they had Park act the fairly convincing role of a potential defector. Throughout, Chernin had remained uncertain how much of Park's professed desire to get out of North Korea was genuine. Even someone of Park's rank couldn't help but want out of that lunatic country. But the intensity in Park's voice when the two shared a smoke earlier in the day seemed forced, artificial. And Park's offer to Mansur of a hundred thousand American dollars did nothing to allay Chernin's suspicions. A North Korean scientist, regardless of his importance, was unlikely to have access to such a sum.

Ultimately, Dmitri Chernin had not been fooled. Despite the fact that they had formed a friendship over the last several months, Chernin thought it unlikely that someone in Park's position would've confided in another person so readily. The North Korean would know that the slightest sign of disloyalty could mean death. He would probe his intended accomplice for any sign of possible betrayal, any inclination toward reporting him. Such a probe would be a long, incessant effort. In this case, though the dance had lasted several months, it hadn't been long enough.

So, as he did with everything else in his life, Chernin had planned and prepared meticulously. A pessimist when it came to human nature, Chernin anticipated that there was a fair chance he would be betrayed by Park. Chernin, therefore, had done three things.

First, using a series of fake identities he had created over the years, he wired equal amounts of the bonus he had received to accounts in Zurich, Nassau, and Montreal. He had amassed a considerable sum from both the project and general frugality over the years—enough to preserve his anonymity and live very comfortably for the remainder of his life.

Second, using a different series of false identities, he purchased several airline tickets—each with multiple connections to camouflage his ultimate destination, a place that had held his fascination since early adulthood. It had all the amenities he required—chief among them impenetrable obscurity.

Third, he coordinated his escape with Mansur. After providing Mansur with the details of the project earlier in the night, he accepted Mansur's offer of a Puros Indios and the two walked onto the balcony for a smoke while Park examined Mansur's rather forlorn collection of poetry inside the apartment. Chernin quietly explained his suspicions that he was being set up by Park along with either Russian or Iranian intelligence—perhaps both. As Chernin expected, Mansur already had a plan in place for getting them both out of the country, if, in fact, Chernin's suspicions proved accurate. The entire discussion on the balcony took only a few minutes. The two had agreed upon a code to activate the plan, extinguished their cigars, and rejoined Park in the living room.

Chernin climbed from the backseat of the Subaru and punched in a number on his cell. Mansur, having heard the gunshots from the street below, picked up immediately. If the caller was Chernin, he knew he would hear him utter a single word.

"Run."

CHAPTER FORTY-SIX

Dwyer took Garin's call in the subbasement.

"Your timing couldn't be better," Dwyer said.

"Been trying to reach you for a while. I need you to check something for me."

"Before getting into that, you should know that Olivia Perry is going to try to take some heat off of you. She or Brandt is going to tell the FBI your side of the story. No guarantees that it will cause them to go in a different direction, but it will give them something to think about."

"Good. Good. What about Delta?"

"That, as you might expect, is a bit more complicated. But she's going to do what she can," Dwyer replied.

"And what does she want in return?"

"A meeting. She hopes you might be able to shed some light on what the Russians and Iranians are up to. And before you start questioning my sanity, I think you should take the meeting. It's a calculated risk. But you take those all the time."

"In this case the risk might be too high."

"Then focus on the reward. You get the help of the national security advisor. Risk-reward, buddy. Besides, you don't have many options, and no good ones."

Silence, punctuated by a sigh. "You're right," Garin agreed, surprising Dwyer. "I need allies and it sounds like Brandt and Perry want to form a coalition. And they're right to suspect the Russians and Iranians are up to no good."

"What makes you say that?"

"Various streams of information. I'll tell Ms. Perry when I see her."

"Does any of it involve Taras Bor?"

"Bor?" Garin asked, a wisp of concern in his voice. "How did that name come up?"

"Clint Laws. You were right—he was trying to tell us something. Apparently, the Iranians who shot Laws report to this Bor. I'm going to have my people run his name first thing in the morning."

"Let me give you a head start. He's Russian. Former Spetsnaz, Vympel unit. As formidable as they come. Supposedly has a scary IQ. I've heard he acts at the specific direction of the Russian president. An assassin, but more than that. He ran terrorist cells in Germany and specializes in regime destabilization. This is not good," Garin said quietly.

"Heard from whom?"

"Contacts at GSG-9. You probably know some of them," Garin responded, referring to the highly regarded German special operations unit. "I'll fill in Ms. Perry when I meet her and she can give you the details. But I suggest you have your people run the name right now and gather all of the information they can possibly get. I don't think we can wait."

Dwyer had known Garin for nearly fifteen years. He had observed him in situations that would make some men freeze and others panic. Throughout, Garin had remained unflappable. It was a quality that helped keep those around him calm and focused on the task at hand. Hearing concern in Garin's tone was an unfamiliar experience, one that made Dwyer uneasy.

"Just how serious do you think the situation is?" Dwyer asked.

"I don't have enough information to say for sure," Garin dodged.

"Right *now*," Dwyer insisted. "With what you know, on a scale of one to ten. How serious?"

"Russians. Bor running Iranians. My entire team wiped out. Look, buddy, you and I don't deal in tooth fairies and unicorns. I'd say it's pretty damn serious."

Dwyer rubbed the back of his neck and abruptly changed direction, a show of resolve, as much to himself as to Garin. "What do you need me to do?"

"I got a flash drive off one of the Iranians. It may be nothing, but I need the contents checked. I don't want to insert it into any of the network computers you have here at the house in case of malware. I'd like one of the tech guys to analyze it and tell me what's on it."

"Not a problem. I'll come right over and pick it up."

"No, you won't. You're smarter than that. Right now you're probably the most surveilled man in the US. If you come here, the FBI, and who knows who else, will follow. So that can't happen. Hell, I'm still having a hard time accepting that your phones are secure."

"My systems are impenetrable. If someone tries to listen in—"

"I know. They'll end up listening to the French prime minister placing an order for truffles with his mistress's chocolatier," Garin finished. "I'll talk to you on your internal lines, but as far as getting you the flash drive, I'll give it to Ms. Perry when I meet her and ask her to give it to you. How soon do you think she and I can meet?"

"She's pretty anxious. You name the time."

Garin needed to get out of his muddy clothes, shower, and grab a quick meal. "Three hours?"

"Midnight it is. Nice. Very dramatic. If that's not good for her, I'll call you back. She lives in Crystal City, so she can get to the house pretty easily."

"Not here. Although I doubt she's being watched, I don't want to take the chance of her coming here." Garin thought for a moment. "Make a reservation at your favorite hotel. Have Ms. Perry call you with the room assignment after she checks in. Then call me back with a room number."

"You don't want her to come to the house, but you're going to march into the highest-profile hotel in Washington," Dwyer declared, shaking his head.

"Would you look for me there?"

Dwyer conceded to himself that the man had a point. "By the way, I take from your comment about where you got the flash drive that there may be a few more room-temperature Iranians about?"

"There may be," Garin replied warily, wondering where Dwyer was headed.

"Piece of advice. Try not to mention that to Olivia when you meet her."

CHAPTER FORTY-SEVEN

The Michael Garin who strode into the lobby of the Mayflower Hotel shortly after midnight bore little resemblance to the one who had been engaged in a gun battle with Iranian agents hours before. Aside from the distinct physique, he resembled a freshman congressman or judiciary committee lawyer more than an elite killer.

Garin was cleanly shaven and well scrubbed, something he hadn't been—at least not both at the same time—since before the beginning of the Pakistan operation nearly two weeks ago. Other than a few rebellious curls along the hairline and nape of his neck, his short black hair was brushed straight back. The simple blue blazer, taupe slacks, and white shirt he had selected from the closet in the master bedroom of the safe house fit surprisingly well.

Garin nodded to the night staff manning the reception desk as he walked through the empty ornate lobby toward the elevator bank opposite the concierge station: a hotel guest returning from a long-running meeting, perhaps a late-night outing. The only guest with a handgun stuck in a holster at the small of his back.

Dwyer had told Garin that Olivia would be expecting him in Room

546. He emerged from the elevator and looked down the corridors. The fifth floor was quiet, the guests asleep. Garin rapped lightly on the door to 546 and waited with curious anticipation. Dwyer, in his usual jocular manner, had warned Garin that Olivia Perry was far more attractive than any woman Garin had seen in a very long time. Still, Garin knew that Dwyer was prone to wild exaggerations when it came to women, so he wasn't sure what to expect.

Olivia Perry opened the door and Garin realized that his friend— possibly for the first time—had embellished absolutely nothing about her. Only those who knew Garin well would be able to discern his astonishment.

In this regard, Olivia held a slight advantage. She had seen photos of Michael Garin and studied him closely over the last several days. She had a fair idea of what to expect upon opening the door. Nonetheless, Olivia found herself somewhat flustered seeing Garin in the flesh. She couldn't remember ever being intimidated by someone's mere physical presence.

Neither Garin nor Perry, however, perceived the awkwardness of the other. Olivia moved to the side of the doorway to permit Garin to pass. "Please come in, Mr. Garin. Have a seat."

The room was dominated by two queen-size beds separated by a nightstand. An armoire that held a television sat opposite the beds. Garin took a chair in front of a small desk near the window. Olivia sat in an armchair across from him. She found herself studying every detail of Garin's appearance. There was an indefinable quality to it that conveyed physical confidence, martial superiority. He had the air, thought Olivia, of someone who looked as if he owned every room he entered. Not arrogance, but the supreme ease of a creature at the top of the food chain. A sound interrupted Olivia's musings, and it took a second before she realized that Garin was speaking.

"Ms. Perry, Dan Dwyer told me you were interceding on my behalf with the FBI and possibly the Pentagon. Thank you. I understand the very real problems it poses for someone in your position."

Olivia shook her head. "Actually, Mr. Garin, it's my boss, Jim Brandt, who's doing the talking. I'm just his aide."

"And I'm sure he wouldn't be doing so if you hadn't persuaded him. You took a professional risk speaking on behalf of a stranger who law enforcement and intelligence have concluded is a killer and a threat to national security. So, again, thanks." Garin leaned forward slightly. "But tell me, given the evident risk to your reputation and your career, why'd you do it?"

The icy intensity that Olivia had seen in Garin's photos was a weak imitation of the live version. It occurred to her she now knew for certain that the man sitting just a few feet away had killed multiple times. Perhaps as recently as today. Olivia tried, unsuccessfully, to suppress a shudder before responding with a calm she didn't possess.

"Two reasons, Mr. Garin. First, I find it implausible that you killed your entire team and then went on a rampage that just happens to target Iranians. It's far more likely that you were intended to die along with your team, and when that failed, they decided you should take the fall. I'm not some criminologist or forensics specialist, but it looks like you were set up—big-time.

"That, of course, brings us to the second reason," Olivia continued. "Why? Why are you being set up? Obviously, it must be pretty important. People don't just go to the trouble of obliterating one of the most elite military units in the world on a lark. Jim Brandt thinks you may have knowledge, whether you're aware of it or not, of information vital to answering that question. Our hunch is that the Russians and Iranians are colluding on a major strike against Israel. We cannot allow them to do so. We cannot allow them to kill with impunity. And we cannot allow them to run wild on American soil."

Now it was Garin's turn to note Olivia's eyes. Already enormous, they grew larger the more animated she became. There was a hint of indignation, even anger, in her voice. This was someone who clearly believed in the concept of good guys and bad guys, perhaps even in vengeance.

"Dan tells me you're very smart," Garin said. "And your boss—well, everyone knows the reputation of Jim Brandt. Now, I'm just a little ole grunt, but I've got a suspicion that the two of you think something more is going on. Am I right?"

Olivia eyed Garin for a moment before replying. "Dan tells me you're also very smart." A smile crossed her face, revealing a perfect set of teeth. "So now that we've established that everyone in this room is above average, what else do *you* think is going on?"

"This goes beyond Israel, Ms. Perry. Precisely how far, I can't be sure. But as big as a major strike against Israel would be, there's reason to believe something even bigger is in the works."

"What makes you say that?" Olivia asked.

"Several things. But, before going any further, am I right that you and Brandt agree?"

"Agree? I'm not sure what you mean. In general terms, yes, we're concerned that the Russians and Iranians have a strategy that goes beyond a strike against Israel."

"How far beyond?" Garin asked.

Another electric smile. "I thought I was going to be asking the questions."

"You will. I'm just trying to get a read on the administration's thought process. It might shed some light on how I got drawn into all of this."

Olivia nodded sympathetically. "I understand. You've had a hellish last few days. Well, for what it's worth, we think the Iranians want to destroy the evil, racist, and rapacious Zionist state and become the undisputed leader of the Muslim world. The Russians, in turn, desire instability in the Middle East to increase the value of their oil and gas reserves, thereby increasing their leverage over anyone and everyone dependent on those reserves."

"Meaning just about everybody."

"In varying degrees. The most pronounced effect, of course, would be on Eastern Europe, followed closely by Western Europe. But a major war in the Middle East also will wreak havoc on the US economy—further consolidating Russian power.

"What about China, India?"

"Everyone will take some kind of hit. China may be able to weather it better than India, or anyone else for that matter, because the Chinese have been making strategic resource investments in Africa and South America for the last two decades," Olivia replied.

"The Russian economy wouldn't be immune, though. They would suffer too. It's not exactly a risk-free proposition for them, either."

"In the short term, there would be some dislocation, that's true. But you know as well as anyone that Russians take the long view. They're not making decisions on a short-time horizon. They believe that they'll emerge from the crisis in better shape than when they went in. That may take a few years, but they're prepared to weather the storm.

"In fact, I believe they're prepared to profit from the storm. Satellite images show massive stockpiles of generators, cable, and other equipment throughout industrial sectors of Russia. But there's no market. It doesn't make sense. Unless, that is, they think there *will* be a market."

Olivia brushed stray strands of hair back over her right shoulder. A recess in Garin's brain noted that the woman had an impossible abundance of hair. But his mind focused on the warehouses.

"What makes you think I know as well as anyone that Russians take the long view?"

"Dan gave me some of your background. I'm sorry. I didn't mean to be presumptuous."

Garin stood. "Do you mind if I help myself to some water?"

"Oh yes, of course. I'm sorry for not offering," Olivia said, gesturing toward bottles of water on the lower shelf of the armoire.

Garin remained standing next to the armoire as he took a long swallow from a bottle and exhaled. "They do take a long view, the Russians. At least a longer view than we do. And they have a willingness—some would say an expectation—to endure periods of suffering." Garin finished off the water bottle and placed it in the metal trash can next to the desk. "Enduring brief economic uncertainty is no sacrifice at all for them. That's one of the reasons why I think, with all due respect, you and Mr. Brandt aren't thinking big enough."

Olivia looked surprised, and then intrigued. Until a few days ago she had never heard of Michael Garin. Now this killing machine presumed to point out flaws in the national security advisor's analysis of the implications of Russian-Iranian cooperation in the Middle East. And not just any national security advisor, but the famed Oracle. This Garin character clearly didn't suffer from lack of self-confidence.

"Just how big, then, should we be thinking, Mr. Garin?"

Garin discerned that Olivia was a bit nettled by his presumptuousness. James Brandt and his brilliant aide were used to being the ones who came up with the novel theories and who found answers to questions no one else had even considered. They weren't accustomed to being accused of thinking too small—and by some pit bull from the bowels of the country's clandestine forces, no less. Garin resolved to be more tactful.

"Dan Dwyer told you that a man by the name of Taras Bor may be running the Iranians in the US, right?" Garin asked.

Olivia nodded curtly in acknowledgment.

"Taras Bor is a Russian agent," Garin continued, "who operates at the direction of President Mikhailov. Why would the Russians send one of their biggest guns to ensure the elimination of the US counter-WMD team? Why make such a bold move if all they're interested in is helping Iran hit Israel?"

"Well, first of all," Olivia answered, "we aren't sure it's Taras Bor."

"Ms. Perry, humor me for a moment," Garin interjected. "The man who gave us that information is as good as they get. So let's assume he's right and it's Bor. The Russians don't need to pick a fight with the US to help Iran hit Israel. Helping Iran pass a UN resolution that inflames tensions to the point of war is all Russia needs to do to help Iran. Yet that's not all they're doing, is it?"

"Maybe assassinating your team was an insurance policy. If Iran is going to hit Israel with, say, a nuke, then it makes sense to clear the path by taking out America's counter-WMD team—to ensure you don't take out Iran's nukes first."

"Plausible," Garin conceded. "But unlikely. Russians play the odds. Wiping out my team is an extremely risky operation that doesn't guarantee the safety of Iran's nukes. Israel is more than capable of taking out Iran's WMD on its own." Garin shook his head. "No, the risk isn't worth the reward for the Russians."

"Maybe they've also disabled Israel's counter-WMD capabilities."

"If they had, then we would've heard about it, wouldn't we?" It was more statement than question.

Olivia sighed. "Yes, right away."

"Killing my team was not about Israel. If it wasn't about Israel, it must've been about the US."

"Utter speculation," Olivia retorted, and then immediately felt sheepish. *Of course* it was speculation. That's precisely what this exercise was all about. "But even if you're right—that it's got something to do with the US—the questions remain: What are they up to and why?"

Garin studied the patterns on the carpet as if he was trying to decipher a hidden code. Olivia was right. He was engaging in pure speculation. But it was speculation informed by experience and instinct. And by adherence to Clint Laws's maxim that there are no such things as coincidences.

Olivia studied Garin as intently as he studied the patterns in the carpet. She still felt somewhat intimidated by him but was becoming increasingly comfortable in his presence. Something about his demeanor and the way he carried himself imparted a sense of security. She also believed Brandt was right. Garin held a key to figuring out what the Russians and Iranians were planning. And she could tell he was on the verge of providing that key.

"There's something you're not telling me, isn't there?"

Garin looked directly at Olivia, contemplating what he could and couldn't tell her. The two stared at each other for several seconds before Garin spoke. "There is something else," he confirmed. "I'm just not sure what it means."

The midday thunderstorms had done little to diminish the heat of the day. The rain falling on the city's blistering pavement had steamed into the air and had remained into the night.

Robert Congo Knox was oblivious to the suffocating humidity, just as in past operations he'd been oblivious to the cold or the snow or the rain or the mud. The only thing to which he was never oblivious was the wind. Wind was the enemy. Wind could affect the mission. But tonight the air was still.

Knox had taken a position on the roof of the Washington Square Building at a diagonal from the entrance to the Mayflower. The range was less than a hundred yards. As he had in Spencer, New York, and at the Crowne Plaza, he worked without a spotter. Given the ranges and conditions, he had no need for one.

Knox had a sober understanding of his capabilities. His superiors considered him one of the best in the world at what he did. Reliable, efficient, and deadly, he was a problem solver.

An al-Qaeda leader inciting an insurgency in Ramadi? Deploy Knox. One shot, problem solved. A heavily protected Serbian war criminal defying capture in a mountain redoubt? Deploy Knox. One shot, problem solved.

He often operated at ranges of eight hundred to twelve hundred yards. The shots had been taken on moonless nights, in rainstorms, and during fierce firefights. In jungles and deserts, on mountains and oceans, in villages and metropolises. The results seldom varied. One moment the target's head appeared in the scope. The next, just a puff of scarlet mist where the head had been.

Knox understood that to deploy someone of his caliber to take out a target at a mere hundred yards meant that the assignment was of unusual importance; there was no margin for error. Other elite snipers might have considered the task an insult to their skills. Knox gave little consideration to such matters. As always, his focus was solely on the successful completion of the mission.

That characteristic made him virtually automatic, a quality that inspired terror in US adversaries around the globe. The bad guys had no inkling of his actual identity. Only that when he arrived in a particular theater, enemies began dropping. He had spent enough time in the wild west tri-border region of Paraguay-Brazil-Argentina that South American drug lords referred to him as El Diablo Negro—a descriptive coincidence since they had no inkling if he was black, white, or some shade in between. Once, when the Colombian Ministry of National Defense spread a rumor that El Diablo Negro was operating in the southwestern region of that country, two leaders of the Cali cartel surrendered to the authorities rather than risk certain assassination. Knox hadn't even been in the Western Hemisphere at the time.

It had been slightly more than an hour since Knox had received the order to take out Michael Garin at the Mayflower. Although Knox didn't know the details, apparently someone had been surveilling a woman with a connection to Garin. The woman had checked into the

Mayflower and, sure enough, a short time later Garin was observed entering the hotel also.

Knox was staying at a Days Inn on Connecticut only five minutes away. A quick recon of the area surrounding the Mayflower had yielded a few promising sites for a hide. He had gained access to the roof of the Washington Square with the use of a proximity card descrambler and a pair of bolt cutters.

After the Crowne Plaza fiasco, Knox was pleased that someone had at least verified that Garin was actually inside the Mayflower. When first told that Garin had checked into the Crowne Plaza, Knox had dutifully reported to work, found a hide opposite the hotel entrance, and prepared to waste a few hours of his life. Knox knew full well that a fugitive with the skills and experience of Michael Garin wouldn't check into a hotel—whether under his own name or any of his traceable aliases—unless he wanted to elicit precisely the reaction that had occurred the previous morning. In fact, Knox was fairly confident that while he was lying atop the PNC building, waiting for Garin to emerge, the target was somewhere nearby watching the pandemonium he had produced.

Knox didn't know Garin personally, but he certainly knew of him. What he knew he respected. The tier-one special operator community was tiny, and the man had a reputation as an exceptional warrior. He must've committed a spectacular sin to be targeted for elimination by Delta, especially on US soil. He knew federal law expressly forbade the use of armed forces personnel within the United States except in extremely limited circumstances, such as restoring order after a terrorist attack, an insurrection, or a national disaster. The secretary of defense could, however, pursuant to the discovery of a nuclear threat on US soil, direct the use of military personnel to eliminate the threat. Knox could only conclude that Garin was involved in some pretty nasty stuff.

Knox was unaware of anything that permitted the *assassination* of an American citizen on US soil, but he assumed that the legal i's had been dotted and t's crossed. Knox's job was not to analyze the legalities. Knox's job was to kill Michael Garin.

And that's what he would do. He had a clear view of the entrance to the Mayflower. He had a comfortable, undetectable hide. Sometime soon a head would appear in his scope. Then just a puff of scarlet mist where Michael Garin's head had been.

Olivia watched as Garin paced the length of Room 546. The gait was familiar to her. She'd seen it often as a little girl when her father's former Alabama football teammates visited, some of whom had been in the NFL. It was the stride of the well-conditioned athlete—smooth, balanced, controlled.

Olivia suspected that the intensity never left Garin's eyes, but his face, incongruously, was calm and his body relaxed. Olivia couldn't help imagining how she would be carrying herself if she were being hunted like Garin. An ordinary person, any sane person, would be tempted to curl into the fetal position in a corner of the room.

Just a few days ago, Brandt had teased Olivia about having a crush on Garin. Although she found him attractive in the dated photo and was fascinated with the history Dwyer had provided, Brandt had been wrong. Even as a schoolgirl, Olivia had never had anything remotely resembling a crush. Not that there hadn't been any handsome, accomplished men in her life. Her looks and accomplishments ensured that successful, handsome, and wealthy men, even the occasional minor celebrity, pursued her. None had ever held her interest. Too often the successful were boring, the handsome vain, and the wealthy shallow. The minor celebrities were usually all three.

Garin, on the other hand, had been in her presence for barely thirty minutes, and she found herself wanting the meeting to continue indefinitely. But any attraction she might have felt was overshadowed by the insistent knowledge that this man was a killer.

Garin turned and faced Olivia, who was still seated in the armchair. The look on his face was a curious mixture of calculation and indecision. He needed her cooperation and for her to understand his theories, but he was unsure how much to tell her.

He examined her face for several long seconds. Dwyer trusted her. And although he liked to cultivate a frat-boy image, Dwyer was a shrewd analyst of character. Garin's own preliminary sense of the woman was more wary. But then, his default mode was wariness. He especially distrusted civilians. Their innocence about malevolence was hazardous. All that was almost beside the point, however, since Garin had no better options than the woman sitting before him.

"My team was involved in an operation a week ago," Garin began before pausing. "Look, you're going to have to fill in certain blanks regarding what I'm about to tell you."

"Michael." Olivia caught herself. "I'm sorry. May I call you Michael?"

Garin nodded as another recess of his brain noted the length and shape of her legs. She was much taller than he had imagined.

"Please call me Olivia. If it makes any difference, everything you're telling me is at the direct request of James Brandt."

"Olivia, we both know that's not really how Washington works. If things blow up, the fact that I spoke to you about a classified operation will be just one of the paragraphs in the multicount indictment that will be brought against me. And it won't matter what a great guy James Brandt says I am."

"I don't dispute that. But if you can help James Brandt and the president avoid a catastrophe, no one will care that you told me about a classified operation. And believe me, Jim Brandt would go to bat for you. Now, what was it about the mission that makes you think the Middle East crisis is about more than Israel?"

"Something that at the time didn't quite compute. Let me give you a little background. The conventional wisdom is that Shiite Iran and Sunni al-Qaeda won't, and don't, work together."

Olivia shook her head. "That may be the media's conventional wisdom, but not James Brandt's."

"Brandt's right. They work together against their common enemy—the US. Are you familiar with the CIA's program to track al-Qaeda operations in Iran?"

"Yes," Olivia replied. "RIGOR, I think it was called. Established after the invasion of Afghanistan. Al-Qaeda operatives were fleeing from Afghanistan into Pakistan and Iran. Iran claimed that it was 'detaining' the al-Qaeda operatives. We had our suspicions about what that meant, so we began satellite, drone, and ground surveillance."

"Right. The agency found that 'detention' actually meant 'support.' Turns out Shiite Iran had no problem providing assistance to Sunni al-Qaeda. In fact, intel from RIGOR showed that the Ansar Corps of Iran's Quds Force was actually running al-Qaeda operations. They—Iran and al-Qaeda—were working joint operations."

"When and where?"

"You name it," Garin replied. "Iraq, Afghanistan, anywhere they found the enemy. Anyway, a week ago a nuclear facility in—you fill in the blanks—is compromised by al-Qaeda and Taliban fighters."

"Rhymes with Baluchistan, I suspect."

"You didn't hear it from me. The intelligence services in that country are supposed to be on our side. Don't get me wrong—lots of them have taken great risks to assist us. But there's an element within the nation's intelligence services sympathetic to al-Qaeda and the Taliban. That element assisted al-Qaeda in gaining access to a nuclear facility. Dangerous stuff. They could've gotten control of nuclear weapons—al-Qaeda's holy grail."

Olivia looked both perturbed and irritated. "That was a major threat. An off-the-charts threat. All I knew was that there was an attempt, not that they had actually gained access. Why didn't I hear anything about it?"

"Because we neutralized it just as they were gaining access."

"How? Why you? Why not the ISI or Pakistani military?"

"First, we weren't sure of the allegiances of their military and intelligence services. This was a bet-the-farm situation. We couldn't take any chances.

"Second, Omega was specifically created and designed to handle such circumstances. We are—were—not just trained for combat, but to dismantle and destroy WMD of every type imaginable, most often without the host country's knowledge. We were airborne within two hours after RIGOR—more accurately, RIGOR's successor program—even had a hint of a problem.

"As to how, what I can tell you is that al-Qaeda fighters had breached a nuclear facility in the unnamed country and had established control over a portion of it before my team arrived. It's likely they would've gotten their hands on the nukes had we not intervened."

It was Olivia's turn to look down at the carpet. "Nuclear weapons in the possession of terrorists." She shook her head. "I didn't hear about any of this, Michael."

"And you wouldn't. Only a handful of people in the country knew anything about it—the president, SecDef, DNI, DCI. It's not the kind of stuff that gets broadcast. Markets tanking and all of that. I'm pretty sure James Brandt knew about it but couldn't share it with you. In fact, my guess is the reason the Oracle put you on my case is because he thinks there could be a connection between what happened in that unknown country and what the Russians and Iranians are up to."

"He sometimes says that the people who call him a genius do so because they only see the end product. They don't see all the plodding work that precedes it. The endless days, nights, and weekends sifting through mundane data . . ."

"The Thomas Edison quote. But I bet even Brandt didn't expect that I'd have much information that would prove truly useful. He probably thought he was just making sure he wasn't leaving any stones unturned."

"He's excruciatingly thorough." Her tone indicated her disappointment about being in the dark about the situation at the Pakistani nuclear facility. Garin tried to soften the letdown.

"Olivia, Brandt couldn't tell you. That's not a reflection on you. That's just the way things are. If he didn't have the utmost confidence in you, he wouldn't have assigned you the job of ferreting out the information from me."

Olivia straightened and brushed back her impossible abundance of hair. "I'm a big girl. But thanks." Her eyes locked on Garin. "Back to your operation. How did you stop them?"

"We destroyed the assault force and secured the facility. We fed real-time video of the dead Tangos to Langley. Some were al-Qaeda. But they ID'd at least one of the dead as Iranian Ansar Corps."

"And what do you conclude from that?" Olivia asked.

"Nothing more than what we've just discussed. The Iranians and al-Qaeda work together whenever it's in their mutual interests to do so," Garin replied. "The Ansar Corps officer who was there isn't what's important. What's important is what was on his laptop."

"I know you're intentionally leaving gaps in what you're telling me, Michael, but I need you to be a bit more linear. You have an Iranian Ansar Corps officer's laptop, and I assume it has certain information that leads you to believe that his country is planning something beyond, or in addition to, a strike in Israel."

"I'm sorry. I sanitized the narrative a little. I'll back up. We were in a firefight with these guys. It didn't last very long—we went in hard, fast, and hot. About twenty of them retreated into a tunnel beneath the complex. They must've been working on the tunnel for quite a while—it wasn't just a crawl space.

"Anyway, we advance and methodically take them down. After we've taken out the last one, we video them and examine them for intel. The Ansar Corps guy has a laptop in his backpack. I switch it on and begin examining the files. A few seconds later, one of my guys starts yelling that he's found a timer. Turns out they'd wired the tunnel. Semtex. We had less than a minute to get clear. We're scrambling, climbing over dead bodies, trying to get out. We barely made it. I lost the laptop in the process. A couple of my guys took some shrapnel, but everyone made it out alive."

"What was on the laptop that makes you think the Russians and Iranians are planning something beyond an attack on Israel?"

"Photos."

"Photos? Photos of what?"

"Jordan Manchester, Joseph Bauer, and Evan Dellinger."

"Manchester, Bauer, and Dellinger," Olivia repeated.

Garin could see a look of recognition washing over her face.

"Manchester and Bauer are missile defense at the Pentagon," Olivia said. "I don't think I know who Dellinger is."

"He's an expert on, among other things, EMP defense,"
Garin said.

"How did you know who they are?"

"Olivia, it's my job to know."

Olivia put a hand to her forehead. She understood instantly the connection that Garin had already drawn.

"Was there anything else in the file? Any text?"

"Not that I could make out. It was in Farsi." Garin returned to the desk chair and sat down. Muscle in repose. "At first, I didn't know what to think about the file. Thought it was peculiar, something that nagged at me. But the night after we returned from the operation, I had other concerns on my mind, like staying alive."

"And then when the Iranians killed your team and came after you, you revisited the matter," Olivia said. "You asked yourself why Iranian agents were so intent on destroying America's counter-WMD capability."

"That's certainly part of it. Like I said before, why take out Omega if your objective is Israel? Also, taking out Omega still leaves the US with SEAL Team Six and Delta, both of which could be tasked to deal with WMD. They've done so before. But it's more than that."

"What else?" Olivia was leaning forward within inches from Garin. He thought he detected a faint scent of sandalwood.

"A couple of things. The Iranians have invested a ton in intelligence but still don't have the assets to conduct an operation as sophisticated as eliminating Omega. The Russians do, although I'm a little surprised they farmed out the actual assassinations to second-stringers like the Iranians.

"The Iranians also don't have a missile capable of coming anywhere near the US. So why would they be interested in our missile defense system? What do *our* missile defense systems have to do with their plan to hit *Israel*?"

"Well," Olivia offered weakly, "we supply Israel with certain missile defense technology."

"Not the high-end ICBM laser intercept defenses that Manchester and Bauer are involved in. That's strictly US missile defense. Again, the Iranians are not in a position to test our defenses. So what's their interest in Manchester and Bauer?"

Olivia shrugged. "Being interested in US missile defenses doesn't necessarily mean that Iran's not going to hit Israel."

"True, maybe they're going to hit Israel. Maybe not. But having photos of America's top missile defense guys on the laptop of an Ansar Corps officer who just *happens* to be trying to access a nuclear facility sure isn't the product of casual interest."

Garin rose suddenly. Nervous energy in the middle of the night. Olivia wondered idly if the man ever needed more than a couple of hours of sleep a night.

"If that's not enough," Garin continued, "now it appears that the guy running the Iranians is none other than Taras Bor. A joint Russian-Iranian operation run by the Russian president's pet dragon."

"We don't yet know for sure it's Bor."

"It's him," Garin countered. "We always underestimate the bad guys and refuse to believe they intend to do us harm."

"I don't disagree with you, Michael. Just playing a little devil's advocate to crystallize what we know." Olivia stood. "The Russians and Iranians are doing their best at the UN to provoke a war in the Middle East. Now they've teamed up to destroy America's counter-WMD team. Is it possible that the Middle East crisis is just a distraction?"

"Olivia." Garin shrugged, palms up. "You're the geopolitical expert. What do you think?"

"No, it's not just a distraction. It's too big for that. But I'm beginning to be persuaded that may not be the only, or ultimate, target."

Garin strode the length of the room again, immersed in thought.

"I don't know what to make of the EMP guy," Garin said. "The Iranians don't have deliverable nukes yet. Their missiles can't hit us. They don't have the ability to hit us with an EMP. So why the interest in EMPs?"

"The Russians, on the other hand, have nukes. Their missiles can hit us. They can hit us with an EMP. But . . ."

"They'd never hit us with any of those in a million years," finished Garin, still pacing slowly.

"Not in a *billion* years. The Russians can do it, but won't. Deterred by the prospect of mutual assured destruction. The Iranians, on the other hand, wouldn't mind doing it, but can't."

"I'm pretty certain of one thing," Garin said, stopping in front of Olivia. "The Iranians—guided by Bor—killed my team because of what was on that laptop in the tunnel. They don't want the contents of that laptop revealed under any circumstances."

"But how would the Russians and Iranians even know you'd seen the laptop? And even if you *had* seen it, that you could read Farsi?"

"They wouldn't. But that itself is significant, isn't it? It means that the contents of that file were so sensitive that they couldn't afford to take even the slightest risk that anyone had seen any portion of it. So they needed to eliminate all of us—and anyone we may have possibly talked to about it."

"That's why they tried to kill Clint Laws. They thought you might have spoken to him."

"Right," Garin confirmed. "Clint isn't exactly unknown in these circles. Given his past and our relationship, they probably thought there was a chance that I might talk to him about it—even if he's not cleared for it."

"And that's also why they were poking around at Dan Dwyer's. They can't take the chance—given his position and relationship to you—that you told him about the laptop." Olivia's eyes narrowed in thought. Garin knew what she was thinking and what her next question would be. "But then why haven't they come after me yet? If they were watching Dwyer, they'd surely have seen me with him. They'd have to surmise that you told him about the laptop, and then he told me."

"Killing you would be too high profile, Olivia. They wouldn't do it unless they absolutely had to, unless they were absolutely sure you had been told."

"Me?" Olivia scoffed. "High profile? I'm just an aide to the national security advisor. I'm not even a deputy."

"You," Garin said, pointing his finger for emphasis, "are the right hand of James Brandt. You're more important than a deputy. They shoot you, especially in the context of everything else that's going on, and every agency but the National Park Service will have people looking for them."

"But, Michael, you just said that they wouldn't kill me unless they were absolutely sure I had been told about the laptop. The fact that no attempt has been made on my life would indicate that they believe I haven't been told. How would they know for sure I haven't been told?"

"They wouldn't. Not unless they have someone in place inside. Someone who would know, for example, that you've told James Brandt that a laptop with incriminating information was discovered during a raid on a nuclear facility."

Garin and Olivia stared at each other in silence for several seconds. Whatever the Russians and Iranians were planning, all signs pointed to it being something of significant magnitude.

Olivia broke the silence. "Do you think they've been watching me?" she asked softly.

"Up until a short time ago I thought it was possible but unlikely. The more we talk this through, the more I think the answer is, clearly, yes."

"Then they know I'm here . . ." Olivia's voice trailed off.

"They do. And that means they know I'm here. So now they have to presume I've told you about the laptop. The risk involved in killing you is now outweighed by the risk that you know and will inform James Brandt and the president about our conversation."

"When will they come for me?" Olivia's voice remained calm, but Garin could see the apprehension in her eyes.

"As soon as they can."

"Here?"

"Maybe."

"They would kill me here?"

"They're not going to kill you anywhere." Garin's voice was low but firm.

"They killed an entire squad of elite soldiers." Olivia looked down at the desktop. "I'm just a policy person."

Garin touched her arm. She looked up. Intensity in a relaxed body. "They couldn't kill me. They will not kill you."

"What do we do now?"

"First, in a minute, I'm going to take a quick look around while you call Dan Dwyer. I'll give you the number to use. Tell him to send all the tac teams he has available. He'll know what to do."

"Why not the police or FBI?"

"Because Dwyer's men can get here faster, heavier, and they don't play by the rules. Besides"—Garin smiled—"the FBI might shoot me."

"Then what?"

"Then you're going to call James Brandt and tell him you've got to see him right away."

"And when I see him I suppose there's something in particular you want me to tell him?"

"There is," Garin said, motioning toward the chair. "Have a seat and I'll tell you a story about Russian winters and warehouses. . . ."

CHAPTER FORTY-EIGHT

CASPIAN SEA, EAST OF AZERBAIJAN
JULY 17 • 9:00 A.M. AZT

Mansur had one more thing to do before he fell off the face of the earth.

The flight from Heydar Aliyev International Airport in Baku, Azerbaijan, to Vancouver would take several hours with multiple connections. Once there, he would take care of business and then disappear forever. He had planned for this for years. The arrangements were made. Provided he remained disciplined over the next few hours, Iranian intelligence would never find him.

Nonetheless, Mansur was a bit troubled. Rarely did he miss clues about a person's intentions. It was one of the things that had kept him alive and out of prison for the last several decades. Yet he had completely misread Park. Granted, he hadn't had much time to evaluate the North Korean, having just been introduced to him by Chernin. But he had sensed nothing amiss. Only after the crafty Chernin had expressed his suspicions when they'd smoked Puros on the balcony had Mansur given any thought to whether Park's motives were sincere.

Chernin should've been a spy, Mansur thought. He knew the Russian was smart, calculating. Yet he had underestimated him.

Chernin had a contingency plan in place. That much was clear. What it was, Mansur could only speculate. A place on the water in a warm climate, somewhere the SVR would never think to look. Somewhere, as Chernin had often said, he could read and drink vodka.

Shortly after Mansur had received the warning call from Chernin, the two met a block south of Mansur's apartment and drove Mansur's car to a small dock on the Caspian Sea just outside Chalus, where Mansur's cousin Jafar was waiting for them in his fishing boat.

Now Mansur and Chernin were sailing to a makeshift dock just south of Baku in relative silence, Jafar carefully avoiding the lanes policed by Iranian gunboats. For Mansur, this was the most nerve-wracking part of his journey. Once he made it to Baku, the odds that he would never be detected and apprehended by Iranian intelligence improved to nearly a hundred percent.

Whatever Chernin's plans were to disappear, Mansur believed his were at least as good. He was traveling under a false passport and had left behind no clues as to his destination. He had accumulated enough money to live the remainder of his days in what most outside the West would consider luxury. Before leaving Baku for his own destination, Chernin would make arrangements to transfer one hundred thousand US dollars to one of Mansur's accounts, an added cushion.

Although Mansur hated the Iranian regime, he loved his country and would miss it. The familiar sights, sounds, and smells were now irretrievably in the past. The few friends he had he would never see again. He had known of this eventuality for years and had reconciled himself to it. But adjusting to life as an exile wouldn't be easy. The reward, however, was freedom. And his life.

CHAPTER FORTY-NINE

Garin took the interior elevator to the Mayflower's ground level. The hotel was still quiet. Olivia was secure in Room 546. She was not to open the door for anyone but Dwyer's men.

Garin walked to the lobby and up the staircase near the front entrance to the mezzanine level, where a bank of curtained windows provided a view of the area in front of the hotel. He pulled aside one of the curtains and scanned the sidewalks, street, and buildings. The only signs of life were the cab drivers seated in the taxis along the curb. The area was clear otherwise. Garin knew that someone could be lurking in an alley, possibly on an adjacent rooftop, but was fairly confident the surveillance-detection route he'd used made that unlikely.

Garin turned to descend the stairs back to the lobby. He needed to get back to the safe house for a couple of hours of sleep before his next step.

Congo Knox was comfortable but alert. The entrance to the Mayflower had seen no traffic in nearly two hours. Nor had there been any motion within the lobby that he could see. He could acquire any target emerging from the hotel doors with ease.

A barely perceptible movement of a curtain in the mezzanine level above the entrance caught Knox's attention. He estimated that it had moved less than an inch, remained in that position for three to five seconds, and then slowly moved to its original position.

He could see no one behind the curtain. There wasn't even a shadow. But Knox knew that Garin would be emerging from the entrance within seconds. No one else had reason to peek from behind a mezzanine-level curtain at an empty Connecticut Avenue at two thirty in the morning. Only a person who had reason to think someone was looking for him.

Knox exhaled slowly and relaxed his muscles. The muzzle of his M110 was trained on the center of the entrance. Although he was positioned at a forty-five-degree angle to the Mayflower's door, he had a full view of the entire entry. He would acquire Garin within a fraction of a second. A fraction later Garin would be dead.

Knox could see shadows of movement within the lobby. The shadows of a dead man. It was a matter of moments now. One shot. Another kill. Then off to breakfast.

As Knox's earpiece crackled, he could hear the screeching tires of fast-moving vehicles pierce the quiet of the night. His scope remained focused on the entrance, where the glass door to the left was beginning to open outward. Knox listened to the low voice in his earpiece as he caught the unmistakable profile of Michael Garin appear in the portal, oblivious to Knox's presence atop Washington Square.

Seconds later Knox's earpiece fell silent. Knox pressed his throat mike with his left hand and gently uttered two words: "Roger that."

As Garin walked south on Connecticut, the vague sensation of being in a sniper's sights haunting him once again, three black Ford Explorers sped past him and braked to an abrupt halt in front of the Mayflower's entrance. Four men sprang from each of the SUVs. Six walked rapidly into the hotel while the remainder fanned out around the perimeter of the building. To Knox, they appeared to be former military. He paid them no further attention.

Garin turned left toward the Farragut North Metro station. At the same time, Knox rose to one knee and smoothly and silently gathered his things to leave.

Michael Garin would not die by Congo Knox's hand this day.

CHAPTER FIFTY

The identity of the amphibian who had accompanied Julian Day to dinner at the Mayflower had nagged at Dwyer most of the night. Dwyer couldn't match a name to the face, nor could he recall where he had seen the face before. But there was something about the man, some vague recollection rattling about in Dwyer's mind, that told him that particular face shouldn't be accompanying Day anytime, anyplace.

Now Dwyer had another puzzle on his hands. Earlier, he had dispatched a tactical team to pick up Olivia Perry at the Mayflower. The operation had gone smoothly, although several of the hotel's night staff were frightened by the sudden appearance in the dead of night of half a dozen large, swiftly moving men.

Olivia had given Dwyer the flash drive that Garin had obtained from the Iranians. Dwyer had promptly awakened Matt and Ray, and they drove to a DGT facility just outside of Quantico. While Olivia remained at Dwyer's place under the protection of the tactical team, a group of DGT technicians began analyzing the contents of the flash drive. At the same time, Dwyer ran the photographs of the frog through the DGT facial recognition system.

Dwyer's technicians told him that a full forensics analysis of the flash drive would take a while, but it was clear that the device harbored a worm—an extraordinarily complex one. The FRS, however, returned a match in relatively short order, and when it did, Dwyer immediately remembered where he had seen the frog before: the Russian embassy on Wisconsin Avenue. He was Yevgeny Torzov, an ostensibly innocuous functionary in the Russian diplomatic corps. Only a select few knew he was SVR.

Dwyer pondered the possible reasons why Julian Day, counsel to the chairman of Senate Intelligence, would meet with Yevgeny Torzov. No matter how hard he tried, Dwyer couldn't think of an innocent one.

A rlo led the national security advisor on one of his frequent strolls along the north side of the National Mall. It was not a daily stroll, the demands of the office being such that doing nearly anything on a regular basis was difficult. But Arlo and his master usually could be found somewhere along the path between the Capitol Building and the Lincoln Memorial four or five mornings a week.

The stroll provided Brandt an opportunity—uninterrupted by aides or conference calls—to sharpen his thoughts and shape inchoate theories. The exercise was a substitute for a cigarette habit long since vanquished. Now the only times he smoked were on celebratory or contemplative occasions. Even then, he indulged in a solitary Winston.

At the moment, Brandt's focus was on, of all things, warehouses. Warehouses in Murmansk. Warehouses outside Vladivostok. Warehouses around Ust-Kamchatsk. Cavernous warehouses filled with inventory for which the market was, at best, static: standard generators, cables, transformers, capacitors, routers, distribution boards, circuit breakers, switchboards. Nothing advanced or cutting-edge. And, as Olivia had insisted, Brandt was beginning to sense there was something troubling about that. Something that he couldn't quite put his finger on.

But something connected to the Russian-Iranian–sponsored UN resolution condemning Israel and to Olivia's conversation with Michael Garin, both of which signaled major problems in the offing.

The night before, the UN General Assembly had voted to condemn Israel. Only the United States, Great Britain, Canada, and Australia had voted against it. Germany had abstained. The resolution provided cover for Israel's enemies and within hours the number of skirmishes between the IDF and Hezbollah had increased dramatically. Syrian troops were massing close to the frontier villages near the Golan Heights. Hundreds of rockets were being fired on Israel from southern Lebanon with deadly effect. Although most political pundits contended that full-scale war was unlikely, they were talking out of terminal ignorance. The National Security Council believed the probability of all-out war was greater than at any time since 1982. To lessen the possibility, the Pentagon ordered the US Fifth Fleet, based in Bahrain, to deploy ships to strategic locations throughout the Mediterranean and Persian Gulf.

As troubling as Brandt found these events, they were dwarfed by what Olivia had told him. The information she had gotten from Michael Garin filled in the blanks in her hypothesis regarding Russian-Iranian cooperation on the UN resolution. In short, the latest crisis in the Middle East was about more than Israel. She and Garin believed the United States was also a target. And that nukes were involved.

The problem with the United States–as–an–ultimate–target hypothesis, however, was that all intelligence indicated that Iran didn't yet have the ability to strike the United States with a nuclear weapon. And Brandt knew that the Russians would never do so.

Nonetheless, Olivia maintained that Russia and Iran planned to hit the United States in addition to Israel. And they planned to hit the United States hard. Precisely how they were going to hit the United States, and with what, Olivia didn't say. But the Oracle, strolling in the warming morning air past some of the most recognizable monuments in the world, was in the process of formulating the answer. Before going to the president with it, however, Brandt needed more evidence. And he needed to consult with Olivia, the one person who probably was closer to the answer than he. Telling the commander in chief to prepare for one of the greatest threats to national security since the Cuban missile crisis required more support than the hunch of a man currently sitting atop the FBI's Most Wanted list.

CHAPTER FIFTY-ONE

Four identical black Ford Explorers, tinted windows shielding their occupants from scrutiny, emerged from the underground parking garage at DGT's facility near Quantico and sped single file onto I-95.

When the caravan reached exit 156, the second SUV in line peeled off and disappeared around the end of the ramp. When the vehicle came to Dale Boulevard it engaged in a series of countersurveillance maneuvers, including three U-turns. The SUV last in line did the same after reaching the exit for Prince William Parkway.

The remaining two vehicles proceeded north on I-95 until the one in front, Dan Dwyer riding in its backseat, took the exit toward Route 1. The last vehicle crossed the bridge over the Occoquan River on its way toward the District.

Dwyer's Explorer was driven by Matt, who spent the next several minutes driving circuitously about Lorton, doubling back twice to flush any tails. Satisfied that they weren't being followed, he parked in the rear of the crowded parking lot of a strip mall featuring a large Sport&Health Fitness Club.

Dwyer and Matt sat in the Explorer for nearly ten minutes, waiting patiently as they surveyed the lot. Neither saw Garin approach the vehicle from the left rear until there was an electronic *click* and he opened the door and slid into the rear seat next to Dwyer. Dwyer and Matt broke into broad grins, amazed and amused that Garin had, as he'd so often done in the past, evaded their detection.

For his part, Garin, holding up the remote he'd opened the door with, was, as usual, stone-faced.

"If I were one of the Iranians, both of you would be dead," Garin said, a hint of irritation in his voice.

"Well, Captain Perfect," responded Dwyer, "before passing judgment on the tradecraft of your inferiors, you may want to take a peek at the roof of the Mexican place to your right."

Garin looked out the tinted windows. Barely visible atop the restaurant fifty yards away was the matte-black muzzle of an SR-25 trained on the Explorer. Had Garin been one of the Iranians, he would've been dead before he had touched the door. A faint smile creased Garin's face. He turned back to Dwyer and the two clasped hands enthusiastically.

"That's Ray on overwatch up there," Dwyer said. "You haven't met him. Hired him after you left DGT. He has orders to shoot anyone approaching the vehicle who looks better than a pregnant rhino. Figured you'd be safe."

Garin leaned forward and grasped Matt's outstretched hand. "Good to see you, Matt," Garin said. "How've you survived for so long working with this worthless SOB?"

"He encourages us to drink on duty. Quite liberally," Matt said, his voice deadpan.

"Matt's been walking on air ever since he met the lovely and talented Olivia Perry," Dwyer said. "Unfortunately for Matt, it appears that Ms. Perry's intrigued only by the Great and Powerful Garin."

"I don't know what you're talking about," Garin deflected. "But if you don't mind, there are a few items more pressing than who I'm taking to homecoming."

"No sale," Dwyer said. "It's our understanding you spent a couple of hours alone with the luscious Olivia at the Mayflower. Matt here, along with Ray, Carl, and every man on the tac units I deployed to the hotel last night, would've killed for that opportunity. If it were up to me, you'd have no business going anywhere near her, no way, no how. But since that ship's already sailed, you have a moral obligation—warrior to warrior—to provide us with details about your enchanted evening, pal."

Dwyer wore the mischievous look of a pubescent boy, a look Garin had seen on Dwyer dozens of times in the past. It was usually a mistake to indulge Dwyer, a former SEAL and savvy businessman who nonetheless had the mentality of a college athlete at a strip club. He strenuously resisted separating work from play, regardless of how serious the circumstances.

"You want details? Here are the details," Garin replied. "My team's dead. I've killed more than half a dozen Iranians in the last seventy-two hours. All hell's breaking loose in the Middle East, and none of these things happened in isolation."

Garin's speech sobered the other two occupants of the car. Dwyer shook his head. "Mike Garin. All work and no play . . ."

"Keeps me alive," Garin finished. He inclined his head toward the former SAS man. "Matt, please drive."

As the SUV pulled out of the parking lot, Dwyer's demeanor became more serious. "Mike, you've been in some bad situations before, but this may be one of the worst."

"What do you have for me?" Garin asked.

"That flash drive you gave Olivia contains a very sophisticated worm. We're still working on the codes, but I can tell you, this thing is well beyond the capabilities of the Iranians. Not that they're that bad. In fact, as you know probably better than most, they've got some serious cyber-attack capabilities. But this thing is next, next, next generation."

"Then who engineered it?"

"There are only about a half dozen countries that even conceivably could have done it: Russia, Israel, China, Germany. Maybe the Brits and Japan. That's about it."

"Then it's definitely the Russians," Garin said unequivocally. "What's the worm supposed to do?"

"I think the technical phrase is 'screw with our defense computers.'"

"You mean disable them? Shut them down?"

"No. This thing is a lot more subtle. Kind of like the Stuxnet worm that wreaked havoc on the computers in Iran's nuclear program, another situation with which I believe you have a passing familiarity. Only this one's even more advanced, more like the Snake or Ouroboros used against Ukraine when the Russians invaded Crimea. Apparently, this worm infiltrates a system like missile defense, locates a certain target, and then knocks it just slightly off kilter. Enough to render it essentially useless, but not enough to be detected," Dwyer responded.

"But even slight anomalies would set off alarms," Garin said. "Besides, we have multiple redundancies in our systems to guard against systems failures and data corruption."

Dwyer nodded. "That's the beauty of this thing—if, that is, you're trying to knock out a segment of our defense grid. It has up to seventy-five submodules, giving it the ability to adapt, to evolve. The worm disguises itself, fools our systems into thinking everything's operating okay. The system's been corrupted, but the data appears normal. We don't know anything's wrong until we get hit."

Garin stared out the front windshield, assessing what Dwyer was telling him. "So, say a satellite detects a Topol-M missile launch from the Teikovo missile base in Russia . . ."

"The worm scrambles the data so that our computers show no launch. Or, it might actually show a launch, but that the missile's trajectory is taking it to China as opposed to the actual target—the US. Point is, we have no way of knowing anything's amiss. We believe the data. And we react—or don't react—accordingly."

Garin shook his head slowly. "How much damage can the one flash drive do?"

"Enough," Dwyer replied. "A bad guy inserts it in the USB port of a defense laptop connected to a particular network and the worm crawls toward its targets. It searches for specific lines of code, attaches itself to it, and does its mischief. It keeps expanding, keeps infecting the system. Keep in mind, Mike, my guys tell me it's unlikely the flash drive you gave to Olivia is the only one. Our bet is that several flash drives have been created—each with its own codes. All it takes is for one to be inserted into any laptop that may be a gateway to a DOD network, and it's off to the races."

"I figured as much," Garin said. "Tell me something. Now that we're on notice of a worm, do your guys know whether we can find out which computers have been infected? Aren't there diagnostics that can be performed?"

"The short answer is 'probably,'" Dwyer replied. "We haven't gotten that far. But remember, we don't know which systems have been infected. DOD's huge. Figuring that out would be a colossal undertaking. That takes time. We didn't know the Chinese had hacked OPM for months. How much time do you think we have?"

"Don't know. As usual, probably not enough."

Matt drove back onto I-95 heading south. The traffic was light.

"Why do you think the Russians want to screw up DOD computers?" Dwyer asked.

"I don't really know. In fact, I'm not sure it's DOD computers or only DOD computers that they're attempting to hit. Could also be NSA, Department of Energy, who knows? But I've seen evidence of Iranian interest in our missile defense systems. The Russians are working with the Iranians. So I'd conclude that the Russians have got the Iranians running around trying to sabotage our missile defense systems."

"And trying to kill you, too, Sherlock. Busy Iranians," Dwyer added.

"But I don't understand why the Russians would want to sabotage our missile defense systems. Why do it? What's their interest?"

"I've been asking myself the same thing," Garin said. "The Russians are usually more subtle. And why enlist the aid of the Iranians? Russians have more and better assets by far. They don't need the Iranians to do their dirty work."

"Maybe for plausible deniability," Dwyer offered. "The Russians always liked to use proxies, cutouts, during the Cold War. East Germans. Bulgarians. You know, the KGB themselves rarely, if ever, killed anyone on US soil, at least not Americans. So they may have farmed out this operation to the Iranians this time."

Garin nodded, not in agreement, but in thought. "Regardless of who they're using, we keep coming back to the same question. Why would the Russians want to scramble our computers—missile defense or otherwise—when they wouldn't dare risk attacking us?"

"Well"—Dwyer shrugged—"have you considered that maybe screwing up the computers is, in fact, the end game? Multiple worms could do serious damage—set us back quite a bit. Stuxnet set Iran back two years. The Russian president is known to want to restore Russia to co-equal superpower status. Resurgent Russia, and all that."

"Maybe," Garin said. "But I'm not convinced." Garin switched gears. "What about Laws? Any updates?"

"He was really in bad shape, Mike, but barring any setbacks, the old horndog's going to make it. He'll be in the hospital for quite some time. Then rehabilitation, physical therapy. They say several months, but I bet the chastity of most of the nurses in ICU will be in jeopardy by the end of the week."

Garin's expression didn't change.

Dwyer said, "I thought you'd be pleased with Laws's progression."

"I am."

"You're thinking about how you're going to kill his attackers, aren't you?"

"I am."

The news about Laws did cheer Garin. "Did your men get any more information from him?"

"No," Dwyer replied. "It appears Laws really didn't hear anything beyond what he already told us." Dwyer shifted in his seat, pulled his cell phone from his hip pocket, and searched for the photo he had taken the previous evening at the Mayflower. "Speaking of updates, you might be interested in who your close friend Julian Day is having dinner with."

Dwyer displayed a shot of Day for Garin, who squinted at the image.

"What am I looking at?"

"You'll recognize the gentleman with his back to the camera, head turned slightly to the right, as His Self-Important Majesty, Julian Day, counsel to the Senate Select Committee on Intelligence. His dinner companion facing the camera, though resembling a well-dressed toad, is actually one Yevgeny Torzov, a member in good standing of the Russian diplomatic corps, currently attached to the embassy in Washington."

"SVR?"

"We think so. Maybe FSB."

"Any idea why Day would be meeting with him?"

Dwyer shrugged. "None. But whatever the reason, it's peculiar, don't you think?"

"No argument there," Garin concurred.

"No coincidences in this business."

"That phrase is starting to become the understatement of the decade.

"Why would Day be meeting with Torzov?" Garin asked, more to himself than to Dwyer.

Dwyer examined Garin's face again. "You're thinking about asking him, aren't you? You hardheaded, stupid son of a bitch. Everybody but the third-shift janitor at the FBI is looking for you and you're thinking about going to make a house call on the chief snapping turtle for the

Senate Intelligence Committee, a turtle who, by the way, has hated your guts since before you were born. He hates the very idea of Mike Garin. In his mind, you're the chief locus of evil in the world. You know that? He'd love to nail you to the wall. What the hell could you possibly accomplish?"

"Might frighten him a little."

"Beautiful," Dwyer said, flinging his arms in theatrical exasperation. "World's going to hell and you want to make a detour to scare a one-hundred-fifty-five-pound lawyer. I'll tell you what, that shouldn't be a problem. As much as he hates you, he's even more afraid of you. I'm pretty sure he wets his pants every time he hears your name."

"Good to know." Garin leveled his gaze at Dwyer. "Consider all the plausible reasons why Day would be meeting with Torzov in a very public place. The most plausible is . . ."

"Hiding in plain sight, obviously."

"Right. And you hide in plain sight when you don't want anyone to be suspicious about what your true motives are. He needs to present a façade of innocence because there's something to hide, something that concerns Russia. At just the same time it appears the Russians are trying to crash DOD computers. Now, what are the odds he knows something, something important?"

Dwyer nodded. "About a hundred and ten percent." A pause, then: "How do you plan on playing this?"

"I don't have many options. When in doubt, the direct method is always best."

"Geez, Mikey . . ."

Garin changed the subject. "Were you able to get anything from the Germans on Taras Bor?"

"What am I now, your personal assistant? Can I get you a hand towel? Maybe some mints?" Dwyer protested. "Yeah, as a matter of fact, I received a PDF file on our way here to meet you, but it's pretty dense. Easier for you to view on a big screen. I'll download it when I get back to Quantico and we can make arrangements to get you the information."

"No need to go to all that trouble. I'll just go with you to Quantico."

"Great move. Outstanding move," Dwyer said, rolling his eyes. "Quantico's got two things, Mike. Just two things. Marines and FBI agents. Thousands of them. Nothing else. Not a friggin' thing else. And you want us to drive you right into the middle of it. They catch you, that makes us accessories. Did you think about that?"

"Just hiding in plain sight."

As Dwyer continued to protest, Garin leaned forward. "Matt?"

"On our way," Matt said, grinning. "Just another ten minutes."

CHAPTER FIFTY-TWO

A ri Singer stared out of the twenty-first-floor window of his room in the Pan Pacific Hotel at the giant cruise ship docked in Vancouver Harbour. *This*, he thought, *is tranquility. This is how life is supposed to be. No missiles. No suicide bombers. Just peace. Normality. Sanity.*

Singer had preceded Mansur to Vancouver for reasons far removed from tranquility. At the outset of their relationship, the Iranian had made clear his aversion to communicating by phone or other electronic devices, regardless of how secure such devices purported to be. Mansur insisted that any substantive communication be conducted face-to-face. He would use the phone only to utter prearranged signals—usually consisting of no more than one or two innocuous words—that would alert Singer to a meeting time or place.

Singer didn't object to Mansur's refusal to use phones. The old intelligence operative hadn't remained alive by being reckless. The Iranian wasn't only cunning; he knew his country. The regime monitored everything. It suspected everyone. A single misstep meant not merely prison, but torture and death.

Approximately twenty-four hours ago, Mansur had called Singer and spoken a single, simple word that set off a silent alarm in the Israeli's brain: "Terminal." The signal conveyed two things: the seriousness of the situation and the action to be taken. It meant that Mansur's life—and, therefore, Singer's—was in jeopardy. A lie had unraveled, a cover had been blown, or a body had surfaced.

Both men had to leave Iran immediately. Do not finish your dinner. Do not pack your clothes. Get out on the fastest conveyance you can find.

The preselected destination in which Mansur and Singer were to meet was Vancouver. It was Mansur's choice. He had never been there but he'd seen videos of the city, fallen in love with it, and pronounced it the place where he would spend the rest of his days if he couldn't do so in Iran. Singer thought the selection a bit impetuous and quirky. Perfect for a man who had spent his entire life being deliberate and methodical.

Singer was unsure when Mansur would arrive in Vancouver, but upon his arrival he would get a message to Singer at his hotel. The Israeli turned from the window and poured a cup of tea from the pot delivered by room service a short time ago. He sipped slowly and decided to try to contact his friend in the United States again.

Singer sat at the small desk next to the window, powered on a laptop, and typed in an e-mail address. A few keystrokes later, he hit send. He had sent several other messages in the last two days but had received no replies. That wasn't unusual. The addressee was a busy man. But he was also a conscientious and diligent man. He would reply, eventually. Singer just hoped it would be sooner rather than later.

Matt turned off Jefferson Davis Highway and drove the SUV about a quarter mile along a narrow drive and down the entrance ramp to the underground parking facility of DGT's Quantico facility—a black, two-story, glass, steel, and granite building situated on fifteen wooded acres a short distance south of the Marine base. At the bottom of the ramp, two guards in black uniforms and body armor, MP5s slung across their chests, stood adjacent to a steel lift gate that spanned a tire shredder beneath. The guards knew the SUV on sight but raised their weapons to their shoulders, tracking the vehicle as it descended the ramp.

Matt brought the SUV to a halt in front of the lift gate as a third guard, carrying an inspection mirror and accompanied by an all-black Belgian shepherd, emerged from a kiosk next to the lift gate and inspected the perimeter of the vehicle as well as its chassis. Matt lowered all four of the SUV's opaque windows and the guards peered inside. The guard at the driver's-side door nodded in acknowledgment toward Matt and Dwyer. Turning his gaze to the man seated next to Dwyer, the guard's jaw slackened slightly in recognition.

"Is everything okay, Mr. Dwyer?"

"This is Mr. Webster from DOD, Gary. He's here to consult on a matter with GSG-9," Dwyer replied, nodding toward Garin. "Is that understood?"

The guard dutifully pulled a smartphone from his breast pocket and scrolled through a list of individuals authorized to enter the facility for the day.

"Mr. Dwyer," the guard responded skeptically, "I don't have any appointments scheduled for a Mr. Webster today."

Dwyer sensed Gary's indecision. He had a job to perform. His boss had just authorized admission of the most wanted man in America, who, according to company lore, also happened to be one of the trio of special warriors who had founded DGT. "This is unscheduled, Gary. I'm personally authorizing Mr. Webster." Dwyer pulled a Browning .45 from a shoulder holster and placed it next to Garin's temple, a theatrical but convincing demonstration that neither Dwyer nor Matt was under duress. Garin didn't blink. "And you will list Mr. Webster's name on today's visitors' log." Dwyer replaced the weapon. "Understood?"

Gary, unsure whether his boss was testing him and his fellow guards, hesitated. The wrong decision could mean his job. Or, if it wasn't a test, his life.

"Okay," Dwyer sighed, yielding to the evident distress that showed on the guard's face. "Let's go by the book, Gary."

Dwyer and Matt opened their doors and exited the SUV, hands raised. The guard on the passenger side opened the rear door and Garin emerged. The effect among the guards was electric.

All three passengers placed their hands against the SUV and subjected themselves to pat-downs, after which Dwyer turned toward his employees. "All right, very good. That," Dwyer said, pointing to Garin, "is Mr. Webster. Got it?"

The guards nodded in unison. Whatever was going on, they understood they were to keep their mouths shut.

Gary punched a large red button on the side of the kiosk, raising the lift gate and retracting the floor spikes. Garin, Dwyer, and Matt returned to the vehicle. Before Garin shut his door, the guard closest to him lowered his weapon and addressed Garin.

"Mr. Webster?"

Garin looked toward the guard.

"Hooyah, Mr. Webster."

Matt drove down three levels to a series of parking spaces marked RESERVED FOR CEO-DGT.

"Those guards back there were hired about two months ago along with about two dozen others. Good men. We're getting lots of applicants from the teams. Some Delta as well, including a few players you might know," Dwyer said.

Garin turned his head, curious. "I'd have thought that with the drawdown in Afghanistan you'd be laying off, not hiring."

"No, business is actually on the uptick. Always a supply of bad guys that need taking down. ISIS, Boko Haram. But we're doing a lot of civilian contracting now—about sixty to sixty-five percent of our gross revenue. We secured several major maritime security contracts, protecting cargo vessels against piracy off the East African and Southeast Asian coasts. We're also providing security for oil companies in places like southern Iraq and South America. Very lucrative. Manpower intensive."

"Impressive. Maybe I cashed out too early."

"I tried to tell you that, but you wouldn't listen," Dwyer chastised lightly. "But, hey, you still did pretty well for yourself."

"Well, sounds like you're staying ahead of the curve."

"It may be hard for you to accept, genius," Dwyer replied, pointing to his head, "but I also have a brain cell or two rattling around up here."

"And a flair for the ridiculously dramatic. Black uniforms. Matching black guard dog. You waiting for a call from Hollywood?"

Matt pulled into the parking space.

"We continue to do our bread-and-butter work," Dwyer informed him. "Still augmenting Diplomatic Security, providing overwatch for high-threat meetings. And we're also doing a fair amount of training for law enforcement, especially SWAT teams for midsize cities like Richmond, Newark, Akron, Pittsburgh, as well as security for major airports. We've hired nearly a hundred people since the beginning of last month alone."

The trio exited the vehicle and proceeded toward the adjacent door to an elevator that opened directly into Dwyer's private office. Dotting the ceiling of the garage at regular intervals was a series of surveillance cameras. Dwyer placed his palm on a biometric pad next to the elevator door and it slid open. The three rode silently to Dwyer's office four floors above.

Dwyer's corner office fit the man: expansive, untidy, but purposeful. Floor-to-ceiling windows stretched across two sides of the office, providing a pleasant view of a creek and woodlands beyond the well-kept lawn of the DGT campus. To the left of the elevator sat a four-by-seven glass-topped desk facing a seventy-two-inch television monitor embedded in the wall. A leather couch sat below the monitor, and Navy football memorabilia and photos were scattered across a long, low credenza in front of the couch. The door to the rest of the DGT facility was on the other side of the office, where dozens of technicians and analysts of DGT's cybersecurity division were hard at work.

Dwyer sat at his desk and began typing on the computer keyboard. He opened a folder marked HEINRICH that contained information on Taras Bor obtained from Dwyer's German contacts and then stood, yielding the chair to Garin.

"This is everything I've got from our German friends on Bor," Dwyer said as Garin sat before the monitor. "Goes back about ten years. Lots of gaps, as might be expected. Also, lots of speculation. What's there, though, says this guy's a very serious player. The go-to asset for President Yuri Mikhailov. Here, I'll throw it up on the big screen."

Dwyer leaned forward and manipulated the mouse. Scanned pages of a German intelligence file appeared on the seventy-two-inch screen. Matt whistled.

"Gent really racks up the frequent-flier miles."

"He ever cashes them in, Aeroflot goes out of business," Dwyer agreed.

Displayed on the screen was the first of a partially redacted, multipage list of dates and locations with brief descriptions of events in which Taras Bor was suspected by the Germans of being involved. The events spanned several continents and multiple countries. The first page listed operations in Hamburg, Berlin, Lyon, London, Cairo, Benghazi, Tehran, Grozny, and Lahore.

Garin clicked to the next page. Rome, Belgrade, Damascus, Mogadishu, Brussels, Managua. Bor's suspected activities ranged from assassinations to fomenting and suppressing local uprisings.

"Obviously, he couldn't have done everything the Germans suspect him of," Garin observed. "But the list's still pretty impressive. Of course, I won't ask how in the world your contact could transmit this to you."

Dwyer nodded. "Don't ask, don't tell. The Germans are thorough.

They don't miss much. Don't you just wonder what kind of list they have on you, Mikey?" Dwyer needled.

"Not quite as exotic as this."

"Yeah, sure. I bet." Dwyer manipulated the mouse again, scrolling several pages down. "Here, look at this. Bring back any memories?"

Garin read the entry, translating the German out loud:

September 3, 2005. Baghdad, Iraq. Subject suspected of training, coordinating and directing insurgents in ambush attack on military convoy escorting US State Department personnel from Baghdad Green Zone to Mosul. Three United States Army Rangers killed, nine wounded. Credit taken by al-Qaeda in Mesopotamia.

The sentence was followed by redactions of the names of several Iraqi informants, as well as a redacted name followed by the legend "MI6."

"Remember that? Fun times," Dwyer said drily.

Garin nodded. "One of our first DGT assignments. Rangers were supposed to escort the State Department staffers to Mosul and hand them off to us. Should have been a straightforward security gig while they were in the city. They're late, we get a call—all hell's broken loose. We jump in the Humvees and hump down the road. When we get there, it looks like Little Bighorn."

"Except with AK-47s and RPGs."

"We lost Bobby Scales that day. I had to inform his fiancée. Not what I'd imagined when we started this outfit."

"We're damn lucky we didn't lose more. We nearly closed shop after that."

"The Russians were behind that?" Garin asked. "Bor? I thought they were staying on the sidelines, just rooting for us to lose. Hell of a risk for them to take if their involvement became known."

"Well, the Germans seem to think they had a hand. Look there,"

Dwyer said, pointing at an excerpt from the transcript of a prisoner interrogation. Although Bor's name appeared nowhere, numerous references were made to a Russian who the Germans, piecing together information, concluded was Bor.

"Looks like hard-core jihadists don't mind being manipulated by infidels like Bor as long as it helps to kill other infidels, especially those loyal to the Great Satan," Garin said.

"Not exactly unprecedented. First they use the help of the Great Satan against the Soviets in Afghanistan. Now they work with former Soviets *against* the Great Satan." Dwyer scrolled down again. "Something I can't figure out, though . . ."

"Interesting. The entries stopped cold two and a half years ago," Garin said, looking at the monitor. "Zero. Nothing. He's on speed up until that point, but then falls off the face of the earth." Garin's eyes narrowed and he turned to Dwyer. "You thinking what I'm thinking?"

"Olivia Perry's got a smokin' body?"

Matt raised his hand. "Yo. Amen over here."

Garin cast his eyes toward the ceiling and paused for the frat boys to air-five.

"Bor's either dead, discharged . . ."

"Or setting up his next operation," Dwyer finished, becoming serious again. "And probably a big one. There's hardly more than a few weeks' break between any of his previous operations; then suddenly he's silent for almost three years."

"A big op. Complex. Maybe deep cover," Garin agreed. "Anyone ever put eyes on this guy?"

"Let's look behind door number two," Dwyer said, clicking on another file. "GSG-9 takes more photos than a busload of German tourists."

A series of about two dozen photos appeared on the monitor. It was apparent that most had been taken from an appreciable distance. In most of the photos, it was unclear exactly who or what the intended subject had been—indicating that Bor hadn't been the original target;

German intelligence had simply collected any photos containing any-one resembling Bor's alleged description and placed them in the file.

Garin began scouring the photos. When he got two-thirds down the screen he stopped, one of the grainy images appearing indefinably familiar. He took the mouse from Dwyer, placed the caret over the photo, and clicked to enlarge. The enlarged results didn't reveal much more than the original. He zoomed in on the man suspected to be Bor and clicked to enlarge further, causing the image to devolve into a blur of indecipherable pixels.

"Even our facial recognition program is useless without a known photo of Bor to compare against," Dwyer said. "Here, try this." Dwyer reclaimed the mouse from Garin and with a series of clicks sharpened the resolution of the enlarged image. As he did so he could see a look of recognition register across Garin's face, its color draining in the process.

The room fell silent for several seconds. "How the hell did he do it?" Garin asked, his voice barely a whisper.

"Do what, Mikey?"

Garin, ignoring Dwyer, continued to scrutinize the image. It was still blurry in spots, but the telltale was clear: a J-shaped scar along the right jawline terminating in front of the earlobe. A scar Garin had seen on a curious onlooker standing behind a police barricade on Fourteenth Street. A scar he had seen during scores of operations and training exercises over the last two and a half years.

"Mike." It was Dwyer again. "You know this guy?"

Garin didn't reply. His mind was trying to process the logistics, the feasibility. The background checks, verifications, fail-safes, and coun-termeasures compromised and breached. An audacious penetration of the most rigorous security protocols in the world.

Dwyer glanced at Matt, who shrugged his shoulders, then back at Garin, and finally to the monitor. He squinted at the image and tried to see what Garin saw. He scanned his memory for faces, playing them before his mind's eye. Suddenly, a look—not so much of recognition but of realization—covered his face. The realization of a seeming impossibility becoming reality. A supposedly dead man whose return to life signaled an unimaginable breach of national security that could place the country in peril. "My God. We're looking at Gates, aren't we? Gates is Bor. Right?"

Matt whistled again. "Un-freaking-believable."

"We have a file photo of Gates. Should we run it through facial recognition against this photo to be sure?" Dwyer asked. "The photo angles and lighting may be different, but the algorithm should give us a pretty good probability—"

"No need." Garin shook his head, pointing to the photo. "See that scar? Unmistakable." Garin stood and, staring down at the floor, tried to comprehend how Bor had penetrated a team whose very existence was known only to a handful of individuals in the US government. He ran a hand through his hair and rubbed the back of his neck.

Dwyer gave voice to what everyone was now thinking. "How the hell is that even possible? How could he gain access to your team?"

Garin spoke slowly, thinking out loud. "I met Gates . . . Bor . . . more than two years ago when he qualified for the team. Backstory was that he was a good ole boy from Georgia, former Air Force Pararescue, and had also spent time in SAD. He passed every background check—FBI, DOD, CIA. He passed every evolution. He was an exceptional operator. Maybe the best on the team." Garin shook his head again.

"This is real Cold War shit," Dwyer declared. "Sleeper agents. Deep penetration. This is more impressive than Aldrich Ames, Robert Philip Hanssen. They didn't have to air-drop those two into one of our units. They were ours. Already there." Dwyer squinted at the monitor. "I thought that stuff ended a while ago. Turns out the closest Gates probably ever got to Georgia was the former Soviet republic." He looked at Garin. "Did you have *any* clue whatsoever?"

"None. At least none that I can think of right now. As I look back, he played it just right. Nothing amiss. Fit right in. Duty, honor, country—but not mindlessly gung ho. A tough, smart, dedicated soldier. Apparently a lot smarter than the rest of us." Garin looked up. "Certainly smarter than me. And now, all my men are dead because of it."

"No sense beating yourself up, Mikey. You're an operator, not a spook. The guy got vetted by the best in the business. That wasn't your job." Dwyer continued staring at the image on the monitor. "If he could somehow craft a résumé that includes Air Force PJ and the Special Activities Division without tripping any wires, no way would you be able to make him."

Garin wasn't persuaded. "They were *my* teams. We drank, hunted, and chewed dirt together. Gates and I weren't particularly close, but if my family were in trouble, there wouldn't be anyone I'd trust more to get them out of a jam. I liked the guy. Tanski even said in some ways, Gates and I were alike."

Dwyer scrutinized one of the images at the bottom of the screen. He clicked to enlarge and then brought up the resolution. "Geez, Mikey, take a look at this."

Garin saw Bor huddled in conversation with a shorter man. The photo appeared to have been taken in the winter. Both men wore heavy coats and scarves. The shorter man resembled a bullfrog.

"That," Dwyer informed him, pointing at the shorter man in the photo, "is Yevgeny Torzov, Julian Day's dinner date at the Mayflower last night."

Matt stood from the couch, sensing that Garin was also about to move. "Now what?"

"Gates . . . Bor is at the center of everything that's going on. I need to let Olivia know. She needs to let Brandt know. The Russians are driving everything. The Iranians may think this is all about them, but they're just tools, puppets doing the Russians' bidding." Garin paused, formulating a plan.

"What else?" Dwyer asked.

"Dan, I need one of your vehicles. And I need to check an e-mail account."

"Then what?" Dwyer asked, suspecting the answer but seeking confirmation.

He received no reply. Only a look he'd seen several times on his friend's face before: Mayhem was about to ensue.

CHAPTER FIFTY-THREE

Ari Singer finished his tea and checked his watch. He was to meet Mansur in ten minutes in the middle of Chinatown. While waiting for Mansur, Singer had also tried unsuccessfully to reach his contact in the United States. In the past, he and Singer had exchanged several useful pieces of data. Singer hoped the Americans might be able to provide contextual information, something to confirm Mansur's. Unable to reach the American, Singer had placed a series of messages in a draft folder in a shared e-mail account.

Singer's waitress appeared at his table with a carafe of tea. "Anything else, sir?"

Singer smiled charmingly. "Thank you. No."

She returned the smile, placed the check on the table, and left. Singer checked his watch again. It was time to meet Mansur. The location was just a short walk away.

Singer paid the bill and left the café. The light drizzle on his face felt good—warm, but refreshing. He walked briskly down East Pender Street. Mansur would meet him in a short alley between two restaurants four blocks south and two blocks east of the café. An alleyway in Vancouver. The old SAVAK agent was wedded to cloak-and-dagger.

Singer turned east. He could see the entrance to the alleyway ahead just past a small Thai restaurant. There were no pedestrians on the street and traffic was sparse.

Upon reaching the alley, Singer kept walking with his eyes forward. He continued for another block before dropping to one knee, pretending to tie his shoes. No one was following. In fact, there wasn't another person anywhere in the vicinity.

He rose and doubled back. A few seconds later he was back at the entrance to the alley. It was a block long with a large Dumpster piled high with plastic trash bags at the midway point, near the rear service entrance of the Thai restaurant. Nothing else but brick and asphalt was in the alley. Mansur, nowhere to be seen, was probably on the other side of the Dumpster or perhaps hadn't arrived yet.

Singer glanced about before cautiously entering the alley. As he approached the Dumpster he realized Mansur was already there. At least his body was, sandwiched among the trash bags in the Dumpster.

Singer's training and instincts told him to leave. Immediately. With his hand on his weapon and his senses on a trip wire. But years of experience told him that he needed to stay, to inspect the body. This time the stakes were too high to let any information, however minor, go unretrieved.

So, in the last minutes of his life, Ari Singer climbed atop a stinking pile of refuse and rifled through the clothing of a man he considered a friend and patriot. What he found scrambled everything he and his superiors had believed about the threat to Israel's existence.

Singer had found a thin scrap of hotel stationery bearing nine words—some English, some Hebrew—taped to the inside cuff of Mansur's left pants leg. The instant he absorbed the message, Singer knew it was vital that it be relayed to Tel Aviv immediately. This one was different from all the other "urgent" messages he'd transmitted over the years. In barely more than twelve hours, the world would change.

He called his superiors, but the call dropped before connecting. He tried twice more and failed to get through.

His anxiety building, he decided to reach outside his own agency, an act that in ordinary circumstances could be career ending, or worse. At the moment, Singer didn't have the luxury of patience or protocol.

He keyed the number for Mike Garin, with whom he'd worked several times before, just as a cab approached and slowed to pick him up. Singer cursed as the call automatically went to voice mail. Opening the rear door of the cab, he paused and then rapidly began to leave a message. As he climbed into the vehicle, the last thing the synapses in Ari Singer's brain registered was the horrified look on the driver's face just before the top of the old spy's skull exploded across the length of the dark brown upholstery of the backseat.

Matt stood next to Dwyer's desk and watched the confrontation, having no intention of getting between two forces of nature. Dwyer stood in front of the door of his office, blocking Garin's egress. Garin stood barely two feet away from Dwyer.

"I don't have to tell you that this is a spectacularly bad idea, Mikey. Spectacularly bad." Dwyer turned to Matt. "Tell him. Tell him this is a bad idea."

The Aussie raised his palms, indicating he wanted no part of the argument that had been going on since Garin had used Dwyer's desktop to access an e-mail account shared by Garin and an Israeli agent and had then retrieved a voice-mail message from the same agent. The normally imperturbable Garin, seated at Dwyer's desk, had shot to his feet, declaring that he needed to contact James Brandt and interrogate Julian Day immediately.

"Move aside, Dan." Garin's voice was even, but his body's attitude bore the menace of a cobra. Dwyer, for his part, was unmoved.

"Mike, I'll make the call. Hell, *you* make the call. But don't go into the District," Dwyer implored.

"I'm going to need you to move aside now, Dan." It was not a request.

"What are you going to do? Go to Day's office at Hart Senate? They'll have you handcuffed before you even get to the metal detectors. Any headway Brandt may have made persuading the authorities that you're not public enemy number one will be gone."

"Last time, Dan."

Dwyer looked to Matt standing next to the desk and nodded.

Matt slid his right hand under the right side of the desktop and pressed a panic button. An earsplitting klaxon sounded. The television monitors flickered, went blank for a moment, and then displayed a grid of six images of guards in the process of securing different sections of the DGT facility. The image in the upper left showed the cybersecurity division's area immediately outside of Dwyer's office. Four guards, MP5s trained on the office door, were stationed behind cabinets and desks within a radius of twenty feet.

Dwyer nodded toward the monitor. "Take a good look, Mike. Even you couldn't make it out of here. Stand down and listen to reason."

Garin glanced at the monitor as a voice came over a speaker set in the office ceiling. "Mr. Dwyer. Situation."

Dwyer looked at Garin. "What should I tell them, Mike?"

Garin hesitated for a moment, coolly scanning the images on the monitor to confirm that any attempt to exit the building would result in significant casualties. Several guards were deployed at every exit. These weren't rent-a-cop security guards, but DGT personnel—all of whom were former military. Garin looked at Dwyer and gave a barely perceptible nod. Matt, who had not dared escalate matters by reaching for the Glock under his shirt, exhaled audibly.

"Situation is Blue Zero," Dwyer responded to the voice on the speaker.

"Say again."

"Blue Zero."

"Copy. Blue Zero. Thank you, sir. Could you please open your door?"

Dwyer opened the office door, permitting the guards to peer inside. Dwyer detected a look of recognition on one of the guards as he spotted Garin.

"Just giving Mr. Webster here a demonstration," Dwyer said as he gestured toward Garin. "Make sure you put that in your reports. Tell everybody they did a good job."

"Yes, sir, Mr. Dwyer." The guards retreated. Dwyer closed the door and turned to Garin.

"Okay. I'm back on your shit list for maybe the seventeenth time. And woe to anyone on that list. But now let's talk about your wanting to rush off and commit suicide by going to see Day at his office."

There were several moments of silence as Garin considered his response. Dwyer, despite his perpetual spring break demeanor, was able to assess the benefits and detriments of a course of action as well as anyone Garin had ever met. He sat on the edge of Dwyer's desk and spoke calmly, as if the pandemonium of the last few minutes hadn't occurred.

"Dan, hear me out. The Russians are working with the Iranians on a UN resolution that likely will lead to war between Israel and several of its neighbors. Bor infiltrated my WMD team and, with the help of the Iranians, killed everyone but me. Then I get a flurry of messages from an Israeli agent whom I've trusted for years asking me to contact him ASAP. A short time ago he leaves me a voice mail that says—ready for this? The US is going to be the target of an EMP strike. You know what that means. Armageddon. And Singer is as reliable as they get. If he says an EMP attack's coming, it means he's worked this to death, eliminating possibilities. But the voice mail is cut off. My bet is Quds Force got to him. So I don't know *where* the strike's coming from, *when* it's coming, or *how* it's going to happen.

"Now, we know the Iranians don't have the capability of hitting us with an EMP strike. Even if they attempted to do so from a cargo ship or other vessel along our coast, we have countermeasures in place to thwart them. Besides, an EMP launch from a cargo ship wouldn't get sufficient amplitude, so it would only affect a relatively small area. The Russians, on the other hand, could do it, but they're not nuts."

Dwyer made a rolling motion with his hand, urging Garin to move it along.

"So we've got Iranians who want to hit us but can't, running around with Russians who wouldn't dare hit us, and a Mossad agent saying we're going to be hit."

"And Bor, the guy in the middle of it all, is in a picture with a Russian SVR agent who just happens to be dining with Julian Day," Dwyer finished.

"And that, my dear friend, is why I need to see Day."

Dwyer understood immediately that Garin was right. If Day had any information about a possible EMP strike, it wasn't going to be pried out over the phone. A personal visit from Mike Garin, however, was another matter entirely.

"I'll concede the point," Dwyer acknowledged. "But let me play devil's advocate for a second. Why not just tell Brandt about Day? He can then tell the FBI and *they* can interrogate Day." As soon as the question left his mouth, Dwyer knew Garin's response—because Olivia Perry had provided a similar one just yesterday.

"Even if Brandt did go to the FBI, what's he supposed to say? 'Hey, you know that guy Garin the entire bureau's been looking for? The threat to national security? Well, I thought you should know he told me the counsel to the Senate Select Committee on Intelligence has been consorting with the Russians. Something about starting a world war.'"

Dwyer sighed. "Well, what are you waiting for, Mikey? Go get 'em. Time's a-wastin', man."

"Really? That fast? After hitting that buzzer and siccing half of the former special ops community on me, you've seen the light that quickly?"

"You knew I would all along, you stinking sack of shit," Dwyer growled. "That's why you backed down so fast when my guards showed up. You knew I'd agree with you." He pointed to himself and Matt. "Now, what do you need us to do?"

Garin turned to the former SAS man. "Matt, keys to the SUV?"

Matt dug into his pocket and tossed the keys to Garin.

"Why don't I have one of our helos take you instead?" Dwyer asked. "Save some time."

"No. Too much attention. Besides, where I'm going, there's no good place to land. Don't worry. If I get stopped, I'll say I stole your vehicle so you won't get into trouble."

"That ship's sailed, buddy. They're bound to find out eventually that we've been helping you. Just make sure you succeed. That's our only ticket out of this mess," Dwyer said. "What else do you need?"

"How do I reach Olivia?"

"Wherever she is, a half dozen of my men are close by. If she's not in her office at the Old Executive Office Building, she's at my place."

"I need to use secure comms to talk to her right away."

"I can only guarantee a secure line if she's at my place," Dwyer said.

"It'll have to do."

"You can use the phone on the desk. You know the number."

"One last thing," Garin added.

"What's that?"

Garin cast a bemused look at his old friend. "Blue Zero? Seriously?"

CHAPTER FIFTY-FOUR

The summer heat and humidity of Washington, D.C., weren't as oppressive as the residents made them out to be, thought Taras Bor.
Still, a nation as great as the United States could've selected a more
temperate location for its capital city. No matter. His assignment was
drawing to a close and he would be gone soon.

Nearly everything was in place. There were just a couple of loose
ends to take care of, and he was on his way to taking care of them, the
Beltway traffic being his only real impediment.

It seemed the only loose end Bor wouldn't be able to eliminate was
Michael Garin. From the very outset, Bor suspected that might be the
case. He knew Garin to be smart and tough. Over the last few days he
had also proved resilient.

It had been a mistake to delegate Garin's elimination to the Iranians. But that had been Moscow's call. The Iranians took offense at any
slights, real or imagined, no matter how small. Giving them the task
of taking out Garin was designed to keep them happy. Bad move. They
were horribly overmatched.

Fortunately, the Iranians' failure proved unimportant. It hadn't
been necessary to kill Garin. He was on the run, discredited. Even

if he had seen anything of consequence in that tunnel in Pakistan, no one would believe him now. Besides, Bor had bought himself an insurance policy against Garin. Something to freeze him in place should he get too close. He wouldn't be a problem. He would be no problem at all.

CHAPTER FIFTY-FIVE

MOUNT VERNON, VIRGINIA

JULY 17 • 1:48 P.M. EDT

Olivia Perry expected the call from Garin to come through any second. A few minutes earlier, Carl had informed her that Garin would be contacting her. Carl then guided her to a room in the basement of Dwyer's mansion that appeared to be a replica of Houston Control. She was seated in the captain's chair in the center of the room, Carl standing a few feet to her left, when there was a buzzing sound. He pointed to the console in the right armrest. She pressed the flashing button and heard Garin's voice.

"Carl and the boys taking good care of you?"

"Couldn't be better," Olivia replied. It troubled her to admit that she enjoyed hearing his voice.

"I'll get right to it. We have a serious problem. I need you to relay what I'm about to tell you to James Brandt. Immediately."

"That may be a problem, Michael. As we speak he's on his way to the White House. I'm not sure how long he'll be there. All I know is that he'll be in the Situation Room and I'm supposed to meet him in the OEOB afterward to debrief. So I'm unlikely to be able to reach him for a while," Olivia said.

"What's going on?"

Olivia detected the concern in Garin's voice. "I'm not authorized to reveal the details. Let's just say that I wouldn't be surprised if recent activities of the Russians are discussed."

"Olivia," Garin said, urgency now in his voice. "I understand your constraints and don't want to put you in a tough spot, but we have an extraordinary situation here. This call is secure. The meeting in the Situation Room may have direct bearing on what I need you to relay to Brandt."

"Michael, I'm sorry. I very much want to tell you. But you know the drill. I can't say anything."

Garin sensed Olivia's distress. There was no time to argue the point. Brandt needed to know about the EMP strike right now.

"Okay. Olivia, you *must* communicate what I'm about to tell you to Brandt as soon as we get off the call. I don't care if he's in the Situation Room, laundry room, or the men's room. You get a message to him no matter what it takes."

"Go ahead. I might be able to reach him before he enters the room."

"First, there may be a worm in certain DOD computers that causes them to give false reads. Tell Brandt we should probably focus on satellite feeds, radar, missile trajectories, and missile launches. Bottom line: We should be concerned about our ability to detect incoming missiles."

Olivia motioned to Carl to get her some writing materials. He retrieved a pen and pad of paper from a drawer under a bank of monitors and handed them to Olivia, who began taking notes.

"Second," Garin continued, "my unit was penetrated by a Russian agent by the name of Taras Bor. He was behind the killings. Remember my theory that the elimination of my team might somehow be related to what I saw on the laptop in that tunnel in Pakistan? The missile defense, EMP guys? Well, that brings me to point three."

Olivia was taking notes rapidly, recording Garin's statements almost verbatim. "Keep going, Michael."

"An Israeli agent whom I've known for years left me a voice mail a short time ago stating that the US is going to be the target of an EMP strike."

Garin heard a quick, pronounced intake of breath on the other end of the call.

"How reliable is this information, Michael?"

"As reliable as any intelligence can be. Nothing's ever concrete. I know you don't want to go to the national security advisor with this kind of information on a hunch. But the Israeli agent is extremely good—given to understatement, not hyperbole. In fact, tell Brandt that the agent is Ari Singer. Mossad will vouch for how reliable he is—maybe was."

"When is this going to happen and who's behind it?"

"Don't know when. We have no choice but to assume it's imminent. It very well may not be, but we can't take the chance. As to who's behind it, that's the mystery. You know the litany: The Iranians may want to, but can't, and the Russians—"

"I know, I know."

"Both of their fingerprints are all over this. I guess we can't rule out anyone who's got the capability—North Korea, maybe even a terrorist group."

Olivia struggled to resist telling Garin that what prompted the meeting in the Situation Room was the detection of a phalanx of Russian nuclear submarines arrayed along the Eastern Seaboard. Garin was right, however, that the Russians wouldn't strike the United States.

"What else should I tell Jim?" Olivia asked.

"Make sure someone gets security around Manchester, Bauer, and Dellinger. If the US is going to be hit by an EMP attack, the top experts on it may be subject to an assassination attempt. The president needs to know this. Get in touch with Brandt."

"Michael, I just heard Dellinger's dead. Heart attack. FBI suspects it was induced somehow."

"*Go.*" Garin terminated the call.

Olivia disconnected and punched in the number for the White House.

CHAPTER FIFTY-SIX

The house was more modest than the assassin had expected. Well maintained, elegant, but relatively small. Much like the man inside.

Bor parked his SUV several doors down, next to a small playground featuring the kind of recreational equipment favored by conscientious, graduate-degreed parents. Padded, rubberized, and, consequently, rarely used by children.

He glided toward the rear of the house and to the side of the back door. Looking through the door's small, dual-paned window, he saw the back of Julian Day's perfectly coiffed head as he sat drinking coffee at a small wooden table.

Bor tested the doorknob. Unlocked. He turned it, quietly pushed the door inward, and stood behind the counsel to the Senate Select Committee on Intelligence.

"Get up, Mr. Day."

To Bor's mild surprise, Day wasn't at all startled. He casually slid his chair back from the table, rose, and turned toward the assassin.

"Hello, Bor. Where are you taking me? A rendezvous with Quds Force, perhaps?"

The look on Bor's face was a mixture of amusement and curiosity. "You were expecting me?"

"Your ilk rarely disappoints. Insufferably predictable."

"My ilk?"

"I've spent nearly two decades dealing with men like you, Bor. The American version, but the same. Regimented. Programmed. You get an order, you execute. No hesitation. No thinking."

"And you know I've received an order?"

Day looked closely at Bor's eyes. Wolf's eyes. "I knew I'd become a liability once all of the preconditions were met, obstacles removed. We're only hours away. I'm of no further use. So you must've received an order."

Bor nodded. "Very good, Mr. Day. A taut analysis. Now it's time for us to go. Time for me to 'execute.'"

"Yes. Time to execute, all right." Day turned his head over his left shoulder. "Gentlemen?"

Three men, each with suppressed handguns trained on Bor, emerged from the adjacent dining room. Bor's surprise was more than mild. He'd never been outmaneuvered before.

Bor raised his arms away from his sides and opened his hands to show he had no weapon.

"He will be carrying a gun, of course," Day said. "Get it."

One of the three men approached and began patting Bor from under his arms down to his waist. The man retrieved a SIG Sauer P226 from Bor's waistband and continued patting him down to his ankles. The man then rose, stepped back a few paces, and shook his head to Day, signaling the Russian carried nothing more.

"Say hello to Al, Tom, and Rick, Bor. Detectives, D.C. Metro," Day said.

Bor looked at each in turn. "Al. Tom. Rick."

Day said, "Al, Tom, Rick, meet John Gates, a.k.a. Taras Bor, the Terror of Tbilisi, the Butcher of Grozny. A one-man blitzkrieg. He's killed more people than . . . well, we don't know how many. But rest assured, it's a lot. Got an early start—what were you—seventeen, eighteen? Somehow aces every qualification test, mental and physical, known to man—or at least the Russians. Became a Spetsnaz *podpolkovnik*, that's lieutenant colonel in Russian special forces. Manages to embed himself in probably the most elite unit in the US armed forces. And kills them all. Beg your pardon. I think he may have let Quds Force kill one or two. No, wait. What am I saying? You don't trust the Iranians' competency, do you, Bor? You probably ended up doing all the killing yourself. Am I right?

"Take a moment to consider that, gentlemen. One man—*one*—wipes out a unit of not just special operators, but *super* operators." Day stared tauntingly at Bor. "Except Michael Garin. I assume Garin's assassination, along with Clint Laws's, was subcontracted to the Iranians? Big mistake, Bor. Big. That's going to be a problem."

Bor shrugged. "It wasn't my call. But it's not a problem. I've made certain preparations in case Garin surfaces. But you, my friend, have a very big problem: What do you do with me?"

"You're not a problem. You're a solution."

"A rather optimistic assessment of the situation, to put it mildly."

"I'm turning you over to the FBI. Telling them everything."

"If you do that, at best you're going to prison for life," Bor said. "Possibly be executed for treason."

"Wrong. I'll be a hero. Celebrated, rewarded. There's no paper trail whatsoever. No e-mails. Nothing. Nothing connecting me to you, or those madcap Iranians of yours."

"There's me, Mr. Day. I know everything."

Day laughed loudly. "For someone who kills for a living, you're spectacularly naïve. I'm counsel to Senate Intelligence. Everyone knows me—senators, intelligence officials, FBI. Vetted a million times over. Trusted with the nation's most sensitive information. Respected. You, on the other hand, are a slimy Russian thug who slaughtered several of America's finest patriots. You're plotting to do grievous harm to

US interests, just like you sneaky Russkies have been trying to do for more than half a century. And as the intrepid counsel to Senate Intelligence, I've been able to piece together your plan, having doggedly investigated all of the compromised JSOC operations over the last two years." Day snorted. "You think I haven't been preparing for this?" Day shook his head. "You're fried, Bor. Done."

"Very good. But you still have a big problem. The FBI will be very interested to know how you came to establish a seven-figure bank account in Saint Lucia. Most difficult on a public servant's salary."

"Wrong again. The FBI will never find out."

Bor shook his head. "I say, again, you have a very big problem. Three, actually. The FBI will never find out *only* if your three friends here don't tell them. And now that they've just learned of your seven-figure account, I'm sure they'll want what's in it. Otherwise, they'll go to the FBI. And then, once they've got your money, who's to say they *still* won't go to the FBI? Now it's not just a slimy Russian thug's word against that of the counsel to Senate Intelligence, but the word of three of D.C. Metro's finest. Very bad, Mr. Day."

"Did you happen to notice that Al, Tom, and Rick are out of their jurisdiction? That's because they're working for me. I've had them with me for days in anticipation of your making a move on me. They already know about the seven-figure account, Bor. They're getting paid—fairly generously—from that very account."

Day turned to Al, Tom, and Rick and grinned. "But they've got an extra incentive to be loyal, right, gentlemen? You see, Bor, I know their secrets. All of them. Hid them where only I can find them. You'd be amazed at the kind of information Senate Intelligence can get access to. Surveillance footage. Electronic intercepts. All kinds of communications. Communications cops shouldn't be having. Not unless they want to finish their days behind bars. Hell, you didn't think I just picked these guys randomly, did you?"

Day gave a satisfied shrug. "So you see, Al, Tom, Rick, and I are the best of friends. They'll each cash in as heroes, just like me. Everyone retires fat, rich, and happy. Except you, Bor. As I said, you're done."

Bor nodded slowly. "We thought you were committed, Mr. Day. What you would call a 'true believer.' Not driven by the money. Or, at least not *just* the money. We miscalculated."

"I *am* a true believer, Bor. It's *not* just the money. But apparently, with your being busy killing people and making the world safe for Russian imperialism, you haven't had time to keep up with current events. The world's been changing. Much more rapidly than we'd ever expected. Without the need for war. Without Russian influence."

Day paused, then waved Al toward Bor. "In the end, a pathetic display, Bor. I don't know how in hell you got your reputation. But now, time for you to go."

"Hands behind your head, jackass," Al said as he moved behind Bor. "Slow."

With a look of resignation, Bor complied. Tom stepped next to Day and in front of Bor as Al pulled out a set of handcuffs.

For Julian Day, what happened next occurred, almost literally, in the blink of an eye.

As the lawyer's eyelids began to close, Bor, his hands behind his head in compliance with Al's command, reached into a nylon sheath sewn inside the back collar of his shirt, pulled out a serrated dagger, and, shifting his wrist, swung it forward over his head as if he were chopping wood with an ax. As Day's upper and lower eyelids met, the Russian jammed the dagger savagely into Tom's left eye socket, splitting the orb as the tip penetrated past the nasal cavity into the auditory canal.

A jet of Tom's warm blood spurted into Day's eyes just as his eyelids bounced open again and Bor was pulling the dagger from Tom's eye socket. A piercing shriek fired from Tom's lungs as he fell backward. At the same time, Bor collapsed to his knees, spun left to his rear, and plunged the dagger into Al's left inner thigh, slicing a deep gash upward from his knee to his groin, ripping the femoral artery.

A tick before Bor's blade severed Al's left testicle, a stunned Rick's right index finger reflexively squeezed the trigger of the Beretta M9 trained at the spot where Bor had been standing milliseconds earlier. The bullet discharged a full foot over the kneeling assassin's head and slammed harmlessly into the wall over the stove.

Day's vocal cords involuntarily generated a primal, anguished noise, his brain only now beginning to register the blur of mayhem before him. His eyelids snapped wide as Bor catapulted violently from the floor, hurling his 215 pounds of bone and muscle, dagger extended, at Rick. The blade drove into the detective's throat just below the Adam's apple, penetrating upward under the chin, through the floor of his mouth, and impaling his tongue against his palate—all of which were shredded by the blade's serrated edges when Bor pulled the dagger out. Rick crashed to the floor next to Tom and Al.

Elapsed time since Day began to blink: a shade over four seconds.

The horrified lawyer stood frozen, watching torrents of blood gush from the D.C. Metro detectives lying on the tiled floor.

Immediate threats now neutralized, Bor paused, expelled a long breath of air, and collected himself before moving from Al to Tom to Rick, filleting each with a series of strategically placed incisions to ensure each was dead.

Day vomited effusively. Ten more seconds had elapsed. Maybe fifteen.

Finished, the assassin rose, shoulders back, thick cords of vein pulsing in his neck. He took a sharp gulp of air before speaking.

"*That*, I suppose, is how I got my reputation, Mr. Day."

Day began hyperventilating.

Bor drew closer. Wolf's eyes riveted on the counsel for the Senate Select Committee on Intelligence of the United States of America.

"You're fried, Mr. Day. Done."

CHAPTER FIFTY-SEVEN

President John Allen Marshall had known James Brandt for more than twenty-five years and not once during that time had Brandt engaged in hyperbole or dramatics when it came to his work. He was deliberate, precise and sober. He had once described the Japanese tsunami of 2011, which resulted in more than sixteen thousand deaths and two hundred billion dollars in damage, as a "noteworthy event." So when the national security advisor made reference to "the immediate end of the United States as currently constituted," he commanded the undivided attention of everyone in the Situation Room.

Those present—Defense Secretary Douglas Merritt, Chairman of the Joint Chiefs Robert Taylor, CIA Deputy Director John Kessler, Director of National Intelligence Joseph Antonetti, Secretary of Homeland Security Susan Cruz, Secretary of State Ted Lawrence, and Chief of Staff Iris Cho—were already on heightened alert. Not only were things unraveling in the Middle East, but less than an hour earlier the USS *Texas*, a Virginia-class nuclear submarine, had detected up to a dozen Russian subs approximately three hundred miles east of the northernmost tip of Maine. Hearing the coldly analytical national security advisor refer to the end of America did little to alleviate the anxiety in the room.

The president was terse. "Jim, explain. What does that mean?"

"Mr. President," Brandt began. "It's our assessment that we're going to be hit with an EMP attack."

There was some stirring among the attendees as Brandt paused, anticipating a series of questions. None came, everyone waiting for the president, who was looking at Director of National Intelligence Joseph Antonetti for concurrence or disagreement. The DNI, like all the others in the room, appeared dumbstruck.

Marshall didn't know where to begin, so he simply asked, "Upon what do you base your assessment?"

"Several factors, Mr. President. But principally, information from Michael Garin."

The room exploded with rapid-fire questions and expressions of astonishment. Brandt sat silently for several seconds until the president raised a hand, quieting the room. "Again, Jim. Explain," the president directed.

"Mr. President, through back channels, Michael Garin has provided information to a member of my staff—information that I find credible—that an EMP attack will be launched on the US. Unfortunately, he doesn't have particulars as to when, how, or by whom."

"Why, then, do you find the information credible?"

"Primarily because Ari Singer was Garin's source. But I concede, quite readily, that I'm biased. It somewhat fits my own assessment of the cooperation between the Russians and the Iranians."

"When were you going to tell us you've been in touch with Garin?" Antonetti asked.

Marshall's face grew dark. "Stow it, Joe. I'd ask you why *your* shop hasn't been in touch with him. *Or* tracked him down. *Or* had any whiff of a possible EMP attack. That's your job, isn't it?"

The room fell utterly silent. The rebuke caused everyone but Marshall and Brandt to look down at the conference table like scolded schoolchildren.

"Who's this Singer fellow?" Marshall asked.

"An Israeli intelligence agent, Mr. President," Brandt replied.

Marshall looked back at the chastened Antonetti. The DNI, taking the cue that he had permission to speak, said, "He's known to us, sir. Very reliable. If Singer told Garin the US is the target of an EMP attack, well, we should assume we're the target of an EMP attack."

Marshall stared vacantly at the opposite wall for a moment. Then he looked at Brandt and asked quietly, "So we don't know who's going to hit us or how much time we have?"

"Again, Mr. President, we don't yet have those specifics, but based on everything that's happened over the last few weeks, the most likely players are the Russians or Iranians. And given the nature of the threat, our operating premise must be that an attack could happen at any time."

"Mr. President." It was Secretary of State Ted Lawrence. "It's simply implausible that the Russians would take such an action. We were engaged in a Cold War for nearly half a century. They wouldn't dare strike us. Mutual assured destruction ensures that. Remember, they backed down in 1962." The pompous secretary of state looked around. Forever concerned Brandt was being groomed for his job, he was determined not to let the upstart national security advisor upstage him. "And they're comparatively weaker now than they were back then. They'd never risk it."

Several heads around the table nodded in agreement. Marshall noted a skeptical look on the secretary of defense's face. "What's your take, Douglas?"

Douglas Merritt was Ted Lawrence's opposite in almost every way. Whereas Lawrence was self-promoting and voluble, Merritt was self-effacing and measured.

"Mr. President, while I agree that the odds of the Russians launching a conventional nuclear strike against the US are prohibitive, what we're talking about here isn't at all conventional."

Lawrence scowled. He detested Merritt. He detested being contradicted even more.

"It's true," Merritt continued, "that the Russians—and the Chinese, for that matter—will be deterred by the certainty of a devastating retaliatory strike. For decades both the US and the Russians have understood that a nuclear attack by one of us—one that killed millions on the other side—would prompt retaliation that would annihilate the other side. If they take out Chicago, we take out Saint Petersburg. If they take out New York City, we take out Moscow. Everyone knows this. We've gamed the scenarios a million times over. Each of us has standing retaliation protocols."

"Your point, Douglas."

The secretary of defense straightened. "Mr. President, an EMP attack wouldn't kill anyone. At least not immediately. In fact, no one would even be injured. No cities would be incinerated, no farmlands scorched. Not a single building would be leveled. Quite frankly, Mr. President, we haven't established an agreed retaliation protocol for these circumstances. Put simply, we haven't been able to justify nuking Moscow and wiping out millions because something went boom and startled pigeons somewhere miles above Manhattan. I don't mean to be flippant, sir. Those are just the facts."

Marshall had an incredulous look on his face. "Do you mean to tell me that in the fifty-odd years we've been aware of the possibility of an EMP, we've never developed a damn response doctrine?"

"That's correct, Mr. President," Merritt said. "At least nothing formal or concrete. The idea, as I understand it, was that we needed to be flexible in our approach, not formulaic. Since an EMP itself wouldn't kill anyone, a full-scale nuclear response would be wildly asymmetrical—escalating matters out of control. It would undoubtedly provoke a massive nuclear counterstrike."

"There are also practical concerns, Mr. President," Chief of Staff Cho piped up. "If the US were to inflict millions of casualties on a country just because that country caused our lights to go out, we'd be a pariah state. We'd be ostracized from the ranks of civilized nations. The world would unite against us. Treaties abrogated, boycotts, embargoes, sanctions."

"Not to mention the political upheaval domestically," Cho continued. "A large segment of the American population thinks we shouldn't have any nukes to begin with. They would go nothing short of berserk if we actually used one."

"But the Russians don't know our protocols, or lack thereof, to something that goes boom over Manhattan," Marshall said. "They can't be sure we *won't* launch a full-scale military response. So how can they risk it?"

Antonetti spoke up. "On the contrary, Mr. President, they have a pretty good idea how we would or would not respond. We'd like to think they don't, but just like us, they've run countless computer models on every conceivable military scenario. They've run psych ops scenarios. Plus, let's face it, despite our best efforts, they've no doubt gotten regular intel on our protocols. After all, we've got theirs."

Brandt cleared his throat and all eyes turned to him. "Mr. President, everything that's been said is well considered. And even though I strongly disagree with Ted's assertion that MAD would deter the Russians from launching an EMP, I don't mean to diminish the consequences of such an attack."

Lawrence scowled again. Too bad if that insufferable egghead couldn't see it. At least everyone else in the room would see the secretary of state's displeasure at being upstaged by this prissy academic.

But no one was looking at the secretary of state. Everyone was focused on Brandt.

"As Doug Merritt has stated, an EMP wouldn't kill anyone or level any buildings. Not right away." Brandt leaned forward slightly, giving greater emphasis to what he was about to say. "But I want to be clear that the cascade effect of the EMP would be cataclysmic, perhaps one of the greatest disasters to befall any nation in history."

"With all due respect," Lawrence interrupted, "that's overstating the matter quite a bit. In fact, we've had at least two commissions studying the issue. As a result, we've hardened a number of assets against an EMP strike."

Marshall's patience was becoming strained. "Gentlemen, you're talking in circles. And frankly, Ted, you sound like you're trying to cover all sides on the issue, as usual. I need facts. And I need them fast. If there's going to be an EMP attack, and we're in the dark—no pun intended—about when, then we've got to move quickly with the best available information. I need to determine a course of action before we leave this room." Marshall turned to Brandt. "Jim, how do you respond to Lawrence's assertion that you're overstating the case?"

"Mr. President, I wish I were overstating the case, but far from it. Yes, just before 9/11, Congress established the Commission to Assess the Threat to the United States from Electromagnetic Pulse Attack. Members of the commission testified before the House Armed Services Committee in 2002 about our complete vulnerability to an EMP attack. The commission recommended specific steps to harden US infrastructure against such an attack. Virtually nothing, however, was done. Congress reestablished the commission in 2006. It issued a report in 2008 warning of the dire consequences of an EMP attack and recommended robust hardening of critical infrastructure against such an attack. Bills were introduced in Congress to deal with the threat in 2009, again in 2010, and twice, I believe, in 2011. They went nowhere. In fact, the Critical Infrastructure Protection Act, introduced in the House in 2014, stalled immediately. Since then, the focus has been on preventing cyberattacks. But we haven't done much there, either."

Marshall's face had a look of disbelief. "So you're telling me we're completely vulnerable to an EMP?"

"Not completely, Mr. President," Merritt interjected. "We've hardened much of our strategic defense infrastructure against an EMP attack—such as our nuclear deterrent capabilities. We would still possess a substantial nuclear retaliatory capability in the case of an EMP attack." Merritt turned to Brandt. "But I largely agree with Jim. In almost every other way, we're vulnerable to an EMP attack, and the consequences would be devastating. Far more than a massive cyberattack. We learned that after the Starfish Prime high-altitude nuclear test during the Kennedy administration. A one-and-a-half-megaton thermonuclear warhead detonated more than two hundred miles above the Pacific Ocean produced an electromagnetic pulse that knocked out power in Hawaii nearly a thousand miles away."

"A high-altitude—say, a hundred- to a hundred-fifty-mile—nuclear burst," Brandt resumed, "above the center of the US would send a high-intensity electromagnetic shock wave through the atmosphere, frying all electronics and communications over most of the continental United States. Telephones, radios, televisions, computers, power lines. Anything and everything that uses electricity would be rendered useless in an instant. Power plants, factories, generators, practically all transportation would grind to a halt—including air transportation, most automobiles, rail. Most emergency backup generators would be fried also. We wouldn't even have the power to manufacture the circuits, fuses, and replacement parts to get those things moving again.

"Banking, oil and gas production, would be compromised. Because we couldn't irrigate and harvest crops, much of the nation's food supply would rot in the fields. Even if we could harvest some by hand, we'd have no means to transport it or refrigerate it. Food shortages would occur within weeks, if not days. Water-treatment and sewage-treatment plants would be inoperable. Disease would become rampant. Hospitals couldn't function effectively. Many, if not most, businesses couldn't operate. The economy would utterly collapse. And the worst hasn't even begun. Imagine what conditions will be like six months from now—in the dead of winter, temperatures below freezing. Most will still be without heat, without power."

Marshall shut his eyes tightly, trying not to erupt in anger. When he spoke, his tone was forceful but measured. "So, essentially, except for our nuclear capability and some of our military and intelligence apparatus, we'll be thrown back into the early 1800s."

"Unfortunately, it's worse than that, Mr. President," Brandt replied. "Much worse. Because back then, society was built and organized to function without electricity—without cars, phones, computers, planes. An agrarian society. A person's job, food sources—most of the staples he needed to live—were within walking distance of where he lived. Seventy percent of the population never traveled in their entire lives outside of a twenty-mile radius of where they were born.

"In contrast, today's society is based on mobility and information. The milk in your cereal this morning likely came from a dairy farm in Wisconsin seven hundred miles away, the fruit from an orchard in California three thousand miles away. We're not built to function without electricity. Where do we find clean water, food? Conservative estimates put the death toll from disease and starvation in the first year after the strike at nearly twenty percent of the entire population. And there's no way to predict the number of casualties from the inevitable civil unrest."

The president turned his head slightly. "But, Jim, by that logic—even though we've never announced we'd retaliate in a major way, the Russians know that the consequences of an EMP are so catastrophic that we'd be compelled to respond. Accordingly, they *wouldn't* launch the attack. So, Ted's right—MAD still governs."

Lawrence, sensing that this argument was prevailing in the president's mind, remained determined to drive the point home. "Plus,

Mr. President, the Russian economy would certainly take a major hit, and that's not something they can afford."

Marshall could barely refrain from rolling his eyes at the secretary of state's transparent attempt to appear relevant. "What about that, Jim?"

Brandt's response surprised Marshall and, once again, angered the secretary of state. "Actually, Mr. President, I don't consider the economic ramifications as a primary deterrent to the Russians. Sure, there would be some short-term dislocations to their economy. But some would argue that after an initial roiling of the markets, the Russians could capitalize on our economic paralysis, fill the breach—so to speak—in several segments of the world economy affected by the turmoil in the US. No, I don't think the effect on our economy is a sufficient deterrent to a Russian EMP."

"Damn it, Jim," Marshall said, exasperated. "Now *you're* arguing against yourself. First you say an EMP is cataclysmic. But not cataclysmic enough to make the Russians think twice about hitting us. This isn't some graduate seminar—trying out theories on your doctoral candidates. This is real. I need guidance, not vacillation."

The secretary of state lowered his head to conceal a whisper of a smile. A rebuke to the great Brandt, apparently trapped in an inconsistency.

"Mr. President," Brandt responded, "I just think—"

Marshall interrupted. "Based on everything you said, I can't believe the Russians would take the chance of hitting us with an EMP. It's much more likely that this Ari Singer is wrong, or was misunderstood by Garin."

"But, Mr. President," Brandt said, but he was waved off by Marshall.

"Let me finish, Jim. In my experience the simplest explanation is usually the right one. It seems to me that an EMP strike is, in fact, going to happen. But it's not going to be a Russian EMP strike on the US.

Instead, it's going to be an Iranian EMP strike, maybe with Russian help, against Israel."

Marshall scanned the room for concurrence. The secretary of state leapt.

"My point exactly, Mr. President. Let's not forget the obvious, what's been going on in front of our noses the last few weeks: the UN resolution, the troop buildups by Iran's client, Syria, the rocket attacks by Iran's proxy, Hezbollah, the border skirmishes—all provocations designed to draw Israel into a war that Iran intends to finish off with an EMP strike on Israel." Lawrence paused, assumed a pedantic posture, and continued. "The EMP would render Israel completely defenseless against an attack by its enemies. And the resulting turbulence in the Middle East oil markets works to Russia's benefit."

The secretary of state sat back in his chair, pleased with himself, as everyone in the room, even Douglas Merritt, albeit somewhat tentatively, nodded in agreement. Everyone but Brandt. The logic of Lawrence's argument, however self-serving, sounded almost impeccable. It was even consistent with Brandt's own argument for why the Russians wouldn't hit the United States. But the national security advisor couldn't bring himself to believe that men as serious as Singer and Garin, men for whom small mistakes in judgment could mean immediate death for themselves or their comrades, would make a mistake concerning the target of an EMP.

"Ted," Marshall said, "we don't know how much time we have. You need to make principal-to-principal contact with your counterparts in Israel and Iran, ASAP. Give Israel a heads-up, in case Singer hasn't already done so. And tell Iran we're onto their plan and remind them in no uncertain terms of the consequences. They know this administration's position concerning an attack on Israel, and"—Marshall looked at SecDef Merritt—"your people should make contact with IDF."

"Mr. President," Brandt said more loudly than was common for him, capturing everyone's attention, including a startled Marshall.

"Pardon the interruption, sir. I appreciate the urgency, but given the magnitude of what we're dealing with here, perhaps it would be helpful to take an hour to run this premise through our respective departments and agencies before we contact any foreign governments? See if we can get more corroborative intelligence before making any statements or taking any action?"

Brandt needed to slow this process down, buy some time so that he might get more information from Garin that would support the intel on an EMP attack on the United States. Perhaps more important, the president needed more intel before he embarked on an irreversible and possibly flawed course of action.

"Jim," Marshall replied, "you're the one who raised the issue of an EMP attack, possibly an imminent one, and the DNI here says your source Singer is practically unimpeachable."

Good, thought Lawrence, the rookie's reputation was imploding. The unmaking of the Oracle was occurring before his eyes.

"Mr. President, Iran is only nine hundred ninety miles from Tel Aviv. Even if we left this room right now, a missile could travel to Israel before— well, to be blunt, it'll hit no matter what we do at this moment." Brandt's ice-blue eyes were cast directly at the commander in chief. "Under the circumstances, *accuracy* may be more important than speed."

Marshall was a decisive man. He abhorred equivocation and delay. Those qualities, as much as his stance on the issues, had set him apart from his opponent during the presidential campaign. He believed that sometimes it was more important to act, even if it wasn't the *perfect* course of action, than to wait or to do nothing at all.

The president was not, however, rash. If he abhorred delay, he hated unforced errors even more. And his instincts told him Brandt's caution was right. If, with incomplete or incorrect information, the United States warned Israel that an Iranian EMP was imminent, it could trigger a preemptive Israeli attack on Iran, possibly even a nuclear one. Marshall realized that he had been on fast-forward since being told of the presence of Russian subs along the coast. He exhaled as if to deflate the sense of panic that had been building throughout the meeting.

"All right, Jim," Marshall said. "Your recommendation?"

Lawrence sank visibly in his chair, but again, no one noticed.

"Convey to Prime Minister Chafetz in a neutral way, without elaboration, the information we got from Singer—that the US is going to be hit with an EMP. We don't know by whom. We don't know when. But the intel comes from Singer.

"Now, given that it came from a Mosssad agent, maybe they know all this already. But my guess is they don't; otherwise, they would've contacted *us* with the same intelligence by now. The Israelis can't afford to make any mistakes. If they come to the conclusion that the EMP strike is actually directed at them, they'll hit Iran and we will have done our part for our ally. If, however, Singer and Garin are right that the EMP is directed at us, well, that's our problem and Israel can't do anything about it anyway."

"And if the EMP *is* directed at us? What do we do besides tell the Israelis what Singer and Garin said?" the president asked.

"Mr. President, that's precisely why we need more time to figure this out. Everyone in this room agrees the Russians won't hit us. Let's use the time to determine, as far as we can, if that's absolutely right."

"What if we're wrong and Russians *are* planning to hit us?"

"That's why I suggest you call President Mikhailov and tell him what Singer and Garin said, that we're the target of an EMP, that we've detected Russian subs on our coast. And, in a nonthreatening way, remind him that despite the previous administration's best efforts, we still have several thousand nuclear missiles aimed at the motherland."

"I've heard enough." Lawrence stood up in a huff. "Mr. President, this is ridiculous. We can't possibly—"

"Shut up and sit down, Ted," Marshall said sternly. The president sat motionless again, staring for several long seconds at Brandt, assessing the national security advisor's recommendation.

"Okay, Jim," the president said finally. "We'll go with your plan for now, but we move quickly. Everyone, go back to your people and gather all information pertinent to this matter with all the speed you can muster. Run the scenarios we've discussed here past your respective analysts. Then stand by for my orders to execute."

CHAPTER FIFTY-EIGHT

At first, Olivia had protested that the protective detail that Dwyer had assigned to her was over-the-top, but she appreciated the feeling of security it afforded. Now that she was actually being escorted to the Old Executive Office Building to meet Brandt, there was absolutely no doubt in Olivia's mind that Dwyer was overdoing it. She felt almost as if she were in a presidential motorcade.

Olivia was riding in the back of one of DGT's seemingly endless supply of black SUVs. Two armed, black-uniformed DGT security guards were in front. Carl was seated to her right. And, as usual, whenever he was around Olivia, he was smiling. The vehicle in which she rode was sandwiched between identical lead and trailing SUVs, each carrying a quartet of DGT security guards armed with MP7s. As Carl had been told by Dwyer, he'd be damned if anything happened to the NSA's aide on DGT's watch. The only threat Olivia could discern, however, was the impenetrable traffic approaching the Beltway. It was nearly at a standstill.

Olivia was on her way to meet Brandt to assess the information provided by Garin. According to Brandt, confusion had reigned in the Situation Room a short time ago. Brandt had succeeded in buying some time before the president decided on a course of action. Olivia was unsure what good would come from the extra time. She hadn't gotten any new information from Garin about the EMP strike and doubted she would. Garin had been clear about the message he'd received from Singer. The EMP strike was going to be on the United States. Israel hadn't been mentioned. From Olivia's perspective, there was little more to analyze. The president needed to understand that the nation he led was the target.

The only questions were, when would the attack occur and from where would it come? Olivia had struggled with those questions from the moment Garin had told her about the EMP. She shared Brandt's conclusion that under ordinary circumstances the Russians wouldn't risk doing it for fear of annihilation. The same rationale applied to every other country with nuclear capability, and those countries didn't have agents running around America killing US special operators.

Olivia decided that without additional information she'd be wasting Brandt's time, causing both of them to waste the president's time. And despite her whiz-kid reputation, Olivia couldn't shake the fear that she was out of her depth. If Garin's information was correct, the United States was facing a titanic calamity, and Olivia was part of the team tasked to prevent it. A far cry from grading undergrad term papers at Stanford.

At least Jim had forestalled the president from taking precipitous, potentially catastrophic action. She decided to call Dan Dwyer and ask whether he could put her in touch with Garin. Maybe he had gotten some new information. Or maybe he had some ideas that Brandt and Olivia hadn't considered. She desperately hoped he did.

Brandt sat in the Situation Room as the president and his chief of staff huddled in a far corner in advance of the president's call to President Mikhailov. Marshall had asked Brandt to remain behind after the meeting had ended. A Russian translator, who had introduced himself as Josh Plotkin, sat opposite Brandt. Mikhailov spoke English fairly well, but Brandt had advised the president that given the stakes, even the slightest misunderstandings couldn't be risked. Plotkin, a tall, owlish Princeton summa cum laude in his late twenties, was to keep silent, acting only as a backstop.

The call to the Russian president would be placed in five minutes, the White House Communications Agency having contacted the Kremlin within the last twenty-five minutes to alert the Russians of Marshall's need to speak with Mikhailov on a matter of urgency, a matter that could involve military action. It was late night in Moscow and it was estimated that Mikhailov would need some time to summon whatever advisors he needed to participate in the call.

Aside from Plotkin, Marshall had chosen to have only Brandt and Cho join him, causing no small amount of distress to the secretary of state, who offered to stay to provide whatever advice and counsel the president might require. Marshall politely declined. The last thing he needed in the room was the distraction of Ted Lawrence jockeying with Brandt for influence. Plus, the president trusted Brandt's sober reasoning. Substance, not political posturing, was what was needed at this moment.

The voice of Major Clayton Cord, detailed to the White House Communications Agency, came over the speaker in the Situation Room. "Mr. President, President Mikhailov will be on the line in sixty seconds. We're told he will be joined by a senior aide and a translator."

"Thank you, Major," Marshall replied as he took his seat. Cho sat to his left and Plotkin moved to his seat at the president's right. Brandt sat to Cho's left.

Brandt's calm demeanor belied a twinge of anxiety. To this point, his involvement in critical issues had always been confined to the background. The importance of this moment eclipsed anything he'd ever done before. He was seated at the table with the president of the

United States, about to talk to the president of Russia. The two commanded the largest nuclear arsenals in the world, enough firepower to extinguish the lives of every human being on the planet. The thought, while producing a bit of nervousness, also sharpened his focus.

There was a click and the gravelly yet urbane voice of the Russian president materialized. "Mr. President?"

"Yes, Yuri," replied Marshall, leaning toward the speaker. "Thank you for making yourself available on such short notice and at such a late hour. I have in the room with me my chief of staff, Iris Cho, and national security advisor, James Brandt. Joshua Plotkin is also present as translator, but I doubt we'll need his services."

"Good evening, Ms. Cho. It was good to meet you at the G20 summit last month. I would like to continue our discussion of insufferable Parisian sommeliers, but given the hour, I gather the purpose of the call is not to exchange pleasantries. I've not had the pleasure of meeting with Mr. Brandt or Mr. Plotkin, but I, of course, have read a number of Mr. Brandt's papers. Impressive. With me are my senior aide Alexei Vasiliev and a translator. I would greatly prefer to videoconference, but, as you might imagine, at this hour, I am not quite presentable."

"Yuri, as you've surmised, I would not have roused you in the middle of the night unless it pertained to a matter of some significance."

Brandt made a downward motion with his hand, reminding Marshall to modulate his tone and not be unduly inflammatory. Marshall nodded absentmindedly.

"We have detected a large number of your submarines very near our coast. We estimate eight Akula class, four Delta IVs, and possibly a Borei. If I recall correctly, the Delta IVs are equipped with sixteen ballistic missiles with four to six MIRVed warheads." The clinical manner in which Marshall spoke gave the statement a heightened impact.

There was a short pause at the end of the line followed by unintelligible conversation.

"John Allen," Mikhailov said, "I do not quite understand. You stated that this was a matter of significance, but you know quite well that for the last fifty years both your country and mine have engaged in maneuvers off of our respective coastlines. It is the norm, not the exception. As tiresome as it may be, it is, in fact, expected. Therefore, I must conclude that this is not the primary thing on your mind. Am I correct?"

"You are correct, Yuri."

There was more unintelligible conversation on the other side. Brandt realized that the Russian president's words with his aide were being electronically scrambled. Brandt didn't know whether any sidebars between himself and Marshall would also be automatically muted or scrambled, so he remained silent.

"John Allen, I'm reliably informed that any Russian submarines that may have been in the vicinity of the North American coastline have since moved well into the Atlantic. I'm sure you can verify this."

"Thank you, we will look into it. But I can assure you, the number of vessels involved indicated that this was not an ordinary exercise."

"Even if true, that would not have prompted you to call me at this hour."

"Perhaps not," Marshall acknowledged. "But that, coupled with another piece of troubling information, has caused some alarm."

"And what is this other piece of information?"

Marshall hesitated, glancing at Brandt. The two had agreed that Marshall would not reveal the source of the EMP intel, just the claim that the United States would be hit.

Marshall replied, "That the United States is going to be subject to an electromagnetic pulse attack."

More unintelligible conversation, then a calm "And when is this attack to occur?"

"We assume imminently."

"And, Mr. President, you believe my country is somehow involved."

The subtle shift to formal salutation was not lost on anyone in the Situation Room.

"The presence of a large number of your subs at the same time we received intel related to the EMP attack, as well as other incidents, prompted us to reach out to you."

"And, if I may ask, who or what is the source of this intel?"

Brandt shook his head. Marshall paused. Before he could reply, Mikhailov continued. "Could it be a Mr. Garin?"

The Russian president's question took everyone in the Situation Room by surprise except Plotkin, who had no idea who Garin was. Brandt shook his head vigorously, signaling Marshall to neither confirm nor deny, but the president decided not to be coy.

"What do you know of Mr. Garin?"

"You do not seriously think, Mr. President, that we would not know that your FBI has been engaged in a widespread manhunt for one of your most elite clandestine soldiers? You may no longer consider us a superpower, but I would wager that our human intelligence capabilities remain vastly superior to yours. No disrespect, of course." There was a slight pause. "Did you know that he is Russian?"

"He is an American," Marshall stated firmly.

"Yes. So he is. America. The great melting pot. I am certain he eats hot dogs and enjoys baseball. But you must admit, his behavior is very . . . Russian. Quite tenacious, I'm told. An exquisite killer. Implacable. Reminds me of the kind of individual who would have survived Leningrad." Another insouciant pause. "I understand he still has relatives here."

Marshall bristled. "What are you suggesting, Mr. President?" Marshall's shift to a formal salutation prompted Brandt to again make downward motions with his hand, signaling a need to temper the conversation.

"Nothing at all, Mr. President. It is not the Cold War any longer. *The New York Times* says we are friends."

"I don't read *The New York Times*. And either way, friends don't mass nuclear subs off one another's coastlines."

Mikhailov's tone softened. "John Allen, Russia is not suicidal. If you had any doubts about this, I am sure Mr. Brandt has dispelled them for you. This electromagnetic pulse, I understand its effect. You would be forced to retaliate with atomic weapons against any nation that launched such a horrible attack. Millions would die. We know this . . ."

There was more garbled chatter at the other end before Mikhailov resumed speaking.

"But if you do not believe me or your national security advisor, perhaps you will believe your spy satellites and your electronic intercepts. Check the satellites tasked over our rocket-launch facilities, or as you call them, ballistic missile sites. You will detect absolutely no preparations for a rocket launch. Our silos are cold. And your National Security Agency will have detected absolutely no communications regarding a rocket launch."

"What about the nukes on your subs?" Marshall asked. "They could reach us in minutes."

"As I have stated, we are not suicidal. The vessels have set a course to return to Yagal'naya. You have my word that we will take no aggressive action toward the United States and we have no intention of taking such action. How many hundreds of nuclear missiles do you have aimed at Moscow at this moment? How many nuclear submarines do you have that could vaporize Saint Petersburg twenty minutes from now? That is your best proof that no EMP will come from Russia."

"Just to be clear, Yuri, this administration's unequivocal response doctrine is massive nuclear retaliation toward any nation that strikes the US with an EMP."

"That has always been our understanding, John Allen."

There was silence for several seconds. Brandt made a slicing motion across his throat, suggesting the call be terminated.

"Apologies for having disturbed you, Yuri, as well as Mr. Vasiliev and your translator. I am sure you understand my concerns. Those concerns, thankfully, have been allayed. We will talk again soon."

"Yes. We will talk soon."

Alexei Vasiliev regarded his boss as he sat in a high-backed chair next to the speakerphone. Yuri Mikhailov was a big man—six foot six and nearly three hundred pounds, a former discus thrower on the 1984 Soviet Olympic team. He had a broad, peasant's face and tended to sway from side to side as he walked, suggesting mild inebriation. After a brief time with the KGB before the collapse of the Soviet Empire, he had leveraged his contacts and position to amass a modest fortune in oil and gas leases. He appeared to those who didn't know him well to be perpetually half asleep, but his mind was fast, exacting, and shrewd.

Vasiliev knew his boss well, admired him. But on occasion, Mikhailov could be inscrutable. This was one such occasion.

"What do you make of Marshall?" Vasiliev asked in Russian.

"He is smarter than his predecessor. Tougher. Clarke believed everything his professors taught him in university. And the lessons he learned there remain impervious to reality. Marshall, however, is guided by his experience in the real world."

"Then that is not good for Russian interests," Vasiliev observed.

"He is tougher than Clarke, but he is still the American president. He leads a fractious people, many of whom expect and demand comfort. His charge is to provide it to them. Inconveniences are not lightly tolerated."

"Therefore, they—and he—can be manipulated," Vasiliev noted.

"To a point. We must not underestimate them. Many Americans, it seems more of them every day, expect comfort as an inalienable right. They think their government can and should provide a subsistence.

These Americans are not our concern. It is the segment of America that expects nothing more than freedom that is our concern. The cowboys. The United States may have its problems, but it still exists. The Soviet Union does not."

"For now," Vasiliev reminded him. "Should we urge some of our friends in the Western media to put pressure on Marshall, criticize his unnecessarily provocative Middle East policies, his confrontational posture toward us?"

Mikhailov picked up a glass from the highly polished mahogany table next to him and sipped the clear liquid slowly. It was not vodka, but water. Contrary to his CIA profile, Mikhailov almost never drank alcohol.

"It is not the American president who is on my mind right now," Mikhailov said. "It is our friend from the American Senate. He has not been as useful as we had hoped, despite being compensated quite handsomely. More importantly, it appears he may now be a liability."

Mikhailov placed the glass on the table and rose from the chair. Stifling a yawn, he turned toward Vasiliev. "Garin should not know about an EMP. That is unacceptable. It is too close. Only hours now. Much too close."

"But Marshall did not confirm that he learned it from Garin," Vasiliev countered.

"That is confirmation itself," Mikhailov said. "Contact Bor immediately. Tell him to find out from Mr. Day how Garin knows about the EMP, and what else he may know. If I know Bor, he is already in the process of doing so."

"Anything else?"

"Yes," the Russian president said as he headed toward his living quarters. "Tell Bor that our association with Mr. Day is yielding diminishing returns and to exercise his best judgment accordingly."

CHAPTER FIFTY-NINE

THE WHITE HOUSE

JULY 17 • 4:53 P.M. EDT

Iris Cho and Josh Plotkin left the Situation Room immediately after Marshall's call to Mikhailov ended. Marshall asked Brandt to remain behind. The president, Brandt sensed, was endeavoring to project resolve and control.

"So, where are we, Jim?"

"It's clear that the Russians are not going to hit us with an EMP, especially now that we've put them on notice," Brandt assured him. "Understand, I don't trust Mikhailov. The Russians are involved somehow. Unfortunately, that call provided no further clues as to the extent of their involvement."

"I don't trust him either. What did you make of his reference to Garin?"

"That's just it. The Russian president should not be able to identify one of our operators by name. It's pretty clear he knows something about an EMP, even if they're not going to launch it."

"What about that crack about Garin being Russian, still having relatives there?"

"You mean, do I think it was a subtle threat that he might somehow hold Garin's relatives hostage?" Brandt asked, eyebrows raised.

"No, I don't think so. Too Soviet. Besides, what could he hope to gain from it?"

Marshall shook his head. "No, I mean, do you think he was sending some signal that Garin is actually one of theirs?"

"Sir, I don't know Mike Garin, never met him, never even spoken to him. I suppose anything's possible in this world. But"—Brandt paused, considering how to relate his knowledge about Garin to the president—"one of my assistants has spoken to him. Ms. Perry. She's provided me with a debrief. Do you know the story about his grandfather's escape from the NKVD?"

Marshall didn't admit it, but he was fascinated by Garin and over the last few days had had DNI Antonetti provide regular updates during his morning briefings, one of which included information about Garin's personal background.

Long under suspicion by Red Army political officers for having the temerity to engage in irreverent speculation about the party's alleged infallibility, Lieutenant Nikolai Garin had been remanded to an NKVD detention facility in the Soviet occupation zone of Germany at the conclusion of World War II. He was held there pending transfer— if he was lucky—to a labor camp in the motherland. Stuffed for months in a dank, suffocating cell of stone and mortar with scores of similarly suspect soldiers, barely enough room to take more than two steps, he waited his turn with the dreaded *sledovatels*. The cell reeked of urine, gangrene, and fear, the prisoners' ears assaulted day and night with the cries of those being tortured in the "Yama," an unseen chamber somewhere down the passageway nearby. Listening to the screams and imagining the cause of a specific inflection or tone was sometimes worse than the physical agony each would eventually endure.

Nikolai was among the more fortunate, for many of his cellmates returned from the Yaama missing appendages or disfigured by hideous burns and lacerations. When it was his turn to be escorted down the corridor, Nikolai succeeded in disabling the guard with a single, powerful blow to the bridge of his nose and escaped out a lavatory window. After crawling under barbed wire and evading sentries, dogs, and searchlights, he navigated through the frigid countryside in a general westerly direction. For nearly a week he had not a scrap of food other than pieces of frozen bread found in a garbage dump outside of a small Bavarian village. Nikolai's feet, several toes frostbitten and the others split and bleeding, had carried him—running, walking, staggering—more than a hundred miles to the American sector. To safety, and, more important, to freedom.

Brandt said, "Then you know that it would be next to impossible to turn a man like Garin. Yuri was right to call him 'implacable.' Seething might be more accurate. Men like Garin are Yuri's worst nightmare."

"I know. Refugees from the former Eastern Bloc countries, Cuba, Vietnamese émigrés, are some of my strongest supporters . . ." Marshall's words trailed off for a moment. "Frankly, Jim, I have to say I've had a hard time believing for an instant that Garin's running around killing members of his own team." Marshall sported a trace of a smile for the first time all day. "Now, if you told me he went rogue and started massacring FSB or SVR agents, I might believe you."

Brandt seized the opening to press Garin's case. "Sir, Garin tells my assistant that he's been set up." A quizzical expression came over Brandt's face. "I can't believe I said that, 'set up.' I sound like a character in a bad mob movie. But even if he hadn't said so himself, it's pretty obvious. Men identified as Iranian Quds Force showing up dead in New York, Virginia—that just doesn't happen every day."

Marshall nodded tentatively.

"Garin's still alive because he's lucky and he's good," Brandt continued. "In addition to Quds Force, he's been targeted by a Delta sniper."

Marshall stopped nodding. "He told your assistant that?"

"He did."

"Then he's mistaken or delusional. Jim, you know that's not possible."

"Maybe so, but he insists it's the case. And what about the FBI?

Why are they still pursuing him? Aren't they supposed to be the best in the world at investigating cases? Masters of deduction? By this time they must've concluded that if Garin killed anyone, it was the Iranians, and in self-defense. Isn't it more logical that Garin killed Iranians as opposed to his own men?"

"The CIA came to that conclusion pretty quickly. But the FBI's getting a lot of pressure from Senator McCoy's staff. I'm told one of his staffers keeps asking for updates to the point of being obnoxious. But I think they're also drawing the same conclusion."

"A word from you, obviously, would help Garin, sir. Not interference with the investigation, just relating to them what you've heard."

"I'll have Iris make a call."

"And Fort Bragg, too?"

"Jim, there's no chance of Delta involvement. I'd know about it. Heck, I would've had to green-light it." Marshall mulled it over a second. "They're going to think we're smoking something. But I'll have Iris call General O'Brien." Marshall looked sideways at Brandt. "We finished with Garin?"

"Yes, sir. Thank you."

"Then, my friend, what am I supposed to make of all this? The Russians aren't going to strike us, so is this a big wild-goose chase?"

Brandt's friendship with Marshall was strong enough that he felt less discomfort than other aides might at admitting he was somewhat baffled. Even if the Russians weren't the actors, there was too much going on to dismiss the EMP threat.

"It wouldn't be the first time. Lawrence seems to think so," Brandt replied.

"Lawrence was all over the map in the Situation Room. He's a human weather vane. But I'm sure he truly believes the Russians would never strike the US with an EMP." Marshall leaned back in his chair. "Beyond the possibility of retaliation, the consequences to the world economy, including their own, would be catastrophic."

"It most assuredly would cause an earthquake to the world economy," Brandt agreed. "But, sir, have you considered the very real prospect that Russian strategy is to profit—both geopolitically and economically—from the quake?"

Marshall's face registered a mixture of befuddlement and curiosity. "How in hell could they do that?"

"Do you remember the previous administration's summit with Mikhailov in Germany two years ago?

"The Mainz Accords."

"Right. Clarke tried to score political points in advance of the election by engaging Russia. The theme was that after the Syrian chemical weapons affair, Russia was no longer an adversary; it was a partner."

Marshall snorted derisively.

"The Mainz Accords," Brandt continued, "were the capstone of Clarke's engagement effort. A series of trade agreements representing by far the largest commercial transaction between the two nations in history. It would revive both our economies and permanently reset our relationship for the positive."

"Lots of words on a piece of paper. But it went nowhere. The Russians produced a ton of product, but nothing that we wanted or needed."

"So we think."

Marshall's eyes narrowed. "You've lost me. Where are you going with this, Jim?"

"As soon as the ink dried on the Mainz Accords, Russian factories started spitting out mountains of equipment: generators, switches, circuit breakers. Ms. Perry tells me they're just sitting there in these immense warehouses. You're right. We didn't need them. Nobody's buying them. And the Russians aren't even trying to move them."

"It takes a while to get the hang of capitalism," Marshall said.

"They also built lots of cargo vessels, cargo containers, trucks, and the like. Presumably to transport product they seem to be in no hurry to sell, let alone ship, anywhere."

A flicker of understanding played on Marshall's face. "If it weren't for the Mainz Accords, we would've been awfully curious about why the Russians were producing so much stuff that apparently was going nowhere. Instead, we chalk it up to market ineptitude, a modern Russian version of the Soviet-era five-year plans. So we don't suspect something's afoot."

"Think about what the product might be good for. It's unremarkable, standard-grade material. But if an EMP were to go off and the power goes out . . ."

"It becomes the most indispensible standard-grade material on the planet," Marshall finished. "The Russians will step into the breach and save our ass."

"Food and essentials won't spoil or rot, because they'll be transported to distant American populations by our benevolent Russian friends in their trucks and cargo containers. Fried cars, planes, factories, offices won't be rendered idle, at least not for long. Russian-supplied parts and generators unaffected by the EMP will get them restarted. Heck, they'll restart all of our essentials, from hospitals to factories to power plants."

Marshall exhaled audibly. "And a desperate US will pay virtually any price and obey virtually any command to get restarted." Marshall's words came slowly and softly. "They'll set the terms, Jim. They'll have rescued us from utter destruction, mass starvation, and we, in turn, will effectively become a vassal state."

Brandt forced a chuckle. "A wee melodramatic there, Mr. President."

"Maybe so. But I see your point, Jim. This may not be so far-fetched after all. They'd be softening the global economic impact of the strike."

"Again, it's just conjecture, sir."

"That would make me feel better, Jim, if your conjectures didn't so often come true."

"It was actually my aide, Ms. Perry, who came up with this. Connecting a million disparate dots. Again, this truly is guesswork, a shot in the dark. It's conceivable that we're being fed that EMP intel as a diversion. The Russians are particularly good at getting people to chase down multiple rabbit holes.

"But I do think we should call Prime Minister Chafetz with our EMP intel. I still believe it's wise not to editorialize—not to state, for example, that they're definitely the target, or that Iran is the actor. It would be helpful to tell him that Mikhailov assures us Russia's not going to hit us. Chafetz knows Iran can't hit us, so he'll conclude on his own that Iran plans to hit Israel."

"But we won't be the ones who say it," Marshall affirmed.

"Right. If they decide to hit Iran, it's their decision. If their conclusion is wrong, it's not our fault. But if they hit Iran and prevent a strike on Tel Aviv, well . . . then we will have provided the critical intel that saves Israeli lives."

"Jim, I'm inclined to offer to have the Fifth Fleet on standby to provide any support he may need. Too provocative toward the Iranians?"

"On the contrary, it may not go far enough."

CHAPTER SIXTY

G arin was proceeding north on I-95 toward Washington after disconnecting with Olivia, but the rush-hour traffic was at its usual crawl. He placed a call to information using the SUV's hands-free feature and requested the general number for the Hart Senate Office Building. Within moments, he was connected and an operator cheerfully answered, "Hart Senate Office Building. How may I direct your call?"

"Julian Day."

"One moment, please."

A few seconds later: "Office of Chief Counsel."

"May I speak with Mr. Day, please?" Garin asked.

"I'm sorry. Mr. Day has left for the day. Can I take a message or send you to his voice mail?"

"No, thank you. Do you know if I can reach Mr. Day at home?"

"I'm sorry, sir, I can't provide you with that information."

"I understand," Garin said. "This is Dan Dwyer."

"Yes, Mr. Dwyer. How are you?"

"Fine, thank you. Mr. Day asked me to get in touch with him immediately if I heard from a man by the name of Mike Garin."

"Okay."

"Well, I was just in contact with him regarding a matter of some urgency. I need to contact Mr. Day at once."

"Of course, Mr. Dwyer. I'm sure Mr. Day will want to speak with you right away. He's at home. I can connect you to his cell or home number.

"Mr. Dwyer?"

CHAPTER SIXTY-ONE

Garin drove down a quiet, tree-lined street sporting modest but elegant houses occupied by some of the junior to midlevel consultants, lawyers, and lobbyists who made their livings, directly and indirectly, from the US Treasury. Julian Day's home was two blocks down on the left.

Garin had spent an exasperating couple of hours on I-95, the traffic at a near standstill due to a single vehicle disabled by an overheated radiator. Maybe he should've found some way to use one of DGT's helicopters after all. While he waited for the traffic to lighten, he had plenty of time to think about how he would approach Day, but he actually didn't need it. He knew there was no time for subtlety.

He came to Day's house, a two-story redbrick affair with a small detached garage in the rear. His neighbors' houses were at least fifty to sixty feet away on either side. Close, but not so close that anyone could overhear a normal conversation or moderate level of noise.

Garin drove past the house and continued for two blocks before making a left turn to circle the block and make another pass. He saw nothing to suggest Day's house was being watched by anyone else or that he was the subject of any other form of surveillance.

After rounding the block, Garin again drove by Day's residence and parked beyond the sight line of Day's home. Turning off the ignition, he remained in the vehicle for another minute or so, checking the rear- and side-view mirrors.

Garin took the SIG from the center console and stuck it in the holster at the small of his back, covering it with his gray T-shirt. He put on a black ball cap, adjusted his Oakleys, and stepped out of the SUV, walking casually toward Day's house. He knew that if Day were looking out his window, it would take him only a second or two to recognize Garin, but he didn't have the luxury of even a light reconnaissance.

Though it was early evening, the heat of the day had yet to dissipate. The doors and windows in all the houses were tightly shut, a discernible whirring noise indicating that air conditioners were doing their best to combat the swelter. Thankfully, this ensured that the homes' occupants were unlikely to hear a wooden door being forced open.

As Garin approached Day's house, he turned into the driveway and walked swiftly toward the rear, removing his pistol after he had disappeared from street view behind the house. Day's red Volvo sat in front of the garage. Fortunately, there was a rear door that didn't look very secure. In one fluid motion, Garin climbed the back steps, opened the screen door, and directed a powerful kick toward the lock. The door yielded easily, with less noise than Garin had expected, and moments later Garin, weapon at the low-ready, was sweeping silently through a hallway, then the kitchen, half bath, office, and living room. No sign of Day.

Garin paused at the bottom of the staircase that led to the second floor, listening for any sounds. Hearing none, he took the stairs two steps at a time and swept three bedrooms, a bath, and a small sunroom. Still no Day.

Garin retraced his steps, returning to the kitchen, where he spotted the basement door beyond the refrigerator. Fifteen seconds later he had confirmed that Day wasn't at home, though his car was still in the driveway.

Standing in the kitchen, Garin began to resign himself to waiting until Day returned, when he noticed a cup sitting on the counter next to the range and detected a wisp of steam coming from the stainless steel coffeepot on the front left burner. He tapped the pot quickly with his index finger and confirmed that it was still warm. Day must've left just minutes earlier. And before he had a chance to pour himself a cup. On the wall just above the range was what appeared to be a fresh patch job. Garin put a finger to it. Still damp.

His suspicions aroused, Garin examined the rear door and determined that the reason it had opened so easily was that it had been unlocked. Garin made a mental note never to mention this detail to anyone, lest he suffer merciless ridicule from Dan Dwyer.

It took only seconds for Garin to find a third telltale that Day's hasty exit had been involuntary: fresh scuff marks on the kitchen's tile floor, indicating resistance. Crouching to get a better look, he detected tiny flecks of a reddish-brown substance in the grout. The floor had been scrubbed but particles of drying blood remained.

Garin had no time to ponder the implications of this, however, because he spotted the tops of two police caps, insignia on their crests, passing a side kitchen window in the direction of the rear door. A neighbor must've alerted police to the presence of a stranger. Since Garin had been in the house for barely three minutes, they were probably responding to reports of Day's earlier abduction.

Because of the height of the kitchen windows, the cops hadn't seen Garin. He stood flush against the wall next to the kitchen door. The cops would no doubt see the signs of forced entry, radio dispatch, and draw their weapons before entering.

A firefight with the cops was the very last thing Garin needed. He placed the weapon in his holster, and assumed his position against the wall. Then he braced for speed and violence.

Eight miles northeast, the convoy of SUVs carrying Olivia Perry and her DGT detail had finally escaped the Beltway and was proceeding down H Street on the way to the Old Executive Office Building, when Olivia caught a glimpse of a man to their left who appeared to be carrying a long plastic tube on his shoulder. Carl saw him too and immediately began shouting something, when the lead SUV burst into an orange fireball, catapulting six feet off the ground and coming to rest on the passenger side of the vehicle.

Unable to avoid the stricken vehicle, Olivia's SUV slammed into the wreckage, and a wall of flames engulfed the front of the vehicle. Moments later the trail SUV also exploded, its occupants blown out of the vehicle as it, too, rolled onto its right side. Amid a swirl of frantic shouts, flames, black smoke, and screeching metal, Olivia was vaguely aware of debris raining down around her and a dazed Carl drunkenly searching for the MP7 thrown from his grasp in the crash.

The last thing Olivia remembered seeing before losing consciousness was the man with the plastic tube, a submachine gun strapped across his chest, aiming a device that resembled a small TV remote at the vehicle. The last thing Olivia heard before losing consciousness was the click of the door locks opening simultaneously.

Garin saw the barrel of the lead cop's weapon first. The officer's extended arms, sweeping from side to side, and then his torso appeared in the doorframe. He entered the kitchen cautiously, passing by Garin, whose back was flat against the wall next to the door. The first cop had gotten approximately three feet inside the kitchen when the barrel of the second cop's weapon came into view, this time at the ready but pointed downward and to the right, away from his partner's back.

Garin shot forward between the two and smashed his right elbow into the second cop's nose and forehead, then slingshotted the same arm forward, driving his fist into the base of the first cop's skull. As the second cop flew sprawling backward out of the house, the lead cop dropped heavily to his knees, his pistol falling from his grasp. The second cop crashed unconscious onto the rear pavement just as the first cop fell face forward on the kitchen floor. Garin swiftly retrieved their respective weapons and tossed them into one of two green garbage cans outside the kitchen door. Grabbing the second cop under his arms, Garin dragged him inside and placed him down next to his partner on the kitchen floor.

It was then Garin noticed a small pool of blood expanding from under the lead cop's face. Garin cursed, dropped to one knee, and checked the man's pulse. Still strong. Relieved, Garin turned him over slightly and examined his face. A nose broken by the fall was the source of the blood.

Garin noted blood seeping from under the head of the other cop as well. He performed the same ritual on the man, determining that he, too, was fine, save for a broken nose of his own. No real long-term damage other than embarrassing explanations at the station house offset by a few weeks of paid leave.

Garin went to the living room and peered outside the window, scanning the neighborhood. Everything remained quiet. He returned to the kitchen and used a dish towel to wipe down the surfaces he had touched before stepping over the bodies of the two cops and exiting the house. He remembered to wipe down the cops' pistols as well as the lid of the garbage can before leaving.

Given the arrival of the cops, he assumed a neighbor was probably still monitoring the scene, watching. There was no point in feigning casualness, so he trotted toward his vehicle. At the intersection he turned left and disappeared around the corner. At least no one would connect Dwyer's black SUV with the man jogging from the house containing two bloody cops.

Garin climbed into the vehicle and sat for a moment, wondering what else could go wrong. The cascade of setbacks and bad news over the last few days was beginning to overwhelm him. He seemed to be making scant progress in either getting answers or clearing his name. Wherever he went, someone seemed to be one step ahead of him or pursuing one step behind.

Garin returned his focus to Day. The working assumption was that Day had been abducted by the Iranians, of which there suddenly seemed to be an endless supply. The traces of blood on the floor were an ominous sign. Where had they taken him? They appeared to have used the cabin on the Eastern Shore as their base of operations, but where had they gone since? Where could an indeterminate number of foreign operatives possibly hole up without attracting undue attention?

Garin caught himself. Maybe he was asking the questions from a false premise. What if the Iranians hadn't moved their base of operations after all? Why, in fact, should they? The Severn cabin was perfect—spacious, secluded, and within reasonable driving distance of D.C. Garin was the only one who knew of it and in his present circumstance he would be considered no threat to them. Even he had assumed there was no reason to go back since he had dispatched the Iranians who were there.

He pulled away from the curb, conceding to himself that this particular theory was more than just a little attenuated. He had simply run out of better options.

Garin navigated toward the Beltway to pick up Route 50 toward the Terrapin Estates. The cast of the midsummer sky was beginning to soften. Nightfall would be approaching soon. He would make an obligatory check of the Severn and then return to DGT's Quantico facility to reevaluate.

He had been driving for a while, making scant progress, when he took a call from Dwyer on the hands-free option.

"Mike, where are you?" There was a distinct edge in Dwyer's tone.

"On 50. Traffic seems to be a mess everywhere."

"Where are you headed?"

"You don't want to know," Garin said, resignation in his voice. "Why?"

"They got Olivia."

"What? What do you mean? How's that even possible?" One of the few times Dwyer had heard Garin's voice register alarm.

"We're trying to figure that out right now."

What else could go wrong? Garin thought.

"We're still debriefing Carl," Dwyer continued. "I'm here with him at George Washington University Hospital, standing in the waiting room. They make you turn off your cell in the patient's room so it doesn't interfere with the medical equipment." He paused. "He's in pretty bad shape. They were escorting Olivia to the OEOB. Standard escort protocol like we used with the State Department personnel in Iraq. Nothing special, but we thought it was overkill for a run in Washington, D.C. Then a guy with a rocket launcher—*a rocket launcher in the District*—appears. Don't know how unless he has drones or satellite feeds, but he just so happens to choose one of the only relatively deserted spots on our route. Hits the lead and trail vehicles. Eight of my men, killed instantly. Olivia's vehicle crashes into the lead. Carl loses consciousness. When he comes to, half of the D.C. Metro force is there, but Olivia's gone. Crowder and Gamble in the front seat are dead from multiple gunshot wounds. Close range," Dwyer's voice cracked. "Carl was hit too, but so far he's hanging on."

That explained the traffic. "How many attackers?" Garin asked.

"Attacker."

"What?"

"One attacker. One man."

"Carl give you a description?"

"Uh-huh."

"It was Bor, wasn't it?"

"J-shaped scar along the right jawline," Dwyer confirmed. "Hold on a second. I'm getting a call from Matt at Quantico."

Garin was beginning to develop a rare sense of desperation. The bad guys seemed to be everywhere at once. They seemed faster, cleverer, and better prepared than his allies. Garin couldn't remember confronting many adversaries like this, Bor in particular. Not only had he been able to fool Garin for more than two years; Bor seemed able to anticipate Garin's every move. Garin had always respected his enemies but never feared them. He wondered if that was about to change.

Dwyer returned to the call. "Matt says we're picking up intermittent data from the GPS nanotracker we sewed into the heel of Olivia's shoe."

"Bor's sure to find it. He's no dummy. He'll wand her first chance he gets, if he hasn't done so already. He finds it, she's dead."

"No way, Mike. It won't register. Its shell is polymer and it emits its signal in microbursts. Unless he wands her at precisely the millisecond it transmits, he'll never detect it. Either the battery's damaged or there's some electronic interference with the GPS, but we did get a brief signal twenty minutes ago near Annapolis. A few minutes later a blip about two miles from there. Nothing since then. The vector suggests she's moving toward somewhere on the Eastern Shore, but the destination could be anywhere within a one-hundred-square-mile area."

The Eastern Shore. Garin felt a flutter of hope. "Keep me updated. Dan, listen, have someone make an untraceable call to the McLean District Police. Tell them two cops are down inside Day's house."

"Geez, Mikey," Dwyer whispered. "Are they dead?"

"No, just bad headaches and bruised egos. They're probably up and back at the station by now. But just in case, they may need an EMT."

"Thank God. Where are you going?"

"Just following a hunch. I'll let you know if it pans out. Let me know if you get any more GPS coordinates."

"Roger that. And, Mike, keep your head on a swivel. These guys are everywhere."

"Tell me about it."

CHAPTER SIXTY-TWO

Arlo led Brandt down the hall toward to the Oval Office. After Brandt had left the Situation Room, he'd proceeded next door to the Old Executive Office Building to meet Olivia. He had been there barely ten minutes when he took the call from Iris Cho informing him of the mayhem that had occurred on H Street.

Brandt's anguish was plain on his face. The placid countenance, the cool demeanor, were gone. Olivia wasn't simply his aide. She was his closest confidant, their relationship more familial than professional. The two of them had been a prolific intellectual team in the comfortable cocoon of academia. Now the real world had intruded ruthlessly.

"They're all inside, Mr. Brandt," said the president's secretary, Maggie Dixon, a note of sympathy in her voice.

Arlo remained with Maggie as Bob Bertrand, head of the president's Secret Service detail, escorted Brandt into the room. The president was seated at his desk. Secretary of Defense Merritt and Joint Chiefs Chairman Robert Taylor were seated opposite him on a low couch. As Bertrand guided Brandt to a chair next to Merritt, Marshall stood.

"Jim, for the thousandth time, you know that Arlo's welcome here."

"The Secret Service insists he stay with Maggie, Mr. President," Brandt replied.

"Hell, I've known Arlo longer than I've known Bertrand here." Marshall cut himself off, not wanting to make light in view of the situation. "Jim, I want you to know we're doing everything we can to find Olivia. We'll get her back. You have my word."

"Thank you, sir," Brandt said as he lowered himself into the chair.

Marshall sat. "I've read Doug and Bob in on our talk with President Mikhailov. I've also spoken to Prime Minister Chafetz and relayed the intel about the EMP threat, just as we discussed—neutral, just the facts. I offered support from the Fifth Fleet if needed. He didn't hesitate. He definitely thinks it's necessary."

Brandt, Merritt, and Taylor sat quietly. Events were unfolding rapidly. Taylor, who had seen a lifetime of military conflict, thought the situation had a certain ominous, martial inevitability about it.

"Chafetz is placing the Israeli Air Force on alert," the president continued. "He said he can't risk a delay. Frankly, I don't blame him. He has no margin for error.

"Now, with this brazen attack right here on American soil"— Marshall jabbed his desktop with his index finger, his voice projecting anger—"barely two miles from the White House, we can't suffer any illusions that we're no longer involved—that this is only Israel's problem."

"What do you need from us, Mr. President?" Brandt asked.

"I need to know from you, Jim, how far you think our support for Israel should go," Marshall replied. He pointed at Merritt and Taylor. "And I need to know from Doug and Bob whether we have the capability."

"Mr. President, do we have any idea who struck the vehicles on H Street?" Brandt asked. "Can they be tied to any state actors?"

"The CIA and NSA are trying to determine that right now. They're reviewing security cameras in the vicinity, electronic intercepts, satellite feeds. So far, nothing. They're baffled, absolutely baffled. It's not like this happened on some country road; it happened during the evening rush in Washington, D.C. Yet no sign of the attackers. They're ghosts. How's that possible? And that's not all. As you know, those were DGT folks that got hit. I've been a little skittish about them from time to time, mainly because of the optics. The press absolutely hates private military contractors. But DGT's men are damned good at what they do and they were wiped out. I'm no intelligence expert, but that looks to me like it requires the kind of skill, logistics, and coordination that can only be pulled off by a state actor."

"If it was a state actor, that's unequivocally an act of war," Merritt interjected. "And we'd be justified in responding accordingly."

"Mr. President," Brandt added, "we may not have the luxury of waiting until we've nailed down—with a hundred percent accuracy—whether a foreign country was responsible. We may never be able to nail that down. We don't know when—or even if—there's going to be an EMP strike, but all signs are that something big is going to happen, and soon. Although you and I both have our doubts about Russia's innocence in all this, I'm concerned that the actor is Iran. If we're caught flat-footed, it could be a debacle. At minimum, Israel could cease to exist."

"So what do you advise, Jim?"

"What specific support did you offer to Chafetz?"

"Logistics, refueling, intel, and, of course, presence of a carrier strike group—the *Eisenhower*—in the Gulf as a deterrent."

Brandt shook his head. "Respectfully, that's not enough, sir. Israel's air force can do a lot of damage. Perhaps take out a majority of Iran's nuclear capability. But they don't have the kind of bunker busters— like our MOPs—needed to be sure that Iran's most hardened facilities are taken out. Only we have that capacity. We need to seriously consider deploying that weaponry."

The president turned to Taylor. "Bob?"

"We're positioned to both assist the IDF and deploy our own forces, Mr. President," Taylor said. Brandt's statement had caused the chairman of the Joint Chiefs to sit at attention. The old soldier was much more cautious, more reluctant to use military force, than anyone else in the room. "But, sir, if I might suggest—strongly suggest—that we not take any action until we're at the point of no return." Taylor held up his hand as if to ward off the inevitable question. "That point isn't easily definable. Mossad has outstanding intelligence on the locations of Iran's nuke facilities. We've also gotten some from the MEK dissidents in Iran. But neither Mossad nor the CIA knows from which site any nukes would be launched. We need to hold off until we get as much intel as possible, before our strike window closes."

"I concur, Mr. President," Merritt weighed in. "If we go down this road, we need to maximize the possibility that we're successful. We can't risk that they'll be able to get off even one of their missiles."

"I don't disagree, sir," Brandt added. "If we—along with Israel—hit Iran, the consequences are obvious; too numerous to mention. The oil shock alone will drive markets worldwide into a tailspin. And that's if we're successful. If we attack and still leave Iran with nuclear capacity"—Brandt shrugged—"well, earlier today we talked political fallout. Many of the Iranian nuclear facilities are located in the midst of civilian populations. Intentionally so. Human shields."

"Doug, do we have any military options other than hitting their facilities with these godforsaken bunker busters?" Marshall asked. "Anything that could avoid innocent Iranian casualties?"

"I'm afraid not, Mr. President. As you're well aware, our missile-intercept programs were stagnant, if not degraded, during the previous administration. Peace through unilateral disarmament. At this moment we have six Ticonderoga-class Aegis cruisers in and around the Persian Gulf. But their design capability is for midcourse and reentry-phase intercepts, not boost phase. That's not going to help Israel. So we need to hit the launch sites *before* any missiles are fired."

Marshall slapped his desk in frustration. He stared vacantly across the room for an instant before collecting himself.

"All right, gentlemen. Doug, Bob, be ready to go when I give the order. Liaise with IDF. I assume we've gamed this with them multiple times."

Taylor opened his mouth to confirm, but Marshall cut him off. "We'll wait until we've gathered all the intel that's available before our window of opportunity closes, Bob's point of no return. I trust you all to alert me when that time approaches. I will then give the order to strike Iran."

The finality in Marshall's voice gave the trio sitting across from him their cue to leave. As they rose, Marshall said, "Jim, stick around. No sense in coming and going every ten minutes. I'm certain to need you." The president turned to Merritt and Taylor. "As you leave, tell Maggie to let Arlo in here. If Bertrand gives you any shit, deck him."

Merritt, Taylor, and Brandt chuckled. All three men comprehended the magnitude of what was transpiring. Each was aware of the crush of responsibility weighing upon the man behind the desk, a feeling only previous wartime presidents could truly understand. Each was signaling respect, not just for the office but for the man holding the office. And appreciation that the man appeared equal to the moment.

"One last thing," the president said as Merritt and Taylor were opening the door. "Where in hell are we going to get that intel?"

CHAPTER SIXTY-THREE

Julie filed the last of the rental forms and shut down her computer for the day. She had agreed to cover the swing shift at the Terrapin Estates rental office for Lori, one of the other rental agents, so that she could attend a Nationals game with her boyfriend.

It was almost dark out. Julie had been on the job for twelve hours, but she really didn't mind the long shift. It had been a slow day and she appreciated the overtime. She'd spent good portions of the shift shopping online and e-mailing some of her friends. The manager didn't mind as long as she got her work done, and most of her work was complete by midafternoon, with only one new arrival checking in after three o'clock. Nonetheless, she was looking forward to going back to her apartment, taking a long shower, and relaxing in front of the television with a glass of wine. A movie she had wanted to see was debuting on pay-per-view, one she'd missed at the theater because Justin, her lying, cheating ex-boyfriend, had taken her ex–best friend, Barb, to the show instead. Julie had stumbled upon this indiscretion when she found the ticket stub in the lout's jeans while doing the laundry. When Julie confronted him, the idiot unraveled in an instant, incoherently claiming that Barb had come on to him but that the movie had been innocent. The former was probably true. He was an idiot, but he was a really good-looking idiot, and Barb was in perpetual pursuit of pretty boys.

Julie turned off her desk lamp and began making her way out when the rental office door opened and Justin's opposite in every way walked in. This was no pretty boy, although he was at least as good-looking and far better built than Justin. This, Julie thought, was a man— something women in her age group encountered about as frequently as leprechauns. Maybe the evening still had possibilities.

"Well, look who's back!" Julie exclaimed, flashing a perfect set of laser-whitened teeth. "I was afraid you'd fallen into the bay or something. I've seen some of your friends from time to time, even though you all keep pretty much to yourselves, but you must have been practicing your imitation of the invisible man. I thought I wouldn't see you before your rental's up on Thursday."

Garin smiled charmingly, an act that didn't come naturally. He wanted to maintain the impression that he was just an average guy spending the week fishing and hanging out with his college buddies.

"My office called and I had to go back to the District to take care of some business," Garin explained.

"So you took care of business and now here you are," Julie said cheerfully as she came from behind the rental counter, making sure Garin got a good look at her plyometrics-toned body. "Oh, I almost forgot." She stopped abruptly and began walking back to the desk. "Your friends asked me to make sure I called them whenever one of you guys arrived. I think maybe they wanted a head count for a beer run or something later on."

"No need to do that," Garin said with feigned casualness. "They called me earlier and asked me to pick up the beer and some wings on my way back." Garin leaned against the counter. "Anybody else show up after I left?"

Julie looked conflicted. "You know," she said reaching for the phone,

"I'd better call. The one guy—built kinda like you, actually—gave me a fifty just to make sure I'd call."

Garin glided around the counter and placed his left hand gently over Julie's as she began to pick up the receiver. "Had to be Gates," Garin said with a knowing grin. "That SOB. He's setting me up again, I know it. He'll probably have some booby trap waiting for me when I come in the door. He's got me three times in a row now. You probably wouldn't believe it, but he had a bag full of dog crap over the transom last time. Just missed me." Garin reached into his hip pocket with his right hand and pulled out a roll of bills. "I'll give you a hundred dollars not to make the call."

"Whoa," Julie laughed, enjoying the feel of Garin's hand on hers. "Keep the cash, cowboy. You guys throw money around like it's free." She raised an eyebrow. "But I do like your style. I'll just have to think of some other way you can repay me." She placed the receiver back in the cradle.

"Well, Julie, maybe you and I can figure something out."

"At least you remembered my name. That's a start."

"Wrote it in my diary," Garin declared with mock earnestness.

"Not 'hot blonde with the great ass'?"

"Well, that, too."

Julie remained standing within inches of Garin. Most guys she knew would've taken that as a signal to make a move, which typically consisted of some clumsy pawing of her body. It was, after all, a killer body, so who could blame them? This man did no such thing. He just gazed steadily and smiled. Not arrogantly. Confidently. But with a hint of danger.

Under different circumstances, Garin might have had similar thoughts. But he was tightly focused on his objective. His hunch had proved correct. The Quds Force operatives were, indeed, using the same cabin. And it sounded like Bor might be with them. Garin needed to get whatever relevant information he could from Julie before embarking on a course of action.

"So, Julie, how much beer and wings should I get?"

Julie, who had eased even closer to Garin, blinked, snapping back to reality.

"Oh. Well, let's see," she said as she returned to her desk and restarted her computer. "You know," she said absently as she typed in her password, "your friend—Gates, I think you called him? He sure doesn't seem like much of a prankster to me. Real serious. A little scary, actually."

"That's vintage Gates." Garin smiled. "Part of the act. Always putting people on. He's harmless, though. Even a little bit of a wimp."

"And the other guys I've seen aren't exactly rays of sunshine either," Julie said, scrolling down the tenant register. "No offense. I know you guys go back. They just all look like they could use a good laxative."

"Well, I guess we all grew up and got responsibilities. Got serious." Garin shrugged. "That's why we wanted to come out here and unwind a little."

"And some of them looked kinda, I don't know, foreign, you know? Just saying."

"Probably been in the sun, out on the bay."

Julie stopped scrolling. "Here we go. There are"—Julie counted under her breath—"fourteen."

Fourteen. Garin had expected three or four, max. Clearly, he needed support for this operation. He didn't know how to reach Brandt without Olivia, and he couldn't call the FBI. Even if he could, they would take a while. Same with Dwyer. And his friend had lost several men in the last few hours. He could hardly ask him to sacrifice more men and place his organization in legal jeopardy. But Garin had no other options. He couldn't take on fourteen Tangos by himself.

"Plus," Julie added, "I think one or two guys brought their wives or girlfriends. They're not on the register, but when they drove in earlier this evening, I did see a woman. Tons of really long black hair. Pretty. I'll just register and charge them tomorrow morning."

Olivia . . .

Any remaining chance Garin had to wait for the cavalry to arrive evaporated. Bor was going to interrogate Olivia about what Garin had told her and what she, in turn, had told Brandt. Then he'd kill her. Garin had no choice but to call Dwyer and hope he and his men could get here fast. But he needed to move now.

Garin thought quickly. "Thanks. Is there a place close by where I can pick up some cold beer, maybe some wings?"

Julie shut down her computer and came around the counter again. "There's a 7-Eleven about two miles down on Choptank," Julie said, waving in an easterly direction. "Just hang a left onto Waverly as you come out of the access road, go a half mile, and take a right onto Choptank. It'll be on your right, next to Dumser's Bait and Tackle. I don't know about wings, but they've got frozen pizza, cold cuts, stuff like that. The 7-Eleven, that is."

"Great. You've been a real help." Garin smiled again, trying to keep up the charade of normalcy. "Is there any possibility . . ."

"There might be," Julie said with a playful look. She quickly wrote her cell phone number on the back of one of the manager's business cards lying on the counter and handed it to Garin.

"I know you probably want to catch up with your friends tonight and all. But give me a call whenever you have some time. I'm just twenty minutes away; maybe we can grab a beer."

Garin palmed the card, smiled appreciatively, and headed for the door before turning.

"By the way, did you happen to see my buddy Julian arrive? Skinny, glasses, thin light brown hair?"

"Oh yeah, I think so," Julie replied. "Real worried-looking? Like he's marching to the electric chair or something? Now, *that* guy really could use a vacation."

Bor had allotted six hours to interrogate Perry and Day, but he was confident he wouldn't need the entire time. Taking Day's measure, Bor concluded that the Senate counsel would probably be an easier subject than the woman.

Bor stood in the living room area in the center of the cabin's main level and scrutinized Day and Perry, seated together on a small couch. Whereas the frail lawyer was looking downward, pulling nervously at his fingernails, and appeared on the verge of evacuating his bladder, the aide to James Brandt gazed directly at Bor with a look of defiance. That look, Bor knew, was not uncommon for strangers to cruelty. They had little conception of the horrors that their fellow man had the capacity to inflict. That would change shortly.

Bor's primary concern at the moment was the Iranians. While there was no doubt that Bor was in charge, they seemed perpetually perched on the brink of violence. Without Bor's knowledge, a few of them had roughed up Day in the back of the van on the drive to the Terrapin Estates. Upon discovering this, Bor sent a message to the other Iranians by unceremoniously snapping the principal culprit's right arm at the elbow. The other Iranians instantly fell into line. Bor was the undisputed alpha dog of this operation. Nonetheless, they continued to hover about Day and Perry like jackals circling carrion.

Bor much preferred working alone or with a small cadre of his own handpicked professionals. He was most comfortable with a team of Spetsnaz comrades, but he'd been impressed with the Omega operators. They were as good as anyone he'd ever worked with. He'd even grown to like and respect them, particularly their leader, Michael Garin, one of the few men Bor considered a peer.

In contrast, these Quds Force men seemed little more than highly trained thugs, with an inflated sense of their own competence. Not that they couldn't be effective. They were a creditable special operations unit. Provided the mission was relatively straightforward, and their adversary ordinary, they were able to acquit themselves very well. But their limitations became glaringly obvious when tasked to kill Garin.

They'd been thrust on Bor by Moscow, who thought Bor needed help. In the end, Bor ended up killing most of the Omega team by himself anyway. But the Iranians at least provided logistical support.

Bor turned to Atosh Larijani, the senior Iranian. "Take Mr. Day to one of the upstairs bedrooms. We will start with him." Larijani nodded at two Quds Force operatives, who grabbed Day roughly by each arm and pulled him off the couch. The attorney appeared almost catatonic. Although he offered no resistance, his face was tense and his body was rigid.

"*Gently*, please," Bor admonished. "Mr. Day is a friend. We need not force information from him. He will cooperate. We're just going to have a little chat."

Day, his eyes wide with fear, hoped it was true. Why shouldn't it be? He'd already demonstrated his willingness to provide Bor with any information he needed. He'd proven his loyalty and reliability for nearly three years. Why were they treating him like this? He hadn't betrayed them in any way. Not really. He'd only acted defensively. This had to be a show for Perry to frighten her. That was it. Of course, that *had* to be it.

The two Iranians disappeared with Day down the hall and up the stairs. Bor looked at his watch. Ten fifteen. Less than six hours until exfiltration. *His* exfil. A speedboat manned by three heavily armed naval Spetsnaz operators was hidden in a cove less than half a mile away. A fast trip four miles down the eastern Chesapeake shoreline to a waiting helicopter. Then a short hop to a plane located at a small rural airfield in central North Carolina. He had been given explicit instructions to leave the Iranians behind. After all, their presence would be more evidence for the Americans of Iran's culpability in the EMP attack. An attack that would occur sometime in the next eight hours.

Bor walked over to the couch and sat next to Olivia, an almost imperceptible flinch betraying her show of defiance. Bor looked at her a moment, his face inscrutable, then patted her knee reassuringly.

"We will have our little talk shortly, Ms. Perry," Bor said in a calm, eerily detached voice. "As you no doubt have guessed, I'm interested in your conversations with my friend Mike Garin. That's all. Nothing earth-shattering. But first I need to have a talk with Mr. Day. It shouldn't take long. In the meantime, gather your thoughts, and if you need anything at all, just ask Atosh."

Bor rose and smiled down at Olivia.

"Be back in a bit . . ."

Olivia was sure she'd never heard anything more menacing in her entire life.

Garin crept carefully downhill and through the brush toward the cabin housing Bor and the Iranians. The sky was moonless and the densely wooded forest with its thick canopy reduced visibility to barely five feet in every direction but one. Less than one hundred fifty feet ahead, the lights of the cabin illuminated its immediate perimeter and acted as a beacon for Garin, who would otherwise have no indication he was headed in the right direction.

Improvisation. Garin carried a six-pack of beer in his left hand. In his right he carried a cheap fishing rod he'd purchased at Dumser's Bait and Tackle Shop next to the 7-Eleven on Choptank. Wedged between his right hand and the shaft of the rod was his SIG Sauer P226, suppressor affixed. In the dark, from a distance of more than a few feet, the SIG and the fishing rod were indistinguishable.

While driving to and from the 7-Eleven, Garin had made several unanswered calls to Dwyer. The lack of response was unusual, but Garin surmised Dwyer must still be at Carl's bedside, cell phone off in compliance with hospital rules. Garin had left a message for Dwyer, as well as for Matt on DGT's main line, although he knew any operation of this magnitude and sensitivity could be green-lighted only by Dwyer himself. Garin couldn't take down the occupants of the cabin alone, not if he had any hope of Olivia's making it out alive. He desperately needed support from Dwyer's men.

On his way back from the 7-Eleven, Garin had placed his phone on vibrate and every minute or so he'd hit redial. That was fifteen minutes ago, with no response. He had no choice but to begin moving in on his own.

The darkness provided excellent cover as he approached the rear of the cabin. Although the curtains weren't drawn, the main- and second-floor windows were too high for anyone at ground level to see everyone inside with certainty. From Garin's vantage point slightly up the hill, he was even with the main-floor windows but still too far away to see the occupants clearly without a scope. Through the picture window in the living room he could see several individuals standing about, as well as others seated on a couch and chairs. But he couldn't tell whether they were male or female, American or Iranian.

Slowly, Garin moved closer to the cabin but still well within the tree line of the surrounding forest. He expected there would be guards stationed outside, and Bor was likely to have positioned portable motion detectors and pressure plates around the cabin as well.

When he came within seventy feet of the cabin, Garin was able to discern two figures standing at opposite ends of the structure. Two more were likely stationed on the other side, but Garin couldn't see them. He needed to take out all of them to ensure getting into the cabin undetected. But to get to anyone on the other side, he first had to leave the cover of the tree line.

Before taking care of the outside guards, Garin had to find out where Olivia and Day were in relation to their captors on the inside. While scanning the windows he continued to move closer to the edge of the tree line, approximately forty feet from the cabin.

There he detected movement in one of the upstairs windows and paused. *Taras Bor.* The Russian's head was cast downward and he appeared to be speaking to someone seated to the right. An Iranian was barely visible to his left.

This complicated matters significantly, rendering a bad situation worse. Garin had expended thousands of rounds in innumerable kill-house exercises, as well as in actual hostage scenarios in both Iraq and Somalia. None had presented the challenges he was facing tonight. It would be difficult enough for one man to take out Bor and the Iranians were they all grouped together in a small area. Taking out the downstairs contingent without alerting those upstairs, and without increasing the already high probability of collateral damage, would be nearly impossible. He had no flash bangs, no backup, and poor intel on the bad guys' positions. He needed support—lots of it—and he needed it now. Otherwise, this exercise would be futile, suicidal.

He hit the redial on his cell again to no avail. Seconds later, more movement caught his eye, this time in the living room window below. He looked down at the ground-floor window and his chest seized with astonishment. Seated on a couch was his sister, Katy. Although he couldn't see them, he knew Joe and the kids must be nearby.

The noise outside the bunker. In the chaos of the last few days Garin had neglected to check on Joe and Katy. The seemingly omniscient Bor, however, had not. Clearly, to have located the bunker meant the Russian had extraordinary resources here in the United States. But that wasn't an issue to be addressed now. Right now, all that mattered was that Bor had located Garin's loved ones and was using them as an insurance policy. Just in case Garin showed up. Freeze him in place. The Russian assassin had covered all the angles. Once again, he remained one step ahead.

Garin felt a rush of adrenaline fueled by a combination of fear and fury. A jumble of childhood memories and emotion swirled in his brain, stoking his rage and causing the muscles in his neck and jaw to tense. The monsters in the cabin were holding the person who knew him best, loved him most. Maybe the only person who loved him. And they had Olivia, too. She'd taken a chance, risked her career, to help him.

So for their crimes they would suffer. Especially Bor. Garin would rip out his intestines and ram them so far down his throat they'd end up where they'd started. He was going to die slowly, in unbearable agony.

And then Garin's training—the cold, steel discipline of Omega's team leader—began to kick in. His training told him that any move he made now, compromised by emotion, would end in disaster. He needed to think, be rational.

His training, however, was at war with his instincts. Long ago, Laws had warned him there would be one or two extraordinary situations in his career in which that would happen. No amount of training, no amount of experience, would help. And on these occasions he would be alone, the correctness of his choice validated only by its outcome.

He sensed he was left, quite simply, with no choice but to act. If he didn't, Katy and her family would be dead.

Katy's eyes reflected seething hatred toward her captors. The animals had thrown her family, bound and gagged, into the rear of a filthy Econoline van and had driven from Ohio to . . . wherever they were. Joe, bleeding from his scalp from repeated blows to the head, had been unconscious for most of the trip. They had stopped only once, Katy presumed for gas. The family was kept locked in the van, and the kids, denied the use of a restroom, had soiled themselves. No food, no water. Nine hours of driving sprawled on the bare metal floor of the van.

The animals had taken Joe somewhere else in the cabin. She hadn't seen him since their arrival, and she suspected the worst after Joe had punched one of the men as they were herding their captives into the cabin. Two of them leapt upon Joe, beating him as the others kept their weapons trained on him. Katy held no illusion that the beatings had discontinued. The kids were sitting together at her feet on the floor, frightened but quiet.

Seated on the couch to Katy's immediate right was a young woman who had arrived at the cabin along with a frail, distraught-looking man a few hours after the Burns family. She had tried to speak to Katy but was slapped by one of the guards for the effort. The leader of the group seemed to take particular interest in the woman, who apparently possessed information valuable to the animals. One disapproving glance from him had caused the guard to retreat submissively.

A total of six guards, each with some sort of submachine gun, formed a semicircle in front of the couch. The one named Atosh sat in front of her in a chair. Two stood to his right in front of the living room window. Three stood to Atosh's left. Katy let them know she was unimpressed.

"Six men with guns to cover two women and three children," Katy hissed in contempt. "Pathetic. You're not men. You're not even cowards. You're beneath cowards. My husband—"

"Will be dead soon," Atosh said dismissively, cutting her off.

"My husband will kill you," Katy continued. "He will—"

"Silence," Atosh commanded. "Your husband, like all Americans, is weak. He is all but dead." Katy heard the soft sniffles of Kimmy and Alex. But Katrina Garin Burns didn't heed the Iranian.

"My brother will find you," Katy continued in a poorly controlled rage. "Every single one of you. You've bought yourselves a nightmare. Worse. You don't know it yet, but you're already dead. There's nothing you can do to change that. Nothing you can do to save yourselves. Because you can't stop him. Can't beat him. No one can." A pause. "But you can still save your families. Let my children go. That's your only chance. Otherwise, every member of your families will be dead." Katy looked at each guard in turn. "Every. Single. One."

A sneer crossed Atosh's face. The impertinence of the American female. She had been a constant irritant throughout the trip from Ohio. No matter, the impertinence would soon be purged from her, along with her life. "You foolish—" He stopped in midsentence, distracted by the chirping of the outdoor motion detectors. And the sound of someone singing.

G arin, vastly outnumbered, decided to hide in plain sight. Unable to see all the perimeter guards, he determined that the risk of being detected before he was able to get into the house was too high. So Garin decided to take the risk of detection out of the equation. He'd simply make his presence known to everyone in the cabin. Garin quietly retreated from the tree line back into the woods. When he'd gone far enough, he began humming loudly and walked to the cabin again, making no attempt to conceal the noise of twigs and branches snapping underfoot.

Just before he broke the tree line, Garin began singing boisterously, feigning inebriation.

Well, I stand right up to a mountain . . .

The guards peered into the dark, standing tensely, with their hands near the pistols on their hips. A third guard quickly appeared from the front of the cabin to check on what was happening.

And I chop it down with the edge of my hand . . .

Garin walked unsteadily toward the cabin, carrying the six-pack in his left hand and the fishing rod camouflaging the SIG in his right. His head down, he appeared lost in song, but through veiled eyes he was assessing the guards, gauging the angles.

As Garin drew closer he saw that one of the guards wore a head mike, his hand pressing against the earbud so he could hear over the noise. Someone from inside must have been inquiring what the commotion was all about.

The guard responded in Farsi to the inquiry coming over his mike. "No, Atosh, no. There is no problem. Everything is under control." A pause, then: "A drunken American. Yes. We will send him on his way."

Garin continued to approach, affecting an oblivious, careless manner. His eyes scanned from side to side. No other guards outside. He looked up as if noticing the guards in the dark for the first time and staggered to a halt, the picture of confusion.

"What . . . Wait, isn't this the Prince George's cabin?"

"Sir, you are lost," said one of the guards without a trace of accent. "This is not the Prince George's. You must move along if you wish to locate your cabin."

"Oh man," Garin moaned. "This is really messed up. I was just fishing . . . lost track of the time. As you can see I didn't catch squat"—Garin held up the beer cans—"except this. And now here I am, lost in the dark."

From the outlines of their torsos, Garin suspected the guards were wearing body armor. He would have to shoot each of them in the head. A neat trick in the dark, even at close range.

"Sir, you must move on," the guard insisted politely. "This is a private rental." The guard pointed to his left. "Perhaps your cabin is in that direction."

Garin turned in the direction in which the guard pointed. "Where?"

The guard took his eye off Garin and turned in the direction in which he was pointing. "Over there."

Garin seized the split second, dropped the beer and rod, and rapidly fired two suppressed rounds into the heads of each of the three guards, who collapsed onto the soft ground without a sound. Garin sprinted toward the cabin and moved to the front to confirm there were no remaining guards outside, hugging the exterior wall so he wouldn't be seen from the windows.

As he moved along the right side of the cabin, he saw a light in a basement window. Staying to the side of the window, he bent down and glanced inside. Joe Burns, blood dripping from his head and face, was suspended by his hands from a wooden overhead beam in the basement laundry. Two Quds Force operatives, their backs to the window, were standing next to him. Even from behind, Garin immediately recognized the one holding a bent wire coat hanger in his hand as Mr. Obvious from the Diamondback. The other had what appeared to be a Mossberg 590A1 shotgun. From what Garin could see of Joe's shredded, blood-soaked clothing, the Iranians had been beating Joe's head, legs, and torso with the hanger.

Garin passed by the window and completed a circumnavigation of the cabin. No other guards were outside. He approached the rear door from the side and took a quick look in the door's small window. Seeing no one, he carefully opened the door, stepped inside, and closed it. To his left, a flight of stairs ran up to the main and second floors. To his right was the door leading to the basement.

Garin opened the basement door slowly, praying that the hinges were well oiled. From the top of the stairs he could see the lower legs of the two Iranians and hear them talking in Farsi. Joe would be hanging a couple of feet to their left.

Taking a breath, Garin descended the stairs swiftly and silently. He reached the bottom just a few feet from the Iranians and began firing before they realized he was there, double tapping each. Both were dead before they hit the floor.

Garin stuck the SIG into the holster in his waistband, pulled out a SOG tactical knife from his left boot, and cut the ropes from Joe's hands. Joe began to collapse but Garin steadied him with his free hand.

As Joe rubbed his arms, trying to get the feeling back in them, Garin ejected the half-spent magazine from his pistol and seated a fresh one. His next move would require him to engage at least six targets at once, and he wanted to reduce the need to change magazines in the middle of the fight. Garin looked over at Joe, who was doing his best to mask his pain.

"How bad is it?" Garin whispered.

"About as bad as it looks. They got my legs pretty good. I'm kinda wobbly. I didn't tell them anything, though, Mike. Not that I had anything to say."

"Can you handle one of those?" Garin asked, pointing to the Mossberg.

The sergeant major gave him a withering look.

"Katy and the kids are on the next floor. There are half a dozen of those bastards covering them. On the floor above that, there are at least three more. It's not optimal, but I'll need to use my pistol—I can't use the shotgun and risk spraying Katy and the kids. Can you get up the flight of stairs?"

"I think so."

"All right. Take a position on the landing inside the back door and smoke any bad guys that try to come your way."

"Like hell. That's not gonna happen. Those are my wife and kids up there in the living room. I'm coming with you."

"Joe, listen. I need to move fast. Really fast. No margin for error. Even then . . . Look, I just can't risk having you slow me down."

Joe eyed Garin with an intensity he'd never before seen from his brother-in-law. "That's my family up there," Joe snarled. "You better not slow *me* down."

Garin knew he was wasting precious seconds and that he wouldn't win this argument. He conceded to himself that he needed help. Even with a second gun, the odds of pulling this off were not good.

"Okay, I'll go up to the first floor and wait in the hallway leading to the living room." Garin picked up the shotgun and handed it to Joe. "You continue up to the second floor. There's a light on in the bedroom directly above the living room. There should be three bad guys standing in there, plus a skinny blondish guy who's probably sitting in a chair or on the bed."

"I saw them bring him in," Joe said.

"It would be nice if he came out of this alive. Try to avoid hitting him if you can. But you're not trained for this, so don't be cute. When you're ready, you go into that room blasting. Take out all the bad guys."

"I've never been accused of being cute."

"One of the guys in that bedroom is *really* bad. If you hesitate, even for a millisecond, you're dead—we're all dead. Got it?"

"We're wasting time," Joe replied impatiently.

"I'll wait until you've made your move first. When you start firing that cannon, I'm counting on it to startle the enemy in the living room just long enough to give me an edge."

Joe nodded. Garin proceeded quietly up the stairs to the landing at the back door. Someone was talking in the living room. Garin poked his head quickly into the darkened hallway. He could see the kids seated on the floor in front of the couch twenty feet away. An Iranian seated in a chair facing the couch blocked his view of someone Garin presumed was Katy.

Garin motioned for Joe to pass him and continue up the stairs to the second floor. As he passed, Joe patted Garin once on the shoulder.

Garin slid slowly down the hallway toward the living room, hugging the right wall, weapon extended at eye level. He could hear his sister cursing the Iranians. Balls. He stopped—remaining obscured by the shadows of the hallway, three feet from the entrance to the living room. If he stayed to the right side of the hallway when he moved forward, he'd have a clear shot at the three Iranians facing the window and the one sitting in a chair with his back to him. At the same time, the Iranians standing to the right, in front of the window, wouldn't have a clear shot at him. He decided to start with the men on the left and then move to the other side of the hallway, engage the seated man, and finally the two in front of the window.

Garin inched forward. Alex's eyes widened as he noticed Uncle Mike standing with a pistol in the shadows of the hallway. Garin shook his head curtly and Alex obediently cast his eyes downward just as a series of deafening explosions sounded from the upstairs bedroom.

For Garin, the next five seconds unfolded in a slow, dreamlike sequence. He stepped forward and fired six rounds at the Quds Force operatives standing to the left. Each round found its target, sending the three Iranians tumbling backward and landing in a tangled sprawl on the floor.

Katy reflexively dove on top of the kids to shield them from errant bullets. Olivia dove next to her. Atosh, the seated Iranian, wasn't able to turn more than halfway around before two shots from Garin's weapon tore the top of his head off, blasting him from the chair and onto the floor next to Olivia.

Mental clock ticking, Garin stepped to the other side of the living room entrance and pivoted to his right to engage the two Iranians standing in front of the window. Before he could lock onto either target, he realized that the one closest to him had already raised his weapon and was about to fire, when the living room window exploded and the skulls of both Iranians burst simultaneously into a pink mist, sending their lifeless torsos crashing to the floor amid a cascade of shattered glass.

Sniper fire.

Garin rapidly checked the six corpses, ignoring the ringing in his ears and the cries of his niece and nephews. He took a brief glance at the women and kids to confirm that they were unharmed, then bolted up the stairs to the second floor, taking three steps at a time.

Reaching the landing, he jutted his head into the hallway and, seeing nothing, moved to the bedroom door, where Joe was standing, chest heaving, Mossberg held at his hip.

Joe turned urgently to Garin. "Katy and the kids?"

"Scared witless, but good as new."

Garin peered into the bedroom to inspect the carnage. A kaleidoscope of blood was splattered across the walls behind two bodies lying on the floor. Neither body was Bor's.

To the left of the door, Julian Day sat cowering in the corner, hugging his knees to his chest. The counsel for the Senate Select Committee on Intelligence stared at the mangled bodies of the Iranians, eyes wide and his face frozen in terror. Flecks of blood covered his right arm and shoulder.

"What happened to the third Tango?" Garin asked Joe.

"Only two were here. I shot the two that were standing and tried to avoid the skinny guy like you said. He might've gotten nicked by some shot, but he'll be fine."

Garin looked at the slightly open window with no screen and understood: Hendrix. Taras Bor, the former Omega operator, had recognized the song and the singing. He'd come to the logical conclusion that Garin wouldn't have assaulted the cabin without overwhelming force, and coldly made the most rational decision. He was gone and would not be found.

Garin's cell vibrated in his pocket. He pulled it out, answered curtly, and heard a familiar voice. "You still playing Lone Ranger or is it safe to come in?" Dwyer asked.

"I thought it was you out there but was a little worried it might somehow be the FBI," Garin said. "It's clear. Everyone moving in here's a friendly." Garin ended the call.

"Cavalry?" Joe asked.

Garin nodded. "Go take care of your family."

As Joe hobbled painfully down the hallway, Garin called after him. "Hey, Sergeant Major."

Joe turned.

"I'm glad you married my sister."

Garin stuck his SIG back into his waistband, noticing for the first time that he'd been grazed by a shot at the right hip. He walked over to Day, who recoiled as Garin grabbed him by the collar and pulled him to his feet.

"Shape up, Julian. We've got work to do."

Garin pulled Day along the hall and down the stairs to the living room, where half a dozen of Dwyer's black-clad men were moving efficiently about—searching, then covering the bodies of the Iranians and administering first aid to Olivia, Katy, and the kids. Dwyer stood in the middle of the room, flanked by two men carrying M110 sniper rifles. The man on the left was Matt. Although he'd never met the man on Dwyer's right, Garin recognized him in an instant.

"Meet the man who saved your life," Dwyer said as Congo Knox extended his hand. Garin stood motionless, bewildered. Slowly, he relaxed his grip on Day and moved warily toward Knox.

Dwyer, recognizing Garin's hesitation, said, "Mikey, of all days, today's Congo's first with DGT." Dwyer chuckled nervously. "Baptism by fire. You know he's no longer with Delta? We signed him up this morning and he wasn't slated to start with us until next month, but I played a hunch. He didn't have to come on this assignment, yet he agreed right away when I told him what it was. Heck, he insisted on coming. He took out the shooter who had you dead to rights."

"Mike, Congo Knox," the sniper said, hand still outstretched. "Dan told me you thought you saw me in New York and D.C. You were right. He still brought me aboard, figuring the assignment to take you out wasn't my call. I'm sure you have a lot of questions, and probably want to punch me. Maybe worse. But I don't know where the order to take you out came from. An order like that doesn't originate at Bragg or MacDill. But that's the extent of my knowledge."

After several long seconds, Garin grasped Knox's hand. "I'm not going to make happy talk with you right now. Even though it wasn't your call, it'll take a while to process. And, yeah, I may have to clock you to get it out of my system. But I understand. Unfortunately. Been there." Garin turned and glared at Julian Day. "I have an idea who might know where the order came from, though."

Garin then pointed at Dwyer. "Just when were you planning on telling me you were bringing the guy who was supposed to kill me to DGT?"

Dwyer looked sheepish. "Mikey, like I said, it all happened in the last twenty-four. The word in the community was Congo was becoming a free agent, so we tracked him down as fast as we could. Found him down at the Green Beret Parachute Club. Figured it was better to have him on our side than on someone else's ticket. So we took him off the market. Hey, in the end he saved your life."

Garin did not look placated.

"What about Bor?" Dwyer asked, anxious to change the subject.

"Gone."

"I'll send some men after him."

"Forget it, you won't find him, even with NVGs. He had a plan, and he's prepared for just this."

Garin saw Katy approaching from the other side of the room and turned back to Knox. "We'll talk," Garin said as he pulled Day forward and thrust him toward Dwyer. "Keep an eye on him for me, will you, Dan?"

Katy crossed the room and embraced Garin. "Not bad, little brother," Katy said, trying with surprising success to remain composed. "Pop would be proud."

"Not bad yourself. It's a good thing you're so pretty," Garin said drily, "because you're one scary chick." He tilted his head toward Kimmy, Nicholas, and Alex, who were hugging Joe. "Traumatic situation. How do you think they'll hold up?"

"They're kids." She shrugged. "They're resilient. I'm sure there'll be a nightmare or two. We'll talk to them, probably with Father Augustine and Sister Frances Marie. But trust me, within a week it will be Kimmy, Nicholas, and Alex's excellent adventure. They'll be the envy of all the neighborhood kids. And on top of that their dad's a hero."

"Ah, yeah, about that . . ."

"Don't worry. We won't let them talk . . . much. You think you're the only one with a brain in this family? No 'operational details,' as you call it. Just the part where Dad saves them. Heck, that's all they really know anyway."

Even as Katy spoke, Kimmy, Nicholas, and Alex, showing little evidence of being shaken, gravitated to the imposing figure of Congo Knox, whose smart salutes they repeatedly returned with increasing precision and enthusiasm. *The Burns family's version of crisis therapy*, thought Garin.

Noticing Katy looking over his shoulder, Garin glanced back and saw Olivia, still visibly jarred, standing behind him.

"I didn't mean to interrupt, Michael," Olivia murmured, her eyes watering. "I just wanted to say thank you. You were . . . Well, thank you."

"I guessed you two probably knew one another," Katy said as she brushed by Garin to comfort Olivia. Embracing the aide to the national security advisor, Katy looked expectantly at her brother. "Mike?"

"I'll make introductions all around later," Garin said, trying his best not to sound brusque. "But right now we need to take care of some urgent business. Olivia, I assume you can reach Brandt?"

"Yes."

"Stand by. I'm going to"—Garin searched for the right word—"*debrief* Julian Day."

Garin walked over to where Day was standing between Dwyer and Knox. The kids immediately left Knox and hugged Garin's legs.

"Awesome, Uncle Mike!" Nicholas squealed. So much for trauma.

"I had my eye on you guys," Garin said, tousling their hair. "You're the bravest soldiers I've seen in a long time." He gently pried them from his legs and steered them back toward Knox. "Right now Uncle Mike's got some work to do. We'll catch up in a little bit. Okay?"

Garin turned to Dwyer. "Dan, have some of your men take the Burns family back up to the rental office," he said quietly as he grabbed Day by the arm. "I don't want them to hear what happens next."

"Got it, Mikey. But do what you have to do fast. I figure you've got no more than"—Dwyer examined his watch—"fifteen minutes before every CIA, DIA, and FBI agent within one hundred miles shows up."

Garin jerked Day roughly down the hallway toward the kitchen. Olivia, alarmed at the sight, tried to follow, but Dwyer placed his substantial frame between her and the kitchen. The dour look on his normally agreeable face told her not to press the issue.

Upon reaching the kitchen, Garin slapped Day hard across the face, causing him to stagger against the refrigerator. The lawyer, nerves already frayed from Bor's interrogation, yelped as much from dread as from pain. Grasping Day with one hand, Garin ripped through the drawers under the expansive kitchen counter until he found a stainless steel cleaver. He turned to Day.

"Let's review, Julian. With your assistance, Taras Bor and his Quds Force friends killed every single member of my team, a team vital to protecting America's national security interests. They were good men, good Americans. Doing a job you despised and hounded them for, but without which you wouldn't be able to go to the theater, grocery store, or ladies' room without fear of getting blown to bits." The words, though spoken quietly, were steeped in unmistakable malice.

"You also assisted Bor and his goons in kidnapping my sister's family, using them as bait and insurance against an attack by me. They beat my brother-in-law half to death and abused my sister, niece, and nephews. I have no doubt they would've killed them all once they'd served their purpose." Garin seized Day's right wrist. As he spoke, Day avoided looking at Garin's eyes and the cleaver in his hand.

"Now, you're going to tell me how you did that and who assisted you. But before you do, you're going to tell me everything I need to know about the EMP attack that's going to hit us. You didn't think we knew about that, did you? Of course you didn't. How could we? We're just ignorant grunts, tools of American hegemony, exploiting and violating the rights of kind, peace-loving people everywhere. While you, on the other hand, are the brilliant legal avenger, making the world safe for the perpetually aggrieved, the righteously entitled, and the morally superior."

Garin's voice grew softer as he spoke. Day, bizarrely, found himself straining to hear what Garin was saying, lest he miss a threat of imminent disfigurement.

"Here's how this is going to work, Julian," Garin continued. "Speed is critical. So first you'll give me the big picture: time of the attack, where it's coming from, and where it's going to hit. Then we'll get into the enemy's delivery vehicles, countermeasures, stuff like that. Finally, we'll talk about how and with whom you orchestrated all of this."

Day struggled futilely as Garin held the lawyer's right hand atop the granite counter. A foul odor wafted into the air. Garin angled the blade above Day's pinky finger, using the edge of the counter as a fulcrum.

"If you lie, a finger comes off. If I *think* you're lying, a finger comes off. If you hold back anything whatsoever, a finger comes off. Got it?"

Day clenched his fingers protectively. Garin responded by repositioning the cleaver over Day's wrist. "All right," Garin whispered. "Then this is how we'll play it. If you lie, a hand comes off. If I *think* you're lying, a hand comes off . . ."

"Please," the terrified attorney pleaded, sounding utterly drained and defeated. "This isn't necessary. I'll tell you everything you want to know."

Garin drew his face to within inches from Day's and studied the man's eyes for several seconds. There was no deceit, no resistance, only exhaustion and resignation.

Garin returned the blade to the drawer, pulled Day to the doorway, and called out to the living room. "Olivia, get in here right away."

N o one present in the Situation Room was sitting. It was a maelstrom of nervous energy.

After receiving a call from SecDef Merritt approximately twenty minutes earlier, Marshall had recalled to the White House all the attendees from the earlier meeting. Merritt had just received a call from Dan Dwyer, head of DGT, advising that he and his men had located James Brandt's senior aide, Olivia Perry, at a cabin along the Chesapeake. Dwyer informed him that his snipers were positioned around the cabin and were prepared to engage hostiles. Secretary Merritt was well aware that he didn't have the authority to give Dwyer's men the green light but calculated that there wasn't any time to send the matter through appropriate channels. Deciding to act and deal with the consequences later, Merritt granted Dwyer permission to engage. What Merritt hadn't known at the time was that Dwyer had placed the call a full minute *after* Matt and Congo Knox had already taken out the two Quds Force operatives in front of the living room window. Dwyer, too, believed it was better to ask for forgiveness than permission.

Minutes before everyone had assembled in the Situation Room, Prime Minister Chafetz had called Marshall to inform the president that Israeli F-15 and F-16 stealth fighters were manned, fueled, and prepared to strike Iran. Israeli agents and electronic surveillance had identified a frenzy of activity at suspected Iranian missile sites. Silos at two sites appeared hot. Marshall, in turn, informed Chafetz that the Fifth Fleet's USS *Eisenhower* carrier strike group was closing in and would provide any support Chafetz requested.

Shortly after Merritt had spoken to Dwyer, Brandt received a call on his cell phone from Olivia, stating that she had reliable information on the Iranian EMP plans. Brandt informed Marshall, who directed White House Communications Agency Major Clayton Cord to arrange a secure call back to Olivia in sixty seconds and to place the call on the Situation Room speaker. Major Cord's voice came over the speaker.

"Mr. President, we are now connecting to Ms. Perry."

There was a click, then: "Mr. President?"

"Ms. Perry, this is President Marshall. You are on the speaker in the White House Situation Room. Among those present are Secretary of Defense Merritt, Secretary of State Lawrence, Director of National Intelligence Antonetti, DCI Scanlon, Joint Chiefs Chairman Taylor, and Jim Brandt.

"We're all grateful that you're all right. Jim tells me you have information on a planned Iranian EMP strike on Israel. As a preliminary matter, Ms. Perry, what makes you believe that the information is reliable?"

"Mr. President," Olivia's voice sounded strong and confident to everyone in the room except the person who knew her best. Brandt recognized that Olivia was both nervous and scared. "The information comes from Senate Intelligence counsel Julian Day, who confesses to working with the Russians and, by extension, the Iranians, to coordinate an EMP strike."

Expressions of amazement covered the faces in the Situation Room. "And how did you obtain this information?" Marshall asked.

"Mr. President, Michael Garin obtained the information from Day. Mr. Garin is standing next to me right now." The expressions of amazement became more pronounced. Several individuals leaned toward the speaker.

"Where is Mr. Day at this moment?"

"He's in another room nearby, guarded by DGT personnel."

Marshall scanned the faces of everyone in the room. A few nodded as if to somehow validate the legitimacy of the information Perry was about to convey.

"Okay, Ms. Perry. Time is of the essence. Just give me the headlines."

"Mr. President, within the next eight hours, Iran will launch several missiles, all but one of which carries a nuclear warhead with a yield approximating the bombs dropped on Nagasaki and Hiroshima. Missiles will be launched—I'm having Dan Dwyer forward the precise coordinates to Secretary Merritt and General Taylor as we speak—from sites in northern Iran between the Caspian Sea and the North Alborz Protected Area . . . and all but one of the missiles will detonate over various targets in Israel."

"All but one?" Marshall asked.

"Yes, Mr. President. The final missile, with a one-megaton yield, will be launched toward the United States. It's set to detonate at an altitude of one hundred twenty miles somewhere between Kansas City and Chicago, creating an electromagnetic pulse that will cover two-thirds of the continental United States."

The room fell into stunned silence for several seconds as its occupants sought to absorb the enormity of what they'd just heard.

As multiple questions began to percolate among them, James Brandt knifed through the confusion. "Olivia," Brandt said. "Jim here. Two questions: Iran's missiles do not have the capability of hitting the United States. They can barely be certain to hit Israel with any degree of accuracy. Am I correct in assuming that the Russians provided that capability to the Iranians?"

"That's correct, Professor. The Russians and North Koreans have been working with the Iranians for the last two and a half years—Day says to modify the Shahab-3, increasing both distance and accuracy as well as modifying the Shahab's payload capacity for a larger warhead to detonate over the US."

"Second," Brandt resumed, "an Iranian nuclear strike on Israel can destroy enough of that country's strategic capacity that Iran could survive a retaliatory strike. But surely the Iranians know that they wouldn't even make a dent in our nuclear capability, and a retaliatory strike by the United States would annihilate them. How does Day explain that?"

"The Iranians don't know they're hitting us," Olivia replied.

"What in the world do you mean, Ms. Perry?" Marshall asked.

"Just a moment, Mr. President," Olivia said, handing Dwyer's phone to Garin.

"Pardon me, Mr. President. This is Mike Garin. Sir, the Iranians don't know that one of the missiles is targeted at the United States because the Russians controlled the project—the development of the nuclear missiles. They never let the Iranians get near the computers, guidance, telemetry, or anything but the material for the warhead. And they let them work on the warhead only because they didn't want the payload's nuclear signature to be Russian.

"The Iranians believe *all* the missiles are targeted toward Israel. The strike will all but obliterate their enemy. Iran is willing to accept the losses from whatever limited retaliatory strike Israel may be able to mount. The mullahs believe they'll be heroes for destroying Israel.

"The Russians, for their part, will have total deniability regarding the EMP attack on the United States. The United States and every other country in the world will be tracking the missile launch from Iran that detonates over the United States. Everyone will blame Iran. It's an Iranian missile, launched by Iran, from Iranian soil.

"Mr. President, the missile aimed at the United States is located inside a foothill near Mount Azad Kuh, south of Chalus. To my knowledge, it's not a site previously identified by either the CIA or Mossad.

There are two other sites previously unknown to us located at Shah-rud and another at Gorgan. Those sites, among others, will hit Israeli targets."

"Mr. Garin, one moment, please," Marshall said.

The president pointed at Secretary Merritt and Chairman Taylor. "Gentlemen, I gather you have the location for this Mount Azad Kuh?"

"Yes, sir," the men responded in unison.

"Do anything and everything you have to do to destroy that site right now. *Go.*"

The two men moved rapidly toward secure phones at the other end of the room. Marshall pointed to Ted Lawrence. "Tell Prime Minister Chafetz everything we've just heard. Wait until the Pentagon informs you that our forces are in the air, and then inform our NATO allies, starting with the Brits. Meanwhile, I'll have a talk with President Mikhailov personally. Have Carole Tunney demand an emergency meeting of the Security Council. *Go.*"

Marshall then turned to his chief of staff. "Iris, we'll need to address the American people contemporaneously with our attack. Have our—"

The president abruptly stopped speaking. He and everyone else in the room were startled by the distinct sound of multiple gunshots coming over the speaker.

CHAPTER SIXTY-FOUR

By the time Garin got there, it was over. Dwyer, Knox, and Matt were standing on the right side of the living room, still holding their pistols. Two other DGT men stood behind them. Differing degrees of disbelief registered on their faces.

Julian Day lay dead on the other side of the living room. Several entry wounds were grouped around his chest and abdomen.

Garin lowered his weapon and gave Dwyer a puzzled look.

"What could the son of a gun have been thinking?" Knox asked no one in particular.

"He went for one of the Iranian's weapons," Dwyer explained. "Crazy effin' idiot. In a room full of operators, the lawyer goes for a gun. What kind of odds did he think he was playing?"

Garin walked over to Day's body and kicked the gun away from his side. Out of habit, Garin checked for signs of life before securing his weapon.

Outdoors, the forest came alive with lights and sounds as a spotlight from a hovering helicopter shone on the cabin. Looking behind him out the living room window, Dwyer could see more than two dozen uniformed FBI HRT personnel moving about as an amplified voice announced their presence and their intention to enter.

"Did he actually think he had any chance of getting away?" Dwyer asked.

"No chance whatsoever," Garin replied. "No, he knew exactly what he was doing. Suicide by cop. Or in this case, by operator."

"What the hell are you talking about?"

"Some criminologists say that suspects sometimes provoke cops as a way to commit suicide. Whether or not that's true, Day knew he'd be cut down in an instant."

"Day never struck me as the type," Dwyer said. "But, hey, what do I know? I'm just a guy whose life he's made miserable for the last five years. As if I needed another motive to shoot him."

"He was looking at a possible death penalty for treason anyway," Garin said. "And big-time public disgrace. Senate Intelligence Committee counsel working with the Russians to topple the United States. For someone used to running in the elite Washington circles, that alone would be terminal."

Garin knew that his best chance of finding out who, if anyone, had been assisting Day died with the man. Although it was possible Day was the Russians' primary contact, the operation seemed too sophisticated and complex for just Day to be pulling the strings. Then again, with a man like Bor executing directives from Moscow, perhaps Day needed no other assistance.

As the sounds of several FBI agents coming up the stairs echoed in the living room, Dwyer motioned for his men to lower their weapons so as not to accidentally provoke the new arrivals. Garin turned to go back into the kitchen.

"Yo, Mikey," Dwyer called after him with a mischievous grin. "Aren't you going to stick around for the FBI? I'm sure they've got lots of questions for you."

"Can't. Gotta call holding."

"Who?"

"The president."

"Well, look at you. From America's most wanted to American hero in thirty seconds . . ."

CHAPTER SIXTY-FIVE

FRESNO, CALIFORNIA

AUGUST 2

In the two weeks since the bombing began, American and Israeli forces had substantially degraded Iran's nuclear capacity and had caused serious damage to its overall military infrastructure.

The first targets hit were the hardened sites identified by Garin as those that would launch missiles against the United States and Israel. B-2 stealth bombers dropped several fifteen-ton bunker busters—specially reconfigured versions of the bomb known as the Massive Ordnance Penetrator—on one Iranian site alone. The weapon, by far the largest conventional bomb ever produced, was designed to penetrate hundreds of feet of mountain rock as well as the concrete and steel protecting the fortified silos before exploding. And that's precisely what they did. Ground intelligence confirmed obliteration of the facility.

The prudential destruction of Iranian nuclear facilities followed next. Even Western antiwar and environmental activists conceded that both the Israeli and American airstrikes were impressive in avoiding the release of nuclear material into the environment. Still, the predictable denunciations ensued.

While the Israelis focused much of their attention on devastating

Iranian command and control, US AGM-86 and BGM-109 Tomahawk cruise missiles targeted nuclear enrichment plants throughout the country. Bunker busters also hit processing plants in Arak and Parchin. Even so, Chairman of the Joint Chiefs Taylor advised President Marshall that several more weeks of bombing were necessary to completely eliminate the Iranian nuclear threat.

When the joint US-Israeli assault began, massive protests erupted in major cities in the United States, Europe, and the Middle East, only to collapse once the US government released hundreds of photos of the interior of the mountain facility. The photos revealed in exacting detail the purpose and scale of the project. The source of the photographic evidence remained classified. In truth, the source was unknown. But the photos, including those of known Iranian nuclear scientists working on warheads within the facility, presented nearly irrefutable evidence of Iranian plans to launch nuclear weapons against its enemies.

As expected, world markets took a substantial hit but began recovering sooner than expected. Energy markets continued to remain volatile but began showing signs of stability after US, British, and French naval forces secured the Strait of Hormuz. The Saudis, relieved that action had finally been taken against their chief rival, Iran, announced a significant increase in oil production. Curiously, even the Russians, who the experts had expected would try to capitalize on the interruption of oil flow, worked feverishly to neutralize the adverse effects on the oil markets. Much of the Iranian population initially rallied around the regime, especially after propaganda of civilian causalities was circulated. But barely a week later, support began to ebb. Brandt, however, cautioned the president not to expect a regime change anytime soon.

During the first few days of the air campaign, most of the world, including its nastier elements, watched in fascination. Garin knew that in a short while the bad guys would try to exploit the world's distraction in order to make strategic mischief. Scattered reports of clashes in Pakistan's Khyber Pakhtunkhwa Province suggested that it might be the next region to explode. Whether Garin would have any involvement in containing the situation was yet to be determined.

For the moment, Garin's life was in a holding pattern. The first few days after the takedown of the Iranians at the Terrapin Estates cabin were occupied with briefings at Langley and attending the services for Dwyer's men killed by Taras Bor. Then he'd spent a few days at Katy's, before he and Dwyer flew to California to check on Clint Laws, who had been released from intensive care and was finally able to receive visitors.

At the moment, however, Laws was unaware he had visitors. Garin and Dwyer sat patiently in his room while Laws slept through a good portion of visiting hours. He appeared to Garin to have lost at least thirty pounds, and his skin looked dry and sallow. The trauma seemed to have aged him ten years. Laws finally opened his eyes and, upon seeing Garin and Dwyer sitting next to the bed, drawled, "Lord, I've died and gone to hell."

"Hell wouldn't take you," Garin said.

"Well, this sure ain't heaven, that's for sure. Otherwise, you two dummies wouldn't be here."

Garin and Dwyer stood so Laws could see them better. It was a gesture of respect as much as convenience.

"This is where you guys are supposed to tell me how good I look. Didn't your mamas learn you any hospital etiquette? Geez, you two are hopeless."

"How long are you going to be in here, Clint?" Dwyer asked.

"It'll be a while," a nurse who entered the room to check his vitals said. "He's recovering well, but he's still got a long ways to go. Needs lots of rest. This wasn't a case of the hiccups. He stays awake maybe ten minutes at a stretch, so don't be concerned if he falls asleep on you; it's normal. By the way, no rush, but visiting hours are almost over."

"I'm perfectly fine," Laws countered. "They just can't bear for me to leave."

"His *hands* are perfectly fine," the nurse agreed. "They've been all over every nurse in this ward. Can you two convince him to keep them to himself? Or we'll have to put him in restraints."

"Darlin', you just want to put me in restraints so you can have your way with me," Laws said with a wink.

The nurse smiled over her shoulder as she left. It was the same smile, Garin noted, as the one the waitress at the Diamondback Bar had flashed.

Laws watched the nurse leave before turning to Garin.

"What's next for you, Chief?"

"I haven't decided, Clint."

"He had a meeting with the secretary of defense himself a few days ago," Dwyer interjected. "At the request of the commander in chief, no less. He won't say what it was about, but my guess is they want him to take some low-paying job, risking his life for God and country. I've been trying to convince him to come back to DGT as a full partner, where he can make lots of money directing others to risk their lives for God and country."

"So, back to the private sector, Chief?" Laws asked. "Make some more money?"

"He's absolutely got to if he's got any hope of escorting one *Ms. Olivia Perry* around Washington," Dwyer said. "You can't entertain a woman like that on a government salary."

"Whoa, whoa, hold up. Olivia Perry?" Laws asked, looking genuinely impressed. "Fat boy's right, Chief. I've seen her on TV sitting behind James Brandt. Yeah, buddy. Now, *that's* a woman. Way out of your league, though, son."

"That's what I've been telling him," Dwyer agreed. "Wait. Fat boy?"

"She's a star, Chief. She's being groomed for bigger things. By the end of the president's first term she'll be an assistant secretary of . . . something or other. Guaranteed. That means Georgetown cocktail parties, state dinners. She sure as hell can't be dragging an embarrassing specimen like you to those things."

"Tell him." Dwyer nodded emphatically.

"Do you even know how to use a salad fork? I mean, for something other than severing someone's trachea?"

"Save your breath," Garin said. "Nothing's happening. She has absolutely no interest in me. Besides, I don't think operators are quite her type."

"Now, that's the first thing I've heard since this thing began that makes sense," said Laws.

"And, sorry to disappoint you, but I've got no interest in her, either," Garin added.

"I call bull. Big-time. Everyone's interested in her," Dwyer said.

But the tone of Laws's voice, to Dwyer's disappointment, turned sober. "So, what's it going to be, Chief? You going back to work with Dan?"

"To lead a long and prosperous life?" Dwyer added.

Garin didn't reply.

"Dan," Laws said, tilting his head toward the door.

"I'll be down in the cafeteria," Dwyer informed them, to no one's evident surprise. "Bring you guys anything?"

Laws and Garin each shook his head and watched as Dwyer turned to leave. After a moment, Laws shifted his gaze to Garin.

"You weren't meant for a long and prosperous life, Mike. Not you. Your life will be strenuous and short."

Garin wore a faint sardonic smile. If only Clint knew. "'To every man upon this Earth death cometh soon or late.'"

"And you're not going back to DGT."

"Don't jump to conclusions. I haven't decided what I'm going to do yet, Clint."

"There's no decision to make. We both know that. We both know exactly what you're going to do."

Garin cocked his head slightly, considering Laws's statement. "*I* don't know that."

"Tell me something, Mike. If you can."

Garin nodded for Laws to continue, knowing what the question would be.

"Did you kill Bor?"

The two men stared at each other for a long moment. Then Garin shook his head almost imperceptibly.

"He had help on the inside, Mike," Laws said, his voice raspy. "High up. Way higher than Julian Day. Day couldn't have authorized Congo Knox. It had to come from one of only two places. You know that."

Again, Garin's nod was barely visible.

Laws exhaled wearily. "A short life, Mike. Remember that. Yours will be a short life."

"Get some sleep, Clint."

The old warrior's eyes closed slowly. Garin watched him for several minutes before turning to leave. Upon reaching the door he heard Laws whisper, "Mike."

Garin paused and looked back. Laws lay perfectly still, his appearance cadaverous. With his eyes still closed, he turned his head in Garin's direction and spoke, his voice barely audible but clear.

"Kill them all."

CHAPTER SIXTY-SIX

ATLANTIC SHORELINE, DELAWARE

AUGUST 3

Sunrise was half an hour away but already pale shades of orange and pink painted most of the cloudless eastern sky as threads of dawn shimmered over the calm ocean. The air was still. The beach was deserted, but only for a couple of hours more. It was going to be yet another hot day.

A lone figure stood smoking a cigarette on the second-floor balcony of the large beach house situated on the northern end of Bethany. Tall and lean, the smoker had a patrician bearing. His movements were casual, unhurried, a man in control of himself and his circumstances.

The news during the last two weeks had been dominated by the bombings of Iran's nuclear facilities. The Americans' and Israelis' devastating attacks would likely continue for several more weeks, precisely as he had expected. He watched closely the rate at which the US forces expended their munitions as well as the type and amount. Several times each day he studied detailed reports about the progress of the air campaign and the state of US military readiness throughout the rest of the world.

The reports generally pleased him. In fact, the course of events in the last month had generally pleased him. Not everything had gone according to plan. But he had been around long enough to know that there would always be detours and glitches. In this case, nothing had detracted from the overall success of the plan.

The first phase was nearing completion. No other obstacles remained. The United States had behaved exactly as he had predicted. In a way, it was somewhat disappointing. A superpower shouldn't be so easily manipulated. But then, he'd always been two moves ahead of his adversaries.

It was time to initiate the next phase. They had spent several years meticulously plotting every detail of the entire operation. Although he wasn't aware of every aspect of the plan, he had executed his portion, the most vital portion, flawlessly. They had determined that the first phase would take a bit longer to execute than it had; nonetheless, they were fully prepared to begin the next step.

He flicked the cigarette onto the sand below and opened the sliding screen door. The house was dark and quiet and would remain so for a while.

Standing for a moment in his study off of the balcony, he decided to first get himself a cup of coffee. Padding down the stairs to the kitchen, he paused on the landing to listen at the window facing the driveway at the side of the house. Although he couldn't see them, his acute hearing picked up the quiet conversation of two bodyguards from his protective detail standing next to one of two black sedans parked outside of the carport.

At the bottom of the stairs he turned into the kitchen and poured himself a large mug of coffee, taking a sip before returning to the study. He sat in a high-backed leather chair for several minutes, cradling the mug as he faced the brightening sky.

They were on the verge. The vast intelligence apparatus of the United States had been misled and outmaneuvered. Now they would be caught flat-footed. There would be nothing they could do to prevent what was about to happen.

The house was swept twice a day for listening devices. The windows were specially constructed to frustrate any surveillance by laser microphones or similar devices. Nothing he said in this room could be heard by anyone but the intended listener. Nonetheless, obsessive about security, he exercised extreme caution, as a man in his position must, whenever speaking of the operation.

He pulled an encrypted phone from the pocket of his robe, pressed a series of keys, and waited. When the call was answered he spoke a single word.

Then he terminated the call and finished his coffee.

EPILOGUE

For the first time in longer than Dmitri Chernin could remember, he didn't feel like a character in a Chekhov play. Rather, he felt . . . optimistic. Content, even. A rare feeling, perhaps a first. He took another sip of Smirnoff, sat back in the lounge chair, and opened his senses to the ambient sights, sounds, and smells surrounding the open-air beachfront bar on a spit of sand between the Costa Rican jungle and the Pacific Ocean.

The light mist from the surf spray did little to temper the heat of the midafternoon sun. Still, Chernin declined an umbrella from the beachboy as he had every day this week, spending hours in the sun, luxuriating in the tropical heat. As a result, he sported the only tan of his adulthood. It looked good. He looked good. In fact, better than at any time in his life. He had grown a closely trimmed beard; his thick graying hair was combed back from his face and fell below the collar of his white linen shirt. His features appeared roguish, a dramatic contrast to his ascetic appearance over the last several decades. It was a look that during the Soviet era would've been considered decadent.

To his delight, the seemingly limitless supply of beautiful women sunning themselves on the startling black sands of the beach also found his new appearance extremely attractive. Women of every hue, age, and nationality. The tall blond Dane, for instance, who was doing a swimsuit layout for a sports magazine declared he had "a look." Not that there weren't scores of handsome, roguish men populating the miles of beach between Dominical and Ciudad Cortés. But they, she said, almost invariably wore insufferably vapid expressions, an observation that Chernin found had something of a pot-kettle quality about it.

Presently, he was involved with a woman named Marisol, the stunning, fortyish ex-wife of a Mexican telecommunications magnate. She had introduced herself after listening to him hold forth on Cold War politics during an impromptu party of vacationers at a cantina in town. She had pronounced him fascinating and invited him up to her estate in the hills approximately three kilometers from the beachfront. He emerged three days later utterly spent. It had taken the physicist nearly six decades to learn he was "fascinating" and had "a look." Given the rewards those attributes had conferred upon him in the last few weeks, he was determined to cultivate them over his remaining years.

He would have an opportunity to do just that later this evening. Marisol was throwing another of the interminable string of parties that seemed to be this corner of the earth's purpose for existence. She delighted in showing him off to her guests, all of whom were card-carrying members of the Union of Beautiful People and who, among them, may have read an entire book. Marisol was distinguished from the rest of them by Chernin. His presence at her side said, "See, he is smarter than all of you put together, and his brilliance chose *me*."

The last of the partygoers would filter out shortly after two A.M., and then Marisol and Chernin would retreat to the master suite with its spectacular view of the ocean for another exhausting round of bedroom gymnastics. The next morning Chernin would steal back to the beach for a morning swim and breakfast at the beachfront bar. He would then spend late morning and early afternoon exploring the edges of the jungle and marveling at its flora and fauna before wandering back to the open-air bar to gaze upon acres of tanned female flesh while sipping from a large frosted glass of Smirnoff.

Eventually, he knew he would tire of the routine. He'd been here only a few weeks and already he sensed stray tendrils of boredom creeping into his brain. The rich dilettantes and aimless surfers who lazed about this place appeared comfortable with idleness, with purposelessness. He was not. Chernin's life had had purpose and direction up until this point. He had accomplished notable things in his life, even if only a handful of people understood or even knew about them. Indeed, perhaps his most significant accomplishment was known only to himself. An encrypted file containing hundreds of photos he had taken of the project had been sent to an Internet account Mansur had given to Chernin as they had sailed the Caspian to Baku. He knew only that it was an account accessible to a friend of Mansur's Israeli contact and that the release of the photos would mute opposition to the bombing campaign he hoped would ensue.

When he finally became bored with paradise, Chernin would retreat to the small home he had purchased on a hill two kilometers from the beach. There, he'd keep up online with the latest scholarship in physics and continue challenging his mind. He would still make occasional forays to the beach, go sailing on a sixteen-foot dinghy he'd spotted up the coast that he intended to buy, and do a little fishing. He had more than enough money to last the remainder of his lifetime, however long it might be. And Chernin was increasingly confident that it would be a very long time. He had covered his tracks well. All evidence of Dmitri Chernin's existence had been erased. He was now Vladimir Petrov, retired mathematics professor from Novosibirsk.

Chernin would refrain from traveling and would remain vigilant. Despite having employed his prodigious intellect toward ensuring that Dmitri Chernin had disappeared from human existence, there was always a possibility, however small, that an assassin would find him. Consequently, he always examined the new faces that showed up at the bar.

The Russians might send anyone. Perhaps it was the frail, bookish man in his late sixties speaking to one of the waiters at the far end of the bar. Or maybe it was the robust younger man with the J-shaped scar along his jawline who had been sitting alone on the veranda for the last few hours. Of one thing Chernin was sure. The cold, bleak existence of his previous life was gone forever.

Chernin finished his Smirnoff and got up to leave. The remainder of his life promised to be an adventure.

ACKNOWLEDGMENTS

Many thanks to the outstanding team at Dutton, particularly my editor, Jessica Renheim; my copy editor, Eileen Chetti; and, of course, Ben Sevier. I am grateful to have a remarkable agent in Scott Miller of Trident Media. Many, if not most, authors acknowledge their respective publishing teams as the best in the business. Unless such authors have the same publisher, agent, and editors as I have, those authors, respectfully, are sorely mistaken.

Several others deserve mention, especially my father, now deceased, upon whom Nikolai "Pop" Garin is based; Joe Stimson, whose record of service to the country is the inspiration for Mike Garin's exploits; and my wife, Kathryn.

ABOUT THE AUTHOR

Peter Kirsanow practices and teaches law and serves part-time as an official of a federal agency, having received both presidential and congressional appointments. He is a former member of the National Labor Relations Board and has testified before Congress on a variety of matters, including the confirmations of four Supreme Court justices. He lives in Cleveland, Ohio, where he is wrapping up the next Mike Garin thriller.